SEVEN
POOR MEN
OF
SYDNEY

Christina Stead

ANGUS & ROBERTSON PUBLISHERS

AN ANGUS & ROBERTSON BOOK
An imprint of HarperCollinsPublishers

First published in Great Britian in 1934
Reprinted by Angus & Robertson Publishers, Australia, 1965
This Australian Classics edition, 1978
Reprinted 1991
CollinsAngus&Robertson Publishers Pty Limited (ACN 009 913 517)
A division of HarperCollinsPublishers (Australia) Pty Limited
4 Eden Park, 31 Waterloo Road, North Ryde NSW 2113, Australia
HarperCollinsPublishers (New Zealand) Limited
31 View Road, Glenfield, Auckland 10, New Zealand
HarperCollinsPublishers Limited
77– 85 Fulham Palace Road, London W6 8JB, United Kingdom

ISBN 0 207 13654 8.

Printed in Australia by The Book Printer, Victoria

5 4 3 2
95 94 93 92 91

CONTENTS

THE SEVEN POOR MEN

JOSEPH BAGUENAULT	*a printer*
TOM WITHERS	*a printer*
BARUCH MENDELSSOHN	*a printer*
GREGORY CHAMBERLAIN	*owner of a press*
MICHAEL BAGUENAULT	*a ne'er-do-weel*
TOM WINTER	*a librarian*
KOL BLOUNT	*a paralysed youth*

Introduction

CHRISTINA STEAD is an important Australian writer whose early books, though well received both here and overseas, have unfortunately been out of print for many years. There is no other twentieth-century Australian novelist of comparable stature whose works have become so difficult to obtain, and no other contemporary writer of ours who deserves to be more widely read. Up till now none of Christina Stead's work has been published in this country. She left Australia in 1928, but her writing career, despite certain earlier efforts, did not really begin until five or six years later, and she has never returned to the land of her birth. Most of her fiction has been published in both England and the United States. Two of her books have been translated into other languages—*For Love Alone* into French and Italian, and *Letty Fox, Her Luck* into French. This edition of *Seven Poor Men of Sydney* is an event to be welcomed. It makes available her first novel (and her only book set completely in Australia) to those who have long admired her work and to the younger generation to which she is either unknown or known only from accounts given in critical essays or histories of Australian literature.

Christina Ellen Stead, eldest child of David G. Stead, an eminent Australian naturalist, was born on 17th July 1902 at Rockdale, N.S.W. Her mother died while Christina was still very young; her father married again some years later and Christina grew up at Bexley and then, from 1917 onwards, at Watson's Bay, along with a younger family of six children, four half-brothers and two half-sisters. Watson's Bay, which she came to know so well, is the Fisherman's Bay of *Seven Poor Men of Sydney*, and the locale again for much of the first part of *For Love Alone*. Christina developed strong literary interests as a young girl. At the age of thirteen she began to learn French and was soon an impassioned admirer of Guy de Maupassant, whose work exerted a powerful influence in the early years of her life. She was a pupil at Sydney

High School, where she edited the school magazine, and then attended the Sydney Teachers' College. She taught for a short time only and afterwards became a demonstrator in Psychology at the College. She had always been a lover of books and by now had read widely in the English, American, and European classics. *The Salzburg Tales*, a collection of stories arranged in a manner reminiscent of *The Decameron*, shows a fascination with European folk-lore and legend, which almost certainly goes back to her early years. She was interested too in Nietzsche (Catherine's quotation from Nietzsche, "They are alien, so alien, that they cannot even speak their difference to each other" might be taken as the epigraph for *Seven Poor Men of Sydney*), in modern psychology, and in the writings of the economists and social reformers. Determined to travel and work overseas, she then found employment in an office and took a business course at night and (like Teresa, the heroine of *For Love Alone*) practised the most severe economies till she had saved enough money for her fare to England. She left Australia in March 1928 and was fortunate enough to find a job soon after her arrival in London with a firm of grain merchants. In 1929 she went to Paris where she obtained secretarial work with a bank in the rue de la Paix. She stayed with this bank for five years and became envoy extraordinary, travelling between Paris and London on many confidential missions, thereby gaining first-hand knowledge of the world of European finance, which she was later to draw on for her novel *House of All Nations*.

The Salzburg Tales (1934), Christina Stead's first published book, takes its setting from the city she had visited during the festival season. In *Seven Poor Men of Sydney* she looks back upon her homeland; but in her next novel, *The Beauties and The Furies*, she returns to the European scene to write a story of student life and love in Paris. The last of the novels of this decade is *House of All Nations* (1938). In this period she had paid her first visit to the United States and had married William Blake, novelist, and author of books on economics. She and her husband were in Spain at the outbreak of the civil war and then moved to London. She lived in the United States during the war years of the forties, and the novels written in this period, with the exception of *For Love Alone*, all have American settings: *The Man Who Loved Children* (1940); *For Love Alone* (1944); *Letty Fox, Her Luck* (1946); *A Little Tea, A Little Chat* (1948); *The People with the Dogs* (1952). While in the United States Christina Stead also worked for a short time in 1943 as Senior Writer with MGM, Hollywood, conducted a course, "Workshop in the Novel", at New York University (1943-4), and wrote literary criticism for *New Masses* and the *New York Times*. She returned to Europe at the earliest possible moment, in 1947, and since then has lived on the Continent and in England, where she has continued writing fiction (though she has not published a book since 1952) and has done reviewing for *The Times Literary Supplement*.

Apart from the works listed above, Christina Stead has published separate short stories and translations from the French, and has done some editing as well. The most interesting work outside her own fiction is the story anthology, *Modern Women in Love* (1945), edited with William Blake. This volume, subtitled *Sixty Twentieth Century Masterpieces of Fiction*, is a first-class piece of editing; its selections, which range widely over English, Continental, and American literature, are made with great skill and tact, so that the book grows through the accumulation of material and the contrasts of viewpoints and styles to a work with its own particular kind of unity. Christina Stead gives most of the credit for this anthology to William Blake, who composed almost all the notes and supplementary guides to the writers represented. None the less, she did her share of the reading and the choosing, and *Modern Women in Love* is just the kind of anthology anyone with a knowledge of her fiction would imagine her helping to compile. She has always been sophisticated and cosmopolitan, but not (despite the remarks of more consciously nationalistic writers such as Miles Franklin) in a second-hand and imitative way. It is partly these qualities and her impressive individuality of style that made her first books stand out with such startling effect in the Australian literary scene of the 1930s; for the best-known fiction of that period was, generally speaking, conventional in manner. With Christina Stead came a new (and strange) voice, fresh subjects, and a different approach. To appreciate their originality we should see *Seven Poor Men of Sydney* and *The Salzburg Tales* against the background of the more typical Australian fiction of the 1930s written by Miles Franklin, Katharine Prichard, Kylie Tennant, Vance Palmer, Leonard Mann, and Eleanor Dark. *Seven Poor Men of Sydney* has an Australian setting but, significantly, the setting is the city, not the small town or the bush; furthermore, its characters seem to inhabit a different mental world. And *The Salzburg Tales*, in some ways a greater achievement for a young Australian writer, is even more strikingly different from the other fiction of the day.

These books both came out in 1934, and the story of their writing and publication is worth telling. While still at the Sydney Teachers' College Christina Stead wrote what was intended to be a volume of short stories, which she failed to get published in Australia. Soon after arriving in London, where she was so ill she thought she would not survive, she began writing *Seven Poor Men of Sydney*, not with any thought of publication, but because (in her own words) "I said to myself, 'I am not just going to fade away, I am going to leave something'." Peter Davies eventually saw the manuscript in Paris and said he would publish it if he could have something else first. It was then that Christina Stead set about writing *The Salzburg Tales*, which was to become her first published book. *The Salzurg Tales* included four of the stories from the earlier Australian manuscript, which had in the meantime been lost in Paris. These were the only stories from the original group that she could remember in detail : they are readily identifiable as the only stories in *The Salzburg Tales* with Australian settings—"The Triskelion", "Morpeth Tower", "On the Road", and "Day of Wrath".

H. M. Green, believing that Christina Stead's talent fades after *House of All Nations*, considers *Seven Poor Men of Sydney* the best of all her work.[1] Many readers will disagree; some will place *The Salzburg Tales* higher; others, finding in *For Love Alone* and *The Man Who Loved Children* a greater concentration of power

---

[1] *A History of Australian Literature*, Vol. II, p. 851, p. 1070.

and deeper exploration of character, will rate these books superior to her first novel. *Seven Poor Men of Sydney* is, nevertheless, a fascinating book in its own right, quite apart from the special interest it is likely to have for Australian readers. Two worlds, the external and the internal, are depicted in this novel. Its characters are placed firmly in the Sydney of the late 1920s: the solid, material world of Watson's Bay, Woolloomooloo, the harbour, parts of the North Shore, the Domain, the city and inner suburbs is vividly realized, and the heat-laden atmosphere of the Australian summer is captured in passages of fine, evocative prose.

Seven Poor Men of Sydney is a story of poverty in a modern city, but, unlike most Australian novels of its time, its stress falls less on the sociological picture than on an exploration of the inner life and the frustration of human relationships. This is that stranger world—none the less real for all its apparent insubstantiality and its refraction through fantasy—represented by the intense soul-searchings of various characters of humble origin. First among these are Catherine Baguenault and her illegitimate half-brother Michael, both introspective misfits who struggle in vain to come to terms with ordinary existence. As he follows their fortunes the reader is taken again and again into that phantasmagoric region of experience which is a characteristic feature of Christina Stead's earlier work.[2] Baruch Mendelssohn, the most intelligent and balanced of the seven poor men, talking to Catherine after Michael's suicide, observes, "What an underground life was that!"—a remark that is likely to awaken echoes of Dostoevsky's *Notes From Underground*. Christina Stead had not, in fact, read this particular book at the time of writing *Seven Poor Men of Sydney*, so there is no question of direct influence here. There is, none the less, quite a striking parallel. Like Dostoevsky's underground hero, Michael is the victim of an *ennui* born of excessive sensibility; profaner and rebel he is, too, a man deeply divided against the world and against himself; his plight made even worse by the threat of incestuous love between him and Catherine—though he, characteristically, plays with this

[2]See e.g. pp. 9-12, 229-36, 264-75.

passion as an idea, while for Catherine herself it is all "too real". In *Seven Poor Men of Sydney* fantasy and reality jostle, in places merge one with the other, and this shifting of planes is most likely to occur when Michael is the centre of the author's attention.

The intensely charged imagery of certain descriptive and analytic passages, and some of the curious dialogue, seem to spring from the personal dilemmas explored. There are many occasions where Christina Stead abandons naturalistic dialogue and, in the interests of psychological truth, allows her characters, when speaking of themselves, an eloquence that goes beyond realism. This same desire to plumb the emotional life accounts also for the unusual structure of the novel. There is little plot in the conventional sense, but the book, growing out of the apparently random interactions of the lives of its main characters, develops a unity of its own.[3] Michael and Catherine, the rebels, the passionate searchers, are doomed to defeat because they deny so much: "Disorder, Lord of the earth", of the madman's tale in Chapter 11, Catherine knows is their epitaph. Joseph, the dull, good cousin, simply accepts in the end, so his destiny is a safe, humble job, marriage, and a front garden with its "cement paths and standard roses". And in between the nay- and yea-sayers fall those who seek outlets in other ways—Mendelssohn in scholarship and the world of ideas, Winter in a vision of communism, the well-to-do Folliots in their hobby of socialism, Withers in his perverse personal scheming.

Seven Poor Men of Sydney is a first novel and bears many of the marks of youthful aspiration. In the boldness and intensity of its feeling it risks the distaste of readers who favour traditional Anglo-Saxon reticence; its style is sometimes strained, as if a poet's love of colourful and unusual words has tempted the writer into self-conscious brilliance and (notably in certain of Mendelssohn's speeches) into displays of intellectual fireworks. But, like the early fiction of D. H. Lawrence, *Seven Poor Men of Sydney* has the courage of its convictions and a reckless sincerity that braves ridicule.

---

[3] This is well treated by B. Eldershaw in the chapter on Christina Stead in *Essays in Australian Fiction*. Melbourne University Press, 1938.

A fuller treatment than is possible in this Introduction would analyse the achievements and the shortcomings of the novel's style, and would consider, too, the symbolic significance of the patterns of imagery, of dark and light, in Michael's story. As a boy Michael has strange dreams on white, moonlight nights; his story ends with his dreams on a night of storm, and he goes to his death over the Gap to become part of the darkness that awaits him below. Again, Catherine is given a long speech, after Michael's death, in which she tells Mendelssohn how Michael confessed his love for her and described his vision of the world in the same twofold imagery.

The poetic exuberance of Christina Stead's early books, a force that threatens to run riot in *The Beauties and The Furies*, is curbed in *House of All Nations*, which plants us firmly within the recognizable world of European high finance. From then on her fiction becomes increasingly naturalistic in approach and the style a good deal plainer, the distinctively picturesque qualities now finding expression, in more subdued tones, in the vivid dialogue.

The particular achievements of the later novels are outside the scope of this Introduction; there are welcome signs of a reawakening interest in them too. *The Man Who Loved Children* has recently been reissued in the United States, with a long introduction by Randall Jarrell, by Holt, Rinehart and Winston (1965). It is most appropriate that *Seven Poor Men of Sydney* should be the first of Christina Stead's books to be published in the land of her birth. Today we may well see it as a signpost to important imaginative developments that have since occurred in the Australian novel.

RON GEERING.

1 🐝

Fisherman's Bay. First days of the first poor man.
An October night's dream.
A stirring sermon has no effect on an ill-fated hero.

THE HIDEOUS low scarred yellow horny and barren headland
lies curled like a scorpion in a blinding sea and sky. At night,
house-lamps and ships' lanterns burn with a rousing shine, and the
headlights of cars swing over Fisherman's Bay. In the day, the
traffic of the village crawls along the skyline, past the lighthouse
and signal station, and drops by cleft and volcanic gully to the
old village that has a bare footing on the edge of the bay. It was,
and remains, a military and maritime settlement. When the
gunners are in camp, searchlights sweep over the bay all night,
lighting bedrooms and the china on dressers, discolouring the
foliage and making seagulls fly; in the daytime, when the red
signal is flown over the barracks, the plates and windows rattle
with the report of guns at target practice. From the signal station
messages come down of the movements of ships and storms.
Flags flutter and red globes swing on its great mast, which is
higher than the Catholic Church, higher than the Norfolk Island
pines, higher than the lighthouse and than anything else which
is between the rocky cornice and the sandy seafloor. In dark
nights, from the base of that enormous spectral pole which points
up any distance into the starry world, one looks down on the city
and northern harbour settlements, on the pilot-lights in the
eastern and western channels, and on the unseen dark sea, where
the lighthouse ray is lost beyond the horizon and where ships
appear through the waves, far out, lighted like a Christmas Tree,
small, and disappearing momentarily; and where, after half an
hour of increasing radiance, the yellow rim of the great sub-
tropical moon comes up like a lantern from underneath.

Early in the morning, through the open window, the people hear the clatter of anchors falling into the bay, and the little boys run out to name the liners waiting there for the port doctor, liners from Singapore, Shanghai, Nagasaki, Wellington, Hawaii, San Francisco, Naples, Brindisi, Dunkirk and London, in the face of all these old stone houses, decayed weatherboard cottages, ruinous fences, boathouses and fishermen's shanties. Presently a toot, the port doctor puts out in the *Hygeia*; a whistle, the Customs launch goes alongside; a hoot from the Point, and that is the pilot-ship returning to its anchorage. A bell jangles on the wharf where the relief pilot waits for his dinghy, and the ferry whistles to clear the dinghies, rowing-boats and children's canoes from its path. The fishermen murmur round the beach-path, fishing-nets dry in the sun, a bugle blows in the camp, the inspected ships draw up their anchors and go off up the harbour, superb with sloping masts, or else, in disgrace, flying the yellow flag, to the rightabout, with nose in air, to Quarantine, under North Head and its bleak graveyard. Butchers' and bakers' carts rattle, an original milkman yodels, little girls gabble on the way to school, the wind with hands in pockets whistles a tune, and the day goes gaily and blatantly forward.

There is no place in the estuary, though, so suited for an old tale as this fish-smelling bay, first in the port. Life is poor and unpretentious, life can be quiet. The sun rises just over the cliff, and sailing vessels roll in and out as they have done for a hundred years, and a quarter of a mile away unfurl their full sails to catch the Pacific winds.

There was a family there named Baguenault, which had settled in the bay directly after its arrival from Ireland thirty years before, and had its roots growing down into the soil and rocky substratum so that nothing seemed to be able to uproot it any more, so quiet, so circumspect in the narrow life of the humble, it lived; but disaster fell on it, and its inner life, unexpressed, incoherent, unplanned, like most lives, then became visible as a close and tangled web to the neighbours and to itself, to whom it had for so long remained unknown. Who can tell what minor passions running in the undergrowth of poor lives will burst out

2

when a storm breaks on the unknown watershed? There is water in barren hills and when rain comes they spurt like fountains, where the water lies on impermeable rocks.

Michael Baguenault paddled through his childhood round the beaches, helped the fishermen haul their nets, often rolled out of his warm bunk at four o'clock in spring and autumn mornings to waken the wooden-legged fisherman, Pegleg Jack, who lived near them in a cabin by himself, to light his fire and cook his bacon. In return the Pegleg called him "my little mate", took him across to George's Head with the fishermen and gave him black tea for breakfast. He gave him chunks of cedar and taught him to carve model racing-yachts and on his eighth birthday presented him with a fisherman's knife and sheath. Michael went always on black, rough feet, whose horny skin was split into deep cracks, bleeding in the crevices, from which the winter's dirt could never be washed. He ran with other little boys in frayed trousers to the beach to collect driftwood and coke for the kitchen, and would return late for breakfast with blue hands; he had chilblains and a running nose all the winter. There were straggle-haired little girls with dirty pinafores and pink skirts. They were all cold; they grasped their sponge-boxes and playtime biscuits, called out the names of teachers in brittle voices and squabbled over hopscotch tors.

The beach provided not only fuel, but also dead fish, swollen fruit, loaves, pumpkins, shoes and socks, broken straw-boaters— all varieties of food and clothing cast up from ships and sewers. Once, when a five-thousand tonner was wrecked near the Gap, a hundred tons of butter floated mildly in to the beach. Pegleg salvaged it and sold it. Cases of condensed milk collided with their frail canoes, manufactured in backyards, of canvas and corrugated iron. They went outside the Heads and brought in a butcher's block, and came back, all their coracles white with flour. They could all swim and were absolutely fearless, despite the frequency of squalls and sharks, paddling all over the harbour in unseaworthy tubs. There were crabs in the rock-pools, little oysters spread all round the bay, and the waters were rich in fish. "If this were a desert island . . ." thought all those verminous little heads joyfully, seeing the bounty of the sea. There was even a great house there, in the last stages of decay, weathered by wind and sea, and standing in a neglected garden with old trees, in which they all could have lived at ease, a pirate brood. The front part of the house, of stone and heavy timber, had been added to the large stone military stables at the back, which had served in the early days. The fences were down, and the house was inhabited fraternally by human, barnyard, and vermin tribes. The goats, ducks, geese, dogs and horses left wandering about the streets of the neighbourhood oftener wound up in the backyard than in the pound, and the children after school found the forbidden front garden, with its tall trees and old bushes, the best spot for playing bushrangers.

Annie Pennergast lived with her family in part of the house. The little girl was thin, with black eyes and hair. She scratched her head and body all the time, and always smelled of ingrained dirt. In the corners of the house bats flew, swallows dropped mud and dung from every beam, and from all the cracks of the great whitewashed stones at the back ran cockroaches, beetles and rats. Cockchafer beetles, cicadas and mosquitoes shouted loudly in summer evenings in the tall trees; large spiders hung in the outhouses, and fearsome-looking, but innocent, crickets and slaters dwelt under the bits of wood and sheets of corrugated iron fallen off the roof into the grass. The house attracted Michael and the other children with the same charm as a stagnant gutter.

The little girl, Annie, took him over the house one Saturday afternoon. The windows were starred by stones which now lay on the naked flooring inside. Annie preceded Michael up camel's-back staircases and adventitious flights of steps connecting the old house with the later front apartments, through heavy doorways pierced in the stone walls. She showed him windows that looked over the barracks, hill and bay, windows without glass or shutters, some surprisingly placed in small cupboards, others letting the dust, sunlight, seeds of weeds, and the swallows into whitewashed landings. Upstairs they went through rooms with sloping roofs, skylights, whitewashed beams hung with old webs, and dusty floors on which their bare feet made tracks. They looked out through open doorways straight down three stories on to the backyard full of plantains and thistles. She led him into the stables, smelling of dung and damp, and held on to his hand with a soft persistence. A stair began in the corner of the stables, passed old plastered walls and withering landings, and ended at last in a garret. In the garret she said, "Do you want to kiss me?" with indifferent naivety. He looked out at the light spring sky which a puff of smoke and a swallow crossed, and at the open door leading on to a silent landing and sunny attic. He kissed her carefully on her cheek, and they went on with their metallic clatter about the bay, school and personalities.

Rats came up from the waterfront and lived all over the house, with mice and all kinds of small things, bugs, snails, slugs. On a summer night the cockroaches scurried in and out of holes where the cracked asphalt footpath led into the stables' foundations. Michael pored over them full of languor and content for half an hour and more, kicking his heels and watching the officers going home to the barracks and the couples walking with their heads together; when they went past he sometimes hooted at them. Up the hill went the soldiers clinking their spurs. He stood at the corner one fine summer evening, the year he was ten, watched the eight o'clock ferry trail its golden lights out of the wharf, and studied the little creatures running about in their long-tailed suits. The dusk gathered and the street lamps yellowly came on. The cockroaches streaked out of their holes with a slow rustling, flittered round the lamp and dashed in through open windows at kerosene lamps burning in the old cottages; mosquitoes sang. Annie came out of the only side-door on the street and trod on a cockroach or two as a conversational opening. Michael ducked as a bat swerved through the air. Annie calmly disentangled something struggling in her hair; it was fearfully hot and Michael perspired.

"Bats," said Annie, "are worse than cockroaches. If they get in your hair you can't get out the tangles. That was only a beetle."

"Bats don't get in your hair, they get in your garret," Michael jeered.

"Orright, wait till you see; but you don't know, your hair's short, like a monkey." She turned her back and began to jump up and down in the gutter, chanting a nursery rhyme: "Bat, bat, fly into my hair, big, black bat."

"There are bats that suck your blood," volunteered Michael to the dancing back.

"There ain't."

"There are: I saw in a book; they have beaks."

"Beaks! You're dopey."

Michael began toying with a gold tie-pin his mother had given him from his father's dressing-table, carelessly letting it play in the lamplight.

"They say I'm your girl!" said Annie, standing sideways and rolling her hair on her finger.

"Who says?"

"It's written on the fence"; she pointed to the opposite fence. They both went over and peered at the feebly-illuminated legend. He hung about her house a few evenings that summer, swung on the gate after school pretending to take an interest in local affairs, would loaf all the afternoon on the verandah pretending to read, or carve a boat, and his heart would beat hard if he saw her go past in the street without speaking to him. If she cooeed to him, or shouted "Ullo, Michael," he would whisk inside, take his hat and scoot off up into the barracks, without a care in the world, and pleased to get away from her without further conversation. His mother scolded him for hanging round with that Pennergast girl. He was puzzled to know how his mother knew. He assumed that his sister Catherine, called Kate, had told on him. "Kate has a boy," he said. Kate slapped his face and punched him on the temple, which hurt very much; in return he hit her on her budding breast. She tripped him up and pummelled him all over the face, her own face purple with fury. Kate was twelve, and outrageously bad-tempered. His two elder sisters were mild and kind.

The hot sun addled his brains. He said one day to a friend, Tommy, as they returned from a long red afternoon in the weatherboard schoolroom, full of the drone of voices and occasional blue hornets, and smelling of wattle pollen and the salt sea:

"I used to think I would fly home when I was a little kid."

6

The little village shone below them, through the pines, in the afternoon sun.

"Me, too; I dream I am flying," said Tommy.

"Perhaps you could, with wings like a kite; but I would like to fly just like that." He raised his arms.

"Perhaps if you tried," said Tommy.

"Perhaps by will-power," concluded Michael.

And when he sat at home later and looked up the green and yellow hill where the school sat, and the road home with its houses and bits of bush, he wished that he could see himself on the road home, where he had been a few minutes before. He pretended that images of himself were still marching along every stage of that much-travelled road, and would have liked to see them from this distance, familiar mannikins.

Reason was awakening in him and in Tommy, like a lazy apprentice who will do freakish things with his tools but doesn't want to use them just yet. He will do a little work and then try his skinny legs, play truant, graduate as journeyman, traipse round the world, get drunk and disorderly, knock up the mayor and dignities, and cry, Why not? Life is very dull for a journeyman so freakish and full of fun. When he has spent all he has, he will beg; and, then, after a few years, he will know himself for what he is, a sober workman in a dull world, and will settle down.

But happily for Tommy and Michael, at this day, he was just stretching himself under a bush; and looking across the mountains, he thought, "Why, they are so near that I can cross them with a hop, skip and a jump." And mounting like a stowaway in the satchel of the childish giant Fancy, he found himself in the next town and boasted that he had flown there by his own power, across the mountains in the twinkling of an eye, and almost believed it himself.

Michael's father had a bull-roarer, a vane on a cord, which when whirled in the air produces a loud whirring and shrieking noise. It is used by the Australian blacks in their initiation ceremonies. When his father and mother were out he took out the bull-roarer into the backyard and whirled it round and round his head, while its shrieking got louder and louder, and let it die down, like a dying wind, and rise again, like a wind howling in a crevice. Then he put it down, and leaning against the fence laughed with tears in his eyes, or rushed out into the street to find some boys, his lips bursting with shouts, with witticisms; or his heart would beat so hard that he could hardly breathe; this feeling was the greatest pleasure he knew. He rolled a dozen times down the grass slope that ran down to the beach in front of the house to get the same sensation, of brains turning and wits glittering. But he had to be alone to do it, because his parents found it silly and dangerous. They noticed, too, that if he had to pick up something for his mother under the dresser or sweep under the table, he always came up looking slightly dazed.

"That is a weakness to be cured in childhood," said his father firmly, and dragged him out with his sister Catherine, across country, up and down slopes and on the edges of the cliffs. Once he made him descend the cliff at Rosa Gully, a precipitous opening in the cliffs, formed by the crumbling of a basaltic dyke, where a few rocks stand in the waves and make a fishing foothold. His sister Kate sprang down without help, but Michael stuck half-way almost dead with terror and vertigo, and his father, though furious, had to carry him the rest of the way on his back. Michael closed his eyes, and after a long time found his feet on firm ground; he looked up at the tall cliff, shuddering. The waves dashed and whistled in the narrow cleft. His father carried him back up the cliff and never tried his great cure for vertigo again. But Michael, impressed with the horrors of that day, often went to the verge of the highest cliff, sat under a sandstone boulder and looked out at the smooth blue sea and flawless sky, to feel adolescence creeping on him, and the surges of excitement which made him at one moment want to throw himself savagely at the lawny slopes and bite them, like an animal, and at the next, to leap from the cliff among the seagulls, ending fatally but sweetly in the sea.

He said to his mother, "Am I your son?" and at her startled question, only replied: "I don't know why I said it. I can't believe I'm anybody's son. I feel as if I just grew out of myself."

"Don't be silly."

His father thought the time ripe to inform him of the mysteries. He was himself an amateur naturalist and gathered orchids. Taking his son before the pots of orchids arranged in a glassed lean-to at the back of the house, he explained to him pollen, ovule; he vaguely called in the help of the sparrows engaged in flirting on the guttering.

When he was twelve, his father inherited five thousand pounds from a childless bachelor friend of his named Bassett, a retired surveyor and amateur astronomer, who was a little queer in his last years and built himself a hut in the bush on the North Shore, in order to work out a system of divination by the movements of planets. The legacy caused surprise, for the old friends had not corresponded since Bassett's retirement, Bassett's peculiarities making him cranky and misanthropic. With part of the money the Baguenaults bought themselves a house in the new suburbs of the North Shore, where the ground was cheap, the soil good, and the bush almost undisturbed. Michael's two sisters now had scholarships at the University, Kate was put in a boarding-school, because she had got out of hand, and Michael was alone at home. Mr Baguenault speculated in gold and oil shares and made money. Their house was airy, with wide verandahs on three sides, and stood far back from the street, in a partly cultivated garden that looked over a gully. They seemed to have the mild wilderness to themselves. Across the street was visible from the top windows a flourishing, spacious graveyard. Michael's mother began to be regarded with consideration in the community, because of her interests in charity, and her two clever daughters at the University. Catherine was not mentioned, nor Michael, who was sent to an undistinguished private school recommended by an ambitious priest whom Mrs Baguenault met at afternoon tea.

Michael was weedy at twelve. He caught diphtheria at the school and was ill a long time. The still hours of convalescence bred light fancies, and these returned to him, rounder and brighter, when he drowsed. He was outside lying on a long chair one morning and came to himself to observe his father standing stockstill among the sweet-pea stakes, looking at him intently. When he saw Michael move, he closed his eyes and then opened

9

them, remarking that he had been thinking there in the sun about sweet-peas. There were too many blooms, he must carry a handful to Mrs Vickers, who had none. The peculiar glance of his father turned Michael's thoughts into a gloomy channel. His father, obtuse in his sympathies, was maliciously alert when he found people depressed. Michael did not like him at all. Now, after looking at him again with an unusual persistence, his father said unexpectedly :

"Take care of yourself, Michael; you have been at death's door," and sauntered down towards the orchard, singing "The flowers that bloom in the spring, tra-la, have nothing to do with the case."

Someone had said before that he had been at death's door, and that metaphor, yawning, produced many ideas of solitariness, cold, fear and mental penury. He now said to himself that his hesitant, susceptible, timorous nature would be his ruin; for example, his father, whom he despised, with his orchids and surveying, still had entire dominion over him. If he spoke an idea out aloud and his father guffawed, he felt nauseous: "I will never be any different," he said now, in his convalescent weakness. Yet that same morning as he lay on his couch he felt a new crystalline person arise out of him, as if he had given rise to a new third. He had found a time-yellowed book among his father's old books and read that "the maniac was merely too much awake, as a man possessed by a demon would have excessive strength, excessive malice". He felt his head swelling with each successive phrase like a bud.

When he looked over the edge of the woven rattan at the garden, everything was more lively than a moment before. The dusty leaves blazed, the grass reared itself with a pugnacious thrust, the plants were marshalled, the snail crawled over the leaf with a rushing voluptuous impulse, and all animal and vegetable creations were aware of the sun, wind, sky, shadow, and of their neighbours and of the footfalls and shadows of men, through prehensile senses. A ladybird on the melon-leaf looked like a tortoise; the melon, scarcely pressing the grass, rolled in space as a green universe, self-creative. He thought of the growth of the melon, and immediately saw it bounding towards maturity. The veils of the flesh were torn; he saw the sun pouring in torrents through translucent creatures with millions of cells. Dehiscent seeds burst, pods split, sheaths flew back, grass sprouted, ants scurried, the sun leaped, the sky vibrated, sap hissed, the eucalypt at the foot of the path arched its foolish light head, and the cicadas shouted to turn one's brain. At the same moment that he feared he would lose this pitch of vision, indeed, the phoenix passed over the house, leaving no more than a bright feather, a brilliant hour, for him ruefully to contemplate. He felt dimly that he had in his bosom, if he could only force it out, the secret of greatness; that if he could always be as he had been that moment, his mere word would sway vast crowds of men.

His father often quoted to him: "And they, while their companions slept, were toiling upwards in the night." He stayed awake that night to see if he could toil upwards in the night. A slight fever aided him. The night passed. He slept a little in the day and tossed. The night approached again, and when all had gone to bed he got up and smoothed his pillow.

He stood a long time at his window looking over the garden, street and churchyard on the second night of his vigil. The river of heaven flowed wide, deep and windless, and the suffocated stars rolled slowly on their white flanks through the celestial currents. It was October; the strewn silver meteors shaken fresh from the airy crests went silting and glinting down through the signs of the zodiac, and the hoofs of the Centaur, plunging and curvetting, beat up the dust of the Milky Way. The early morning moon in its last quarter sank gradually to the foot of the sky and entered the feathery boughs of the churchyard yews. Its sallow beam stole over the scattered tombs like bones, sunken in wet clay and smirched with mosses; it drew out the coarse grass and ivy-ends in shadows. Sleep crouched malignantly over the houses. Many bodies in disordered beds struggled with the phantasms abroad; the feeble beam which now entered Michael's bedroom horizontally showed his bed distinctly on its four legs as if ready to career off bewitched. The sheets were smooth and the pillow unpressed. The moonbeam laboured from the open book on the table beside an extinguished candle to Michael's shoulder and on to his pale quarter-moon cheek, capped with black hair and deeply graved in profile.

A slight noise began in the garden. The wind, after raising itself irresolutely three times, moved across the sill and passed over the page which lay curled upon Michael's hand; a faint sound was heard. Michael stirred, pressed his fingers into his eyes and struggled up out of the sickly lethargy into which he had sunk. The breeze reflectively turned over one more page of the book. Michael's eyes swam in their orbits. He looked without interest at the dull moon and lawn. Then his glance moved to the top of the torrid flood of air. His wits turning topsy-turvy rolled upward along the eyebeam, and once more began wandering and stumbling about among rhythms and numbers hideously mixed: visions had long deserted him and he was now in a chaos of tottering gulfs and complex mazes. His heart went on counting stupidly, plom-ploum, plom-ploum, but except for that one earthly thing, he was lost. He seemed to sit in a conciliabule of black extinguisher hats looking at processions of abstract geometrical forms. He reeled against the pane and stood thus, drunk with fatigue. A cock crew, the moon lay on the horizon, the large hole which someone had cut for the turf in the graveyard looked black and deep.

The daylight began to grow in slow undulations. Michael dreamed. The slow, wilful wind rose and sank around the foundations. Moths hovered round the persimmon tree, crickets zithered in the sourgrass, lizards scit-scuttled on the path, and purple-stained wingcases filled the shrubbery night with a slick, minor lightning; all bewitched garden Lilliput, motley and flea-brained, continued its multitudinous creeping and exhausting razzle-dazzle.

Michael lighted the candle. But the bare edges of the table obliterated his dreams; he blew the candle out. In the south he heard faintly the continued droning of the metropolis, and beyond the valley at the bottom of the orchard came the ribanded shrieks of freight-engines labouring towards the city. Beneath the wind was the delicate chipping of the leaves against the stucco wall; an occasional soft surge disturbed the sleep of the turpentines on the next hill. Their street lay drugged in sleep and the churchyard was dark, freed from the dead eye of the lunar world, now dropping out of sight. Hours ago the last footfall had gone rapidly along the pavement; it was the footfall of a woman, he knew, for the light and unequal tapping left the pavement when it came to the church and hurried along the middle of the road where the moon then shone clear. He waited. A cock crew again. Another answered him, and he heard the call going all over the district, diminishing and increasing, moving in discords of twos and threes, and ending suddenly in silence, close at hand, when the first cock crew last and for all. A smile of beatitude flowed over his face; he put his face against the cool plastered wall and tears trickled out; morning was at hand. At the same time he heard someone coming down the street, a firm, crisp, lonely tread, the tread of the early workman. He did not look out of the window again, he was too weak, but he heard the steps surprisingly near till they resounded as if the pavement had been hollow : they lessened and passed on in the distance. Michael, ravaged by waking dreams, thought the man had passed through his breast.

He fell into bed like a log. He opened his eyes a little while afterwards and saw half a red-hot platter risen above the horizon; the birds were making a deafening clatter. "The sun is up," said Michael, and fell dead asleep until twelve o'clock, when his mother, frightened, wakened him. "Let me sleep," said Michael, "I will be better when I wake up."

His mother told her friends of the miraculous sleep that cured him entirely. For a few months he was happy. His parents took advantage of his good days to give him moral advice, to urge him to work at school, and to vaunt him to their friends. "Michael has changed so much; you know at this period . . ." He thought it patronage, got angry with them and with everyone about the house, wanted to live alone, in a forest, on a hill-top. He hoped his father and mother, or at least his father, would die so that he could live alone and free. He wished he had been born a Bedouin to range the desert like a lion, or in some tribe of natives where the little boys were all lodged and taught together. He moved circularly. He learned along the courses of his passions. To himself he seemed either curiously talented with mystic virtues, or a tatterdemalion. He was untidy about his dress, never cleaned his shoes, hated washing his hands and feet, and felt his clothes unbearably thick, clumsy and ill-cut on him; and for this he blamed his parents. He had a very poor grasp of ordinary life: he could not bear a reproach, and would have killed a person who remonstrated with him if he had not feared the prison or reformatory. He was thrown off his balance, and suffered headaches and nausea many times on account of arguments or scoldings. He cried out at night, dreaming that he was suffocating or being attacked by bears, or being followed by gigantic funereal phantoms, and he had half a dozen tics, twisting his hair, biting his cheeks, scratching his gums with his nails, plucking his knee. He had austere ideals. He would not cry out when the door shut on him, when a boy stuck a pin into him, when the doctor came to sew up a wound where a dog bit him: but he would cry when his father said something insulting to him, for a joke. He scarcely spoke to the other children except to say, "The reason is . . ." "That comes from . . ." or in analogy, "Cloth flows like water. . . ."

He did not play much at school, could not bear to take part in the gang quarrels of the boys, liked to sit behind bushes and enter into long colloquies with friendly children, about marbles, history, the sky, ghosts, the characters of the teachers. He was inarticulate in his love-affairs and suffered intensely for them. He preferred to maunder about amongst rocks, trees, pools of water, beside the sea, in the wind, in the bush rushing with storm where he could divine or imagine presences, voices, miracles. At such times he would feel a rush of saliva in the mouth, and his jaws would work of themselves as if it were imperious for him to cry aloud, to make a speech, to chant. And when he was alone in his room at night, drowsy, he heard long conversations carried on between his teeth and his tongue, between the towel and the washstand, the mosquito and the ceiling he was hitting. Whenever he stood on one foot gazing into the garden, or propped himself against the door looking dreamily about him, or pored a long time over some stuff or surface examining its grain, he was listening with half his mind to these interminable, stupid conversations which went on inside him.

"Floor, you are dusty, but I am dustier still."

"Mat, I know you are dustier still, but that is because everyone treads on you, your design will soon be worn off and you will be nothing but dust."

"But it is good dust, worth having, the dust off the feet of these great creatures."

"Pooh, they got it in the garden, where dogs have pissed and cats stink."

"What do I care if I'm dirty, that's my mission; I don't mind accomplishing my mission."

"I prefer to shine with floor-wax."

This inaudible whispering would keep up for hours; and if it was not a dialogue between two objects or creatures, it was an argument between himself and some creature, an ant, a cloud, a coat. He liked to be alone.

He was lively on birthdays, on Christmas Day, when he was sure to get some presents. He awakened in the early morning, gay, tingling, full of jokes; the whole day he was flushed and amiable, helping his mother, doing whatever his father wanted, complimenting his sisters, making them gifts. If he got a new suit, he would be merry too, and if there was a party given in the house, he hung about, did tricks in the doorway, and recited poetry until he was reproved and sent away. He received twopence a week to spend, and would spend it gladly every Saturday, looking over his new possessions all the afternoon, eating slowly and pleasurably the sweets he had bought, and hating to give any away.

Michael now took to science and would engage with any of the teachers in religious, philosophic and logical discussions; his long years of fanciful reasoning had given him an agility in argument; he found himself in his words, the schoolmen's world, the world of pure verbalism. In Botany, once, having drawn thirty diagrams of the stages of union of two cells of the gutter-weed, Spirogyra, which is thin and long like a green hair, a kind of frenzy took hold of him. He looked through the microscope and saw that not only was the series, taken as a series of poses, like a cinematograph, infinite, but that even with all his care and preoccupation he could not seize the important moment of change, it was not there, it seemed to him mystic. When he saw a person going downstairs and compared the last appearance of that one's head with the empty space when he was no longer there, the change seemed to him infinitely great, even impossible, a freak that could not take place in the natural world in which he breathed. In his imagination a thing was, and then disappeared, dark remained, and in between was a space of dreams, of nonentity. He held up his mind, a cracked and yellow mirror to reflect the machinery of the world, and in that dark space the world ceased for a moment to exist.

But at these times especially, he would fall back against his seat or lean on his elbow looking out of the window at the trees, and powerful visions would pass through his head; he laboured automatically to increase and perfect these visions, to make them logical, grandiose. He believed in intellectual miracles. He suffered states which were ecstasy, although they were not joyful but rapt and inhuman. In those moments he gave out cold as a genial person gives out warmth and love.

One day when the school was out on a picnic, the headmaster walked a little way aside with him. "Your character is like that ship," said he, looking down from the heights of a bay; "it can be guided by you, your will the pilot, or cast away, for the immediate gain in a cheap profession, or the pleasures a young man likes, or cast adrift and someone, man or woman, may earn the salvage of it."

"I will never be captain of my soul," said Michael, interested in the subject. "I began, and will end, a beachcomber—spiritually, I mean," he added at the schoolmaster's start; "guide as you will, Nature is stronger."

"You should wish to oblige—Nature, if you don't believe in God."

"I am surprised you don't think God superior to your will," answered Michael. "I assure you if I believed in God, I would do nothing at all, but sink into his bosom. Be reasonable; any action

16

at all would be away from God. The wells of nature, love, ambition, understanding, sleep, gush in us as oil and water in the world and blood in the heart. I follow them lamely; it is I who do their bidding, in following my bent. Listen, is the world full of spirits, as the mind? I see no will or obedience in anything, only the abrupt, spontaneous will and generation; to a certain point water is water, then it is steam or ice, there is no slow change, as I used to think, it is abrupt, and it is mystery. How blunt our senses are, how many thick veils hang between us and the world. How will we ever refine our eyes to see atoms and our ears to hear the messages of ants? There is plenty that we miss; I feel my brain turning to think what we miss. When I see order I am amazed, it seems unnatural, I feel uneasy, as if I were looking at a thing artificially perfect like a china doll's complexion. You know how astonished you are when you turn a kaleidoscope and see a perfect design fall together by chance. As if harlequins, a drunken mass of masks and ankles, fell tumbling together into a colour wheel. I wish to watch the ordinary movement of life and I see only a succession of dead, shed moments without inter-relation : like a man walking through a hall of mirrors and seeing a thousand reflections of himself on every side, each one a shell of himself, and insubstantial. Time, tide, order, I cannot under-stand; I would go mad; I would rather believe in fairies."

"It is this new country," sighed the schoolmaster. "You have no notion of history; you began yesterday and you all think you are the first men. Doctrine, constitution, order, duty, religion, you have to find them out by long and droughty explorations in the spirit."

"You pursue me; my mind is not strong. Leave me alone!" cried Michael furiously.

The headmaster turned back helplessly.

His mother, who had stayed away from church for years to please her husband, was now about forty-five and began to have vagaries. She read books of religious edification and spent all her household money on charitable fêtes and collections. A nosing priest found Mrs Baguenault in this state of mind and came to visit her every morning, to have tea, talk scandal and improve her chances of salvation: she had already participated in two Catholic fêtes, and caused a lot of talk in the district. Michael came home from school one day before lunch, because he was sick, and found the priest there. He looked at him: shallow blue eyes bright under thick banded lids, a long snout, small at the bridge and lobed at the point, a round helpless chin and face, but a lemony skin and sprouting reddish beard on a jaw stupidly prognathous like a foetus, and the low-placed mouth shut tight and as if strapped in by the pale lips. He was of medium height with medium shoulders, and a belly protruding already: taken with his sleepy, shut-in, absorbed face, this gave him a pregnant look. A woman, said Michael. He stood at the door studying the couple, who were sitting in the bay-window. His mother bent over some knitting she was doing for a fête; the priest was talking easily and uninterruptedly. One divined that he had been talking like that for an hour and would go on until lunch-time; he had an imperative note and ran on like a sewing-machine. His mother smiled, blushed, and laughed clearly like a young girl.

"And Michael," said the priest; "so you think he is cut out to be a teacher?"

"I would like it so much," cried the mother. "It is a learned profession, it is well paid and safe. He is a quiet sort of boy and would do better in a quiet profession. I would not like him to go into the city where the young men run round to races, poolrooms and all sorts of horrors."

"And is he more spiritually minded?" said the priest. "If he would accept it, perhaps I could talk with him."

Michael came into the room.

"Hullo, mother; I had a belly-ache and came home. It must have been your rissoles."

"Michael! Father Bingham, this is Michael; you know him by sight. Father Bingham called in to ask me to do something for the fête," she said hurriedly to Michael. Michael nodded, sat down on the window-seat, and said:

"No teaching for me. Imagine! Hang yourself on a pothook, run around brandishing a ruler over a lot of little fellers dirty as cockroaches and smelling of urine: no! You stand up in front.

'Pi is a surd,' and the whole class begins to laugh and shout, 'Pi is absurd.' 'The first principle of economics is supply and demand,' you say, but Brown is whispering, 'Hey, Sniffles, what do you want for your dictionary of slang?' The bright ones only look for a chance to catch you napping, to mystify you..What would I do if I found myself face to face with a kid who was really smart? Lie down and let him talk? But I'm paid for talking to him. Besides, no pedagogy for me, it's too spiritual: the multiplication table is close to metaphysics: I'm going to be a counter-jumper."

"Teaching is next to the work of God, almost as spiritual as religion," said the priest.

"Spiritual? Look at the Mass, no spiritual elements there: wine, blood, bread, flesh, statue, God the son. Funny thing all religions turn round eating. In that, I must say, the monks used to be very religious; every supper was the last till the next. How do you prove it's an extra holy day? By eating grass instead of flesh. How do you celebrate the rising of Jesus? By eating stuffed duck! Where did Peter get his money? Out of a fish. Where did the Virgin get her child? From a dove. It was called the spirit, but it was a dove. God is a spirit and has no passions, but if you say, God damn, he gets angry enough to roast your soul in real, red fire. He has no nose, but he likes incense; and no ears, but he likes prayers and psalm-singing. He is praised because he created physics and geography, because he made his prophets write down rules about what women should do during their periods, after child-bearing, and that there should be no love between sheep and goats, or something like that; I won't mention it in full on account of mother here, but you're a technician, Father, you know what I mean. And God likes virginity, but what meaning can virginity have to a spirit? And he prefers to be worshipped in church: but what can the Lord of the angels want with coloured glass and crochet lace? Where can you find me a single abstract idea in the whole of practised religion? or a single logical one that a modern working man wouldn't demolish in two words, if he bothered about it? You can fuddle my poor Mumma," finished Michael, getting up and sidling behind the priest's chair, "but I assure you she's your last conquest."

The priest had a mean look, and on his lardy forehead were faint beads of sweat; his mouth was tighter than usual. Mrs Baguenault held her heart as if she thought she would faint.

"Michael, how could you!"

Michael laughed and went out of the room. His mother drew a few loud breaths and ran from the room; they heard her vomiting on the verandah. The priest came into the passage, said nothing for a minute, and then said with a serpentine motion of his neck, very quietly:

"Don't think you've shocked me: you have only not considered one thing, which all your moderns neglect—Mystery. There is an element in life and in deity which surpasses all your reasoning, however logical it is, that is the Mysteries, the Symbols, the Miracles, the Ineffableness of Deity. What you see is only the surface; there is something underneath which you do not see. Do your men of science understand how thought acts on the muscles, how men can receive the notion of God if he does not exist, and how life starts? And as for your men of science, Faraday——"

"—prayed for rain. I know, thanks! I used to find those problems a poser when I was a kid: now I know you don't approach them in that light."

"It's a matter of approach: you must have the grace of God, and that is a pure gift to be obtained by self-sacrifice, prayer, and because of the merits of Jesus Christ . . ."

Michael laughed outright.

"Mr Bingham, don't you see that it's all over with me? I'll never believe in that hocus-pocus again. You're a fisher of men, aren't you? You ought to recognise an empty catch and take the day off to mend your nets when you see you're wasting your time. You know you despise the women you convert, and that if your family had had the dough to put you into business, or give you a profession, you wouldn't be trailing around in skirts."

The priest turned his back. Michael heard his mother and the priest communing for a while, the priest brief, his mother apologising. He went back on tiptoe to hear what his mother was

20

saying, ready to interrupt again rather than have her humiliate herself for him. In a low voice she was saying,

"Catherine ran away from home when she was fifteen, and now Michael is a rebel: my two eldest girls are such dear good girls. Do you think it is possible for such young people to be—sinful?"

"It's easy and very common, unfortunately," said the priest nastily. "As a mother, you are neglecting your duty."

"I feel I am being punished myself," said the woman.

"No doubt," said the priest.

"It is about Michael," said the woman. "He was born in, he was born out of, his father was not . . ."

The priest's traitless face showed a shade of interest, malice, revenge and victory.

"Not here," he said, "but if you wish to come to me this afternoon, at the church, in the chapel of St. Joseph . . ."

"Ah, the bastard," said Michael to himself, "he won't get her: I'll stop her."

"Ah-ha, a bastard," said the priest to himself; "I'll get her, nothing will stop her."

He got up with a satisfied air. She fumbled around in her dress, the woman, her neat hair slightly disordered, her eyes with their swollen tear-sacs, suffused. She looked older than she had a few minutes before. The priest full of spite and pride walked slowly down the garden path along the roses. "So that's the way the land lies," he said to himself. "Look at those roses, those French beans: very nice. So that's how the husband got his touch of satire: well, foh, foh, it's always the same. These meek dames and meek husbands, the devil gets into one or the other with great ease." He looked at the roses with a vicious smile, as if he accused them for the soft effusion of their unreligious saps.

"Not bad," said he.

Michael was joyful.

"Then the old orchid-king is not my papa," said he to himself. "What a blessing! And Cath, too, the other sinner. But no, she may be my half-sister."

He speculated about his father, but could not imagine who he might be. He looked at his mother with respect.

"Who would have thought that the old girl had it in her?"

Michael refused to return to the high school, but would give no reason, except to say that the principal was a dummy and he couldn't stand the staff. He showed an unexpected resistance to his father's command, carried himself with a lordly air as if the key of the family strongbox were in his possession, and loafed about the house.

It was a great spring for Michael : his courage was up. The sky was more purple in the evening than he ever remembered it before. He awakened early in the morning with the birds and insects shouting, or slept until midday and got through the day frowsily without his parents reproaching him. This false calm charmed and frightened him. The day when he must get a job came closer and closer, like the strip of dark blue wind-stirred water to the rowing-boat rowing in the calm. He got fatter, with a bit of colour in his cheeks, sang in his bath, although his voice was still weak, took up water-colour painting, fretsaw work, and went swimming in the river. Catherine came home for two months in the summer, tired out with her jobs. She had been working temporarily at fruit-packing on an orchard, at knitting by machine in a stocking-factory, and at dishwashing in a private kitchen, during the year. At home, she relaxed, played the piano, went out painting with Michael; in the bush put wreaths of clematis on her long black hair to pose for Michael, tried to get through the day without arguing with her mother, and ignored her father entirely. Michael informed her with pride that he did not know his real father. Catherine said, "Poor Mother, I don't blame her, but I never knew she had the guts; I've misjudged her." She began making discreet enquiries and presently told Michael that his father must have been the lonely bachelor, the astronomer and mathematician who had left Mr Baguenault a legacy.

"Go on," said Michael. "The family owes all to me? I always felt I had a secret virtue. And your father?"

"I am legit.," said Catherine.

After the vacation Michael went to a business college, but left

22

in six months asserting that the course was a fraud and that he had already learned all their courses through. He went to a large soap-making firm in Balmain, as filing-clerk, and gradually learned the idiotic routine of the office and the obscure jargon used to dignify business letters in their baldness. The soap-making firm had a director of welfare and culture. The directors liked to see their employees reading the classics of economics written before 1840 and the classics of literature written up to 1902. Michael joined the debating and dramatic clubs, read *Hamlet* for the debate about Hamlet's sanity, and the *Pickwick Papers* for the parody session of the club. He debated about equal pay for equal work, the effects of drunkenness, the relative influence of instinct and environment, and free trade and protection. But he was unsuccessful as a debater. He joined a physical culture class, and started to learn French and Esperanto, but dropped both. He took an interest in the white-slave and drug traffics, and in medicine, in venereal diseases. He bought handbooks on the care of dogs, home-plumbing, french polishing, wireless telegraphy, and the terms used in architecture. He collected old iron which he intended to sell to the junk man in order to pay for a bicycle, and stamps, with the hope of finding a Mauritius blue. After eighteen or twenty months he got a job in an advertising firm downtown and found he had a knack for it; his mysticism of the past aided him.

At eighteen Michael met Tom Withers, then twenty-four, at a smoke-concert of press lithographers, cartoonists, commercial artists and others. Withers was tall, round-shouldered, starved, with a large mouth and soft deep-set eyes behind pince-nez. He wore a good but unpressed suit, and was unshaved. He wore his hat almost all the time, concealing an early baldness. He smoked cheap cigarettes, wore a gold signet ring with a coronet in the seal, and took long, debile steps in old shoes down-at-heel. Except when he was speaking excitedly, or muttering in a friend's ear over a drink, he sat back with the deathmask face of the over-wrought and overworked. A soft moustache drooped round his red lips, his small teeth gleamed like pebbles in his red gums. Tom Withers dropped down by Michael this night, anxious to

23

acquaint himself with the newcomer. He sat by him for hours, slightly fuddled, telling interminable and apparently inter-related histories from the *Iliad*, from Pietro Aretino, from Terence, Horace and Livy, recommended to Michael special editions in English and Latin, assured him he had a genius for the classics, recited a whole bibliography of obscene books of the most brilliant kind, told Michael all true art lay there, quoted recipes from the unexpurgated *Arabian Nights* and similes from the Kama-Sutras, revealed the secrets of exotic religions, secret sects, the obsessions of the Flagellantes, the monks of the Thebaïd, the habits of S. Simeon Stylites, and the private history of the Magdalen. Mixed with his erudition were common-room parodies of psalms, epigrams and limericks, all horribly obscene, and adventures, which he said were his own, of thunderstorms of quartz-pebbles containing gold, rivers blown skyhigh leaving the fish baked in baked mud-beds, human monsters hideous but brilliant in wits, and idiotic beauties seduced on roadsides, married women of the highest social class swimming with him by moonlight in a sand-bottomed river, and pearls of girls sleeping with him in the underbrush or in a cave lighted by phosphorescence. There was a night, he said, when he, Tom Withers, alone was abroad, the Aurora Australis shone and comets streaked the sky. He found an old tramp woman, took her to a Greek dive for food, found her to be an ancient actress, formerly a toast, in distress, and lived with her platonically for three weeks. He had spilled on the ground the milk of milkmaids returning from the cow-pastures, drunk lachryma Christi with the son of a noble Italian family exiled in Australia for unnatural loves. He knew a boy of the best stock who wore two golden armlets bearing spikes on the inside, so that his arms were always covered with blood, to mortify his flesh. He had met funerals at nightfall with lamps and native instruments in the islands, had lived with lepers, rowed nine hundred miles in an open boat to a coral atoll, and had run aground in a merchant-tub in the Solomon Islands. He knew the habits of the Ming dynasty and the authenticity of marks on ceramics. Talking of these things, the voice of Tom Withers flowed almost inaudibly on and on. Michael, astonished

24

and decoyed, listened many hours on many days afterwards to the soft-dropping babble of this troubadour, and was convinced that he had met the most remarkable man in the city.

But sometimes Withers got into a high passion, began squealing in a female voice: he would not stand this and this, he would do anything to teach that bastard a lesson, they had better be careful, he knew too much about them. And the diarrhoea of defamation then flowed from his lips. He knew everyone's weak points, who slept with another man's wife, who was cuckold, who had an illegitimate child, who went to bawdy-houses, why the talents of each one would never get him on in life, what was the brand and catchword treacherously passed round among friends, summing up absent friends, what diseases each one had, how they had made their money, and why each man had married each woman. Nothing was too low for Withers to repeat. He chewed each arch remark, dipping his moustache in beer, chewing his tongue, like a boy chewing sugar-cane until it is dry; his brown eyes shone softly and his face was fully awakened from its mortuary repose.

Withers rarely got blind-drunk. He pretended there were a hundred stages of drunkenness and that he knew which degree would produce in him a certain state of mind. He liked to stop drinking when he was glowing within, light on his feet, and when his lips talked of themselves. He never told the same tale twice in the same way: something new, foolish, foul, extravagant, had always just occurred to him to embroider the theme.

He liked to backbite the successful, glorious, ambitious and proud, but his work was cruder with them; his real artistry was called forth in the backbiting of the mean and unfortunate. He suggested solutions of their personal problems in accordance with the most advanced social theories, knowing well that it was impossible for them to solve their problems. He would act the false comforter to these unfortunates, urge them to run away from their wives, disown their children, give all they had to the poor, join the Communist Party and forget personal troubles in a life of self-sacrifice, join the Catholic Church, join the Single Tax movement, drink themselves to death, take a mistress, murder a rich uncle, hold up a banker one dark night. He proffered these solutions with the utmost seriousness, and almost took himself seriously. He would have been pleased to help in any of these adventures. When he had irritated these friends in need, had poured into their ears a host of stories and examples, made them restless with desire and disappointment, given them a drink and tailed them home to be sure they crossed their thresholds with a dismal face he would go home and sleep softly. But he did not do it to do harm; he did it because his life-blood flowed from his tongue and he wished to have as many audiences of as many kinds in as many moods as he could find in a too-short life; and human nature was sluggish—he was obliged to goad it on. If a person were really sick, alone, or in danger of being gaoled, Withers was always there, with his theories, his advice, a hot-water bottle, and an aspirin tablet. He fixed bandages, recommended sleeping-draughts and washed babies' napkins with the equanimity of a trained nurse, all the time relating that one of his friends was sick in hospital with typhoid got through eating oysters, and a friend's mistress had broken her leg while kneeling down to say the Lord's Prayer; that another friend had shot her husband with a pearl-handled revolver and had only succeeded in removing a mole which had disfigured him for years on the side of the face; that a doctor he knew went to bed with all his women patients and made a fortune by abortions; that a friend of his in Medical School had just discovered a new cause of paralysis; and that the President of some South American republic would fall soon because he had general paresis. Then he would sit down to amuse the patient, tell him picaresque stories, broad jokes, and show him experiments in chemistry and physics; he could describe to him the nature of bacteria and discuss the principle of life. Strange Withers, womanly, corrupt, fantastic, sottish, shrewish, treacherous, faithful; a person to throw up his chances for a quixotic motive and to undermine the reputation of his nearest and dearest friend; a man to borrow fifty pounds for you from a usurer, if you needed it, and to sponge on you for five years, if you were in funds.

Withers had not always been on his uppers. Until the age of

fifteen he had lived in expectation of a small legacy from an aunt, but the aunt had died poor. Cranky at this disappointment, he had knocked about from pillar to post, had been kept by a rich woman for four months in order to get to Italy and had there deserted her on the landing-stage to make his way by a hundred curious means to Germany and England. Yet he was a good workman; inside the walls of his printing-works he was as crazily methodical as a superannuated book-keeper: he was in a continual pet, was careful of his dignity, took a pleasure in scolding the boss, and saw that things were done to time. He was a tyrant for the minute details, and laid down the law. Yet he had no pride in his work, ran it down, never consorted with workmen, but with the boss, or friends outside, with artists and students, laughed at unionism and hated the Labour movement.

This pernickety man charmed Michael. Withers, taken with a new fancy, having no bosom friend at the moment, buttonholed Michael and started to run through his tricks with him. Withers liked fishing. Michael invited him to Fisherman's Bay one Saturday, saying that he had relatives there, who would give them tea. On the ferry, Withers said that he knew two nice girls in Fisherman's Bay.

"That's yours: she's just your meat," he said, chuckling, and offered his notebook, in which Michael read:

"Mae Graham, 16, address, 14 Pound Street, blonde, handfed, dances, typiste, no mortgage."

Other names appeared above and below, with different indications, and physical peculiarities were not spared.

"That's the girl for you," said Withers, enjoying Michael's astonished examination of his notebook. Michael blushed to the roots of his hair.

"You're pretty frank, aren't you? What does that mean, 'handfed, no mortgage'?"

"Handfed means she has doting parents and shows it," said Withers; "and no mortgage means she isn't engaged in heart or hand."

A month after, Michael calculated that he had been in the Bay fourteen times on various excuses since that Saturday, had seen

Mae only once, the day he had gone out with her and Withers, and had seen his relatives, the Baguenaults, thirteen times. Mae was always "engaged".

One day Michael saw her walking with her boy, lanky, serious and deeply in love. Michael knew that they both went to an art class in the evenings: Mae even posed, as other students did, in drapery, at times. She was extremely sensual in face and body. Her face, large below the brow, with a full lower jawbone and strong round chin, caught the eye. Her hair was brassy, rolled on the nape of the neck, with curls at the roots. Her skin was most exceptionally white. She had a light-rose cheek, quite full, but on which appeared already a faint shade, the shade of fatigue and bad light in the office. Her eyes, sunken in the socket, but with globular eyelids, clear blue and liquid, were already ringed faintly. Her red painted lips, narrow but full and fleshy in the corners, shut tight over her regular white teeth. She had, in repose, the expression of a young woman languishing a little at the end of a passionate honeymoon: Withers called her "the odalisque". When she laughed, as she often did, tormented her friends, or became eager over an outing, generously wept in the pictures, got excited over a history of the cruelty or heroism of love, her face had a very intense expression of enjoyment. She thrust her head forward, with her lips pouted and parted, as if she was trying to bite into a ripe fruit and suck it. She was plump but still small. She walked with a beautiful bounding step, having long and fine legs, and her round thighs moved under her dress freely. She did not move all in a piece like thick-set women, with their heavy basins and ungainly skirts; her silk dress fluttered like a veil on her. When left to herself, she had a half-smiling abstraction, like a sleeping child.

Withers watched the growth of his affections with a tender satiric pleasure, and tried to bewilder him by taking him out with other girls and by making him get drunk; but Michael came back from these parties wretched, sick with palpitations of the heart. He began to say to Withers, "Go without me. It's not for me, I don't like it. Find someone else." Withers, who never discussed and never burdened his life with other people's problems, let him go, and gradually gave up seeing him.

Michael's father stood watching him from the door some mornings early as he cleaned his boots outside before going to work, frowning over his work with his thin dark cheeks compressed, answering briefly and crossly when they spoke to him. He turned into the wide hall where the mother sat waiting for breakfast, and said:

"He is crotchety, Michael, an unstable boy. Sometimes it turns out all right; sometimes they go completely nutty, like old Bassett. I heard the other day he married his housekeeper secretly some years before he died. You know what a pepper-pot he was. They led a cat-and-dog life and she tried to get a doctor to certify that he was not all there. You couldn't expect a practical woman to put up with his tantrums. At any rate, he left her half his estate and she's doing the genteel widow now in Leichhardt somewhere, going to whist parties and having people to tea on Sundays."

"I didn't know that he was married," said Mrs Baguenault. She took an apron out of the linen drawer and tied it round her. "I'm going to cut some roses," said she. "Do you want to come out with me, Ben?"

"All right." He put out his hairy-backed hand and stroked her arm. She pretended not to notice and went into the kitchen to get the garden scissors. There she sat down on a chair and forgot about her husband waiting in the hall. Michael came in presently through the back-door with a cross face and a bluish face, due to insomnia, or a toothache, or a heart-attack: one never knew what; his works were all at fault.

"Michael," she cried in such a tone that he went to her.

"What, Mother?"

"My baby, no one will ever love you and understand you like your mother: you know that, don't you? There is a special reason, there is . . . why you are a little morbid. Tell Mother your troubles, she will understand."

"Golly, Mother, cut it out," said Michael. "Who told you I'm morbid? All chaps are morbid at my age; it's my heart. Don't notice me, that's all I ask. And there's nothing you can tell me I don't know." He looked at her expressionlessly and went out of the kitchen.

Foolish, hoping to awaken a gesture of love, some haphazard touch that would help her illusion along, that she was cherished, that he was grateful to her for having brought him into the world, for having accomplished her "mission", for having given him suck, she said:

"Michael, Michael, baby, come here; why are you always so resentful? Why don't you speak to your mother? It's not kind. When you were a little boy, you promised to tell Mother everything all your life. You don't know what a mother goes through, Mikey."

"Certainly, I do," said Michael, laughing in the doorway. "You gestated for nine months, you were in travail for eight hours, you had puerperal fever; I know, Mother." He came back and smiled more kindly, as he looked down at the coiled grey hair and the soft wrinkled face, the eyes bleared with facile tears, the mouth drawn with a credulous smile. "And then I puked, yowled, got my teeth, had diarrhoea, scarlatina and convulsions; I had great promise and nothing was too good for me, and my sisters used to love me, I know. I've heard that tale somewhere."

"You love your mother," she said, with her obsession.

"Go on," he cried, impatient. "You always want to be told you're loved; you're like all girls, you never hear it enough, you can't let a man alone: but are you worth all that love? Let me hear what medals for virtue you won."

She smiled to be teased by her tall and difficult son. But she could not stop babbling.

"You haven't really changed, have you? You believe in God, don't you, son? There's nothing unmanly in that."

"Don't bother me with that, Mumma," he replied with fresh irritation. "It's enough that the black-skirts got one member of the family: you can go to heaven and save us all."

"What do you believe, what, tell me?"

"I'm an atheist, have been for years: you know it. What's the good of pretending? And it's only because you're old, Mother, that you're religious yourself: it's a sign of age."

"I'm old, yes, but the old know what life is like."

"You don't bother Catherine with all this, why me? With your little-girl passion for men, I'm all you have in your head."

"Catherine," said the mother indifferently, "she doesn't really mean it: when she meets the right man, she'll settle down. The family, a husband, religion—they go together."

"It's enough to make me sick. You don't know that in Catherine you have a magnificent daughter, a rebel, a gallant character."

"A woman should be a woman. What's the good of her being a rebel? Where did it get her? I hope God will give her a lesson and turn her back to us."

"There's no God, and you know it yourself, but you must amuse yourself with fairy-tales, like all old women. What a breed! it's enough to make a man turn homosexual. Where's any evidence of him? The whole blasted world is a museum of trouble, disappointment and malady, and you expect me to take an interest in a fairy-tale like that. You don't make me respect you any more by running round with priests, Mother. I'm a man, I live with men who make buildings, newspapers, machines, designs for cloth. You housewives are absolutely ignorant of the world; you don't know how stories are fabricated in newspapers or in scriptures, how the house is put together, how cloth is made or dyed. All you know is, religion, home, fashion, some painted mechanical creatures that come all made into the world. The one bit of creation you can and must all do, does itself unconsciously: you think the rest of men's work is like that. Let us alone, Mother. I am thinking in terms of reality, the only ones I know. I suffer; Catherine, poor girl, suffers, and fights; you too. God didn't help you through your labour-pains. That is real, realler than the fantasies of a dreaming God. If he were present, as you say, he would know the degree of misery in a household, the pain of drowning in a fog, firedamp in a mine, cancer, the degree of pain even in a poor creature like me, for instance: all too heady for the thin vessels we are. Are we to be damned for such cruel potions and purges put by him in a phial too weak to hold them? We burst in pieces on the floor. God, anything we can seize here on earth is too little to recompense us for what we suffer."

He put his hand to his forehead, turned about, and rushed out of the room. His mother sat staring at the floor, nodding her head to herself and moving her lips. Her husband came to the door:

"Mary? And the roses?"

"Never mind now."

"Michael's gone without any breakfast."

"Let him be; let him be. Boys get brainstorms." But she continually repeated to herself, "He's like that Bassett: that crazy Bassett. I knew Bassett was undependable: imagine marrying a housekeeper."

Later she said to the father:

"Ben, I think Michael must be in love: I never thought of it before."

In the evening the father took Michael out for a walk to find orchids and to talk with him privately.

"Be simple," said Mr Baguenault. "Don't get drunk with liquor, or with your wits, or adolescent sufferings. After all, they're not very real, compared with true trials. It's called the age of storm and stress, but maturity is for a man; then he has unheard-of troubles, mostly financial: he has to face bankruptcy and black-mail. If you want to know how I have got over many troubles, it is through loving Nature. My orchids have saved me from thinking over human things too deeply. It doesn't do. Nature is free, you can love her as you might love a girl. It is the same thing, it is to love her as she really is, not a painted doll, not a planted park, but scarred with storms and bush-fires, diseases and nests of white-ants, blasted by lightning, dried by the sun: as you love a girl although she has freckles, a turned-up nose and spindly legs and is out of drawing in a bathing-suit."

He was silent. He continued:

"You can be absorbed in Nature, as—as in the sea, as if you melted into the sea and were diffused through the oceans of the earth. There is peace when her mysteries are an open book to you; in her inmost recesses she has perfect peace, even for the most fevered."

Michael bit his lip and said nothing; but in the bush behind the house, when he had left his father, he thought over the old man's words, and poking a stick into the soil thoughtfully, he said aloud:

32

"The old fellow has some experience: perhaps there is peace here."

He looked around. A tall tree, whose topmost tips were now yellow in the setting sun, waved delicately against the pale high sky. Michael lifted his stick to the yellowed leaves, smiling.

"Only teach me to believe that, and I would throw myself on your breast. In the ocean, to melt. But the ocean flows and ebbs twice a day. He sees the sky with a great pearl in her bosom and he follows her round the earth, and if I were dissolved there, I would only circle the earth for ever, salt with desire; I would sleep not more than he. And at night I used to hear long conversations and much lamenting among the waves on the seashore, when the moon was away. And here at night in the bush is interminable bickering and soughing. Then I am not alone with my tears and restlessness and there is no peace."

The next Sunday he went to church with his mother, to please her. The young visiting priest said:

"Should you not in all functions desire only to serve God the master and return to God the fountain? The minerals do not desire to live as individuals, they stay in their colonies, sorts and orders, and accomplish their destinies, part of the common rock, although they are more beautiful than the rock. Their hidden virtues do not require the sun. There are no mineral Peer Gynts. They only wish to come to the end of their foreordained cycle, to be dissolved, to crumble and enter the earth and be sucked into the roots of plants and enter the higher life of the vegetable kingdom and grow upwards towards the sun in green spires. The plants do not desire to vegetate; there is intense life among them, even though their existence is usually brief. They are humble, ignorant, have no voice, yet look how they are adorned when they are ripe. They put on roots, leaves, flowers, seeds, and fall to dust; millions upon millions richer than eye has seen in the jungles and wastes. They do not rebel, they accomplish their pre-destined cycle: but the Lord has them in his hand. And if they were sentient and understood what might be their destiny even on earth, would they not give themselves up the more gladly into the maw of animals and become living flesh and blood, to see,

D

feel, hear, have affections, and praise God? Animals would certainly die joyfully if they knew they were to become part of man, if they could understand the higher sense they would enjoy: reason, sacred love, poetry, music, and if they could have any glimmering of the Soul they would inherit. They do not know it. They ruminate in the fields and the Lord accepts their unconscious sacrifice and works out their higher destiny himself. We should take them for a model, these humble creatures, and put ourselves into his hands without revolt. He will sacrifice us for a higher end. And what is that end? We have understanding, small though it is, we know that he will accept the sacrifice of our life, a poor thing, the life of the flesh, at best, to make us one with him, even as all those lower creatures came up to become part of us. What peace and what joy: to stay in one's place and yet be part of the aspiring universe. What glorious functions, exceeding our understanding, will man not perform, and what divine senses not enjoy, when the final sacrifice is over, his personal will is annihilated to be with God on earth, to be with God in Paradise, at the dissolution of the flesh."

"I see: we eat beef and God eats us," whispered Michael. "The lad yonder does not suffer from indigestion. He must have been a cowherd in old Ireland and worked out the simple mysteries of his faith in the fields, chewing the cud."

"Don't come with me, if you can't feel more reverent," said his mother.

"Thank God, then I won't," cried Michael: and he never did again, but went out each week-end with Catherine in the bush, or to resorts along the coast. They walked often together arm-in-arm, in the evenings, along the red roads that wound through the bush, smelling the young clematis and singing sea-chanties in their weak and tuneless voices. They caught frilled lizards, green tree-snakes and the brown "double-drummer" cicadas that sing deafeningly in the hand. They pondered over mysterious graves, deserted orchards and closed huts, and often went into some rough shelter at night and slept easily on dried bracken or hay. But Catherine grew restless after two months and sang no more. She turned on her bed at night, and hardly replied to Michael's

34

musings. Presently she said:

"I must go back. I must go into the city and work."

She left him in a town in the mountains and took the train back. When he returned home he looked for her up and down the town, and at last, through the direction of a friend, located her in a miserable lodging where she had nothing but a blanket on a wire mattress. She wore her oldest dress, torn and faded, and looked at Michael when he entered as if she scarcely recognised him. Never had he seen her more like a witch or beggar-woman.

"You are starving," he cried, almost weeping, terrified.

"I am earning my living," she replied with scorn.

"At what?"

She smiled before replying and raised to him one of her old bright dominating looks.

"You wouldn't guess. I am a model for an art-class, old Mr Benson's. He knows Father, but I have not let on that I know Father."

Michael paled a little, but said mildly:

"Do you do—all sorts of poses?"

She laughed extravagantly and tapped her foot.

"Yes, you think I'm too skinny: that's what makes me picturesque. Look, one of the students admires me, my type: he gave me the finished picture. It's too bad to go for the Prix de Rome, in any case, so it's no generosity."

She took a piece of sacking off a box in one corner of the room, and stood up an oil-painting on its edge. She looked at it with pride. In it she appeared as a worn, crazy, young gypsy.

"They said I am the perfect gypsy," she said contentedly. It was crude and made Catherine seem bold and coarse.

"It's very good," he said faintly.

She looked at him with malice.

"And here's another, the latest."

She took out a sheet of Michallet paper with a drawing on it in charcoal.

"The young drawing-master is preparing an exhibition of his own: I posed for him privately."

Her vanity was intense. The drawing was labelled, "Fished up", and showed an emaciated naked woman lying dead on the quays, while a curious crowd with caricature faces hung over it and a policeman stood by.

Michael looked at his sister with shame. She laughed again.

"Naturally he gave me that because it's not going in the exhibition."

Michael went and sat on her bed, feeling his beating heart with his hand. Presently he got up, held on to the foot of the bed, trembling violently, and said:

"Catherine, Catherine, come out of all this misery. You are unhappy at home. I'll work for you; we'll get a little room and I'll keep you until you feel ready to do steady work; all my life, if it's necessary."

She slapped the two pictures down on the box and turned round with a furious face, controlled herself, stared at him and laughed loudly.

"You mean well, but you're a fearful weakling, Michael. You don't realise I want to be alone so I can beat my head against the wall just when I want to. Keep me!"

She laughed loudly again, strode across the floor, opened the door and pushed Michael out on to the landing.

"Good-bye, old thing, thanks. I'll be better soon." She slammed the door. Michael hesitated for a long time on the landing, but in the end went very slowly down the bare stairs, listening at each step. He did not sleep all night.

2

*Four passions of a poor man with a weak heart,
ending with an explanation of what love is.*

WITHERS NEEDED a loan of ten shillings some months later
and came to borrow it from Michael. He asked, "What do you do
in your week-ends? I'm at a loose end at present," and accepted
Michael's invitation to the Baguenault's home for the Sunday
following. Withers lunched agreeably with the father and
mother, enchanting both with his tales. Catherine, throwing a
look of scorn at him, rose from the table, taking her plate, and
went to eat in the orchard.

"Your sister has funny habits!"

"You must not take any notice. Catherine makes a point of love
and hate at first sight. She will not debase herself by listening to
a train of conversation that she thinks low or stupid."

"She is not very amusing."

"She is outrageous in every respect," agreed Michael. "That's
her charm."

"Funny thing you get on with a girl like that."

"We get on like a house on fire. We go away in the week-end
together sometimes. With Cath you have real adventures, meet
extraordinary people. My people are two old duffers," said
Michael. "Come out with Catherine this afternoon. She's collecting flowers for a Labour Party bazaar and fête : we are going to
take them in by car. Come along, you'll meet some new people."

"No thanks; no Labour Party shivoos. What do they do? Do
they all get together at the beginning and sing a hymn of hate, or
say the Thirty-nine Articles of Bad Faith, or dance peasant dances:
what? Heh, now I see your evil genius, it's your Catherine.
You're always in her skirts, she's a nun in reverse. It's not religion,
but irreligion that drives her mad; but she'll have your soul in

any case, the female devil. She's like one of those female spiders that eat their husbands. You're her brother, but they don't recognise family relations, those man-eating ladies."

"Don't be a fool."

Catherine took them out to the houses of the neighbourhood to collect flowers for her fête. When the ladies, gracious for religious Mrs Baguenault, heard that the flowers were for a Labour fête, they refused to give any flowers. Withers laughed and Michael was confused. They went down into the bush, and into the house of an old friend of Catherine's, now away at the sea-side, to pick wild-flowers and violets. Michael got a backache picking violets, while Withers sat on a tree-trunk and talked. When they made their first journey home, laden with violets, he stayed on the verandah and drank tea with Mrs Baguenault. Seeing in him a disaffected accidental friend of Michael and Catherine, probably a religious man, from his lean, dark look, Mrs Baguenault began to pour her trouble in his ears. Catherine had always been so difficult, even at ten and eleven she had fooled at school and run away, given lip to the teachers, criticised them at home, parodied her father. Not like her sisters. If some sensible person could give her advice, someone who knew her milieu and appreciated the home atmosphere . . . Withers said :

"Don't worry yourself, Mrs Baguenault, your daughter is built for revolution and will probably serve a few gaol-sentences before she's through : she's a gypsy. They occur in the best of families : it's atavism, some ancient ancestral strain coming out," and he proceeded to tell her tales of freaks in families. In the end Mrs Baguenault felt flattered and ascribed the freakishness of Catherine to her own influence. When Michael returned, Withers said privately :

"Come along out o' this. This collection of skirts will drive you dippy before they've finished : one with her religion, the other with her reds. What a woman's man you are! Why don't you get a real woman and taste their real goods, not all this eyewash? Come along with me, to-night."

"Kate," said Michael, "Withers wants me to go along with him. Do you mind if I don't go with you to the fête?"

38

She looked at him ironically.

"No, go along, Michael. Milt Dean's coming along to give me a lift into town."

"Right-o, we'll be off, then."

"Where are you going with Mr Withers, Michael?" asked the mother.

"To a little dance," answered Withers.

"Where at?" asked Michael, surprised.

"Fisherman's Bay, at the Grahams'. I was invited before, but didn't think of going; now I think I'll drop in."

"I don't think I'll go: I don't feel like it," said Michael uncertainly. Catherine brushed past him furiously.

"Go and play, God damn it, you ought to amuse yourself like all boys of your age. I've got work to do: go, go!"

Michael looked at her, meditating. At last he said:

"Well, I'll go," and he went upstairs to change his shirt.

At Mae's house the same loving cornstalk hung about her. Withers whispered:

"Go on, duckfoot, make her: that's what I brought you for. She's always had a bit of a weakness for you because you're so backward in coming forward, I suppose: women love nice sissies. Now, she's ready for it, she'll probably fall into your arms. Her cavalier, the beanpole, has got her all worked-up, thinks she's icy perfection and doesn't know how to make his approach. I'd cackle if you got her instead of him. You pair of mugs!"

She went past him, in the highest spirits, with another fellow, dancing with swift undulating movements and casting arrowed glances over her partner's shoulder, her flounced skirt circling and floating. When she passed Michael, she pouted at him. His heart leaped and turned over. She pouted at someone else up the room. Mae had gone to her tall youth and came tangoing past with him: people smiled confidentially in the room. She did not look at anyone now but smiled at the tall youth.

"Are you going to the wedding?" asked one of the girls of another beside him.

"I thought they were going to be engaged to-day," was the answer.

Michael gazed before him. His defeated heart sank, his aimlessness and loneliness rolled back on him. His life spent in a cocoon seemed black, dusty, dry-mouthed, funereal. When he left the house, after kicking his heels dismally with the boys, who were smoking and talking about cricket, and dancing dispiritedly with a little serious dark girl, he said:

"They all want to marry and I don't want to. What's a chap to do: I can't go through the mill that other chaps do with a flossy and then leave her with tears, shrieks, and perhaps a kid. I'd rather be a flagellant and suffer for my soul, my own good, forget my turmoil in stripes, than go into trouble on a partnership basis."

He walked through the light mist of the spring night towards the cliff and pictured the necessity for love as a shaggy-skinned infernal shepherdess, a brutal Circe. The famous exorcism of the cloister, or of the scientific overall alone banished her: he was sorry he had not become a doctor or a coal-miner. If a man had a cause to fight for, a battle to win, a discovery to make or brutally hard work to do, he could forget woman and only at odd intervals hear her footsteps, and those of her children, passing far-off, regretful, in the grassy ignorant fields. He stood on the cliff-face looking at the distant lamps. It was not this young woman alone who had come back on him suddenly with all the poignancy of his richest summer, but his weakness and failure in all respects. He went along the high cliffs, where he walked up and down the asphalt path, an increasing pain urging him along. He climbed up to the flagstaff at the signal station. It stretched up beyond its normal height into profound heavens where mists now bowled fast and dimly. In its mast and yards he saw the sign of his future, a monstrous pale tree, bitterly infinite, standing footless in the earth and headless in the heavens, a splinter sterile and sapless, a kind of scarecrow, a rack for cast vestments, a mast castaway: underneath the sea ran. He retraced his steps and stood on the lowest cliffs for a few minutes, leaning on the rail and listening to the waves running into the sea-worn caverns beneath, with a dull sound of artillery, and to the hissing as the water drained off the rocks as the wash receded. The sea was hooded, the air cold and damp, a heavy sea-mist was rolling in and nothing was visible but the dim foamline on the jetty of rock beneath the headland. He heard voices passing on various planes and a girl giggling continuously up the hill. He turned resolutely and went round past the military reserve where the water trickled through the grass and the frogs were singing "Cree-cree-creeee . . ." as long ago when he had lived there. They were cheerful at the hissing rain now falling.

It was about ten at night. Michael walked blindly along, more content to be cased in fog. At the turning of the first street, an old man with a stick hesitated on the corner and was hardly distinguishable, although a street-lamp stood opposite. He gingerly moved his stick one way, withdrew it and softly swayed the other, afraid, perhaps, of the water in the gutter, perhaps of the mist. Michael, loping along, brushed by him and knocked him down. The old man lay on the ground squirming on his side, his hat in the gutter; his red and tan face, with high cheek and nose, shone like grease-paint under the rain in the lamplight. His whiskers were scattered white about his chin, his hands feebly clutched, and his stick lay on the ground. He raised himself on one elbow and tried to get up, without saying a word, as if it were the ignoble fate of old age to be knocked down at street-corners, and nothing else was to be expected. An officer going to the barracks-road appeared up the short street leading from the beach, and ran stiffly and elegantly towards the old man. A little boy, slightly dwarfed and stocky, with an old white face and black eyes, ran over from the side of the street and tugged with the soldier. Michael stood staring at the man squirming like a cockroach at his feet, as if he had been seeing figures in a dream. Seeing the soldier pick up the man's wet hat and clap it on his head, while darting an indignant look at him, Michael started back and began to circle round the old man, sketching with his hands a gesture of regret or impotence. He murmured in an extinguished voice, "I'm sorry, I'm . . . I didn't see . . ." The soldier put the old man on his right path, shook his hands in the air with a gesture of disgust, and stared at Michael, dumbfounded by his silence. A woman came up and said, "What a shame! I saw the accident from down the street there. That young man must be drunk."

Michael went down towards the steps leading to the beach-path at a business-like pace. At the corner he stood and looked back as a commiserating stranger might. Thank goodness, he said, someone is looking after the old fellow. At the sound of brass heels rapidly ringing on the pavement he turned again. The little boy was there offering him something. He stared at the little boy's hand.

"Your purse," said the little boy, "you dropped your purse."

"Jo!" exclaimed Michael. "Is it you, Jo Baguenault?" Jo was nine then.

"Here, come round to Baxter's with me and I'll buy you an ice-cream."

"All right: but I'll have to hurry. They'll want to know where I am." Michael bought the ice-cream.

"Here, Jo; don't tell them at home you saw me!"

"All right."

After this he sometimes took the queer, faithful little chap out when he went roaming.

He wanted to join the art-class where Mae went at night with her lover. Since Catherine had posed there it seemed a place that belonged partly to him. He had to pay off the tailor who dressed him on the time-payment system. He went without lunch for two days, but after that felt so faint that he could not continue it. He went about with holes in his shoes and a front tooth out.

"Time enough to get it in," he told his mother, "when I get a girl." But Withers took him out several times in succession and forced him to spend his savings, so that he was always broke.

The Municipal Library was in the Haymarket Building where the art-class was held. He went there almost every day with Withers, or other fellows, all voracious readers, most of whom had collected library tickets from friends and owned from ten to twenty tickets, instead of the regulation two. Michael did not read much. They entered the great barn of a building from the

42

Town Hall end and passed all the closed shop-fronts where exotic societies, herbalists, mind-readers, jewellers and bootmakers lived, as it seemed, without clients, friends or visitors.

The Library appeared miles away at the other end. In the centre of the building are two large staircases, and a spiral staircase leading to the rooms occupied by the art-school. Just before they reached this staircase, they passed its bare yellow entrance with a bell inside and a small staircase covered with sacking against the inner wall. A girl running up the central stairs, with her light coat tightly belted, a small hat and a roll of paper in her hand, turned the corner abruptly and bumped into Michael, apologised, looked up quickly, said laughing and breathless:

"Oh, Mr Baguenault!"

She hung there uncertainly on tiptoe. It was Mae Graham, of course—not queer he should see her when he was always coming on the off-chance. He stood speechless, nevertheless, before the sphinx. Will I solve her, will she destroy me? At the expression on his face, she imagined she had hurt him. She said impulsively, holding out her hand, a little timidly:

"Mr Baguenault, I'm so sorry . . ."

He moved towards her awkwardly and mechanically.

"No, no, it was my . . ."

Some bond existed between them for a moment. She moved nearer to him, he took a deep breath and forgot Withers standing by. She laughed, however, and said:

"Well, I have to fly, I'm awfully late. See you some other time? Good-bye!" She touched him on the arm and was off.

Excitement shook him from head to foot. He took a step into the entrance. She ran laughing aloud up the staircase, grimaced at him through the banisters at the top and disappeared. An absolutely overmastering passion had him in hand. He stumbled up the short staircase covered with matting, twelve or thirteen stairs, but when he reached the top she had already gone into the room behind the dim studio, where a ghostly row of easels stood in a half-moon, spectral in the subdued light coming through the dark linen drapings of the wall of the farther studio. A shaded light in the ante-chamber into which the staircase had led him dazzled him for a moment, and then directed his glance to a large oil-painting which hung on the wall on his right side. A half-naked woman risen from bed looked searchingly out of the picture at the darkness; it was the only thing visible. Underneath was the title: "Awakened." He peered at the pictures on the other walls, but there were nothing but landscapes—women undressed with men dressed frolicking, tiny affairs, waterscapes and river banks, fit for drawing-rooms. He came back and looked at the "Awakened," and his essential superstition which had shown him the flagstaff burst out again.

He thought: "What sort of a barmy lad am I? She's Jameson's girl, and very friendly with all the chaps there." He thought: "A living woman was the model for this," and began to inspect it fearfully and expectantly to see the form there. He looked at the woman's drooping breasts, with their large roses in the centre, and the vermicular pain which had been in his head and bowels for so many months and even years past became a pang. He struck his head with his open hand, and uttered a groaning, crying sound. Fearing to be found there he went downstairs, tripping and sliding over the old matting. When he got to the bottom, he looked up, but saw no one looking after him. He looked upward into the unlighted dome which hovered above in the roof of the building at a considerable height, saw the dark open door-way into the studio and the still expectant light lying on wall, banister, and stair; nothing moved. He said:

"Awakened! I am that. O God, help me: I have been thinking of her for months."

At this moment Withers came in a little curiously, a little diffident. He was by no means irreligious in the presence of the passions he speculated in.

"Michael, did you make a date?"

Michael did not answer. Withers, smiling to himself over his teeth, gradually becoming stained, put his arm into Michael's and drew him out into the great hall. He went into the library and presently came out, still smiling to himself, and said softly, gently:

"Here are two books you'd like."

One was Stendahl's essay *On Love*; the other was the *Aphrodite* of Pierre Louys.

"Just the thing you need to give you a bit of polish," continued Withers.

"I'm not completely dotty on the subject like you," said Michael crossly, looking at the books.

"These are masterpieces," cried Withers indignantly, and cited long extracts from both which gave Michael a pleasurable foretaste. When Michael felt calmer, after they had walked a little while in Sussex Street and York Street, Withers said:

"Want to have a good time? I'm going to take a young chap over from Melbourne to a funny house, where I know the madam."

"Not on your life."

"Go on; you've attended too many Y.M.C.A. lectures. I'm not going upstairs myself. I'm only going to drink some beer with the girls: I know quite a lot of them, they're good sports. This young chap is sweet on a girl here, a nice little bit of fluff, with her mamma and papa: but she's got some money and he's got to marry her to get her and he's sick of hanging around. She's only seventeen, he's seventeen too: and they can't get married till they're twenty-one. Rotten, isn't it?"

"Silly idea."

"And," continued Withers, on a lower tone, hurriedly, giggling, "I'm going to get them both to go out with me. The mamma and papa think I'm a steadying influence for Willy. I'm going to take them to the house of a chap I know—you know, Banks, the artist, out at Gladesville. We'll give the girl a few glasses of champagne and see if she'll give in: they do, you know, the girls: they can't stand champagne. Funny, isn't it, the effect it has on the female temperament? No woman can stand it: there are other things they can't stand, too: for instance . . ."

"Are you sure!"

"Yes: come along, go on, and I'll show you. Come along with us on Saturday when we take the kid out to Gladesville."

"Not my ticket," said Michael; "not my idea of fun. Sorry I'm such a slowpoke."

45

"You are," cried Withers without ill-will, as Michael went down the street.

Michael did not sleep much at nights.

He called for Mae one evening at her office. She looked him over coolly, then, as he was good-looking, she walked off with him, to make a sensation with the other girls.

"Miss your boat," said Michael, "and have a lemonade with me."

He took her to a tea-room on the quay, a close, ugly room with marble-topped tables. She ate hungrily, laughed to think that her parents would fuss all the evening over her loss of appetite, refused to go out with him on Saturday to the pictures, and looked at him sympathetically as she finished sucking up her lemonade.

"You like me, Michael?"

He flushed: the words "I love you" were just repressed on his lips.

"You know I do."

"You know I'm going to marry Jameson in eighteen months: we're secretly engaged already," she said slowly, half regretfully.

"That big stick," cried Michael.

"You're simply jealous."

"You don't know men: you're only a kid. Don't marry him, Mae: there are plenty of other chaps better than him: there's . . . plenty."

"Who? I don't see the queue anywhere!"

"Well, I make one."

"How old are you, Michael?"

"Twenty."

"Stan's twenty-two. Where do you work?"

"In McKinley & Farley's: advertising. It's the liveliest business there is. When you work up you can go free-lance and make up to £500 on a job. Of course, only the best men get that, but the possibilities are infinite: and it's a wonderful business. You see all sorts of people, business men, manufacturers; they show you

46

through their factories, you get to know the processes. Then, socially, advertising is of the greatest service. It makes the best products known to everyone. Competition drives the manufacturers to make the best goods for the lowest prices and to advertise them as widely as possible. You see how useful that is to poor housewives, poor people in general. I tell you, humanity is much better off than ever it was, even the beggars of to-day have things that the prosperous citizen of other days didn't have, and publicity is the great salesman, the great distributor of all these things. It is the benefactor of mankind."

She laughed immoderately.

"You've advertised yourself to yourself pretty well! I suppose McKinley and Farley set up in business to improve mankind?"

"Of course not; but you have to have a social value to live and make money: otherwise you're out. That's the proof."

"Well, I don't care twopence for all that," she said, yawning. "Let's shake a leg: I don't want to miss the next boat."

He got up hastily.

"What about Saturday, Mae?"

"Ring me up: I'll see what I'm doing."

"What does Jameson do?"

"Stan's an articled clerk," she said. "His father's the judge. His father'll give him money to settle down next year when he gets through his exams."

"They're lucky dogs, these only sons who can always put their hands in papa's pocket. Why don't you marry a real man that makes his own way? You girls are all the same: you don't care whether a chap loves you, you only care to get a house and furniture."

"You're mean," she said. "I don't want to hear about it any more. I know what I want; it's my life. I want a home and I don't mind being a judge's daughter-in-law."

She laughed easily again and shifted her gaze along the sunlit quay, studying the crowds hurrying towards her ferry. Michael had to nag her.

"You're marrying an insurance policy, aren't you?"

"Why not? A woman's got to look ahead. A man only thinks

of himself, unless he's a really nice boy like Stan."

The more stupid and calculating she appeared, the more he desired her. She put on a pair of gloves with petalled wrists. She took out of her bag a diamond engagement ring and showed it to him with pride.

"My insurance policy; Stan paid fifty pounds for it," she said.

"His father did."

"All right, his father."

"You wouldn't look at any man but one who could give you a posh sparkler like that, would you?"

"Oh, why do you torment me?" she cried, exasperated. "I didn't ask you to call for me. You hang round me. You are so mean, you buzz all the time like a mosquito. No one would ever marry you, you're a stinger."

She went down the wharf, forgot her pet, exhibiting her high-blooded prancing before the young boys on the boat. Her lover was upstairs, looking from the cabin window.

Michael called for her again the next day at 5.15, and took her to the art-school the nights that she went straight from the office. He came back for her once after the class when he knew Jameson would not be there and took her home on the boat, in the light of the late-rising lack-lustre moon, at ten o'clock. She let him hold her hand. Trembling, at the gate, he held her hand still. She looked at him attentively for a moment and then kissed him on the cheek. He shrank back, and began to laugh in an overwrought tone.

"Mae, do you love me?"

"No."

"Why did you kiss me?"

"You are very nice to me; I owe you something."

"You shouldn't have done it: I can't bear it! Don't you see I'm madly in love with you?"

"Yes, I do. You'd better not come to see me any more. It's not good for you or me."

"Perhaps you're right."

Withers took him one night to a girl's flat. She had two rooms with a small gas-range. In the living-room an alcove was curtained off. Another girl came in, who had the lip of a motherless foal, a headstrong voice, dark eyes, straight hair and a sallow complexion. She always carried a handbag in her hand, wore a Russian blouse flat over her flattish bosom, and spouted poetry. She retired to the alcove with Withers, when they had had tea, and drew the curtains. Michael sat still and awkward, listened to their regular breathing, thought them both asleep, and started as if he had seen a ghost when they both came out again in a short time. The other girl gave him lemonade. Presently three more boys arrived, young accountants who dabbled in Bohemian streams. The other girl had short platinum hair, a long nose, with round high little cheekbones, and beaming eyes nestling a little too close to the root of the nose. A fine curling red mouth and high golden forehead made up a perfect, sunny, bounteous, indolent and stupid face. She distributed smiles among them. They all left about eleven, with the exception of Purcefoy, a young accountant, who stayed with the beauty.

"She's a whore," explained Withers, "but doesn't know it in her crystalline stupidity; she's the queen of stoopids. Go and see her : she likes boys."

"I am a nitwit," exclaimed Michael, "to be chasing a humdrum little middle-class miss thinking of her pans and perambulators. Look at the queens that walk the street practically, and put her in the shade for looks and manners."

"What a carriage, a Phryne!" approved Withers. "You must go and see her : a sweet girl, every inch a woman. None of your bread-and-butter smell. An orchid!"

Michael went to see her two or three times. She was always surrounded by three or four panting youths trying to forget their boredom by laughing at her sallies. Her smile stood her instead of wits, but someone had told her that she looked like a goddess when sedate, and she often fell into a statuesque pose, while she vainly racked her brains for something to amuse. During these interims the boys looked round the room in search of a subject, or examined each other. Michael dropped off.

"Why?" exclaimed Withers, this time irritated.

"Every time I go there it's like a meeting of preference share-

E

holders. Not for me."

"You're too mighty particular," grumbled Withers, "for a cadet whoremaster. You ought to go through the drill book without jibbing; look at the way I sweat over you, to bring you up."

Withers went to see Mae and drew her a touching picture of Michael's state : how he was fretting himself into a fever for her, how he had thrown other girls in Michael's path and Michael had turned them all down.

"Write him a note," urged Withers; "it would only be a kindness. You know, boys like that can easily get brain fever, or tuberculosis, fretting like that."

"Really ?"

"It's well known. You girls should be careful and distribute yourself around a bit. Have a bit of amusement yourself; you'll be married long enough."

"That's true. I'll go out with Michael one day next week."

Michael, tired of wandering, was almost glad to plunge back into his stagnant passion. He argued with himself when he first received Mae's letter :

"I need a passion, even if illusory, to keep me going. I can't fall into the rut the way fellows do."

He pressed her hard besides, telling her they would be married secretly later on, whenever she liked.

"I have funny dreams," she began to tell him. "I never dreamed in my life before, that I remember. I keep on dreaming that my mother sends me for milk; I have to go through green paddocks and on a hillside there are always horses with glaring eyes and long tails which try to bite me. Once," she said, "I dreamed we were swimming together at Nielsen Park."

"You love me without knowing it."

Before his mind's eye flashed a great Banksia in full dark leaf, the sun shining, the green waters of a still bay with steeply sloping shore, glistening rocks and sand the colour of Mae's flesh. Sliding through the water he saw the pale body of a slender woman and a dark head pursuing her.

"Let's do it, Mae : some moonlight night."

"You're the limit; you always take me so seriously. You know

50

I'm only coming out with you for the good of your health."

"What the devil does that mean?"

"Withers said you would get brain-fever if I didn't."

"He's always got his finger in my pie. So you came for that reason. Then you care whether I'm ill or not."

"Not a bit, but . . ."

"You do; you're playing with me. You're a teaser; it's rotten. Come here."

He embraced her violently. She stayed for a moment quite motionless, as if to feel what an embrace was like: he felt her heart beating. She pushed him away without a word. He breathed and sat rigid.

"This is the last time I ever see you; you take advantage."

"You like it, you . . . you're dying to be my wife. Why don't you: it will be sooner or later."

"Never; go away, you pig."

He left her without another word, walking off with his hat on his head. He felt as if he would burst. Then began a miserable period when he strove to see her. Her appearance was changing. Her eyes were darker and more sunken. She often sat moodily unsmiling, unconscious of her companions, in the park at lunchtime, or on the boat. She wrote him one short note to tell him that her parents thought she was fretting for Jameson and that they had advanced the marriage. He tried to catch sight of her at intervals, to meet her at friends' houses, to speak to her casually, to hear of her even from Withers, or to brush her shoulders, clad in some light blouse, as they hurried away from the office. She refused to go with him, but once started to weep as he stood talking to her, and now often smiled at him timidly, in the distance. It was a time of delusions for both, and for him of the wild hopes of despair. He wrote her, "I will marry you to-morrow, if you'll run away with me." He fell out of love with her at times and then returned under the impression that she alone was his only hope of normal living. He was out of touch with his world. He got up at six in the morning and walked in the bush, or came to town by the earliest boat and went into the Botanic Gardens when they opened. He avoided Withers. The days and nights whirled past in fragments; he could not shut his eye, and he did not know when the day shut his. He climbed with heavy haversack the innumerable mountains of despair, while the blinding working-day ground and crashed in his ears, or dragged bitterly forward in its white dry light, without juice or blood. He worked feverishly but disconnectedly, his entrails burned him all day so that he hardly heard when anyone spoke to him. He spent hour after hour of his leisure tossing the same thoughts in his brain, the same schemes, an eleventh-hour Lochinvar rape, a waylaying as she came from her art-school. He rushed out of his home in the evening, if they questioned, particularly if Catherine was there, as out of a furnace, his brain prickling. He marvelled at the freshness of the air and wind. He read the books he read as never before, marvelled at the flamboyant genius of their writers, at their passion and penetration. His stomach was always on the turn, his heart beat heavily day and night, he trembled and was in a perpetual fever. She became unreal, he wanted to seize her and make sure of her flesh and blood, to be sure she was no wraith-haired vampire, but an ordinary girl, and yet he avoided her to keep company with the hundred likenesses of her and doubles that walked across his path in the city, and the dreams that he had at night. He read a wealth of obscene literature to increase his torments. He looked at solid, red-faced, small or lank, pudgy or cadaverous men in the trains and ferries and thought:

"How is it they all have loving wives and I have nobody? Am I different? Do I look different? How is it they all have got to the haven of life-long closeted connubial love and I have not, cannot, and even will not? I am shut out. What is the matter with me? Am I eunuched of the manly graces?" He examined from head to foot the women by reputation so compliant: they did not yield to him. He often thought of committing suicide, but he could not let the waters close over him without first knowing the sweet profound experience of cleaving to a loving woman's flesh and sinking into oblivion with her. He thought, "I'm a goner, a rank failure, but I'll pass out with the toga virilis."

The war broke out in August, and the young fellows talked

52

about it with excitement and importance as if it were their own private affair.

On August 15 Mae and Jameson were married. Two months after Withers said to Michael:

"I hear Mae's proprietor has enlisted."

Michael stared.

"What for? A man must be crazy to go: it's not a jaunt."

"He's tired, perhaps," suggested Withers gently.

"Or has to show he's a hero; he's that sort of a mooncalf. As if there was anything smart in hoofing it through foreign mud, being a living target for foreign sharpshooters."

"You'll go yet," said Withers, "so you'd better have a giddy time while you can. Go and see Mae. You know in Italy, when the husbands went to the war, they left a *cavalier servente* with the wife: in fact, he was often named in the marriage contract."

Michael's two cousins enlisted, tired, the one of school-teaching and the other of clerking in a Government office. They promised themselves Turkish beauties and French chorus-girls while abroad. The people in Wallawee, Michael's suburb, began to look at Michael with appraisal. He heard the ladies one day in his mother's drawing-room:

"I'm sure it's all you can do to stop Michael from going to the front, Mrs. Baguenault. The boys always want to take up arms for their country: it's young blood. Well, you won't be able to keep him back in the end."

And: "It's terrible, isn't it, to see those boys loafing on the street-corners without a thought for the dear mother country they owe everything to. The way they stand, with stooping shoulders, using bad language, taking the name of God in vain, shows what sort of men they are: rotters."

And: "Slackers," said another. "If I had a son and he was a slacker, he'd never see my door or my table again. I'd—I'd rather shoot him than see him disgrace me."

The bosoms of the nice ladies his mother knew swelled with righteous venom. Michael saw these suggestions working in his mother's mind by the glances she gave him in the street when a uniform went past. She began to work, with her two older daughters, at knitting socks for soldiers. Catherine immediately joined a pacifist league. The pictures were full of battleships loaded to the gunwales with cheering soldiers dipping victoriously through freshening seas. *The Daughter of the Regiment* and other topical musical comedies were revived. Michael was affected by the pictures of gay soldiers and heroic episodes, rousing songs, French estaminets, comics in the pictures showing amusing antics in the mud and other warlike diversions. In the end he began to think he would like to join the rough hearty barracks-life now proper to men. He received by post one morning a package with a white feather, and underneath the name "Mae". His blood rose with indignation. Later in the day he thought he would go and expostulate with her; she was infringing his individual liberty. In the evening he thought "Poor kid, her husband's away; that's what's eating her."

She spent her days idling about her mother's house. When Michael called on her she wore a large sun-hat, a transparent blouse and a light skirt round her plump hips and belly: she had grown bigger. A wide satin sash of red white and blue bound her athletic waist. At the end of the beach, where a small steep path rises over a stagnant creek and a cliff hung with vines, she said she was tired. The summer shades filtered through her straw flophat, dyeing with rich and becoming shades her young face, a little older suddenly, tired. She no longer pranced when she walked. She smiled at him:

"You must forgive me for sending that package. I was so nervous and upset and Tom Withers was here and told me you said Stan only went away to show off."

"It gave me a nasty turn. I didn't think you were that kind of girl. But I'm sure it's rotten for you, alone so soon."

She read him a long letter from Stan, very sentimental. Michael put it away in the end.

"I don't want to hear any more, Mae; he doesn't want you to read it to me."

"Are you—are you going to enlist soon, Michael?"

He looked at her moist lips, the blazing sea, the quiet villas

54

above with their lawns of buffalo-grass, at the hills like smoke in the dazzling sun. The quiet joyful sounds of a Saturday afternoon came over the waters, oars squeaking in rowlocks, the swish of the ferry, the shout of boys in a sailing-boat. He looked down at her, smiling passionately:

"Yes, Mae, if you want me to, if you send me, I'll enlist. But you know what I've suffered for you: be kind to me!"

"I am kind to you."

"Be kinder."

She was silent, tracing circles in the sand with her toe.

"Women are funny cattle. They stay at home and ask men to go and get killed."

"We go through danger too."

"I know; but only once on one day, not a hundred times on a hundred days. That's incredible to me, anyhow, that you can send away your own or other women's children. It's like committing suicide."

"Oh, no; I would never commit suicide."

"But you want me to?"

"It's not the same. If Stan were to die," she sobbed suddenly, "it would be for his country. I wouldn't cry; it is my duty."

"They have sold it to you," said Michael grimly.

"We don't reason, but we have our instinct. Do you think it's easy to give up my husband when I'm just married?"

"You don't seem to mind it."

"It's not very easy to have the folks say your husband is a coward, in their war-fever."

"Cut it out, Mae," he said gently. "It narks me, of course, it annoys me. I wouldn't do it for them, not even for my own mother, but if you join the pack too, I'll enlist for you, I suppose. The war'll be over in a few months, anyhow."

"Will you enlist?"

"Certainly."

"Is it a promise?"

"If you promise to be my pal until I go."

"Of course, I would be proud of you."

His calculations were bad. The war went on, and Mae did not

give him any peace or any comfort until he had enlisted. It was a silly business and he felt ashamed of himself, but his mother was very pleased. The dowagers, the settled women in Wallawee, had begun to show him the cold shoulder. On the railway-station, waiting for his train, their remarks reached and balanced on his ear, not-intended, not-veiled (infamous actresses perfected in their roles overnight):

"A perfect shame—the white feather twice, I heard—a wonder his mother—if my boy— his mother must feel it—for her sake alone—my son writes—the brave boys—the brave boys!"

On leave in London in 1917, Michael met the Folliots, Marion and Fulke, attending an international Socialist Congress. They returned to Sydney before Michael, and Michael wrote to Catherine telling her to meet them and link up with them, since she was always complaining bitterly of a lack of sympathetic friends.

When Michael at last returned, in 1919, he was weathered and self-centred. He had to go to a doctor regularly for nerve treatment, and lived apathetically at home, or in friends' houses, or in places unknown to his family, when the fit took him.

He knit up his friendship with the Folliots, avoided Catherine; his old friends had passed completely out of his heart. Michael spent a good deal of time with the Folliots, helped Fulke in the office, once or twice wrote an article for the *International Worker*, the paper of which Fulke was editor; these were a review of *Le Feu* of Henri Barbusse, which had made a sensation, and a description of his own in the same line. This done, his pen dried up. One day he sold the *International Worker* on the streets. His father and mother heard of it and were sure that his brain was affected.

Marion Folliot had dark hair and a broad half-Slavic face, although she was of English stock. She shook her head, laughed clearly and said: "My deep eye-hollows set skew-whiff were the present of Genghiz Khan to some charming female ancestor." A candle burnt in each eye. The Folliots worked hard organising meetings, trying to organise the seamen, the poorest members of the Australian working classes, and the wharfingers. They carried high the rushlight of their metropolitan culture at the same time, talked Cezanne, Gauguin, Laforgue, T. S. Eliot, Freud and Havelock Ellis. They had a pleasant home in a wood, on the North Shore. The young Baguenaults were often there and heard Marion sing the songs of the great and heroic post-war Socialist movement in Germany and tell how they had visited "Karl and Rosa". They painted the "Young Guard of the Proletariat" marching through the young fir forests of Germany, related how Marion had once in Berlin spat in the face of the mounted police, as they tried to compress the crowd, eighty thousand strong, that followed the funeral of Rosa Luxemburg. Marion intoned the mass-songs of the Social-Democrat and Communist gatherings in German, the proletarian question and answer, thus:

" 'Who are you down there?'
'The people underfoot, the wretched from the mines, the goldgetters, the coaldiggers,
The little ones who work in the mountain,
Dwarfed, black, hunched, spindle-legged, short of breath,
Who give up the sun to get gold,
Who extract coal out of the pitchy night,
Who get nothing, neither sun, gold nor coal, nor bread,
They whom the mountain buries, those the firedamp stifles.' "

And the answer:

" 'Life will be given you again; the earth you will inherit!' "

Behind her high white forehead, in the shadow of her beautiful hair, the film of her life for ever unrolled itself and made her happy. She had run away from high-school and taken a job in Sao Paulo, without telling her family. She returned home, met Fulke and fled abroad with him, both living on a small allowance from Fulke's liberal father, an oyster merchant. Fulke quitted medical school at her instance and joined the Communist Party, working as a journalist for every kind of rag, when the father's allowance failed. In Berlin they addressed meetings and walked through the countries with staves and rucksacks. In Wiesbaden Marion met Dr. Grossherz, who had an invalid wife and fell in love with Marion. He still corresponded with her, sending letters of love which she read to Fulke, full of Heine's poems and Grossherz's. She and Fulke had been sent to the frontier on the occasion of a Socialist uprising. They travelled on bicycles through France, and went to Spain for their winter, being now well provided for by Marion's and Fulke's families alike. After London they went back to live industriously, hard and gloriously, pioneers of the middle-class defection. They were protected rather than harassed by the police, on account of their parents, and Marion had little difficulty when she went down to smoodge Fulke's interdicted books in French and German through the Customs.

The husband and wife did not conceal their passion for each other. The many visitors to the house looked sidelong at their bedroom, decorated with roses, as if at that rare and desirable mystery, a happy union. They were both kind, hospitable and generous. Catherine often lived with them, and Michael visited them. Once when the Folliots were away, Michael found Catherine standing like a statue in the shaded front-room of the villa, smelling of red roses, with a book of Confucius' poems in her hand, gazing at a head of Eros in pastels which hung on the wall.

"Michael," she said briskly, when she heard him, "look at this Eros! I believe Marion did it: it looks like Fulke."

He wondered if Catherine liked the gay, small, plump and mellifluous Fulke. Catherine had had, since he left for the war, innumerable passions for intellectual men, but because her circle was small, she usually picked flashy egotists of unstable temperament. Such had been her passion for Milt Dean, a secretary of philanthropic societies, small, dark, with the face of a dried-up Red Indian tribesman. She talked abstractions with Milt Dean for months, argued with him and listened to his monotonous but persuasive discourses about himself. The return of Michael had partly cured her. She was now wavering in every breeze of masculine talent.

"You are not happy, ever, Cath," said Michael. "What a girl! Born with grit and nothing to use it for."

"What do you mean, nothing! I work my brains out and my legs off. I often have a happiness so great that the happiness of the gods, if there were any, would not compare with it. I feel I have found my path." She glanced unconsciously at the Eros.

"Perhaps so."

"I welter in such happiness. You don't know what life means to me, with all its terrors."

"You are happy, my poor girl, because you are divorced from life. You are free to enjoy your own tantrums in your own vacuum. I am the same, only with me, I let my will and wits be arrested and clouded. In a morbid fog I dream away the days, without thinking of what I have lost, or what failed at. I am extremely happy too; and it is happier than the gods who have always to be concerned with creation, according to our Western notions."

Michael had no opinions. They said loosely that he was a "Socialist" and "Communist", because he was compliant and repeated what he heard said in his circles, and plumed himself on radical opinions at home. Catherine assumed that he had her convictions, but not her ardour. She often called him "Comrade" in the persuasive serious way she had. He drifted about with her and the Folliots, because a fluid personality passed more easily through that unstable society. Michael only said, when pressed too close, "I think so," or "I don't think so at all." He wanted to live quietly, and they let him alone. The only singularity was his friendship with Kol Blount, a man paralysed from childhood, undergrown but virile, whose sweetness, penetration, rebellion and wit attracted numerous friends to his mother's house. Round him congregated the gangling youth. But when the two, Michael and Kol Blount, sat still together in the large sitting-room of the apartment, with the Venetian blinds lowered and the breeze mingling its murmurs with theirs, both dark-eyed and thin, absorbed, the others went into the garden, or home, feeling as if those two sat together in a glass globe. Their metaphysical quiets and their long unlaughing relation gave rise, like all things in this society, to a legend. When Michael was away, the others said to Kol Blount, "What do you see in him?"

Kol Blount answered:

"Michael is like me, paralysed, armless, a brother. Who does not wish to spend his life in communion with himself? What is stranger, more painful, richer, like the three white nights before suicide? If one could live in a cloister with a friend whom he follows through all the tortuous errors of reason, all the perversions of the emotions, the undeceiving world of the imagination, the grey plain of banality which appears at the closing of each day and night, the twilight land, tasting the flat sweet waters of the well of inaction, he would have reached a haven. Reason is hamstrung, the eyes and tongue alone live, the passions are asleep and dream, the will drives us no more into the thorns and thistles; we are one and yet not in solitude."

"What! Your ideal man is not the balanced, fire-hearted liberal, dripping with humanity and sweetness, who loves his enemies because they are men, weeps and fights for pacifism, employs the poor, encourages talent, educates children, and rules his family life like a patriarch; who never vails his crest, blunts his word; who crushes egotism, but pursues his own will through thick and thin; who believes in morality, but runs with a bunch of nettles to clear the haunts of superstition; who reveals hypocrisy even if it rises in his dearest friend?"

What Kol designed was no more than a perverse love of death and negations, a prolonged womb-life, a Brahmin self-extinction, a desire to be lapped once more in one's own excreta, an onanism, if you will. Eagerly, they urged this point on Kol, jealous of Michael's bond on him.

"You can't shame me," laughed Kol. "All those things you describe have their place in life. You can't ask a paralysed man to run about with a burning brand driving the bats and phantoms out of churches. I have found a brother: he runs for me, claps his hands for me, runs with a torch for me, if I want it, and yet he has the same emotions as myself. Thus, I know that my state of mind is not solely due to my inertia. I find that paralysis has cleared my mind. In fact, I never was obliged to believe in the knack that most of you do, to help along the illusion of living. Bobbing up and down before an altar, for example; pretending to take an interest in eugenics when what I really need is a girl. In the night of myself I have not needed any bog-lights: I live with a salutary despair."

"Atheism," said Milt Dean sententiously, "must take its mind-life from the poppy, or some internal drug secreted by the endo-crine glands, for it has no hope."

"Leave me alone with your endocrine glands. I don't need them either to explain why I am a failure in life. They should be called the endoctrined glands, from your faith in them to push you into the steps of the great."

"Jacob's Ladder has no meaning to a paralysed man," said Marion Folliot. Blount continued in his twilight, throwing out sparks of feeling, as a cat seems to throw out sparks on a stormy summer evening.

"You don't like Michael, you only see that he is not brilliant, and don't know that I don't care for his wits but for his qualities as a friend. You blame him for not running about bull-throwing with you all. Why should he? His lassitude has taught him more sense. What is this virtue in company? Why should a man have to like mankind, if he has a universe at home, or in his imagination?

"A thin heart must always be rubbing shoulders with crowds and sitting in the sun to get a little heat. If it does not exercise daily, it is found defunct the next morning of inanition. But a strong passion moves in chaos and associates with death, its foot goes among hermits and ravens. Love, love passing through many frightful experiences, retchings and convulsions, draws susten-ance from them; they only show it the measure of its fortitude. Even so its skin is dyed with the mess it feeds on, but it lives. From the fierceness of its discontent it craves all violences, pains and perversions, and feeds on its disappointments. It shuns joy, sympathy, good; it will rifle, plunder, kill, and always arise purer and more triumphant, and more truly love. It desires to do evil, to crush opponents to death, to stifle critics, to drive the breath from rivals, to cleave the world asunder and let the smoke out that curls in its entrails. Venus should be black : that is the colour of love, the rite of the night. My good sun-born friends, suckled on watered town-milk instead of on blood, as I, unlike me you have not had the time to fathom the heart. I, sitting here so many years, seeing my mother working for me, and friends eddying about me, pitying me and going off to their clerkships and marriages, have had the time to study the few passions that sway mankind.

"What is love? It is the pest in a city : there is no sleep at night, but tolling of bells; the ears do not hear, but they start; the eyes see, but ghosts rage; the body does not feel, but the earth burns and freezes. One is in love with a monster, a creature too much like an angel, too cruel, too feeble, too intimate and too powerful to be human. To love you must dissociate yourself from humanity, as with all great passions. But why should I say all? There is only one."

His friends were timorously silent, shocked even. Only Marion and Fulke sat tranquilly reflective, side by side. He continued :

"I ask myself why I rage, though, and why that which is so sweet to many I should feel so bitter : and in the end I know that I am despairing because no flesh nor word, and in no common hour, not my friend himself can enjoy with me the beauty he makes my mind imagine. Alone in his depths, you wander like a prospector in a canyon, looking for gold and rock-crystals.

"What is as unfathomable as a simple man? And a man with whom one lives daily is daily fecundated and grows, a Hartz monster towering over life, distorted through vapours and tears, enormous as on rising mountain clouds, infinitely varied, a figure for every hour of our life, like the shadow on a sundial, a thousand lifetimes in one. The puerile philanderer, Don Juan is schoolboy's dream : give me fidelity and the endless mystery of monogamy.

"Beautiful is the head of love glancing upwards with the moods of years, dark with yet liquid desires, as the mountain top glows in the night, austere with moderated passions, tender with fidelity, pallid with disappointed ambitions, sorrowful for some passing

62

reason I do not know, as I do not know why children and peasants sing sad lays when they are alone in the grass."

The hearts of the little circle were shaken. They looked at Blount, flushed, some with tears, some toying with the buttons of their shoes and coats. At last, Catherine Baguenault, who was there, said in a trembling voice:

"And does my brother Michael seem like that to you?"

"That is the song of any lover!" responded Blount drily.

"The oddest thing I ever heard in my life," said Milt Dean.

"But touching," added the woman.

"Perhaps there is more in Michael than you see on the surface," said one dubiously.

"There is more in Kol Blount than any of us dreamed. If he could be cured, we would see a miraculous birth," cried Catherine.

3 🦅

A hot morning in Fisherman's Bay.
We find four of our heroes at work in a devil's kitchen
where the word is made bread.

ON A SPRING morning in September Joseph Baguenault came
down to breakfast late and found his mother already seated near
the window, wearing her red shawl. The crickets trilled in the
dewy grass and there was a smell of new perspiration in the room.
Joseph kissed her dry cheek: her eyes were full and light.

"Did you sleep well, son?"

"Yes, after I got to sleep, but it was so wild when I got in that
I lay awake listening to the house creaking. I did not get in till
after eleven from college, because the ferry was late. They broke
two ropes trying to tie up at Nielsen Park, with the swell that
came from George's Head. And then the window blew in, in the
attic, and I had to put a board over it before I finally got to sleep.
Though, you know, I like a wind late at night, when the tide is up
and everyone is at home. You feel that something strange is
going on."

"I thought I heard you call out once?"

"No, Mother."

"I was sure you called. It must have been a dream. I was
worried—I thought you were spending the evening with your
cousin Michael. He has such strange friends—I don't think he
quite realises what they are. He has a good heart, and since he
came home with shell-shock, or whatever it was, he has not been
quite the same. Poor boys, I saw only yesterday in the paper,
where a shell-shocked soldier killed his wife and two little
children. Terrible, terrible, and he had been given a farm by the
government, too. It is terrible. I did hope, Joseph, at the begin-

64

ning, that you would influence Michael; he used to be fond of you. Poor boy—funny, you know, you're boys to me still, even though poor Michael's thirty-two and you twenty-one . . ."

"Twenty-two."

". . . but now I only think of you. I am too old to worry about others. I think, my baby is not home, and in such a storm! Anything may have happened to him. Well, at last the storm is gone."

"Time enough—nice spring weather! But, by the sound in the cove, it will come back."

"Will you say grace, my dear? I have not had my tea yet."

The tea steamed in the sun and skin came over the surface. Joseph said grace, and eyes were shut. He finished: Mrs Baguenault filled her mouth with the steaming tea—a rude pleasure; her eyes got moist, her lips red, her gullet was burned and rejoiced. The breakfast clatter began like a chorus of crickets. Mr Baguenault came in in an apron and laid his boots and a blacking-brush on a chair. The mother discoursed on an infinity of local matters, with the preoccupation of housewives with their five senses.

"I heard yesterday—the radio is so loud—margarine not butter—mine taste better—I said, Where is the smell coming from?—that cheap eau-de-cologne—I saw her hair had been peroxided—you could write your name in the dust—all real silk," and the sixth, "I had an *intuition* her husband . . ." The father read the leading article in the *Telegraph*, through his silver-rimmed glasses, but Joseph listened to his mother's conversation with interest. She was a plain woman. Hearing her speak, the tongue clung to the palate and the throat whirred, one's own ideas dried up, in sympathy. That was the effect of a dull youth, a devout life, an intelligence developed between smoky kitchen-walls, a slow remastication of ancient events to amuse the long tediums. Sixty years of poverty had extinguished that fountain of life which lives in infant flesh and ejects experiment and improvisation out of the mouth. The cheap print which hung over the piano showing Jesus with his sacred heart, in three colours out of register, blood, thorns, a nightgown, worn hands and tears, represented her own life as she knew it and as she was not ashamed to record it. Then, she went to church to know what was going on in the world, to know what view to take, as people used to go to panoramas, bad paintings artificially lighted in a little round hall, to find out what the country was like that lay about them. She saw the workaday world through a confessional grille, as a weevil through the hole he has gnawed in a nut. It might have opened to the thrust, that grille, if she had had the will, or if her husband had had the patience to teach her; but he had not, he thought too little of her brains.

Within, her heart was a stuffed chasuble continually repeating "Om, Om," with censers swinging and the tin cash-box clinking, making a sort of perpetual low mass in her soul—if she had a soul; but it was no soul, it was a dried leaf. It had once fluttered on the tree, but that was in spring; now it was winter. Daily events and catastrophes treading on each other's heels over that dried leaf made a faint crepitation and rustling, like a handkerchief wet with tears slipping into a high calico bosom, the prayer of the sacerdotal minister muttering smoke and incantations, the rustle of the assembly crossing itself and jingling rosaries at the name of the Father, or the slow beating of old sleepless blood on the pillow at night. Who can explain how superstition, proverbs, prejudices lay together, taking the place of sense in this simple old head? The face was wrinkled, blackened by age in the folds, but it hung together well, for the body was firmly moulded on the pattern of peasant ancestors bred to survive starvation, fireless winters and the scratching for crops in Irish tenant farms. But her pock-marked face folded most kindly when Joseph ate at table. The mother's liquid eyes saw that his hair was awry, his tie badly knotted. Her hand, already withered with thousands of household and maternal labours, stretched for the clothes-brush to rub the fluff from his ravelling sleeve. She moved towards Joseph with a fuller motion and she was more graceful with him, she had a faint charm, speaking to him, because he also was dried up and gnarled, but that much before his time. He was the solitary woody pear that sprouted late on the old tree, but he was the very seed of that tree. And she looks at him sentimentally, her blue eyes filmy. Heavens, he thought, comparing her and himself, how

66

can so small a pear carry so grand a universe of suffering in its heart? The reason is, the pear had a thousand, thousand ancestors. In Joseph some of those ancestors, seed of other trees, appeared somewhat different, half-blotted out, by a freak of generation. He had musical undertones in his voice, a pale skin, unbroken patience. But he was dwarfed and seemed to scramble along the street even when he walked straight ahead; and his face was as narrow and feebly-lighted as the evening window of their weatherboard cottage.

Joseph looked at the clock, pushed his chair aside, and put on his hat. His father spoke for the first time.

"I'm not going in till eleven-thirty; Simpson's taking the morning shift. It's Wednesday, school half-holiday; that means there'll be students all over the Art Gallery this afternoon. Personally, I prefer it to sitting all the week, without seeing a fly, not a fly, but Simpson don't like them. He says they clutter up the place. I said to him, They're students, it's for them. It makes no difference, he said, they clutter up the place; it's nice when it's quiet. So on Wednesdays I've arranged to take the afternoons."

"Well, good-bye," said Joseph.

"Jo—your uncle Baguenault wrote to me this morning about your cousin Michael. Because you go out with him, your uncle reckons we see more of him than his own home. At any rate, he wants to know if any of your friends can get him into journalism, or as a proof-reader. He wants something quiet, because Michael can't stand the rough-and-tumble. Do you want a proof-reader or something?"

"No, I told you before, we don't want anyone, we're practically overstaffed, and Baguenault wouldn't thank you for getting Michael into a place like ours. Besides, he's too old to begin in our game: and they've got lots in all the places to do proof-reading, doctors of philosophy, M.B.'s, engineers, lots without a job. A journalist—I don't know if he's got the style. At any rate, he knows more journalists than I do. The Folliots——"

"Not a rag like their sheet—a paper like the *Telegraph* or *Smith's*. Your uncle's an alderman, don't forget. In any case, you should try to get Michael away from that set of trouble-makers, it'll get him nowhere, and your uncle blames you. He says, Jo takes him into a set of rascally working-men, without home or religion, foreigners, and even Communists, from what I hear. Now, Jo, I don't like your uncle to have any basis for saying that, however wrong-headed he may be. I know it's not true, myself. You had better give up seeing Michael."

"I don't see him. And if I did—he's ten years older than me, and he's seen plenty more than me: it's rot. But I'll see if I can find out where he's staying if they're anxious. Though why his sister Catherine can't locate him better than me, I don't know; she knows the same crowd. But I know Uncle Jim, he doesn't know what it's all about. It's his fault that Michael and Catherine are always away from home. Anyhow, I've got to go."

"Have you spoken to your boss about your back pay yet?"

"Not this week."

"Tell him you've got to have it: two months—it's a disgrace. Suppose you weren't living at home?"

Joseph kissed his mother mechanically and went out. The gloom of the interior dropped from him. He walked smartly round the beach-path while the coral-trees along the shore, wrapped up in themselves, murmured without wind and dropped dead calices on his hat. It was low water; a transparent wave two inches high rang its air-bells along the sand. The receding tide had left dark lines of flotsam along the beach. The poor children of the district and their mothers, with sacks in their hands, were raking through the deposit with their fingers, gathering coke, chips, and even vegetables thrown overboard in port from the vessels. Temperate sun and cool shadow divided the air. The sea-gulls paddled in and out of the water without a cry, and the fishermen pottered about sluicing and scraping their boats. During the night, the tide had risen over the path; there was a broken oar, a boathouse cradle, and part of the gates of a harbour-side bathing-pool. Miles away, south-west, between the side-drops of Bradley's Head and Shark Point, the city sat in miniature, glittering, without a trace of smoke. Blue-blooded spring was everywhere.

The ferry had not yet come in. Joseph waited outside the Italian fruit-shop at the end of the wharf, looking at a dead shark drawn up on the beach. It was responsible for the first bathing casualty of the season. It had torn off the buttocks and right leg of a bather the day before, and had been caught with a meathook on a clothes-line tied to a buoy, during the night; the bell on the buoy had rung for over an hour. The fishermen were all gathered there, with clusters of school-children and a barman from the hotel. They stood talking amiably and endlessly, like a collection of blue-bottle flies. As Joseph lounged on the railing, Black Jack, the negro fisherman, came up flat-footed, dropped a word in one of the groups and shrugged his shoulders towards the sea-cliffs. A fisherman in the group scratched his chin, hitched up his belt, and planting both broad bare feet on the beach-path spat into the sand. Then he strolled up the shady side of the short street leading to the cliff. There is the Gap, an indentation in the sea-wall, at the foot of which is a shale platform standing out in the waves, a place for fishing at low tide. The Gap is dangerous for shipping on a dark night, because it looks like an opening in the cliffs. Iron hooks in the rocks permit lines to be thrown down, and fishermen climb up and down in any weather. Here have been wrecks, and here is the favourite suicide spot of the city.

Two more fishermen plodded up the street some hundred yards after the first. The school-children pushed and jostled with upturned faces. Another fisherman left them and went up the street, walking on the same side, with his eyes on the ground, meditating and limping on his swollen bare foot, poisoned by a puncture from a stingray spine. The school-children milled round Black Jack, who was spinning out his tale with pleasure; a moment more, and all the little boys had left him and ran shouting towards the Gap, with the little girls at their tails. The pilot-ship gave a long shriek and started for the Heads. Soon they all appeared against the sky-line on the edge of the Gap, motionless, except for a couple of boys pushing their way in to a better place, and all looked downwards at the sea. Amongst them stood three nuns in black. Black Jack sat on the shark's head and bit into his plug. It was a sort of dumb-show, the lazy men walking with heads dropped, their time- and weather-beaten faces, naturally sad and grotesque, now creased with interest as if they went to an entertainment, but not a new one.

The ferry whistled and Joseph had to run down the wharf. The school-children came tumbling down from the Gap, and a boy shouted to the deck-hand, "Hey, Nosey, a man committed suicide: there's a man over the Gap." The passengers looked round and then took out their papers and began talking cheerfully to their usual companions. A suicide at the Gap was a commonplace affair. Everyone knew why a person committed suicide: if it was a man, because he couldn't pay his bills or had no job; if a woman, because she was going to have a baby. The boat chugged into town through the glaze of the harbour on the darlingest, dazzlingest day of spring. Morning smoked on the hills, and the trees rose up to meet the sun as if to return to their primal essence and be dissolved in light. The morning was already hot; at Nielsen Park she lolled under the still leaves, the milky tide reflecting her in pools of curdled light. The *Città di Genova*, bound for Naples, rode out across the eastern channel, her masts rising higher every minute, her flanged bow emboldened by the sun, until she overtopped the little craft on the starboard bow, almost running her down. The engine-room telegraph rang furiously, the engineer shouted down the speaking-tube. They passed under the great red nostrils where the anchors hung, and the schoolboys yelled insults at the blackshirted Italian command. The cicada skirled in the foreshore reserves, the remarks of the season-ticket holders became drowsier and foolisher, and Joseph dreamed. O, lovely estuary with little hills, never to be approached, never to be altered in perspective, as if they sprang from the artist's brain and straightway came into life and breath upon canvas—but such canvas, as if blooming under glass, respiring and yet unearthly. Doubtless those windows on the bays reflect beings of some sort, for we see smoke blowing from innumerable small chimneys built over innumerable small kitchen fires, and swinging this way and that in the wind which so lightly agitates these plumy gardens and casts shadows on white sea-garden walls.

The light is tempered by the early season, but the rays neither deflected nor diffused reveal the smallest details with the accuracy of a miniature painter : small rounded bosky copses, walls loaded with creepers, pure flashes of deep green between pine-trees, and a multitude of red roofs swarming over the hills. Between the pine-tops the grey towers of the Rose Bay convent rise, whose buttresses are planted in an evergreen scrub running down to the edge of this still water. Corsica hardly looks into a more lilied and reflectant tide.

The ferries flock into Circular Quay each morning at eight and nine o'clock. The people burst out of the turnstiles in streams which go twisting uptown through the narrow streets. Some walk in the cool and some choose the sun. The office-boys in worn school jackets, the clerks in unpressed slop suits, the girls in light blouses and thin floating dresses, are already sweating and flushing with the heat. Near the quays is Lachlan Place where there is a small triangular park, generally filled with sunlight, where all day starlings and occasional flocks of mountain magpies chatter in the trees. The place is cool and old, surrounded with old bonds, warehouses and shipping offices, in part let out for shops, and bounded on one side by a large sombre Government building.

Joseph came up the place this spring morning taking short steps and putting his feet down flat to hide the holes in his soles, with legs slightly apart so that the trousers-cuffs should not be further rubbed, but doing this as a matter of habit and all the time glancing up at the blue sky over the new bank buildings. Several times he bumped into people.

"Sorry," said he, and "Sorry," said they.

The air was still and warm. The red flannel which his mother still made him wear was too hot, and prickled. Already office-boys loitered in the park, and the tobacconist stood at the door of his shop fixing the awning and whistling, "Funiculi, funicula." The hyacinths, roses and sweet-peas in the florist's window reminded him of his mother's garden. The boxed luncheons. with sandwiches, a cheese tart and a piece of fruit, priced one shilling, seemed expensive delicacies to him who had, as usual, his hunks of bread and meat-paste wrapped in newspaper in his pockets.

A wide old doorway opened beside the tobacconist's shop, and over it was a name, white on blue, "Tank Steam Press, Ground Floor." The tobacconist owned the old single-storey building and rented out to several establishments the mouldy apartments of the ground and first floor. In the attic was the man who did heliogravure. The building had once been a private house. Its court was now a cart-dock and opened into the other street. Its first-floor bathroom at the head of the stairs contained the old water-closet, used by all the workers in the house, a gas-ring to make tea, and the usual broken chairs and out-of-date telephone directories. The distinctive smell of the building came from this closet and from the printing-ink.

Joseph asked the tobacconist for the key, and when he was told, "Old Williams has it," he bought a packet of used razor-blades for twopence. The tobacconist, who was also a barber, looked at his bristly chin and said:

"Shaving soap?"

"No thanks; I have some."

Joseph walked through the old doorway, went by a staircase and entered the large airy double room occupied by the Press. He opened the glass back-door and moved about among the presses, curiously inspecting the jobs in their various stages, picking up a paper, looking through the bills on a bill-hook, putting his finger in the dust in the little glassed-in office of Chamberlain, the owner, and shutting off the stove, lighted by the cleaner, because the day was warm enough.

He hardly allowed himself a minute's glance into the sunlit place, yellow through the dark passage and door, blue through the high windows in front. He went about the room with the unhurried motions of one who has worked for a long time without pleasure at the same tasks in the same place. He carefully hung up his coat, grown yellowish, a schoolboy's Norfolk jacket with short sleeves, and wiped the band of his hat. The warm air drifted in through the street-door bearing odours from the park and the Botanic Gardens. His mother's garden and the yellow pumpkin flowers in the grass, thick with bees, swam back into his half-adjusted mind: there was a tall paling fence beside which he lay all Saturday afternoon.

"God, I wish I had a holiday: you can't go on for ever!"

He heard old Williams sluicing down the yard. He stood looking at a German printer's catalogue of papers and inks brought in since yesterday, no doubt by Mendelssohn, one of the printers. There was a great A in red, shovelling coal into a furnace-mouth made of a black M, and G in glue was marching off the page: "Wo gehst du, G?" He was going to get Müller A. G. coal, although it didn't say so. It was a beautiful job done on an offset press on thick paper. If you had travelled like Mendelssohn, even as a tramp, even with I.W.W.'s, even riding the sleepers, you could find amusement in any hole and corner. You had to be a flathead like him to stay in one hole for seven years; and that without even a holiday. A mug.

Chamberlain drew up outside in his Bentley with a frightful whine of brakes. He ran into the office lugging a suit-case which split open in the doorway. Jo helped him put back his ties, underpants and so forth, all crushed in anyhow, and nothing freshly laundered. Chamberlain plumped the bag in his office, while Effie, his daughter, a childish coquette of seventeen, took off her fur coat and put a bunch of violets in a glass. Chamberlain hung up his hat beside Joseph's, damped his hair which always fell into his eye, and which he viewed now with love in a blighted jag of glass; he rolled his sleeves over his round hairless white arms, adjusted his eyeshade and called irritably:

"Williams, give my desk a wipe, can't you? Morning, Baguenault. Oh, morning, Mendelssohn. What have we ahead of us this morning?"

The girls were arriving and hanging up their hats.

"Finish printing and bind Jones's catalogue: cover in colours of the wire-netting magazine."

"Are the pages done?"

"No, we're waiting on the blocks that were sent back; we ought to change blockmakers, I've never got blocks on time," said Joseph.

"Ring them up: I'll ring myself. That's sabotage: I know that little red-faced Benson, the foreman, takes a pleasure in disobliging me, because I'm not a mason. I told him, I'll take my business away, last time. I'll break the contract: there's sufficient cause. Where's the telephone? I'll ring him up, I'll tell him . . ."

"If you want another lawsuit, but you're the lawsuit king," said Effie.

"They're coming right away," cried Danny, the boy of fourteen, who came in at this moment. "I remembered to call in on my way here." He had called in at the blockmakers as an excuse for being late.

"Good, good, that's the ticket; now, boys, whistle and ride. You ought to be through by about eleven, eh, Jo? You don't need me, do you?"

"I need help," said Joseph tartly; "Mr. Withers is out all day. There was no one here yesterday afternoon but Danny and Mendelssohn."

"I was damned busy yesterday afternoon. Clients, clients, complaints, complaints, all day. I often wish they'd be here one morning to see how the demon gets into the works; everything tuned to concert pitch and nothing working. Then, after they give an order or two, the very office-girls become experts in printing: should I change the paper, don't the blocks cost too much? I got orders too: I may get the business from a new publishing firm that Montagu knows. Little books of poetry, belles-lettres. The money's safe, because the authors pay for their own printing costs. Well, no cheques at any rate in this morning's mail, Effie? That's our style, isn't it? You've known me for seven years, Jo; you've seen me in my ups and downs. Money only flows to mercenary types, and I'm not that. There's more of the workman, artisan, artist, faber, in me. Well, we'll see each other through. And now, what are you waiting for? I don't know what those travellers do. Oh no, they don't need to produce any references, they're so smart, a week's trial will convince—only they need an advance on the first week's commissions. They must see I'm a soft-hearted duffer. Then, good-bye, it don't suit. If I only could spend all my time drumming up business, it would be different. There's something in me gives people confidence: it's that very lack of avarice I mentioned. I've never had a business relation for a long time where my partner didn't actually love me; they realise I'd do anything for them. But you can't be the whole works, 'The bosun, the cap'n, the midshipmite and the crew of the captain's gig'—you know the old song."

"Give it a breeze," said Effie.

"Put your lipstick away and do some typing."

Joseph's face had a stone-deaf expression.

"Let's see: what have you got there? the wire-netting magazine?"

The presses worked with a low grunting and soft click-click.

"No, we're waiting on the blocks."

"Of course, of course." Chamberlain came and stood by Joseph.

"Yes, of course. How is that new ink? Reminds me, Withers— Withers is still out, of course—given him an inch and he takes an ell. He is an expert on prints, of course, and he detected two yesterday that Montagu himself didn't recognise as reprints, had the plate-mark, ageing, everything. He said (I saw him last night on business, Montagu) he said, there are more original etchings in Australia than in the rest of the world put together: ha, ha! His collection . . ." Chamberlain wafted a kiss into the air. ". . . a peach. I'll get him to show you one time, if you're interested. I have an instinct for it myself, and in these things it's very often the instinct that counts. These forgers have the experts in mind when they forge, but the instinct for artistic value is what you can't so easily fool. And then, yesterday . . . Mendelssohn, stop that press a moment, there's no hurry: I want your advice; these things are in your line. I've picked up a fine Persian rug. I waited more than two hours in the auction rooms, because Montagu tipped me off. It was patched, of course, but the real thing, knotting, design, seal, you could use the back—superb. If Effie thinks of settling down, eh, it'll do for the kid's house. Montagu persuaded the valuer it was false, so got it auctioned as imitation and I got it for nothing practically. Montagu gave his own note. I owe him, of course. It's a good job he feels bounden to me, he's got a whale of a lot of I.O.U.'s of mine by now. But a friend is a friend, friendship dissolves hard cash, and sometimes washes out even I.O.U.'s: it's a powerful solvent. Eh, Jo? Eh? Ha, ha!"

Joseph said nothing. Chamberlain looked at him on top of the ladder loosening a screw in the paper-feeding rollers. It was the new press imported from England at a cost of about £4,500, and only allowed through the Customs because Chamberlain had agreed to give the pattern to a local engineer. It was cemented in the floor and stood in an oil-bath: it could turn out forty thousand impressions the hour at top speed. It was Chamberlain's pride and he had already based two overdrafts on it. Chambérlain watched Jo's expression, and anxiously repeated, "Eh?" Jo remained silent. Chamberlain frowned. Joseph climbed down the ladder, released a lever, and the bed of the press began to move indolently back and forth. Danny, the devil, seated in front of the machine, took a sheet or two as it settled in place, and then pulled the string which stopped the press.

"What is it?" asked Joseph calmly.

"Over-inked on the top right-hand block."

They went on for over an hour on the large press, making proofs and frittering away time, before it ran smoothly. Towards eleven, when Effie was making tea in the lavatory upstairs, Chamberlain, who had been trying to go through his accounts, came and stood beside Joseph and said, quite low:

"I must tell you, personally, that things are bad with us. I like to confide in my workmen; and then it concerns you. I'm trying to find a buyer; someone to run things and take the financial worry off my shoulders, to keep me as manager. In that event we might find we had no need of Withers. He's always with Montagu, anyway, and he's beginning to get my goat. And he is too irritable, it upsets me. Then, all this financial business, over-drafts and inventories, is too much for me. I'm the practical workman, nothing mechanical beats me, there's nothing in print-ing I don't know, but I'm beat by the banks, the mortgages, the interest: money should be free. Now, if anyone comes and asks about our financial situation, don't say anything about the over-draft, and tell 'em business is booming, because they always poke around amongst the workmen—see? But, of course, if another chief wanted to change round the staff I'd have nothing to do with it; there'd be no telling. But you live at home, Jo, don't you? So you're all right. And take my tip, a little change

76

does no one any harm; it's no tragedy. You ought to get all the experience you can when you're young. If I were your age, well, never mind. But perhaps you're counting on buying me out, eh, Jo? You're a quiet one, you're a canny one?" He chuckled at the dig. Joseph got very pale.

"I have no money, and although I live with my people, I need a steady job like the others. We are poor; I need my money terribly bad, sir, joking apart." He blushed; his legs trembled so that he could hardly stand. If it came to giving them the sack now, with their pay two months in arrears, and so many out of work, he would not know what to do. In an instant of terror, he reviewed all his relatives and friends, all his possessions: he could not raise any money at all. He could not face the prospect of tramping the city, as he was, dressed like a tramp, and personally, far from engaging.

Chamberlain looked at him demurely.

"We're all poor, old boy; but I'll see what I can do this week. It's a bargain: any money that comes in we split *pro rata*."

Someone who had been standing by the door for a moment, ran up to the store on the first floor, sneezing. The person rummaged about overhead and ran down again. Chamberlain called:

"Withers? Come in, we're all at sixes and sevens. What in hell are you doing? You think you can come in any time of day?"

"Where's the motor-oil?" asked Withers. "Oh, who put it with the ink? Silly trick."

"I suppose Montagu's outside," continued Chamberlain. "Well, I'm paying you; I'll take the motor-oil out myself. That son of a gun can't take my men like this for his chauffeurs, private secretaries, jackals and other servants he needs to get along in the world. Now get on the job, Tom. Look at those girls sitting with their hands hanging; now then, buckle down, girls: lots to do."

When he returned, he smiled ingratiatingly at Withers, seeing him tapping at a forme with contained rage. After a brief silence, he inquired:

"Everything all right?"

"Quite all right."

The blocks had at last come in. They tacked them on to the perforated steel backing.

Chamberlain came near and looked at Withers closely.

"You should fix yourself up a bit better before you come to work, you're foreman, and I'm expecting someone. I want the works to give a good account of itself. Understand? Especially with the hour you roll in. You look as if you'd been sleeping in the Domain all night. You're a sight and you're half-soused at this time of day. You spoil the look of the place."

"Ya? Well, I've got other rats than that to bite me! You'd like me to come in a morning-coat, perhaps. Let me tell you this is all I've got; when I put my overalls on it'll be decent enough. We're workingmen, aren't we, not lounge lizards. Who is it coming? Somebody of Montagu's, I bet; yes, he said something about it. If you don't want to lose your pants and your underwear, keep out of any deals with Montagu's friends. You shouldn't need me to warn you."

"You're a friend of his yourself!"

"You bet! For the same reason the others are: I get a commish. If I didn't, I wouldn't know where my next counter-lunch was coming from—in this joint."

"Don't harp on that: you do better than the others. I'm doing my best; you get money when I don't, and Effie and her mother have to eat tinned salmon for Saturday night tea. I should expect some co-operation from my workmen; I treat you right."

"Listen," shouted Withers in his hysterical voice, through the plunging of the big machine which was now working at top speed. "You got to fork out this week. My landlady wants the rent, and although she's a bitch, I don't blame the old girl, and I'm tired of dodging her. I did sleep in the park last night, if you want to know, with a lot of other deadbeats: only they're smarter than I am; they don't sweat their guts out for a chap who buys his daughter a fur coat and himself a new car when he's up King Street. You ought to damn well consult us before you let yourself in for expenses like that: we're your creditors. You think I didn't nearly stay with the Domain dossers? I blew in all my cash, by the way, on them," continued Withers calming down. "God, I had a glorious night, all the same. The tales they told me, enough to make a monkey bite its mother. They're a lot of philosophers and remittance-men, sons of belted earls and what not. Fun, what? I'm sick of Montagu and you and the whole caboosh. And you, you poor dope, sweating and groaning and letting Montagu fleece you gently, without even a tarpot. And you still think he's a great man. He says so himself, of course, but he's got other names for you: sucker, for instance, that boob Chamberlain. And for himself too, if it comes to that. He's the sort with three passports, Canadian, English and American; and if the truth were known he's officially domiciled in Luxemburg. I know the twinkle of that Napoleonic eye; I can see behind it a police dossier as long as your arm in several European countries: no one but you would trust him farther than your nose. When I look at you it makes me sick to see what a muttonhead you are, Greg. Does he want a little cash to entertain his flossies in a cabinet particulier? Call on Bobs. Here's a little Persian mat, here's a Japan-lacquer cat, here's a sticky-stucco vawse and a little yaller god with a little emerald eye, palm them off on old pal Greg, fork out Greg, dear old Greg, instinct Greg, aesthete Greg: and you allus does the needful, don't you, Bobs?"

"If you think he robs me, you should tell me," said Chamberlain, wretchedly. "You're an amateur, you know the stuff: why do you let me be taken in, then?"

Withers laughed under his breath wickedly, bitterly, through his soft, dark, drooping, dirty moustache; his dark eyes shone under lowered lids. Solaced for a moment, he crossed the floor indolently, impudently tore some papers from a girl examining a returned proof, and took them to the window in front, sucking his lower lip so that his decayed teeth, blackrooted in his gums, showed beneath his moustache. His shoulders were bowed and he stooped, but still looked his six feet. His face was long and grandly ovoid, his high forehead ran into his thinning dark hair. His blue cotton shirt, torn on both sides of the collar, was marked with sweat-stains, and his greasy grey waistcoat, which he wore for decency, even in this heat, to cover the dirty shirt, was wrinkled like a pig's skin. When he had a new suit only, he straightened up and kept himself clean for a few weeks. The boys called him the "younger son" or "the diseased lord", for he had then an air of debilitated cunning, of acquaintance with usurers and of ingrown baseless vanity.

Chamberlain came over to Withers, bent over him to see the paper, and quickly took a step back, for Withers smelled badly of sweat, drink and indigestion. In a few minutes while Joseph and Williams, the old odd-job man, were still working on the new job, they saw Chamberlain slip some silver into Withers' hands, the clinking concealed in the noises of the workshop. They were talking quietly, Withers was smiling and telling some tale. Presently they both went over to the typist's desk, took out a bottle and drank some brandy with their backs to the room. Effie helped herself to some brandy and drank it openly.

Williams, a mild old one, old though not more than sixty, who always whispered and went about in black felt slippers in which holes were cut for his bunions, wiped his dry hand across his mouth and winked at Joseph. Joseph nodded, smiling at the "poor old chap". ("Me in forty years," he sometimes said to himself, "but I won't be so lamblike. Poor old beggar, the way he waits round on Saturday mornings with his cap in his hand at twelve, when it's all a bustle and a hurry to get out to the car, hoping for his pound-note and never daring to ask for it, it breaks your heart.")

Danny stopped the press, and Joseph went round to look at the sheet. When he went back to his own end, he kept saying, "Primus inter pares," the motto pompously introduced into a trademark on the sheet: the press repeated primusinterpares, primusinterpares. Joseph's mind began to wander with the regular sound and the approach of lunch-time. He remarked to himself, "Contra audentior ite qua tua te fortuna sinet," a motto the priest had written for him in his prize at school, the only prize he ever got—one for handwriting. When he was alone as now, in the noise of the machines, in his room, on the boat amid the rush of wind and water, on Saturday afternoons lying in the grass, he liked to go over his little store of recitations. He had picked them up from the church service, from his Latin grammar at school, and from three little books bound in silk and stamped leather which his mother kept on the round table in the front room when visitors came for dinner. He had picked some up from Christmas cards and some from the title-pages of books. The great charm of his phrases, which were all in foreign languages, was the uncertainty of their meaning, the adumbrations and suggestions which hovered round them in his mind. Where he understood them, they had the same axiomatic standing as proverbs have for old women; and where he did not understand, they were abracadabra to show him he had power too, whenever he felt saddened by his smallness and weakness. He said now, "Labor omnia vincit."

He had spent innumerable long hours of his infancy alone, by the sea, among the bushes on the cliffs, staring at things from a distance, the fishing-boats like peanut-shells, the foam on distant bluffs, sea-gulls and sea-eagles deep in the sky. He had got used to talking to himself, and conversed only at odd intervals with poor and old-fashioned people, like the brothers at the school, the priest, his mother and father. Even when the little boys came together for catechism and skylarked round the church, he always stood aloof. The headmaster of the Catholic school refused to have any notions of modern science taught in the lower classes. Joseph, leaving school at twelve, moved all his life among old things; his Latin tags were even comforts to him, recalling those quiet, sad old days.

He had learned his catechism by heart easily. He loved music, resonant words, the greenish sunny light and shadows of his little hillside church, the wind as it passed outside in the grasses, the cricket which would begin to chirp and stop hearing a footfall on the road, the rattle of the milk-cart, the cry of a boy under the wall. He loved the Sunday masses, the respectable smiling people, the bustle of their clothes, the priest in his vestments and the repetition of the ritual that he knew so well. The ritual allowed its participants to enjoy the exaltation of inspiration, although they had none, as each phrase moved to its oft-rehearsed conclusion and the sacred words were born living on their lips. They were a second transubstantiation, the word becoming spirit. Different from his mother, who muttered her own prayers and plaints, he went through the service like a celebrant. Each moment of the mass perfectly absorbed the small amount of mental energy the quiet allowed him, and the end left him peaceful, quiescent, in a state of grace. The confessional purified him and made it possible for him to live without thinking at all. On Holy Thursday when the cross was exposed on its catafalque and the crowd filed past to kiss it, he would stand aside under a pillar, for half an hour or more, filled with a tremendous joy, only spoilt when some sentimental woman kissed the shoulder or knee of the figure; he would then go past himself, kiss the foot, and thereafter go all the day through his work feeling liberated, like a prisoner who has been in gaol for a long time and is let out on the appointed day. He had been a choir-boy when small; he mingled with and sometimes led their voices now, and was glad to be nothing but a voice.

Joseph stood beside the window looking through a sheet which had just come wet from the press, his eyes assiduously trained on the print. He kept glancing at the clock, it was nearly lunch-time; and there was running through his mind at the same time a bright current of images which arose out of the sunshine and from one of his phrases, "Orta recens quam pura nites," the legend of the New South Wales coat-of-arms which he saw on the Bent Street Library when he passed to go to the Cathedral.

Coloured spokes and plates whirling past on cars in the street were confounded with the wake of the morning's ferry, boiling silver, and the oily eddies at the side, with flakes of blinding light, like a dragon in plate-mail. The direct ray of sunlight separated him from the rest of the workshop. He now felt no more the irritation of the quarrel between Withers and Chamberlain, the disorder and his misery. It often happened to him in church too, when the light fell on him and he seemed to be alone and in a heavenly choir. Now while he worked with his hands, back at the machine, his mind floated out over the harbour and wove invisible skeins in the invisible fine air. He was busy fitting together his future like a jig-saw puzzle. He thought of sailing outside the heads and going to the old countries, where the morning sun gilded domes, palaces, royal parks and hives of cities, bigger ports, and where men had a history that looked through millenniums. He looked at the ugly letters on the yellow and blue cover of the magazine, and saw between them the bright features of an elzevir Utopia. Why, he was a man, it was not so bad. As the years go on one gets older, one is not so stupid as before; everyone is out for himself, some predestined to high and low life, grouchers only make it worse for themselves, and the poor in spirit inherit the kingdom of Heaven. So one graduates without knowing it into the adult world; mere living makes a man wise. The trouble we have had is not as bad as that we shall see before we die, so we must be prepared for it with a stiff upper lip. But Joseph wondered if it would be possible to stow-away, or get a job as steward on a ship. This had never occurred to his sleeping seaside brain before. There it came again, the mirage which leads people from country to country. His future was a procession of days, laying down line after line of clear print, with a few errors, no doubt, each year a sheet sidling into place and followed by others from the press of the Lord. And the whole printing-world is not like this miserable workshop. There are giant workshops with hundreds of men, artists, engravers, lithographers, electric etchers, superb lights blazing like suns in the roof, workers shut off in gauze covers, benches yards long covered with clean trays of brilliant cast lead, linotypes by the half-dozen. There are great buildings for the printing of books and newspapers, where the lights burn all night, as if in a palace, and reporters and photographers run in in shoals; where the news goes in towards the editor through circles of decreasing diameter of rewrite men, the seven spheres of editing, and runs out again through the corridors of the monstrous newsprint machines, through which printers wander as through a forest. There are hundreds of kinds of printing-works—no industry in the world is so varied. Is it possible that he will stick for ever in one wretched place, where one learns nothing and is maltreated?

Joseph looked at the clock—five minutes to one. He paused for a moment again over the German printers' magazine. A red knight on a green horse rode through an iron-brown and steel-blue countryside: it filled the eye and the mind with flame. These Germans, thought Joseph, understood that letters were not letters alone; they gave them characters. They are robust, brawny, squawk, joust, ride; they have pedigrees, religions, countries, political parties; they are dour, civic, frivolous, refined and oblique, square-footed, conservative and with money-bags; they have tongues and elbows, chitter, jostle each other too close at law, or march in open formation to make a show when they have little to say; they are disorderly and blatant for a bargain sale and, for a seizure, humdrum but with a lamentable look; they innovate, become austere, have rules of good taste unsuspected by the uninitiated, live altogether in a world of their own within our own. His eye, long used to feeling its way round the shapes of window-saints, conventional and bright as the pack of cards, and the rough Gothic capitals with their foliations in yellow sandstone and yellow light, understood the lustier vigour of the cartoon; the same comic symbolism was there, the same impropriety and escapades of virtuosity, the caricatures of mean bosses and shrewish wives, a fumbling after and fabling with facts, and the workman's practised, hardy, imaginative implement ascendant. This power of the workman in his element pleased him, relieved him of a Promethean pain, small (for an eagle is a gnat to a god), but often dimly felt within.

The recurrent squabbling of Withers and Chamberlain rose through the great press's lunging and the rotary colour-presses with their brief roll. Chamberlain went into his office to find his hat saying:

"You're so touchy, I can't talk to you"; and Withers came to Joseph, repeating in his soft lip and moustache:

"Silly old woman, his mother ought to've put him in petticoats. A Methody parson; Sunday at eleven our dear sisters will meet for prayer, I will be there; Sunday at three our dear ladies of the Dorcas Society will meet to cut out pinnies, I will be there; Sunday at six the young men will meet for the weekly uplift, I will not be there. A good job I got him, printing a thousand copies of a book of gay ladies, 'The Silk Stockings of Susan'. I know the chap who sells obscene books, it's upstairs in—I'll take you there, one day. A good price, and naturally a commission for me: but he's humming and ha-ing. We'd have to work after hours without the boy and women. The police would find out, and then good-bye. If the bank found out, it would call in the overdraft; I don't know what other excuses for not looking a few quid straight in the eye: he likes bankruptcy, it must be his middle name. Listen, I wouldn't mind going in for it, buying a little press, if I could get someone else to go in with me. I knew a chap in Göttingen when I was there, he did nothing else, and wonderful stuff, private translations of Aristophanes, Aretino, funny too, mind you, not only for the purple patches; and illustrated anthologies of obscene drawings and poems, first-class art, let me tell you, because when an artist does that it's for his own fun and he lets himself go. Rembrandt's best work is obscene, Raphael too, and the great Flemings. He made a wonderful living."

"Where is he now?"

"Well, the police closed the press on the complaint of German printers in the town who lost the business. He was expelled; a wonderful chap, sensitive, brilliant. He had a market all over Europe, but he sold the greater part in Germany itself; the Germans are mad over it. Now, Gregory has the chance of a life-time, and turns it down. He can't stand an investigation, I bet, that's it."

Chamberlain frowned, poked over his untidy table and pulled dozens of dirty little papers out of his pockets, looking for some instructions from a client.

"My best customer," he said suddenly, putting his head on his hand. "It's all over, I'm beat: I'm always like this, I'm no good as a business man."

"Keep your pecker up, Papa," said Effie, putting her hand on his poll. "Come and take me out for lunch, you'll find it after." They went out.

Withers giggled, went into the office and imitated Chamberlain: nobody looked. He came out.

"Why do I stay in this hole?" inquired Withers witheringly of Mendelssohn.

"Like to know myself: you give a chap a pain."

"I'll let you into the secret, then. Six pounds a week in the air and a half a dollar a week to go on with. Another good reason is to see the livestock lodging in the extra-Persian rugs don't escape, or to take 'em out for a walk if you want a beer, until you wish for the provident Scotchman who gave his Hielan' brethren scratching-posts, because they were all lousy. Also I have to receive the influx of orders by telegram and cable, while Greg goes gambolling and gambling in the second-hand artchopsueys of the Rt. Hon. Silkbreeched Montagu. Sylvester B. used to be a private adviser, that is office-boy, to Whistler's patron. Because of Whistler we must stagger under a swag of phony art, the boss must blow himself to a Bentley to transport Montagu's goods about, and we may go and hang ourselves on the nearest fig, if we don't like to work for the family. There's a clean kronk reason for a crank's open season: Kyrie Eleison—that's for Joseph. Where the deuce is the hammer? Here. Keep at it hammer and tongs, mate, till doom cracks, but no crying alack. Keep up the old ensign, brothers, the skull and cross-bones for ever; the ship's sinking. But we are working men, the bread of the world. So Greg says in his expansive moments of brotherhood. We'll soon be driven to eating our own behinds, in that case. And we are merry printers' devils, ta-ra, tay-rum, ta-ra, tay-yay."

Williams, standing behind Withers, made the sign of tossing off a small glass, and chuckling, doubled over his belly, as he stole off to the back door where workmen from a forage store were boiling his billy for him. But Withers was not drunk, only more exasperated than usual. As they went out, Joseph asked bitterly:

"You don't have to stick here; why do you?"

Withers said, "Ah, that's the question," and ambled out.

Pleasant days, pleasant company, jolly little conversazione. Baruch Mendelssohn, the third printer, turning out the covers on the small rotary press, stood quietly taking the last of the leaves as they fell, like a dark angel telling the Lord's tale in the fall of the year. He stopped the machine and put blotting-paper over the top of the pile. He knew these men backwards: he knew all their cues and their speeches, and he knew their condition. No journeyman's dreams were his.

At lunch-time, in the park, Joseph read the newspaper wrapping round his lunch while he ate. In this way he always got the news, although a few days or even a month late. Presently he unwillingly drew out his algebra book and worked through the examples set for the evening class. At night, if he had any difficulty in getting to sleep, he resolved $(a+b+c)^2$ in his head, and always found himself falling asleep before it was done; and he more often nodded with sleep than acquiescence in his night-class.

He was now joined by Baruch Mendelssohn, an American born of European parents, a young man a little over five feet in height, with a white skin, lively brown eyes, and a black stubble springing all over his round cheek. The excessive heat of the advanced spring on an empty stomach made him sick. When he sat down, Joseph observed large tears balancing themselves on his eyelids. Baruch did not wipe them away, but closed his eyes so that the tears ran down his cheeks and dried off in the sun. He opened his eyes unashamed.

"Sick again?" asked Joseph.

Baruch nodded. One would have thought that he did not intend to speak: not Joseph, who knew him. Joseph waited, with eyes roving in the distance, his ears open. Baruch opened his mouth and the words tumbled out:

"What a *fantasque* economic system! We all stand about helpless waiting for great Jupiter to descend in overalls on the stage and plaster his bricks into their courses; in the meantime, we act like common clay. Hum! you know the parables? The oldest son of the world goes off voluntarily and keeps pigs and lives on husks. When he decides to come home and get a square meal, his father wants to give him a veal cutlet, but his brother, who's been running things all the while and expected to see brother cut off, sulks. Gosh, what a morning! Chamberlain's not a bad egg, you know, but his weakness is vicious and he'll sacrifice us any day for his old man of the sea, Montagu. And then, say what you will, he indulges his fantasies at our expense. A man goes mad but his wits are still with him, he knifes someone else: he hasn't forgotten how sharp a knife is. However weak-minded an amiable man is, he buys his own groceries first."

"It's his business," objected Jo, "he put the money into it."

"A philanthropist," exclaimed Baruch irascibly, "look at you! You can afford to keep Chamberlain in Corona Coronas. You pay for a fur coat for Effie without turning a hair : but you don't buy one for mother—that simply shows you're unfilial and hate your family. You save your pennies, don't you, Jo, to give a penny on Saturdays to the first beggar you see, and to put something in the box on Sundays? You can afford also to support the Church of Rome. You see a business so prosperous that it can afford to keep hundreds of square miles of uncultivated land, hundreds of giant buildings of the finest stone, richest workmanship, with priceless treasuries, laces and coloured windows, with paintings, carvings and woodwork, enough to say masses to all eternity for all the souls on earth, so rich that it can keep regiments of idle, big-footed lumpkins to tinkle bells and recite a few Latin words that you know as well as they, and has coveys of devout females to work for nothing all their lives, scrubbing, laundering, teaching, without a decent bite of food or a piece of soft linen to cover themselves; you see an institution that conducts prosperous businesses, has printing-presses of its own, ships at sea, casinos and expensive schools, that has laws enacted to protect its interests, that pays no taxes and levies an irregular toll on millions of people, mostly ignorant and wretched. And what do you do? You save your money to put something in the box on Sunday. Yes, the poor are charitable, the poor are religious, the poor have bottomless purses. They buy gold dishes and gold telephones for the Pope and fill the Vatican with priceless marbles that they will never in their lives see or appreciate. They keep silk-robed youths, fat and rosy, singing songs and learning pseudo-history, in all the proud seminaries of Rome. They keep Cardinals' mistresses and Pope's nephews on the Seven Hills. They buy satin banners for Santa Maria Maggiore and a broom for the Scala, possibly Santa, and before they pray for their own relatives in distress, pray Heaven to protect the Pope, some black-bearded dago who doesn't even know they exist and doesn't give a damn. Does the Pope keep beggars, or the Vatican police hand out alms? Not on your tintype! But you do, Jo. And you likewise give money on Hospital Saturday, and also, I believe, for the missions in China. There's a world-embracing philanthropy for a poor man who doesn't have enough to sole his own boots. What characters we all have, the poor! They tell you poverty keeps you from temptation; it certainly does : but what you need, my poor friend, is a little temptation. Items : pride, in belonging to a dominant class; covetousness, in respect of a new pair of pants; lust, enough to make an appointment with a pretty girl; wrath, when you find you're trod on; gluttony, for a beefsteak; envy, of the bounding health of rich children; sloth, the lying all day on a yellow beach staring into vacancy and getting brown. But the Church has cleansed your heart of the seven deadly sins for working men. You have pints of character, so much that you're scarcely fit for human conversation, Jo. Who forgive the judge who gaols the Socialist?—the poor. The Socialist's disturbing the natural order, they say, he's envious. Who admire the state plug-uglies in their uniforms and lick the hand that snaps on the iron bracelet?—the poor. He's to protect us, you say,—your pocket-books, your safety-vaults, no doubt. Who tremble when they enter a private bank with portal twenty feet high made out of white marble, dug out, shipped and put up by workmen without a second pair of socks? Why, we do : the poor do. It's stupendous, we say, how rich he is! And if the banker should pass us on his way to his automobile, we respect the chauffeur's servile salute, and feel as if Jove had just walked that way. And our imagination opens out into innumerable white marble halls, hung with curtains, with bits of bronze on bits of marble, where tea is served on relatively infinitesimal tables to relatively minute ladies with neat hair. Our soul yearns over all that. Yes, it does; and your precious church, with its yawning vaults and thunderous doors, where you may walk, but may not talk or laugh, has given you since the cradle a holy respect for clinkers, the gold, the jewels, cash and plate, that it would take me years to clean out of your head. But here," cried Baruch, "in this country where you are technically all free, where you all vote and think yourselves political governors, where the land is free and you have no complications, if it weren't for your crazy bounties to protect what won't grow

89

cheaply and your tariffs as high as the moon to protect the uneconomic industries of cheap capitalists, you should live in an earthly paradise: you shouldn't have to think of any other heaven. And what do we see? Beggars, tramps, thousands of workless in misery, poor mothers whelping yearly generations who get wretcheder, gaols full of criminals, madhouses of madmen, extravagance, superstition. You might as well be in the depths of Bulgaria."

"Madmen and criminals," said Joseph, "can't be helped; you get them everywhere."

"Certainly, I recognise the doctrine," replied Baruch; "the natural, the child of God; the criminal, the hounded of God; the madman, the scourged of God. Our psychologists in America have re-established the Binet-Simon test of intelligence which shows infallibly that poor children are ten per cent. below the average, middle-class children at par, and rich children ten per cent. above the average. That is the democratic way of putting the old doctrine; and it proves that foolery and knavery corrupt the most serious of men. This doctrine is intended to and does crowd 'human beings into noisome cellars, and squalid tenement houses, fills prisons and brothels, goads men with want and consumes them with greed, robs women of the grace of perfect womanhood, takes from little children the joy and innocence of life's morning.' I didn't make that up, that's from Henry George. Henry George was himself a journeyman printer and was goaded with want and saw his wife ill and in want before he wrote that. He got a political secretaryship and there got his experience, in California, at the time California was ruined through the Civil War. After that he developed his political economy. You should read it, Jo: so clear, the weft of natural reason, the pure style of English, which a few have had—Hume, Berkeley, Shelley, Bertrand Russell. And he had no more luck than you or I: a poor man, but observant."

Baruch's eyes sparkled; Jo sat silent and doleful, perhaps touched by this discourse. Baruch thought he found it dull and tried to amuse him.

"But it isn't an economic relation at all, ours here, it's a connubial one. We're married to Chamberlain, or we're his concubines. He pets us, snarls, he sees to the general supplies and we get no pin-money at all: I am convinced that he looks at it as housekeeping. We can always eat, he says. He keeps Bovril in the cupboard and occasionally stands one or other of us to a meal. But I object to living in a harem, first, from natural jealousy, second, because I carefully surveyed myself in the glass this morning and I can certify I'm not an odalisque."

"You are right," said Joseph, "and my father is bothering me about it too. He's getting old now and he gets fretful. It's pretty thick."

"Thick? Yes, wait though, listen: what a man! This morning he wrote to his mother. He showed me the letter, being proud of his naturally eloquent style: 'Dear Mother,—As I write to you from a foreign land, I look out of the window at the bay leaves and think——' 'Bay leaves?', I said, looking at the fig tree. He was really hurt. 'What does it matter?' he says; 'she would like to think I was looking at bay leaves: there was a bay tree in the garden at home.' 'But,' I said, 'what foreign land are you speaking of? Isn't your mother English and you too?' 'Certainly,' he said, quite nettled, for he is proud of his phrases, 'but it seems a foreign land to her: she thinks there are hundreds of blacks running round the streets.' Oh, I had to laugh: he is a human after all, although such a dumbbell. To improve my opinion of his learning, he offers me an old copy of *Les Chouans*. 'You read French,' he says loud, so that the paper-carter waiting in the hall can hear, 'you might like to look at this,' he says: 'what does it mean, "Les Chouans," some sort of natives, isn't it?' 'Mr. Chamberlain,' said I, 'let's be vulgar—and frank. Before the mind some matters, before letters, let's start with bread, reversing St John by a simple process of the oesophagus. When are you going to let us have the dough, the specie, the shekels? We'll take it in any currency or form, bullion, Treasury Bills, Argentine bonds, George III pennies, new mint, anything but I.O.U.'s or tram-tickets. I mean, I know Montagu is a worthy character and society ought to keep him on the strength of his having known Whistler's exploiter, I realise that: but why assume the duty of Society? I mean, what about your honest toilers? Otherwise, Chamberlain,' I said to him, without making any bones about it, 'we'll strike and we'll put up a notice outside saying why, and then good-bye to your buyer and the bank'll come down on you.' I wouldn't, of course; but we certainly should have struck before. At any rate, next Saturday, the 20th inst., you, Mr. J. Baguenault, will get one month's arrears."

"Go on!" said Joseph, flushing.

"Yes, does that make a difference?" Baruch smiled with satisfaction, and related the incident again in different terms, with varying illustrations and pithy comparisons.

"Yes," he finished, "I thought to myself, the shop is going to blazes, and he's going to get into such a mess one of these days, with Withers, Montagu, the bank, or all three, as mankind has not seen the like; the wreck of the *Hesperus* will be an ocean regatta in comparison. I like to help you, Joseph: I'm sure you'd do as much for me any day. Wouldn't you, Joseph?"

"I would," said Joseph.

"Take Withers," said Baruch, pleased with himself; "he has a kind of moral and perhaps financial pressure, the insidious pressure one weak man has on another, knowing the weak points in his skin and not being ashamed to jab into them, and he has some blackmail up his sleeve for both of them, from what it appears (singing, the French call it, and Withers sings small in all rôles), running about with that greenish look he gets often, like a girl at the wrong time of the month. A defeated woman he is, in fact. And you, Joseph, you're too humane. I'm not criticising you at all, it's a fine trait, but it will never get you anywhere when misapplied. You're the most advanced case of purseless philanthropy I ever saw . . ."

Joseph always found himself paralysed before any half-dozen consecutive sentences, and now under this torrent of speech gazed blandly at Baruch, wishing to show he understood and was grateful, and only looking vacant. Baruch had now gesticulated himself into a perfect good humour, had forgotten his sickness and empty stomach; he laughed lovingly at his audience, showing his white buck teeth.

"Yes, you may not believe me!" he concluded, beaming.

Joseph opened his mouth once or twice, like a fish taking in air, as reflections of words came into his mind and involuntarily contracted the muscles of speech, but by now he had no ideas at all. He felt that there must be holes in any of the traditional remarks he usually brought out and he said nothing. Baruch had come to a stop. Joseph recalled himself with a tremor and said:

"Oh, really, it's awfully decent of you: thanks. I never know what to start with, when I ought to talk to a fellow: I always say the wrong thing."

"Come down to tin-tacks; that's the right thing. It's natural to me, for I am a Jew: we are realists."

Joseph smiled to hear the familiar phrase "for I am a Jew". It meant that Baruch had entered an intimate train of thought. Joseph looked down at his algebra book, and shyly showed the examples, hoping that Baruch would do them for him. But Baruch explained the problem for him, choosing his words simply, glancing up quickly through Joseph's glasses on which the sun shone brightly, to see if he understood the reasoning, patting his arm, threshing out fine seeds of thought from the golden harvest in his head, till his head presently overflowed again, and he sat chin-deep in a flood of exegesis which bewitched the pupil, his eyes, voice and body mobile with the love, wit and understanding of his nature.

"Grasp this and this, and you have invaded the whole question. More than that, you are on the road for the capital city, you can take the kingdom, you border on all that is known in science. Not so much is known, don't think it, that you can't make your way. The body of science is full of holes, ragged and clear-obscure like a moonlit ghost; but it is there, even if in the moonlight, even if a phantom of a shape that has been. If you make a stab at it, you'll find the stuff it's made of."

Joseph laughed. "You put things in such a way, nothing is serious to you, but then you have the brains; nobody ever thought me smart. Everything is really hard for me."

"Joseph, this is so simple. Here, you have a simple 4—four you have known since you were a baby and counted four fingers, four connie-agates, four sails in the bay; even savages of the most primitive sort have a word for 4. But that is their ultimate, and you, you can count to 10,000 and more with ease. You can multiply, divide, take the square root and calculate prime numbers! Why, your world, by that fact, is infinitely more complex, has many more dimensions. You understand already, without knowing you understand, thousands of relations that savages can't. But take 4, a simple thing, a final thing. You can begin to philosophise about 4—thus, there are four right angles all the same to a square, never more nor less. Fortresses and palaces, railway lines, skyscrapers, are built through confidence in that principle. Look, doesn't printing consist of ems and ens, simple measures. Then, with + and —, there you have a very important idea. A man talks. 'I like this, I don't like that, Rembrandt is a great artist, Velasquez is a rotten painter, El Greco puts one eyebrow higher than the other, Boucher represents the corruption of the court, Boudin paints the light that is on sea and land.' Don't be alarmed, that is only + and —; he makes a song about it, but that is all it is: that is aesthetic criticism, for the most part. If you read the paper, you see (and you get bored with it), 'France has so many submarines, England has less, Germany has armed forces disguised as sporting clubs, Switzerland is swollen with the world's gold deposits, Russia is spending millions on foreign propaganda,' and whether they'll go to war or not, with whom, for what, where, when, it's only a question of plus or minus, guns, wheat, bars of gold, soldiers, markets. Thus: 'the French loan went up to-day'—that's plus a few votes given to the Conservative Party in a by-election; 'the Prime Minister is expected to appear in the birthday honours'—that's plus a lordship and minus a party; 'riot in Austria'—that's bread plus three groschen. Even in the crimes, when you read, for example, 'woman kills man who jilts her,' you should only read it as 'woman minus a regular income, gentleman minus his mortgages.' My ambition has sometimes been to issue a newspaper like that, but it would be suppressed; the professions, the whores, judges, journalists, usurers, kings and commons would be putting a tailor-made halter round my short neck. If the clouds should

94

roll away from poor hearts there'd be too sudden a change to suit the gentry. Pray don't think mathematics is a mystery, Jo, it's the bunk that's obscure."

Joseph, surprised, gay, much agitated by the oddities of the young man, stubbornly fought out each problem, confusing and disentangling in turn mathematical conventions, stumbling over the conjugation of an exact idea of multiplicity with an unknown, mystified, but suddenly breaking open the rock so that understanding gushed out and watered earth barren and virgin. For a moment his eyes were opened, a pure stream broke through into the light, a new diagenetic principle began to work and he became aware of science, dimly, palely, because the light passed still through the clerestories of superstition; but it was as a ray of sunlight he had once seen crash through a memorial window in the village church, when he had wandered there with Michael, as a little boy, showing up a middle-aged mystery and the rusty black of devout kneeling women, a light even to the blind.

Baruch left Joseph to post a letter to an uncle in America. Joseph lay on his back in the sun and fell into a pleasant doze. He heard the rustle of papers being folded and went back with the workers to his workshop, blinded and irrational with the heat. The sun motes hopped about relentlessly all the afternoon, and it was true that his mind was a disk, as they often show to students in the University. The presses clanked a crazy refrain, "Chirk-chank-cho, Chirk-chank-cho, Chirk!" in a sort of mechanical lockjaw Choctaw chinwag in which they conversed among themselves all the afternoon. Graham, a commercial traveller, new to the business, whom Chamberlain had taken on as a freak, that week, brought in the copy for a handbill:

University Extension Courses.

A Course of FIVE LECTURES will be given on
LIGHT

by Professor A. MUELLER in the Physics Lecture
Theatre at the University, Camperdown.
Single lecture, 1s.   Course, 4s.
and so forth.

Baruch called Joseph over.

"Like to go myself; would you go, Jo?"

"It's too much, and I wouldn't understand."

"Tom Winter sometimes gets tickets sent down to Communist Hall. I'll see if I can get a couple from him or the Folliots. The first lecture you can get deadhead tickets to attract a crowd. They reckon they get for the course a fifth of the first crowd."

Joseph sighed. He knew that Baruch would try to drag him to the lot, that this invitation to the first lecture was a trap. He was so tired and lectures were so dry; he would try to find some way of crying off before the evening. It was best. He looked at himself between his hands. The sole of one boot was attached by a hairpin, the worn knees of the trousers showed the colour of his pale skin when he sat down. His hat was an old one of his cousin's. The rest of his attire fell in with these items and produced a sort of harmonious costume, the uniform of misery. The children of Fisherman's Bay shouted after him, "Joey, Jo, Jo, Ullo Jo," when he went past in the evenings. He knew what this song meant; it meant, "You are rubbish thrown out by men, and we are allowed to play with you, no one even has a salvage interest in you." The Clown of the Universe had produced a man in his image. The accumulated misery, shame, hunger and ignorance of centuries straddled the path as he advanced against the evening sun, and they shrieked with laughter to see his hat getting taller in the new lamplight and his coat more uncouth as his shadow fell backwards towards them. He was a stranger. It was marked in his face, which, of a dingy pallor, by some effect of skin or reflection appeared with the masterly distinction of an etched face, it was grotesque but more real, more human than the high-nosed, red-skinned, clapper-voiced, mussel-mouthed faces around him. It shone by the quality of its pain, incongruity and isolation. In certain men the flesh is as expressive of emotion as the eyes and voice. The flesh is most responsive to passion; it shows then how thin is the garment the blood puts on, and shines with a white lucent glare in a moment of agony.

Thinking of his debts at home, his clothes and the children, his face now took on this pallor of excitement, which Baruch remarked:

"Baguenault, you remind me of someone come of an old family: you have the colour of a race worn thin."

"I have."

"You mean, the human family is old?"

"No, my cousin Michael Baguenault told me some long tale, that my father and his had French ancestors. In France they were Huguenots and were persecuted there. Some fled to England, some to Ireland; those in Ireland became Catholics because they remained in the south and were very poor. My father says the story is not true, the tables of genealogy show that the last of the French family in Ireland died in 1808, and since then there is a complete blank. It doesn't make any difference, not to me; but Uncle Ben, Michael's father, spends a good part of his time trying to work it out because he says there must be still estates in France belonging to the old family. Uncle Ben found out that his wife is descended from an illegitimate daughter of Charles II, and he has the tree hanging on the door of his clothes-closet. My aunt pretends to hate it, but she shows it to you in secret. That beats me; don't you think it's childish."

"Charles II has been an unconscionably long time dying, that's a fact," answered Baruch, but he looked at Joseph eagerly. "Wonderful," he thought, "antiquity is in the blood of the Jews and in his, that is why I am drawn to him. He is the concentration of the troubles the family has known: his mother's ageing womb and the long-memoried germ made this masterpiece in her late-born."

4 ❧

The bucolic pill. An unfortunate polygamist.
Personal appearance of Mr Silkbreeched Montagu.
A family discussion. The seventh poor man.
Reflections of Joseph in shop-windows.

MR WILLIAMS trailed in after Joseph, with his red lunch-tin, and began washing out his billycan.

"Good morning, Mr Williams," said Joseph, "this is good weather for rheumatism. Don't you wish you were back at Goosebridge in your orchard?"

Williams sat down on a pile of paper near the back-door and wiped his wet moustache. He smiled slily, and fixing Joseph with his faded blue eyes, began:

"That reminds me, a stoker went downstairs, to Hell, you know. So the devil starts 'im stoking, and after about a thousand years, 'e says, 'Bob, you're a devil of a good stoker, yes, a devil of a stoker—there, I'm not so black as I'm painted, I'll give you a 'oliday, you can 'ave a rest, but I can't give you any pocket-money, so you must work, and since you're so black you must work where the men are black.' So 'e wafts the stoker to a cotton plantation, and after working an hour, although 'e's next to a pretty nigger girl, 'e says, 'Gee wiz, this is 'otter than 'ell,' and the girl says, ' 'Ow do y' know,' and 'e says, 'I come from 'ell just lately.' And the niggers take 'im for a revivalist and they begin to gather round 'im in the evening. The planter comes along and says, 'Out y' go, nigger, I don't want no 'oly joes,' and the nigger says, 'I'm doing the devil's work, not the other's.' The planter says, 'Thanks, I don't need no 'elp,' and out 'e goes. Then 'e goes to Central Hafrica w'ere there are a lot of darkies doing voodoo dances and 'e knows the lingo since 'e's dead. 'E tells them a lot about 'ell and they all gather roun' 'im and begin to trem'le, but out comes the chief and 'is medicine man. 'What'r you doin' 'ere?' 'I'm tellin' them about 'ell and the devil, the chap who invented voodoo,' says the stoker; 'I know all about it, I come from there.' 'Go on,' says the chief sarcastically; 'well, you're going right back there. Listen, I'm the only one that knows about voodoo. I invented it. You ain't comin' poachin' on my preserves, not with no fancy tales about 'ell and a devil. I am the devil.' 'E gets his warriors to seize the stoker to burn him, but there's nothin' the stoker don't know about fires and 'e escapes. Then 'e turns up in a coal mine. 'E don't see nobody and nobody sees 'im. They all pick and chop and lift out the coal with their lamps on their 'eads and their wet batteries under their arms, and presently the stoker gets so dam' tired, 'e says, 'By jingo, I been done. I don't see no sun, no grass; I'm not on earth at all. That blankety devil is foolin' me, I'm in one of 'is fancy 'ells.' The miners next to 'im says, 'Shut y' mouth, don't be yellin'. What y' raisin' 'ell for; where y' come from? You're a *provocateur*.' 'No fear,' says 'e, 'I'm a poor devil minin' a bit to get m' livin' 'cause I been through 'ell and the old devil's givin' me a rest.' 'You bet 'e is. You'll be restin' on y' back one of these days, with the roof saggin' in the way it is,' says the miner, and goes back to choppin' on 'is knees. But when they come up to the top, one of the miners, a sneak, tells the boss, 'There's a troublemaker, throw 'im out,' and two bullies come along and throw 'im out. 'You better be careful with me,' says the stoker, 'I'm from 'ell, and I'll get my frien' the devil after you.' 'Go on,' cries a woman, 'you c'n do a lot! 'Ell would be a 'oliday compared with this boss's place.' 'A fat lot you know,' 'e says, and she starts to bawl 'im out, so orf 'e scoots. So after a few more experiences like this, 'e gets a job as stoker, and 'e stokes so remarkably well, through 'is long expert hexperience, that the chief engineer talks o' throwing orf all the other men and only keepin' 'im. Then the other stokers just take 'im and throw 'im through a port-'ole into the sea. 'Come on, devil,' shouts the stoker, 'take me back!' When the devil gets 'im back, 'e says, 'Why 'r you so anxious to come back so quick?' 'By jingo,' says the stoker, ' 'ell is the only place left where a smart man like me can keep a job. Yes, 'ell is the only place left where a smart man like me can keep a job. Yes,' 'e says to the devil, 'the reason I called out to you to take me back is I found that 'ell is the only place I can keep a job.' Eh?"

"Yes," said Joseph.

"Well, it's like that with me and my orchard. I tried a lot o things, I was my own master, and it's like 'ell to me to work in menial jobs like this, but 'ell is the only damn place I can keep a job : I'm too smart. They want stoopids, yes-sir and yes-sir, certainly-sir : but now look 'ere, sir, there's somethin' wrong. You know what they do in the fruit business? A honest man can't make 'is way be 'imself. If 'e ain't a member of the Fruitgrowers' Association 'e gets all kicks and no 'apence. It's always 'is fruit that's thrown out for specked, always 'is boxes that go astray. 'E 'as to pay freight ninepence, and gets a return sixpence; 'e's out of pocket threepence a consignment, not countin' market dues. But I don't like to be under nobody's control : I always wanted to be a free man."

"Where was it, you said?" asked Joseph.

"Goosebridge, you know, 'alfway to Newcastle."

"It was a pity," remarked Joseph slowly. "I'd like to have a bit of land : you can't die, you can grow things on it."

"You can't grow the rent or the interest on the mortgage on it," said Williams. "Thank goodness, I owe nothin'. I sold it clear and paid all my debts to the townspeople. They get taken in enough without me. Nobody lorst anythin' but poor Halice, my poor little girl. I'll tell you all about it one of these days, Jo. Even 'er mother blames poor Halice, but the girl 'ad 'er bad luck."

"Her husband was killed, wasn't he?"

"Yes, that's w'y we 'ave to look after the family now; it's 'ard when you're old like Mother and me, but she's our daughter. If we made a mistake spoilin' 'er, and ruined 'er life, we should 'elp 'er now, although Mother and I are along in years and should be thinkin' about livin' quietly."

The orchard had not paid in any season; they lost money on the sale. Montagu kindly referred to old Williams as "the bucolic pill". It was a fact that Williams knew nothing about fruits except what he had seen of dried apricots and Christmas raisins. Williams found no work; at his age, they briefly told him, he was out of the question. He came to his relative, Chamberlain, cap in hand. Chamberlain said:

"Bad luck, you've had your ups and downs. I'd bet on you if you were a bit younger even now, but hard times are here. Look, take five shillings, all I've got on me. I'm broke, as usual, and I've got three concerns to think of, the home, the workmen, and an outside business, art dealers I'm interested in. Have you got anything to eat at home? Come up on Saturday night. Don't mind telling me if you're in need of something: I'm your relative in a sense, blood is thicker than water after all."

Williams said:

"You're a good sort, Gregory, but I want a job. Naturally we still 'ave almost 'alf the proceeds of the orchard, but I must get a steady job of some kind. How about a packing-room? something in your art dealers' place, wrappin', cartin', anything."

"Come out and have a nip. I'll ask Montagu, a friend of mine. Would you take a janitor's job?"

Williams came back the next day.

"Did you 'ear of anything, Gregory?"

"Bust it! I clean forgot it."

"I can't get work 'ere. I went for a caretaker at a factory in Surry Hills; there were three hundred applicants, and a lot of them young fellers and young married men. One of the chaps told me I ought to try a packin'-room but I've been all round: they don't want an old man. They call me old, although I feel as young as I ever did. I met an English newchum 'oo said 'e 'eard down Sussex Street in a seed shop they want an older man because they don't pay them so much. I said I'd just come from the country, I'd go. But it was filled. There are plenty of commercial travellers wanted too, and they say twenty-five to fifty: I can take off five years easy, but I don't think I could run round all day any more."

Chamberlain grimaced over the white head and slight stoop:

"Come and have a bite. I'll make a memorandum and let you know to-morrow, if you're in town."

"I'll be in town."

Chamberlain clean forgot him after lunch, and was dismayed to see old Williams the next day at eleven.

"Did you 'ear of anything, Gregory?"

"Look here, old chap, I can't afford it, but I'll take you on: you can clean up, run messages, anything and everything, while you're looking for something better: it's all I can do. I'm so terrible busy now that I can't go looking for something for you even if I would."

"I'll be glad to, Gregory."

"I'll give you a pound a week; it's not much, but it's more than I can afford. If you ever tell you're employed here and say what you get, you might get me into trouble, so mum's the word, eh? You're my relative helping me, for nothing, because you've got nothing to do with your time. Is that O.K.? I suppose you'll be worth it to me."

"I 'ope so, Gregory. I'm not dead yet; there's life in the old dog yet. I sailed before the mast for ten years and rounded the 'orn three times. I've still got an A.B.'s muscles. And I don't s'pose I'll be with you long."

Now old Williams had been there for six months. Nobody knew what he did all day long, except that he sometimes had to run trembling up and downstairs three or four times very quickly when Chamberlain's car was waiting:

"Hurry up there, Williams. God bless me, he's a useless baggage. He's really not worth a pound to me. But there you are, keeping a family. Got to be kind to the poor old beggar, awful when you're no good to anybody any more. If not for me he'd be on the State and Alice's kids too. Got to do your duty: blood's thicker than water."

"I'm comin', Gregory. There, there, everything's there. Don't get so nervous, you've got all day before you."

"I'm in business."

But old Williams got his pound note regularly, while the others waited. He did not know that, and now, reflecting on the unemployment problem and Gregory's pound, he ventured out from the corner where the inks and oils stood and said mildly to Joseph:

102

" 'E's a good heart, whatever 'e says. 'E flusters and blusters, but 'is bark is worse than his bite. Like a lawyer who visited an old lady. No law 'ere, she says, get out o' this, and the bulldog runs after 'im. Outside the fence the lawyer says, You can be sued for this—settin' a savage dog on me. Savage, she says, laughin', go on, 'is bark is worse than 'is bite. No, ma'am, says the lawyer, I am going to prove that my bark is worse for 'is bite. Hi, hi, hi: my bark is worse for 'is bite. Well, I don't mean that for Gregory. I'm not an ungrateful man. And I've begun to realise I'm gettin' older: a man does. If only Halice finds a nice man, I'll be contented. I'd even keep 'er three little kids with me to 'elp 'er out."

Joseph fitted three long galleys into their old galley press and Williams began to make the copies.

Presently there was a breeze on the stairs. A dark, robust, aquiline gentleman strode into the room, said, "Chamberlain out?", sat down at Chamberlain's desk and began looking through his drawers. He had a roll of drawing-paper in his overcoat pocket. When he had inspected all Chamberlain's papers and read the latest pages of his diary, he began fingering a book on tapestries which Joseph had got out from the Municipal Library and had been forced to lend him. Montagu felt himself a misplaced *grand seigneur*, but he made up for it as well as he could by riding roughshod over his friends and swiping any money or any virtuosity manifested in his sphere. Thus, he conned the book on Gobelin tapestries before Joseph had been able to look at it. He would presently sniff loudly through the aquiline, make a smart aesthetic remark to Baruch in a superior tone, as if they had an intellectual lien between them which united them above Joseph's head and would hand the book back, with a "Good, but cursory, of course: a popular edition."

He whistled various airs, balancing his plump fingertips before him, with his eyes lost somewhere in space, to show that he had been to the Italian opera then playing in town, and called out to Baruch to know if he had seen the "Frank Brangwyn exhibition" up the street. He told Withers that he had just had the luck to pick up at Potts Point what he believed to be an unlisted Meryon, that he was getting an Elioth Grüner for Jonah Ragfair, the soft-goods millionaire with a private gallery, and that he was having a commercial attaché smuggle in some old Chinese white jade snuff-boxes. He had just had the good fortune to pick up some marvellous stuff, marvellous. He walked to the front window, looked down into the park, and came hastily back to the office, saying:

"Sacred shades of the virgin, mine eyes fell below and beheld— Grahamovitch, that sucker. Look at him, will you, Withers, a puff-ball, a sunfish, a fleshy geaster, meditating on his phony lacquer and his sorrows like a pale fat Keats. Missed him by a minute! How many times has he been here after me, Baguenault?"

"Three or four days, sir!"

"How can he sit there so long with Mort staring him in the face? 'Born, arrived, died,' the history of a successful monument."

Chamberlain walked in, looked sour, said:

"Wait on, Montagu, I happen to have some business to attend to."

Montagu whistled, pulled out a brochure entitled "The False Van Goghs", read a few lines, with huh-huh and ha! and walked round the shop. He told Baruch a tale of Whistler when broke, astonished Joseph by a story of an authentic Gainsborough double which he had detected, in fact made a special journey to England for, ignored Withers and patted Williams on the shoulder saying, "How goes it, old boy; still on deck?"

Meantime, Chamberlain was fidgeting, turning out his pockets, piling his desk with bits of paper, string, spare nuts, looking for a pencil, tossing his files upside-down (they were already a mass of undated lists, notices of sales, domestic bills, auction-room debits, instalment payments receipted, tickets and orders scribbled on the edges of newspaper and of all those).

"Can't find it!"

Nobody took any notice. The usual thing happened. He questioned them all, sent Williams out to search the car, got Montagu to look through the mess of papers again, which he did daintily with invisible finger to nose, got red, plumped into his chair, and said:

"What's the use? I've got no system; it's no good, I might as well give up the game: a man like me is bound to lose."

He suddenly brightened, put his finger in his vest-pocket and dragged out the missing paper, which had the details for a large order of letter-heads and envelopes of several sizes.

"Bon, not so bad," he affirmed; "here we are again. A fine order! I do better in one afternoon than those Jugginses in a week. Everything is not up the pole. Mercurial, eh?"

Montagu elevated the aquiline, strolled to the window and hastily came back.

"Damn him, I'm positively being hounded. Here's Graham coming in. Tell the boys to keep him outside. Tell them to say I'm not here. I don't want to see him."

Montagu retired through the back-door. Graham entered the workshop. He carried two Chinese vases, one of red lacquer, the other of cloisonné ware, half-wrapped in paper. He placed them carefully on the floor and said dismally:

"Is Montagu about, Mr Chamberlain?"

"No; why?"

"These are 'is junk. He told me to—at any rate, 'e sent me with them to an address where they weren't wanted. I 'ad to deliver them at three yesterday afternoon and get cash on delivery."

"Who told you to run his errands?"

" 'E met me in the street, said 'e'd stepped out without a cent, and 'ad to have lunch with Ragfair. 'E borrowed ninety per cent. of the invoice from me and told me to reimburse myself, for my courtesy with the 'ole. I knew 'e was a good friend of yours, Mr Chamberlain. When I get there—no savee, not for them, Montagu's a name that's new to them. What it is all about I don't know. I know Mr Montagu wouldn't let me down, but I'm a poor man, and when I bring them back to the auction-rooms the chap there said, We don't want 'em, you're the owner, aren't you? No; but I look on the invoice and I see it's receipted, received from A. Graham, and so on. But I need the cash. Then last week— but no matter. I'll wait till I see him if I wait till Doomsday."

Withers listened to the tale with a sly pleased air, like someone who hears, by eavesdropping, news he has been waiting for.

Chamberlain walked out into the workshop.

"He might be here about six," said Effie, ignoring her father's nudge. "Put the vases down there."

"No," said Chamberlain, "I won't have any more rubbish here. It's not the Old Curiosity Shop. But if you want to see Montagu he might be here this afternoon—I can't say for sure. Put those damned vases somewhere around; I hope something falls on them. What you're doing with them, I don't know. Are you doing my business or Montagu's? I thought you were getting orders for me, not him; I'm sick of this; I'll tell him straight."

Graham took his vases and started for the storeroom.

"Graham, take a straight tip. Keep out of Montagu's way if you want to keep your health. People who do his business land in funny ports."

"I will, you bet."

When he came back Chamberlain and Withers were hobnobbing at the end of the room, with intent cross faces. Graham came to Joseph.

"Have you seen Montagu?"

"Here, about half an hour ago."

"Really? Can you beat it? Chamberlain told me . . ."

"I'm not interested in him. Perhaps it was longer then half an hour. We all know him and stay away from him; he's poison."

Graham with his fat puckered face and greying hair plucked Joseph's sleeve.

"Be a pal: I'm in a terrible mess. I don't know what to do, honest. I could burst out crying. That s.o.b. Montagu got me the job 'ere, you know. I introduced him to a friend, a commercial attaché, 'o said 'e'd bring stuff in for 'im from China, Japan, Singapore and so on. Montagu got me to sign a sort of letter to 'im, saying, that 'is name could not be mixed up in it since the Customs House was suspicious of 'im due to 'im 'aving innocently imported some silks for a friend, bales of silk in which drugs were discovered—God alone knows the length of Montagu's imagination and lies. The upshot is, that 'ere I am indebted to this man for nearly £500 of stuff, and what stuff! What do you suppose? A Chinese coffin, fourteen original Mandarin robes, an assortment of topknots that they used at court to show their rank, cork pictures, 'and-worked banners, bronze gongs, some Batik strips, some ceramics, which are smashed, by the way. *What* am I to do with it? Montagu will only take delivery of part of it on spec. and I'm responsible. Now the commercial attaché talks of suing me. 'E has a friend in the Customs and that end is fixed up for him. I say I'll sue Montagu, cause I 'ave a letter of 'is; but 'e says, no, nothing is specified, it ain't the right stuff. 'Is lovely friend, your boss, if you'll excuse me saying so, but I don't suppose you 'ave any illusions, is shielding 'im too. Yesterday I rang up this dump; I'm dead certain it was Montagu answered the 'phone. 'Is that you, Montagu?' 'This is the S.M.H. Packing Room,' 'e answers and rings orf. And rings orf. Smart devil, but 'e leaves too much stink of 'is trade around: 'e'll be so smart one of these days, 'e'll trip over 'is own feet, running orf.

"Be a good pal and let me know if 'e's coming back 'ere. Honest, I'm in a 'ell of a mess; my wife. It's terrible, I 'aven't the 'eart to keep going; my wife wants to shoot me or divorce me—she'd rather do both, because I was in the Gardens with another woman and her husband came in on us—a coupla weeks ago in the Botanic Gardens about nine o'clock one morning. You'll see it in the papers to-night or to-morra. I've got to get some money, I 'aven't a penny. I'm an 'ard worker. I never 'armed a fly in my life, and now I've got everything on my 'ead. This other woman—Bessie—is a magnificent woman, a friend of mine and my wife's. It's true I'm fond of 'er, you couldn't 'elp it yourself, and a man ain't a saint, but I swear I never 'armed my wife. It's a love affair, I love 'er and she's crazy about me. If I 'ad money I'd just give the 'ole pack the slip and take 'er orf with me. We'd make a living in some other place. And yet I like my wife; that's funny. If I only 'ad money—money washes out all spots; I seen *Macbeth* once—'Out damned spot'—if Macbeth'd 'd more money be'ind 'im there wouldn't 'a been any damned spot, and that was a bloody murder. That's the reason I went into this goddamned sickening business with the commercial attaché. I'm smart, I could manage some'ow, but I'm poor: a poor man 'as troubles all 'is life and 'e never 'as anything but a poor, miserable, wretched, untidy, un'appy life. They don't let 'im even be honest or 'ave a friend, if someone wants to pin 'im.

"Well, I'm making you a moan. I'll ring you up this afternoon or to-morrow, I'll talk through my nose, they'll think it's someone else; and you can tell me when Montagu's coming. You've only got to say, yes, no; I'll ask the questions. I'll stick 'im yet. I know somebody 'o'd like to call 'im to account. It's a dirty business, but look what 'e's done to me. What can you do? The jungle must be a decent place beside a pack of men. If they don't like you they roar at you to let you know, but a feller 'o's going to let you down, smoodges and smears you with rosy lingo to begin with; or snapping at each other's 'eels like nasty mongrels, the dog being a sight less decent, clean or honest than a jungle beast. Well, you've got to work. I'll amble along: I'll ring you. Goo'bye; I'll see you again."

Graham patted Joseph dolefully on the arm and trotted out again. Withers said:

"You're a great friend of the boss, aren't you? Why couldn't you tell the poor devil, Montagu is out in the cart-dock waiting for him to go: let 'em have it out."

"What chance has he?" asked Joseph doubtfully.

Baruch said: "God help us, they're all in the same boat. Chamberlain is another edition of Graham. Montagu's down and out for all practical purposes. Give them all a break; I can't see men fight."

Joseph said, "He's going to ring me up, I'll let him know next time."

Withers growled: "His heart can break till next time. Stick by, chaps, solidarity, solidarity, no imparity."

Chamberlain put his sandy head in.

"Has he gone?"

No one answered.

"He's gone!"

Montagu and Chamberlain came back and went into the office to argue. Withers hung about to catch the drift of the business. All sorts of squint-eyed tales, clumsy business plots, mean usurious combinations between friends tumbled out of their mouths like dirty little bits of paper and danced round the room in the soft summer breeze. Meanwhile the city ran on outside. Typewriters tapped, loiterers and unemployed men lounged in the little park, a hydraulic lift wheezed up and down in the cart-dock. The City Council took up and put down tar paving which would not set on account of the heat. A man opposite developing blue prints turned on his heliotrope light, the whistle blew for the cranes working on the Harbour Bridge, ferries whistled, a liner coming down the harbour to berth at midday bellowed, cars rattled past, the messenger boys went out for the lunches, the swallows chased each other off the red roof of the new yellow and blue building opposite which had the blue escutcheon of the Chilean Republic's consul on its walls. The heat increased, the machines meshed their rhythms, the coursers swerved round the track towards midday and the offices sweated. Presently Montagu stalked out of the office in noble indignation and Chamberlain stretched out his legs and said:

"What a pig!"

Then it was lunch-time.

Baruch went uptown to look at sailing schedules of the Union Steam Navigation Co. and Withers lounged off to one of the popular ninepenny tea-and-pie shops on the quay, leaving Williams to eat his bread and apple and to drink his black tea by the back door. He brought the tea in his billy-can, with a string tied to it, from the back of the court where some friendly gentle-men who lunched uproariously every day in the doorway of the warehouse, and who told him "always to call on his cobbers for tea". The cobbers talked Union talk and swapped narratives and conundrums of an interesting nature which made poor Williams grin a bit as he listened and dreamed about his scattered life. He leaned his head on his hand in the hot sun-ray that came through the chimneys of the warehouse and invented plenty of easy tricky schemes by which he could make money, be his own master again, get back to the old country with his wife, to visit Maidstone once again before they got too old, marry off his Alice buy a cottage with a half-acre of ground up on the North Shore or over in the new suburbs by Balgowlah. His wife and he went there on Sundays inspecting new subdivisions. He drank his black tea, and presently took out his can to his cobbers for more hot water. Then he took the *Telegraph* out of Chamberlain's office and read the political articles; he was seriously concerned with the fate of "the Empire".

Meanwhile Joseph walked up Macquarie Street, which is fine and broad and looks over all the Harbour and towards the sea. Down at the left is the Cathedral, in yellow sandstone. Joseph thought of the cool inside the padded doors, of dipping his fingers into the holy water, of the light which always blazed through the stained windows: so he went down there to rest for half an hour. There was nobody there but a thin young man of whom Joseph said "Dago, they're pious," and a young woman in black. Joseph stood at the first station of the cross. A woman in dirty clothes came up; he heard a noise like the whirring of a very old clock about to strike. He discovered that the old woman had spoken to him.

"I beg pardon."

"I said, young man, would you like to come to a retreat?"

"A retreat?"

Joseph stared at her. He didn't get the sense of the words, looking at her bent witch-body looped in black rags. Dismay filled him—what hellish invitation . . .

"Y'know, the Jesuits . . ."

"No thanks, really, no thank you, not to-day," said Joseph, and felt silly: he said that to the greengrocer.

He hastened down the aisle and came behind the high altar. There he sat and contemplated the candles; his heart was beating. It was strange and submarine up there in the gloom with the diffused lights. He sat there for perhaps a quarter of an hour as if asleep; the candles danced in his eyes and the sun shone through the western windows all at once, having passed the meridian. He could scarcely pierce the gloom under this volley of light, to see the three or four darkly-dressed women kneeling at the rail. Here the church kept its images, as in a grotto, and here the most simple-minded knelt. Another dropped a penny in the little tin box, lighted a candle, and started to pray. The smoke went up like a prayer. As he sat there the sun wheeled and fell through a broken leading in the window, smiting his eyes and forehead. He sprang up and gazed up at that effulgence, that miracle—he thought, so I might see the throne of God. Outside the trees murmured, the doves cooed, the purple jacaranda trees were in bloom, and through another small chink he saw the fair blue sky. He remembered how it was outside, the sloping Domain, the far headlands with blue-grey and yellow rounded rocks in Fisherman's Bay, visible even from here, the soft grass which one sees through the arcades of the Art Gallery in the Domain, the orphanage children in red and blue, exactly as children were in the Italian pictures of virgins and saints.

"O God of infinite majesty, I adore you," he said, without thinking what he was saying; the words burst from his lips. He went away from the crouching black women who were as if dead, the penny candles and glowing windows, and stood at the top of the central aisle watching the sun turn the architect's design to motes and confusion. One morning long ago, before Michael went to the war, when he was sometimes devout, Joseph went with him into the Cathedral. The sun was up, a stone in the flagged pavement was red and yellow with reflections: Joseph was only eight then, and sleepily gazed round over Michael's black head. There was a young woman standing against one of the pillars gazing towards them or at the altar. Michael had looked up sombrely, seen the light all around, said in a quiet voice,

"They even pierced windows in this den," and risen up.

He started to walk towards the door, when he looked quickly at the young woman as if he had just caught the glimmer of her skirt. He looked at the pavement and continued towards the door.

"Hey, Michael, hey, Michael! look, it's Catherine, your sister."

"Come on," said Michael.

"It was her."

"I don't care: come on!"

Joseph had often thought, why doesn't he take things normally instead of making things difficult for everybody? Now that was Catherine, but he couldn't say hullo to his own sister. He was ashamed of being caught in a church: he was always under her thumb. Certainly, that is it. As for me, thought Joseph, I have enough to be blue about, but I'm not; and I pray as I—as I piss: it's no great moral question to me. He burst through the doors. The top of the radiant sky blazed over Elizabeth Street, the air lifted his hair and blew dust in his eyes, the tram tracks glittered, his heart leapt into the air and he ran down the steps and along the hot asphalt path, his eyes full of blue sun-spots. At the same time Williams dreamed of making a fortune, perhaps picking up a nugget in the slag of the goldfields. The exaltation lasted all lunch-hour, although he got dreamier and dreamier. It was the sun that did it: the sun is very powerful in those parts and intoxicates the soberest natures. Joseph's gaiety passed out with a last flutter. He trotted back by Philip Street, which has small low houses and runs down a hill. The students stood outside the Law School joking with a spirited air. A young fellow with curly chestnut hair, high colour and a lovely smile was saying:

"You can image him brought up in a brilliant foreign court, not caring two straws for the dun, glum nation of subjugated Celts and Jutes, of whom Thiers wrote . . ."

And in another group a dark-skinned thin student said in a depressed voice:

"Every honest man admits you can't get on without influence."

Joseph shambled shabbily on. How far was he from the bottom of the ladder? He was a long way from the top. All that was true, with the professions organised and education so expensive, with a family depending on you, and no money even for a decent shave, what chance had he? Look at the way the fellows jabbered. He didn't even know what they were talking about, and supposedly they were both using the same language. Yes, with the world organised into watertight compartments what chance had a dunce like him? A man needed influence to get on, influence and money; even those young lawyers said so. A man such as he was would spend all his fertile years scraping together a little sum to pay the mortgage on his father's house or to save up for a wife. After that, nothing; he was done for: only the dreary round of anxieties and every new acquaintance a new responsibility. He did not see how he would ever afford to have a wife and child, for example. Courage, said his conscience faintly, a good heart, cheerfulness, hard work, trust in the Lord.

"O Lord, sweet well of all blessings, who know and see yourself my needs"—does he? is it possible? "God is a pure spirit, because he has no body and he cannot be seen by our eyes, nor touched by our hands. God," said Joseph to himself, with the sun beating down on his head, "is above all that: a funny relation, a pure spirit and a dunce. I wish I did not believe in religion, I would feel more insignificant, I would be freer. Bosh, I am a dead man if I go on like this: let's not think about it." He tried the poor man's catechism all the way to work. There he sniffed the ink, the musky flooring, the faint familiar odour of urine, and his spirits rose. He ran in and began to make proofs from the galleys. It was a fine job, it was cool inside, he was glad to work.

Withers came in holding his jaw, and angrily and mournfully set to work.

"What's up?"

"All my teeth are aching, and my back too."

"Take an aspirin."

"No, I won't, I don't want anything."

Withers chewed on a pencil and got flushed under the eyes: he kept watching the door malignantly. Presently he stopped the machine, said pettishly, "I'm *done* with him," and sat down on the little boy's chair.

"Give it a breeze," groaned Joseph, "it's like a hundred mosquitoes buzzing to hear you."

"This is too much, the last straw. If you had my worries you wouldn't feel so clever."

"Yes, worries you have, no one can deny that," remarked Baruch.

"I sweat and I sweat, I worry and I worry, to make a go of this rotten dump. I work more than all of you put together, I do ten men's work. The whole organisation of the place is due to me; I can't sleep at night for thinking of it. Any money that comes into this place, I earn. I ought to get a percentage, as a matter of fact, of the profits. My £60 may as well be counted a dead loss. But I can put him into bankruptcy for £60 and I've a good mind to."

"Don't be an idiot: you'd have to examine your share of the

proceeds with a microscope."

Chamberlain came in cheerfully, waved his hand:

"Hullo, boys; hullo, girls."

Withers chewed his moustache, flushed, with a naughty expression for a moment, and stalked darkly into the office.

"See here, Gregory, I'm fed up. I want my money, and then I'm quitting. I'll see about the £60 later."

"Well, quit: what are you moaning about?"

"I want my money, and now, and you've got to give these other beggars their pay too; you must have it. Jacobson just told me he paid his bill at the beginning of this week. Now, where's the dough? If you've given it to Montagu, or bought anything else on the instalment plan, I'll—I'll strangle you." Withers' high thin voice began to scream.

"I haven't got it; it's in the bank."

"Go to the bank; or give me a cheque, right away. I'll cash it."

"I had to pay Montagu, he was pressing me; and I had to give him something to help him out with this Graham fellow."

"You didn't, you couldn't have, with your workmen almost starving: you're mad. I'll take you into the courts."

"I haven't any money. If you insist, I'll have to sell my car, my home, and see my wife and child on the streets."

"That's a lie. Chaps like you are bankrupt and still live a hundred times better than men who pay their way. Gee, like a fellow I met on the Melbourne express once, in the dining-car, Baker of Baker & Teakes, the week they were filed in bankruptcy. I knew him at school. He was dressed in a £16 hairline-stripe grey suit, hand-made shoes, hair scented, first-class imported stetson. 'I see you're broke, Baker,' says I. 'Yes, I am.' He looks serious and then, after taking a squint at me, he grins, 'There are five and sixty ways of disguising the malaise, and every single one of them is right.' He orders the best brandy and drives to the Grand Hotel. You couldn't be broke as well as that, you're not in his class, Greg, but you'd do pretty well, pretty well. Now, fork out!"

At this moment, Mrs Chamberlain, a fat, timid, florid woman of forty, and Effie came in. Mrs Chamberlain always wore a spotted veil to conceal a skin disease on her face. Effie, hearing voices, motioned her mother to a seat outside the door, and sat down beside her.

"For your £60, I'll give you the car, you can sell it. It'll be an excuse for me not to drive Montagu around. I've always got to pay the gas anyway."

"Garn! You got it off Dave Jonas, don't be funny, and you've never paid for it. He'd be seizing it on me in a week. And what would I do with a car? I can't pay for beer, let alone gas."

Chamberlain was silent. At last he said:

"Don't make a row: I'm settling with the men this evening. I'll send you to the bank and send Jo over to Montagu."

He looked grey. After an effort he said:

"You don't know what a fix I'm in. But I can't have this discussion going on; it's killing me."

He thought again and continued:

"Withers, I've a good mind to let you take over the business end and put everything in your hands. I get such terrible headaches, I feel like putting an end to it all, sometimes."

"If you want to look at it that way," said Withers beginning to cheer up.

"It's not that I'm indebted to you—if that were all my worries!—but I'm terribly fond of you, Tom, and I can't stand you fighting with me like this. I don't know how I'd get along without you, that's the truth. Yes, you were right this morning. I suppose I could have scraped together the money I owe you, over a period of weeks, borrowing here and there, getting the wife and kid to save, but I was afraid to lose you. I thought you'd be off as soon as you got it, after our scraps you know. You're bitter, Tom, in what you say, and I'm thin-skinned when it comes to friends. I take it to heart, although I should know, I suppose, it's nothing but froth that you blow off a good glass of beer. I want you to stay near me, Tom."

"Why should I leave you, if I'm treated with at least the same consideration as Montagu or Graham? But it makes my gall rise—you give Montagu money for Graham: why Graham? By Jesus, it's maddening."

"It sounds weak, but I'm fond of you like a relative, Tom. I even hoped, in the early days, you'd take a fancy to Effie, you know. But if you're thinking of settling down, any time, really settling down, I'll manage things so that you'll start off right anyhow; you need it, Tom, it's steadying."

"You mean your little girl's to offset your debt. I don't want to be a relative of yours, and I don't want Effie. I'm not the right sort for the Kid, and she's not for me. No one is for me: I'm a natural deadbeat. Besides, you know as well as Danny that Dave Jonas only lets you off the car payments and runs round signing I.O.U.'s for you in consideration of being looked upon as your son-in-law; which he is already, in fact. And Effie loves Dave. You're a moral specimen, aren't you? Rather than try to curb one of your impulses—my God, you've got a wonderful business here, if you'd attend to it—you'd sink your own family and Effie's respectability. You don't give a damn what Dave Jonas does with Effie as long as you can peddle around in a nifty car."

Mrs Chamberlain was shifting into the farthest corner, and Effie patted her hand.

"Papa is a fool: I'm going in. Let me go, Mother; I'll settle their hash." She went in.

"I heard every word. Sit down, Papa, you're simply foolish, you're a laughing-stock, everyone can wind you round their little finger." She looked in a business-like fashion at Withers.

"I'm not ashamed, but you should be. Dave Jonas is my boy, he does everything for me and for Papa. He doesn't get out of it any more than you, and he's the only benefactor this blighted family has seen since I remember. He got Papa out of a corner six months ago by signing a note, and he's lent him his savings: he's lovely. You pretend to be Papa's friend, and you're always hand in glove with that shark Montagu. How I hate him; I'd kill him if I could. And the bank is after poor Papa: wants to get back his overdraft. No wonder he's worried. Why don't you try to help him a bit instead of nagging and nagging? He offered you to run the business, didn't he? Why don't you take it? Run it your own way, if you don't like his. Nail him down, take him at his word; we'll all be better off. But you've got no more character than he has."

116

Withers answered softly:

"You don't know what you're talking about, Effie: you've got someone to keep you. You've never been down and out."

"I'll raise that money for you somehow and you can get out. Get out; we'll be better round here."

"You couldn't raise it in a month of Sundays; Greg's cleared you all out," replied Withers, smiling slightly, "but you win, kiddo. My excuses. Don't be too rough on me. Bad luck sours the temper. I've got an unpractical streak myself, and I'll always be worse off than your Dave will ever be. Have you got the cheque, Chamberlain?"

"I'll telephone Montagu."

"I'll go and see him at the same time," said Withers.

Withers went out and presently returned. A flush of joy went over the workshop; they looked at the office where the money was being counted. Presently, Chamberlain came round and paid them all. Each one felt against his thigh the little wad of paper, the weight of the loose coins, and at the end of the afternoon they were whistling and chaffing. Joseph walked up Pitt Street with Baruch, to find some little place to eat. Baruch was talking politics, but Joseph noticed how splendidly the shop-windows were lighted, how richly dressed in crumpled silk and polished ashwood. There was an inlaid tortoiseshell cigarette-case that he stopped and stared at dully, for the pleasure of looking at expensive things while he had money in his pocket. Baruch came unquietly alongside and peered at the objects in the window without interest. There were things Joseph had never noticed before, or had not noticed for years, he thought, "gossamer" shirts for the heat, blue and buff silk underwear with pleated waists. There were suits with satin revers "For the Evening Wedding", "For the Afternoon Wedding", "For the Evening Reception". He examined with surprise the styles of waistcoats, corded, white, black, satin, brocade, piqué.

"That's absurd, isn't it?" he said severely to Baruch, pointing to a waistcoat with revers of satin.

They both halted before the readymade tailor's to compare the cut and patterns of the £2 2s. suits; there were others at

£2. 17s. 6d. "made-to-order with two fittings". Joseph looked
out of the corner of his eye at the crowd passing him and studied
the styles of suit worn by other small men; for instance, a sac suit
rather neatly cut at the waist. A blonde girl in an organdi blouse
and high heels tapped along beside the sac suit neatly cut at the
waist. And shoes, with a small foot; he could look well in a rather
classy pointed toe : as to the heels, perhaps they could raise them
a little. There were hats, "merino-felt" and "pure hare felt"; but
he knew a man in a hat factory who would get him one at cost
price. That would come after. Oh, to spend it all in one splurge
and turn out the next morning, fresh, clean, neat, a three days'
wonder for the boat; a gag for the mouths of the little skipping
girls. That was the rub, in fact; they would only laugh again to
see him trying to conceal himself; Jo, for the boat, was that seedy
dwarf that he now saw walking with him through the window-
mirrors.

Baruch kept on talking, glancing quickly to see what kept Jo's
attention straying: he once, even, with kind courtesy, dragged
Jo to a shop-window and said :

"That's what I could do with, a badger brush with a silver
handle : they never wear out. And look at that razor with the
tortoiseshell handle : wouldn't we be the beaux of Lachlan
Place?"

He then rapidly took Joseph from the window and plunged
into his political discourse again. And Joseph, from long habit,
said :

"Yes, yes, of course I do, you bet,.too right," and made affirma-
tive noises when the cadence of the voice required it. He quizzed
the crowd. What harem-scarems they were, the skinamalink
office-boys, making their fingers squeak on the glass, hurrying
home to mother's Irish stew. A father with two little children
all looked in at a fine drawing-board stretched with white paper;
above were snapshot kodaks, decorated with cherry ribbons. As
Jo's step unconsciously lagged, Baruch hurried him on. There
were old men by themselves carefully comparing the prices of
shoes in half-closed shoe-shops; there was a huge "boot-
emporium" for the populace, decorated with hideous cartoons in

green and red, of tramps with red noses and their toes out of their shoes, and women in laced boots with bursting breasts and big behinds.

"I'll get a pair of socks," said Joseph, seeing a man with an open case at the corner of a side-street, "and to-morrow I'll get a pair of shoes."

"Let's get them here." Baruch stopped in the middle of a period and pushed him hastily forward.

"Are they good value, do you think, for a shilling?" asked Joseph.

"Yes, yes, at that price, they're all the same. You know what you're getting, don't you? They can't rob you at that price, it's an advertisement of quality, that price. There you are, take that pair." He hurried him on, and Joseph for a minute paid attention to Baruch's remarks, while the paper bag swished in his pocket.

Splendid were the silver shops, with their iron grilles half-up already. Grotesque but beautiful baskets in silver, receptacles of all sorts whose use he could not imagine, all decorated with scrolls, flourishes, chrysanthemums, cherubs, all punched out and pressed in, chased, embossed and pierced; fruit-stands, with lace d'oyleys and wax fruits, etched drinking glasses and champagne glasses, goblets, carafes, great silver dishes, heaps of fruit-knives with mother-of-pearl handles; signet-rings, mourning-rings, wedding-rings, diamond rings, studs, necklaces, magnificent opals like fire and milk lying on white satin pads, Arabian bangles for the girls. Inside the lights shone brilliantly on the cases, the polished wood counter, the purple velvet necks decorated with pearl necklaces, and the numerous mirrors. A small old white-headed man was there, noting the people who stopped outside, and a dandy in glazed collar and lacquered hair kept passing out and in of a swinging glass door with trays.

"What do you think he gets for that job?" asked Joseph.

"Oh, he's probably the son: you have to be introduced, and you learn the trade," responded Baruch in a breath.

"And pearl-handled revolvers," said Joseph in surprise.

"Yes, they exist outside the novelettes," smiled Baruch.

Joseph was embarrassed to see a young couple hesitating before a bedding shop, brilliantly lighted, where an automatic demonstrator was showing the advantages of a pillow containing a fine spring. How can they look and not blush? he said to himself, in his modesty. In fact, the young man brusquely took the arm of the lingering girl and moved on. Joseph breathed more freely. There in a chemist's shop was boricated vaseline, the sort he preferred, and a lotion for the hands, guaranteed to whiten them. His own had been very white, but now they were always dirty. There was a double tooth-paste guaranteed to whiten even difficult teeth, but he had no need of that, for his own teeth were beautiful. Weighing what he needed and did not need, he felt how round and complex was his personality. He almost felt the ebb and flow in the markets, the jostling in the streets, the polishing of counters by elbows. Supply and demand——— Or what was Baruch saying about supply and demand? Something, but never mind, he'll tell it again some other day. There were pearl-pills for virility, with a diagram of the male organism showing a red line from the brain to the small of the back, and there were very odd rubber things, perhaps for women, perhaps for childbirth. Those things were the drawback with getting a wife, of course. He did not like these things, and they went on. At last Baruch gave up.

"You're window-shopping, Joseph; it's the most satisfying and least expensive. You've never done it before. Strange is the influence of Marx on character."

"How do you mean?"

"Come along in and have an ice-cream soda," replied Baruch, and they went into one of the numerous Italian fruit-shops, attractive with their glass windows full of glass shelves and fruit, cool drinks, ice-creams, sundaes, frosteds and what not. They each had a peach-melba: Baruch was a sweet-tooth, Joseph had not remembered that peach-melbas were so good. Afterwards, Baruch walked more slowly and attentively discussed every window Jo looked at. "Look at the nightie in pink silk: that whole outfit costs more than we could save in a year. Don't you wonder how the girls do it? Or the boys." In the other window were babies' clothes. Two hardy girls passed and tittered.

"Oh, you naughty boys," said one; and the other, "No, silly, they're two young fathers out shopping." The girls disappeared into the crowd. The boys blushed a little, laughed and went on.

They reached the less-frequented regions, they turned out of the shopping districts down by Paddy's Market and the Technical High School. Most of the shops were closed. Three young men with hats in their hands played leap-frog outside a closed bar. A pool of blood on the pavement, with several clots, made them look around : opposite were two streets in which were houses of ill-fame—a fight between bucks, a girl having a baby, a bleeding nose? They walked on, the light gradually becoming less, crossing and recrossing the road, dodging the little traffic. They were fatigued now. Baruch had walked for some minutes without talking, looking very pale, limping slightly. They stopped to breathe outside a lolly-shop brightly lighted, in which were purple, mauve and red boxes of chocolates with gilt filigree paper. Going with one of those under your arm to a red plush parlour, a daguerreotyped aunt in a red plush frame, to a girl: looking at the boxes Joseph had an affection for all girls. A doorman smoking his pipe, with a thick lined face, looked through the boys as they passed heavily. His red-braided coat was open down to the stomach, he slumped on his seat, and his polished big boots were unlaced; his wife played solitaire, through the machine-laced curtains, on a red fringed table-cloth. A welldressed girl came up with them and passed them; she hesitated, looked at Joseph and walked on a few steps ahead, the high heels tapping impatiently, marking time. She turned down a side street; who knows? They have to earn their living. How did she know Joseph had just been paid? A broken ostrich-feather, pale blue and grey, lay on the pavement under an open window on the second floor; in the window was a pink blind drawn, on which a woman's head-dress darkly moved. They passed a lighted entrance, with polished handle, varnished door, and two whitened steps. Baruch was silent. Who knows? thought Joseph. This is my city, here I was born and bred, I cannot be lost here, nothing can happen to me. I am Joseph Baguenault of Fisherman's Bay. I know the stones, the turnings; I know where the Markets are, there to the right and behind.

The lights were on dimly to light a little the interior dusk and still to admit what remained of the daylight; the street was not yet that covered way which is endless and mysterious at night, but the city had become warm, hospitable, a city of hearths and yellow-silk lighted interiors; spoons clapped on soup-plates, spoons clanked in cups, sugar-basins revolved. An old man out walking with a cane looked friendlily at the two boys, with the friendliness of a Biblical comment, "Look, what you are experiencing the prophets experienced in their adolescence two thousand years ago." He went stooping on. I am young, thinks Jo. This is what the old man intended him to think. The street-lights were switched on and glowed warmly in a slight thick dusk, as if to prove conclusively that the day had knocked off work and gone home. Near an old garden, he noticed how the trees had taken on an inhuman air with something wild in them, as lions have, sitting unreconciled in the back of their cages licking their paws, in the zoo. He heard again the tapping behind him of the nocturnal prostitute just beginning her beat: fresh, odorous, with shining curls and a big bow on her neck and frilled elbows, pretty, dainty. She smiled unconsciously as she tapped with vanity past him. More soft steps and, rubbersoled, came the lamp-lighter who had just got through the district of gas-lamps. Tea was preparing everywhere; night had begun.

"I am hungry," said Joseph.

Two old dowdy women huddling to each other, both thin, beaked, satin-hatted, and hatpin-eyed, passed him and looked approvingly at him because he was shabby, dull and modest. Joseph, too, felt comforted; his life had been passed amongst old shabby women. They would do him no harm; they would make tea for him.

"I'm dog-tired," said Baruch.

"We'll eat," answered Joseph.

They looked in at the Greek restaurant and tea-shop at the corner of the street. The walls were dark green, the tables marble-topped; the electric bulbs surrounded with scalloped paper shades, cut out of grease-proof paper, were covered with fly-specks. Bred in the heat, small cockroaches scuttled about the window glass in front of the fruit, pastry and sandwiches.

"Here, if you like," said Joseph, looking at the prices.

"We'll go home and buy something on the way; I'll make tea," answered Baruch, wiping his forehead with a brown, twisted, nasty-smelling handkerchief.

"I'm so tired," admitted Joseph, his legs trembling.

"Can you walk back to the station?" asked Baruch. "We'll take a beer and get a bus from the station. Your own bus will land us on the other side of St. Mary's Cathedral; we'll walk from there. The fresh air of the Domain will do you good."

"Right-o."

As they came back past the Technical College a short dark man with a high boot hailed them from the other side of the archway.

"Hullo, comrades!"

"Who is it?" asked Joseph.

"Winter, librarian at the Communist Library," explained Baruch, as he hurried delightedly across and shook hands with the man.

The man was thin, ill-looking, poor; his face gave him thirty-five years of labour, but his voice and manner showed him to be only twenty-five, or even less.

"Coming home with us?" asked Baruch hospitably.

"Not me; I'm going to a lecher on experimental psychology; Hewitt's."

"What's he like?" asked Baruch.

"He's the son of a working-man: he's worked his way up in the University. He lechers with a real Australian twang: he ain't ashamed of it; we workers understand things better in it. He not only gives us the whole thing from Munsterberg to Binet-Simon, Yerkes, Taylor, Ford and Bedaux, form-boards, puzzle-boxes, traffic-signals, reaction-times, colour-wheels and all, but he lets yew see, although he can't go too far, that the whole science only sprang from the need for rationalisation and saving on workers. Gods, it's fascinating; come along."

"We haven't eaten," said Baruch, "otherwise we would: and Joseph here is tired."

123

"Yes, I'm tired."

"What's your job?" asked Winter passionately.

"I'm a printer: I work with Mendelssohn."

"Gods, that dump. Do you belong to the Union?"

"Eh—no."

"I don't understand yew, Mendelssohn, why aren't yew fellers organised? Yer a bloody intellectual, yew ain't got no class-consciousness. And why aren't yew?"

"I'm an intellectual," said Baruch firmly; "and I want to be a scholar: there's no disgrace in it. Besides, I'm a Union man."

"Yer clever," said Winter angrily, "and the masters make use o' yew to subject the workers. Yew'll be a scholar and yew'll leave us behind. The mind even in poverty, misery and slavery rises superior to its material conditions, that's the old gag. 'The clever child,' says Goddard, that feller that works for the corporations, 'will always rise, however many obstacles he has to encounter; we should not waste too much time worrying about his difficulties of temperament or family situation.' Those who dew arise are the smart ones; those who don't are the duffers. Yew would arise whatever yer conditions, and yew'll believe their bloody propaganda before yer much older. I only believe in the workers, and in the Australian workers, the first sons of 'the first sons of modern capitalism', as Marx said. Yer no more good to the proletariat than a beautiful girl who's so swell that she can live off of men without workin' is good to her workin'-class sisters. She don't know their problems, and no more dew yew know our problems. One of these days yew'll be seein' yer name, Dr Mendelssohn, and yew'll be lechering on Social Theory, and sayin', I was onst a workin'-man, comrades, and they'll be cheerin' yew. If yew don't look out yew'll be a traitor to the workin'-class."

"What makes you think so?" inquired Baruch anxiously.

The brown evening gathered round them under the archway. The light shone at each end. Working-men with shoulders slightly stooped and with serious faces passed them on the way to the Technical College, now brightly lighted.

"You've heard me speak," continued Baruch warmly; "you

know it isn't in me to betray the working-classes, even if I'd been born in the lap of luxury. I'm a natural Communist; everyone is my brother."

"That's what's the matter," said Winter bitterly, "yew orter hate the upper classes; they're our natural enemy. Can you imagine chaps goin' to war and sittin' in the front trenches and sayin', 'I haven't got any warrior feelin', I love the Huns like I love my brother. Suppose yew do, yew get shell-shock, or yew desert, or yew fraternise on yer own before the rest o' the army's ready, or yew get safe through the war and fer the rest o' yer life tell the folks back home that the system is wrong, but the Huns are nice people. No, yew got to be uncommunist towards the capitalists: yew got to hate the capitalists. That's just it; that's just it. Yew want to make the workin'-class movement respectable by fraternity, by sincerity, by scientific socialism, by ease, by opportunist pacifism. But worst of all, yer on the make. Yew want to be a scholar. Am I a scholar? Er all them thousans and thousans of miners an' dairy-farmers an' boundary-riders an' painters an' truck-drivers an' wharfies scholars. There's only one book yew need to know, an' that's Marx, an' only one exegesis yew want to read an' that's Lenin on Marx. Yew don't have to read Greek to know the shadder o' the Acropolis fell on slaves, or Latin to know that when the Roman grandees left off studyin' geography an' began to study astrology, Alaric wasn't far off. Yew don't have to read Hebrew to know why no rich Jews are killed in pogroms, or French to know why the aristocrats were scared shitloose an' began givin' away their privileges on the eve of the Revolution. Yew only got to read Marx, and study what's under yer nose."

"But," said Joseph indignantly, "Marx studied it all for you, and that's why you know all those things. Marx didn't do a thing for thirty years but read in the British Museum."

"Are you a Marxian, comrade?" asked Winter, his face beaming.

"No, he told me that."

"Well, so yer teachin' your feller-workers," said Winter, turning to Baruch. "That's all right: if yew do that, it's all right. But

I'm suspicious o' all intellectuals, and we got a right to be. We been betrayed too often. It's too easy for yew fellers to pass over into the other camp, an' be a barrister, a writer, a historian, a clever journalist. Wot's the fate o' so many labour-leaders? the whole world is acquainted with them; the upper classes laugh themselves sick over them. They rat : like MacDonald. And then, are they ashamed? No; they are lonely, misunderstood spirits, self-sacrificed to duty. Well, I got to go. Ross is havin' a few o' us at his house next week : do you want to go? I'll call for yew after work?"

"Thanks," cried Baruch; "I'd be delighted to meet Ross, and Joseph will come too."

Winter scurried along the street towards the College.

"I feel so sick when I look at the College," said Joseph. "I'll never get through. I've failed twice, in two courses, the last three years. I'm a dunce all right."

"You'd be less of a dunce, and feel less sick if you had some supper. Come along, step out, make it lively, old boy, we'll soon get home."

"Who's Ross?"

"You don't know Ross, the secretary of the Miners' Federation?"

"Oh, Faker Ross?"

"Yes, want to meet him?"

"Oh, I—if you like," said Joseph dismally.

"We'll go to the Castle-Palace pictures to-night if you like," suggested Baruch.

"O.K."

But after supper Joseph went home. He took the bus and arrived in the Bay after nine. He was so tired that he did not even turn to look out of the bus at a garage on fire. He was awakened at the Bay by the people pushing past him. As he passed the confectionery shop on the beach-path the little girls were still skipping on the step, saying, "Tinker, tailor . . ." Joseph stopped a moment to look in at the pastry and fruit : would he take his mother a tart? The little girls stopped and peered at Joseph : his drawn face with his hat stuck on slightly askew made him look very funny. They began their song again softly, and when they

126

came to "beggarman . . ." giggled. Joseph took no notice of them; as he went on they started to cry in their thin voices, "Jo, Jo, beggarman, thief."

"Why doesn't he go round by the back road?" asked a young girl coming home from the boat with her brother.

"Why should he?"

"But those little wretches . . ."

"Aw, kids will be kids."

5

*A southerly buster. Baruch at home. The tongue's
ephemeridae. Baruch in love. A patriotic demonstration.
Catherine in love. A female argument. Withers kicked out.
Defence of murder. Baruch is very sentimental.*

IN THE OFFICES of the *International Worker*, in George Street,
journalists and typists raced each other over the typewriter keys,
tired irregulars, come with special reports, walked along the corridors and peeked through doors saying, "Sorry," and a visitor
took off his hat and sat down on the one chair in the waiting-
room. He stared fixedly at the banners standing against the wall,
spelling out each letter as if he could not read. They were the
placards recently used in a procession of striking seamen. When
he had finished with the banners the visitor found obscure names
in the map of Australia on the wall and fidgeted. Catherine
Baguenault loitered about the corridor and peeped into the room
from time to time with affection. She had made up the banners
and printed them by hand. Fulke Folliot, the editor, presently
came to a door and said:

"Can you wait another minute or two, Kate? Marion's doing
some shopping with some friend of her mother's, and I am up to
my neck in it. Liffle's drunk and has sent in some first-class
material on the seamen's strike, but I have to make head or tail
of it. James hasn't sent his telegram on the Melbourne strike yet.
I've got a police inspector coming at 2.30—nice of him to let me
know, at any rate. Winterbaum will be in later; he's laid up. I'll
be late going to press, I know it."

"Why can't I help, Fulke?"

"Oh no, thanks. You can't invent details of the strike, can you?
You rest, you're worn out. We want you to conserve your energy

for when it's really essential. My trouble is all absences. Marion'll be back soon. Liffle's actually here, sobering up, with a towel round his head in the wash-room. But you can do something, if you'll take a toddle," added Fulke, seeing Catherine looking grey, and standing against the wall as if her legs were going to give way. "I knew I wanted to ask you something. Go out and get Dr Plato Lerne's article on the Playway. I want to slash it. In last Wednesday's *Herald*, I think."

Catherine started up and made for the door. Fulke dismissed the visitor in a word and added to Catherine:

"We'll see you to-night at the meeting, comr'de! Marion feels there is something missing if you're not there."

"You know you'll see me, comr'de," answered Catherine, with smothered impatience, but in a moment flashing a bright smile at Fulke. Her white good teeth were a surprise in her worn face. Heinrich Winterbaum came plodding in, untidy, rolling with a slight sea-gait under his great barrel. His uncombed greasy hair fell down under his hat put on awry. He had a puffed, stupid look, for his eyes with long lashes, usually very lively, were now sunk wearily in his head, and his small, Mongolian forehead, compressed at the temples, was drawn with exhaustion. In the office, every third day, Winterbaum was laid up and Fulke was in a pickle, shorthanded. Winterbaum was his assistant-editor and represented on his own account the professional photographic workers. He had stomach and intestinal ulcers, and drank too much for his condition, although he was always sober. Fulke looked after him when he had time. They took it in turns to relieve him when he was ill. Heinrich was an art photographer himself, had two rooms in a condemned building in Phillip Street, and got paying effects in his good moments by making portraits in which eminent men looked haggardly with one eye from a superfinished photographic haze. Heinrich could invent a profile, cure baldness, give a complexion like a peach. Heinrich held the swing-door for Catherine and smiled tenderly at her. He said softly:

"How are you, Kate? How are you personally? I'm not asking after the movement when I ask after our Catherine. I am glad to see you. Do have lunch with me to-morrow. I want to see you oftener—talking with you straightens out my ideas. My brains are wool and yours are a bobbin. Or do you know what I feel? I only photograph Reality with studio-light and art effects, and you perceive it stark, harsh. And we will talk about *your* reality, to-morrow, comrade. You avoid us. You live in your cave of the winds. The undercurrent is not carrying you away? No? You're a raft, not a straw. We know, eh? I'm your friend, Catherine? It's agreed on, then; to-morrow at 'The Black Cat'."

"Ah, no, Heinrich," cried Catherine, who was now halfway down the outside corridor. "That's so devilish arty. Can't you pick somewhere else? The 'Medina' at noon. I'll be there if I can."

Winterbaum followed her towards the lift. She went down the stairs, being too impatient to wait for the lift, although it was coming up. Heinrich leaned over the stairhead and breathed down at her,

"Certainly; wherever you like. And by the way, I want you to read over an article I have on the bourgeois origins of Freudian analysis. Your experience with these lay confessors would be most valuable."

"All right. Till to-morrow, Heinrich. Auf wiedersehn!"

"Auf wiedersehn, liebe freundin!"

His soft voice finished, he heard her laugh down the stairs. He smiled again gently and padded towards Fulke's office. An early baldness made him appear older than he was. He was poor, and his only comfort in life was to dabble in the private affairs of his wide circle of acquaintances. He never took liberties; he had an affection for them all and a passionate love for his closest friends. His intrusion was with pure altruistic intent. He sorrowed over the sins and sorrows of the world, and tried to fish his friends out of what he called "the undercurrents". He now turned quickly, hearing a firm light step at the door. There was Marion Folliot, Fulke's wife. Heinrich made the German bow he always affected, which gave him dignity although he was so fat. He went into his own room. Marion had no troubles she could not solve, and she discussed them without mystery or coaxing: not his meat. He stayed in his office for half an hour, although he was anxious to see Fulke. At the end of thirty minutes he appeared in Fulke's office. Marion picked up her scarf and put it down again.

"Fulke," she cried, "Mrs. Baguenault met us in Farmer's. She spoke so timidly, so tremulously, of our trying to get Michael a job. She looked me all over, found me exceptionally respectable for a Communist's wife, warmed up to me and in a low voice begged me to tell her if there was anything wrong with Catherine that I knew, that she found her so queer and the family could do nothing with her. Then she looked Patty over, admired her style, as it appeared, and kept us fully ten minutes telling us what a trial Catherine and Michael are to a modest and respectable family. But about Michael, it was funny. She dared not say, 'I don't want him to work on your paper,' but she said, 'He should do, preferably, very sober, steady work, in an office where there are a lot of hardworking busy men he can take an example from, for he easily gets depressed and excited.' What do you think, Fulke? Can you get him on something? Do you think Beresford would get him on the *Guardian*, or *Smith's*? No, he's not live enough for them. What about Oxton's wire-netting periodical, or one of the country papers?"

Fulke was typing all the time she was speaking, and went on typing as he replied:

"I'll see, I'll see. Leave me alone at present, darling, and I'll be with you at lunch; then you'll go over it with me. You know I'll try to think up something for your Michaels, for all your protégés. But tell Michael, no job unless he stops giving you the glad eye."

She laughed.

"Imagine calling such a dismal expression the glad eye."

"I'll send him up country so that he can't be hanging around you!"

"Silly, I see him not more than once a month; and I like him, he's quite kind and interesting."

"Why don't you marry him then?"

"Oh, you're stupid. Send him up country then on a country newspaper. As if I cared! But I do; I'm sorry for the poor boy."

"He's thirty-two."

"Oh, it would rebuild that boy," cried Heinrich joyfully, "and yet I don't know. Something in Michael is unhinged or missing, and I think for good; perhaps it never was there. He's one of the derelicts left by the flood-tide of war. Since he tried to be a teacher in that private school and got into such a mess, with his classes running wild, and had his nervous breakdown, he seems paralysed. He's a clinging vine that someone has always supported, I imagine, anyhow. He must have been a soft forest ivy even in his best days. His only real resort at present is Kol Blount. He doesn't care for women very much, despite your charm, Marion. He hasn't Kol's impotent passion, Kol's hardness or ability. If Kol could be cured of his paralysis, you'd see they have nothing in common. I've often thought personally," continued Winterbaum in a confidential tone, "that Michael was nothing but a shadow of Catherine. What a picture! The shadow of a vagabond on a wormy wall!—there, there you have it! They are like twins. They are shadows of each other, close shadows, warm shadows, one of those with whom the master exchanges his personality. Still, Catherine is a fine soul, a vagabond queen. Catherine is the firebell clanging, and Michael is its echo in an empty house."

"Hey, get out of my office with your clatter, will you?" cried Fulke with good-humoured irritation.

They went out into the hall, as Marion was saying impatiently, "But all this doesn't get Michael a job," when they found Catherine at the door. Catherine looked maliciously at them, pleased to have overheard their remarks. She said in a ringing voice:

"No, Winterbaum, you're sometimes right and more often wrong—you see a single gesture and you build a saga out of it; you see a person faint and you invent a debile universe; a toothache and humanity, a lazaret: from a crooked bone invent a crooked genus! You're no naturalist. Michael is better than I, but it is all overlaid, and by all you chatterers. You tear each other to pieces, and all in kindness. Michael burrows into the earth, and he might go too deep. I fly off the handle. You're killing us both!"

She looked at them both with blazing eyes. Winterbaum

looked a little shamefaced, and at the same time watched Catherine with an irrepressible curiosity and enthusiasm, as if he saw a new facet turning to the light, a drama rounding itself out.

Marion spoke.

"You are right, Kate, there is none of your brother on the surface. Perhaps he is like you underneath. At any rate you understand him best. Good-bye, I must be off." She put her hand on Winterbaum's arm for a moment. "I'm going to the club." She addressed herself to Catherine. "You're going to work here, aren't you, with Heinrich?"

"Yes."

Marion arranged her scarf on her shoulders.

"Good. I'm going to sleep for half an hour at the club, get my slippers for gym., and I'll meet you all at the meeting at seven. I'll have lunch with Patty and tea at the club. Heinrich, see Kate gets tea before she comes to the meeting, won't you?"

"Of course, of course."

"Thanks, Marion," said Catherine with great politeness, and pushed open Fulke's door before Marion had got out of sight.

Catherine was tired, but she worked away at the old scrap-iron typewriter under the dying bulb in Heinrich's room. Presently she and Heinrich went into Fulke's room and ate a sandwich. The afternoon sunlight fell across the green oilcloth. The window looked out at the back of the building, over Hunter Street, beyond some low roofs. The smell of flowers and summer grass came in on the close air. The telephone rang. Heinrich went through the files to find out the antecedents of a parliamentarian making a bid for fame at the moment, a dairy-farmer from the northern rivers, demanding the constitution of a new northern state. The sky tarnished, doors banged, somewhere a glass vessel fell to pieces, picture-frames rapped on the walls, a banner clattered to the floor in the waiting-room, and dust went whirling over the house-tops. There rolled rapidly through the sky a long torpedo cloud.

"A southerly buster," said one of them, "it's been due."

When they were ready to go at five o'clock it was very dark outside as if a cloud of dust enveloped the city. Swollen clouds bowled low over the cold, wildly-blustering streets. The palm-leaves in the Hunter Street garden could be heard lashing in the intervals. Abruptly through the broadcasting programme they heard the reedy piping of an S.O.S.

"Somebody turning turtle," said Heinrich.

They waited. At five-thirty Catherine persuaded Heinrich to go out and have some coffee. Heinrich had to eat every few hours. Heinrich smiled at her wisely, looked at Fulke's bent yellow head, and nodded.

"I'm a bad cavalier, but Fulke will take my place, I hope."

"Don't worry about that," said Catherine with curling lip, but she cast a soft side look on the yellow head.

At six o'clock Fulke got up and said to Catherine:

"Not afraid of getting wet, Katkin? Then let's turn this in and go and eat."

"I'll go down and get some buns and we'll eat here," suggested Catherine.

"No, I've got to have nourishment," protested Fulke. "I eat like a whale. I can't live on rice like you. Do you know, I believe there was a Chinaman in your ancestry."

Downstairs, Fulke ate steak and kidney pie and Catherine had a bun and a glass of water. When they came out, Fulke was glowing with a happy digestion, and said:

"Let's walk down to the rocks in the Domain. We'll get wet anyhow, and I'd do anything for a breath of fresh air."

They battled up Bent Street and into the Domain. The drive was strewn with large leaves. A bundle of rags in the roots of a giant fig indicated a beggar-woman sheltering there. Fulke began to sing, and cried:

"Magnificent in this wind! The roots of your hair tingle."

The wind blew loudly, the rain came down in sheets. Catherine called:

"You feel free in storms! Nothing binds me then!"

"I need to sometimes. With giving the Socialists patch-patch on the behind and the trades union secretaries a flea in the ear, with following the strike like a detective, and unmasking private interests and public scandals, entertaining bobbies and proving I'm not a candidate for quod, and neither is Heinrich, I look at the city with a regular jaundiced eye. Why worry? I often think. Take life simply, I say to myself; float and the tide floats with you, for upstream you swim alone. Make no provision for wife, family, or mankind, run off to Tahiti and live under the palm-trees with a hula-hula girl; mankind will be saved just as soon without you. Or engage as supercargo and tramp round the world for ever and aye : that's the happy man's life. What is Fulke, the Peter Pan of his father's house, doing in the hurly-burly?" He sighed. "But I can't give it up : once you're in it you're ashamed of yourself to desert."

Fulke's sibilant light voice came fitfully through the wind.

"If we could do everything we had a mind to," remarked Catherine, "if bread grew on trees, no one would recognise his brother or lover; we'd be a race of angels. You struggle and struggle for years to make a place for yourself, to work out your destiny, to justify yourself, and at the end, nothing is right. You find yourself in a false position even with your friends, even with your co-workers."

They passed along the lower path in the outer Domain opposite Garden Island. In a cave two unemployed men, rolled in news-papers, lay behind the embers of a small fire.

Fulke threw out his hand gracefully.

"Can't help it, we'll never be free. My secret thought is—but I never tell Marion this—this struggle will never cease, it will go on generation after generation. There is no system without its error, its revolting seed; the best will fall to subsequent revolt. What am I fighting for? I feel tired to think of history."

His pale small face moved along the drenched bushes. Catherine looked at him pityingly, but could not help saying with her customary pride,

"I feel I am history : that's how I feel."

"We are such slaves."

"Why," she said, taking his large, beautiful and pale hand, "here we are : there is no need to go back. We can sleep here if you want to. Now we are free!"

They both laughed : "Impractically practical Catherine!"

They were drenched. The silk dress clung to Catherine's legs, and the blood bloomed like a carnation in each cheek.

"Let's take off our shoes; no one is about."

"And if someone were?"

They planted their shoes in one of the fig-trees and went to the waterside, under the thick unpruned trees at the foot of the rock called Mrs Macquarie's Chair. Catherine swallowed sweet drops of rain and apostrophised the rough harbour water that swallowed the rocks.

"Come, sweet sea!" She added: "Come sweet death, I mean." She lay back on the grassy slope, sopping wet. "That is the sort of death I would like, to go down in the swilling storm-waters, ough, guff, gubble, gup, and you're drowned: that death I could die a thousand times. How thirsty I am!" She put her mouth to the driblets of water coming from the rock and trickling through the grass.

"Come, sweet death. I'm so goddamned tired, Kate, I could die too, only I feel too damp. I've a good mind to go for a swim to get rid of the damp feeling."

"Go on, then; I'll come too."

"No, how would we get dry?"

"There are some small caves perhaps unoccupied."

There were some moments of silence. Catherine waited uneasily. The rain was not falling on them but across the rock. A draught blew on them and they shivered. Fulke got up and strolled to the lamp above the rock to look at his watch, and while he was away, Catherine said to herself:

"I would do better to throw myself into the water and swim to the other side of the harbour so that he finds nothing but darkness and rain here when he comes back. The evening is spoiled, everything is spoiled." She tightened her long hair, which had come down, and stood up. Fulke came hurriedly round the rock.

"It is late."

There was silence for some minutes; they only heard the fresh waves in the rising tide washing higher up the rocks. Tears were streaming down Catherine's face mixed with rain. Her cheeks burned. Fulke looked at her, noticed her face working, and said, to say something:

"I hope we don't keep Marion waiting: she worries about us, you know."

Catherine began to sob.

"Catherine, what is it? Don't do that, I can't bear it. Whatever is it? What is the matter?"

She stopped and turned to him. She smiled wrily and put her head lightly on his shoulder for a moment without otherwise touching him, then lifted her head, rearranged the loose ringlets which fell over her face, and said gloomily:

"Fulke, I am so insupportably lonely."

He looked at her compassionately, but nervously, and said stiffly:

"We all are, we all are."

At the top of the drive, she turned to him with a smile:

"You'll have to forgive me, comr'de. I'm not coming to the meeting. My teeth are chattering and I'm beginning to shiver. My heroics don't suit my physique."

"Go home quickly," said Fulke. "I don't want you to catch anything. If Marion finds out what I've done to you she'll be fearfully anxious and cross with me, too."

"Don't tell her then."

Catherine left him at the word, swung down Macquarie Street towards Hyde Park. She had a room in an old building in Elizabeth Street, left her for the moment by a tubercular friend then working as boundary-rider on a station in the country. There she dried herself, put on a waterproof, and after walking nervously up and down the room for ten minutes, looking gaunt and feverish, walked down to the meeting and stayed at the back of the hall, sitting on one of the long benches, among seamen who were housed in the hall during the strike. Marion and Fulke left early and did not see her. As she returned late to her cold room, she looked over the park towards the Cathedral and Woolloomooloo and said:

"I am getting into a mess: I must see someone new. Joseph knows Baruch's address—and they say he is ardently interested in economics."

Baruch lived in a room on the fourth floor back, in a side street in Woolloomooloo Flat, not far from the old public school. His window commanded the Inner Domain, the Art Gallery, the spires of St. Mary's Cathedral and the Elizabeth Street skyline. On the right hand, as he looked from his window, were the wharves of the German, Dutch, Norwegian and Cape lines. In the backyard was a wood-and-coal shed covered with creepers, pumpkins, old tires, kites'-tails, buckets and old scrubbing-brushes. There was a clothes-line across the yard, on a clothes-prop, and upon the line the tenants' garments, washed by the woman on the ground-floor, appeared in regular succession throughout the week. There were in the house a bachelor Government clerk and Government medical officer, a school-teacher with his wife and two children, a navvy, a bartender, a junior draughts-man in the Lands Department, and a widow with a young child. The house backing on to theirs was only three stories high. A cheap chop-suey restaurant occupied the ground-floo , its private assembly rooms the first floor, while the rooms above were for sleeping and for letting out. A couple of ladders reached from the windows of these upper floors to the roofs of lean-to sheds and outhouses. This house was usually very quiet, although lights appeared at the windows at all hours of the night. On Saturdays and Sundays the whole neighbourhood swarmed with children, and everybody was out of doors with sleeves rolled up. Tiny living-rooms with Japanese screens, fans and bead curtains, and reeking of bugs and kerosene, with bric-à-brac, vases, wilting flowers and countless rags and papers, sent out their heat and animal odours and old dust at seven in the evening when the hot day had gone down into the violet twilight, a deceitfully shady moment promising cool, but bringing in the torrid night. Every-where couples lounged about, the waists encircled, the lips together; henna Titians, peroxide blondes, and uncoloured women faded beneath their hair still rich and young; women blowsy and painted, worn and tired, with crow's-feet and unequal powder, fanned their bursting bosoms or their empty sacks of blouses, as they slumped in rickety easy-chairs at their doors.

The doors opened directly into the sleeping and living-rooms

138

and alone admitted air. Little boys argued outside the windows, shrieking and punching.

"My mother is not a whore."

"She is! Why isn't she?"

"No, Willy's mother isn't; she always has the same blokes, and she has only three."

"Yes, and I know who they are; a thin little bloke with freckles and . . ."

"Shut up or I'll gi' y' a lift under the lug."

The onlookers whooped during the set-to that followed. Some father or mother full of ire, separated their darling from the heap of wriggling boys. There were protests, but the boys trailed off, their passions suddenly cooled, and ready in a quarter of an hour or so to begin all over again, apropos of the weather, a cricket hero, or Deadwood Dick. The lamps were lighted. The dwellings on the borders of the hot asphalted pavement were holes in which moved dimly a world of heaving bosoms, gasping mouths, fanning arms. There were visible black-socked feet and bare feet in slippers, bare arms starting upwards from a bush of black hair at the armpit; locks "straight as candles" hung wet and tangled, hairy men's breasts gaped in the vees of open work-shirts. The oil-lamps or gas-jets lighted corsets and stockings carelessly thrown on beds, discoloured with sweat and dirt. The rancid breeze blew in from the wharves with the smell of weeds grown on the piles, beer from the saloons, rotten vegetables from the garbage-tins. There came the clanking of winches at ships' sides, and the fitful songs of men at the waterfront. The last cries of children came from the old streets by the Plunkett Street school or from the other side, where they were dashing up into the rank grass of the Domain to wrestle, smother their giggles, lie on their backs, tell inane tales, sing parodies of songs, and contemplate the high southern constellations through the sensuous summer evening.

The neighbourhood is interesting. One Sunday morning an irritable Italian chased a compatriot through Baruch's backyard with an axe, during a slight difference over Angelina, wife of the first. Sometimes coloured boxers, cheerfully dressed, paraded past with belles of the neighbourhood, and there was a stream of girls, Australian and Italian, large, bright-coloured, buxom, with high heels and transparent blouses. Opposite Baruch's back window, poor Chinese, sailors and loafers could be seen paying attention to females in the chop-suey gambling and lodging-house.

The morning sun rose clear over the wharves, and the evening sky, with its head dark and its scarves of colour, looked like an Italian woman with an orange in her hand.

There was scarcely any furniture in Baruch's room, but on the small pine table were papers for drawing, and inks. There he sat early in the evening, breathing seriously over some small black-and-white design, the margin scribbled with faces, legends and monograms. But it was just as likely that he would be miserably stretched out on his bed in his outdoor clothes. The rarity of his bursts of energy, due to his thin purse and bad food, seemed to syllabicate the sentence of a hopeless fate. He had a wide and wandering vision which showed him all kinds of miseries more than physical, the self-deception of vanity unapplauded, drudgery unrewarded, the mind which for recompense kneels to the tin-tinnabulating priesthood, the symbolist, sick and sunless for ever, the tempestuous who leap from brink to brink and the thin ambitious who wrench their hearts out to put one idea on foot in their lifetime, and those who are for ever in the green-sickness of an unrequited love or desire, and those who work out new-fangled systems to detect fate in her workings, those who are swollen with pride and those who creep in their dejection. He was so wretched to see these people swarming around him, with all these evils added to their burden of poverty, that he often fell into a fever, and this idea was with him, day and night, that he was obliged to relieve them in some way. But he hardly knew in what way. He lived by choice among the sordid southern lives of the native and immigrant poor to get himself impregnated with this fever so that it would never leave him. He suffered at all this misery, but he suffered less in the heart of it, because he thought he was nearer to understanding it and to solving it. He knew by heart the foetid rooms, eyes opening on littered streets, heavy wombs, market-gardeners' carts trailing a cabbage smell, moustaches washed in beer, working-men's tramcars rattling out to brown dusty suburbs, Alexandria, Redfern, Waterloo, pawnshop windows advertising their unredeemed pledges, grimy hands, sweat, unfolded papers relating the latest murder, wrinkles, hands with swollen veins, and eyes thick with the circular lucubrations of the dulled mind trying to escape.

There seemed to him to gleam above all this a city as on an adamant island, where the erudite lived and put the world to shame, told the truth to princes, and wrote tracts to enlighten the slaves. It is true, of course, that they write them to enlighten the poor, but they are usually sold at prices ranging from 10s. 6d. to £2 2s., and the poor are too pig-headed to buy them.

But he doubted his own future. He described himself as "without malice, without cruelty, without pride and therefore without ambition" : he was the pattern of inexplicable insuccess.

"The stupidest writer," said Baruch to Joseph, "can remain alive after his death. Even if he only writes letters, some friend will keep them; if he only suffers from epileptic fancies he may be elevated into Holy Writ; he may have the meanest, poorest and most malicious ideas on earth, be a hypocrite, slanderer, madman, next door to a poisoner, he may indeed be a poisoner, steal his wife's dowry, kill his mistress, rob the state treasury, but has he only a bright and swift pen he can lead the people of a whole country into the maze of controversy, the whirlpool of war; he can be acclaimed as a messiah or at least a fallen angel. But a person like me who talks only, and even becomes warm and radiant in talking, dies with each word as if he spat out nothing but sparks. Look how bright the fire is! It brings wanderers home, it dispels the forest night, it drives away phantoms, it scares away wolves, moths die for it, it revives the mysterious flame of life itself, it prepares a feast with a thousand dishes, it warms wine, it is the source of civilised life, yet it dies in a moment and in a moment more is nothing but a hideous sight, charred ends of wood and grey ashes, ready like an expiring serpent to bite the heel of the child spurning it as he jumps over it. Conversation is the fire of social life, and see how it dies; nothing remains but a few bitter ends to sear some poor souls.

"I have a clear head and my brains often burn, and my heart always. I am not sure whether my brains are in my head or my belly, they burn in both places nevertheless. But instead of burning something on paper, so that even if it had the appearance of a devil's script that is very explosive and unintelligible, like a Fascist proclamation or a tormented futurist poet, it would exist (though God forbid that I should ever produce such a thing), my bright angels go off in smoke, miserable genii without a talisman to call them back. Not that I count on that, but sometimes I think I am like a tree that broadcasts its seeds in every wind, in every respect except in seeing my seedlings sprout. But the tree doesn't care and I do. Oh fitful, fretful lust for materiality, little imp, little brat, the only disease I ever had."

He lived alone in his rented room, and had few friends; he was turned loose on a plain which was barren. When he came home after work loneliness assailed him in every soft spot of his nature. He read long and worked late when his head did not ache, to forget his work and his isolation, and found, to his horror, months slipping past like water, while his situation remained the same and his friends did not increase. He turned to Joseph, that other lonely creature, who was yet so stubborn and secure that he had the appearance of strength. Joseph became his hitching-post in the universal wilderness.

This evening Baruch missed Joseph badly. He sat a while by the open window sniffing the rich air which came partly from the wooded Domain, partly from the wharves. The evening was full of cups clinking, children shouting in the distance, and the grinding of cranes. The crepuscular sky hung from a vast height, with veils of colour. He began to work, drawing his table to the window. He loved to work thus in the gathering evening, without putting the light on, straining his eyes, sitting on a ledge above the surf of terraces. He bent lower over his drawing; there was a woman, robust, white-skinned, dark-haired, with limbs violently agitated: the face and the background were not yet in. On the table in front of him, above the drawing, pinned with a drawing-pin, was a sheet of writing-paper, and on this was written, "Gloss—to Marion!" After this was written twice in a later ink,

"Marion." Then was written:

"There is a miasma that rises out of that lake of old memory at night and makes the imagination pestilential. It is like a drug. One deserts the electric bric-à-brac clapper-trap lustre and upper-crusted tone of all your society and wanders under a cloud too thick for lightning to pierce. Like wool in the ears, it distorts sounds, even sweet ones, and your voice is a sweet one. But by this lake and in your charming company the wrong notes are brought together by my love into a continuous song. There is a plot in it, a purpose, a continual interplay of question and answer. You see into my heart and laugh to think without you the thread ravels by itself. You feel like going away an instant, to come back and see the mischief you have made in an instant.

"It is the dreariest part of life that I am always misunderstood and betrayed by my privileged friends. 'I understand that type of man, yes, he conceals nothing, besides: a brilliant gift, but he doesn't care to use it—sure to waste his life nevertheless. You will see, he will be a failure, you will see,' so I heard you say, kind Marion. And to me, 'I sympathise, I understand, an uncon-scripted man, an unregimented brain—but you are rather too much outside my circle: I cannot stir myself to love. Come in, wipe them off their feet and then—love me!' 'How can I? I am poor—completely abandoned, deserter of father and country; and then, to tell the truth, you are thick, Marion, you understand nothing at all.' 'I know, but between man and woman any question can be settled, everything is resolved, understanding is finer than a needle, clearer than glass. Love me, love me, you can't escape it, because I need lovers.' 'How can I? With your brilliant eyes, your stalwart tread, your adventurous life, those fine scenes that unroll themselves hourly behind your white spacious fore-head, your husband, your Dr Grozherz: an unmarriageable man, I.' 'Love me!' 'You don't love me.' 'I sympathise—and in your condition, with your wasted talent—it might make you.' As mask play, truly."

The lake he meant was the shallow and weed-brown pond at the bottom of the central avenue leading to the University. They passed it at nights coming away from lectures. There was no such miasma—a mist, no doubt, and it was damp there. It was dark under the old figs, and suspicious characters lurked about.

Marion walked down there with Baruch, sauntering a little in advance of the others, while her husband continued his lecture down the avenue in a group of admiring youngsters. Drunks, beggars, slept on the lawns behind the hedges. Men sometimes followed Catherine in that dark spot, as she came down alone, shunning the crowd, taking her to be a beggarly girl, one in their own class. Round the paddocks at one side, in the bushes, hanging on the picket fence, children of the slums of Golden Grove and Darlington found bloody rags and torn clothes displayed by larrikins. There the regulars of the "University Arms" slept off their spirituous heaviness. In this place Baruch always found his passions rising, because it was dark, brutal, strange. A little water flowed under a wooden bridge. In summer there were trunks covered with ivy and water-plants in the shallow brown water, and children joked beyond the coprosma bushes.

Baruch laid his head on his arm and conjured up the picture he would have when the etching was finished. At this moment a knock came at the door.

"Come in!" he cried, sitting up straight, and in came Catherine Baguenault. He looked at her as he knew her, a friend of the Folliots, dark, furious, thin, poor by choice, a woman of revolution without a barricade, with something of the politician in her, an organiser of Labour Branches, a marcher in strike processions, a person who got excited by caucus decisions, a woman who worked in holiday camps and workers' education theatres, always passionately involved in something, always half-sick.

"Your landlady is suspicious of me, comr'de," she announced in a voice which was intended as a trumpet call to the legions of light against Clod sitting in a quagmire, Prosy wrapped in cotton cocoon, and Tradition with fat hams sitting in his pew.

"Of what does she suspect you?" said Baruch, smiling agreeably.

"Of being a woman!"

"She would make a fortune as a detective!"

They began to talk of various things. Baruch did not ask why she had called on him; it was her way to treat everyone as "comr'de". She plunged into the present politics of the Labour Party, the unrest among the Seamen's Union officials. The seamen were in great misery and sleeping all over the place, many in the streets. She went to make soup for them. She talked for half an hour, then stopped, smiled a very sweet smile, sighed, and began on a different tone:

"Last week I had a dreamy night, Baruch!"

"Yes."

"I was at the Folliots' house. We went home late from a meeting at Communist Hall. We walked from the station with bare feet. The night was fine and full of smells of the bush. When they got in, they found that some person, probably a friend—but they did not ask, they have hundreds of strange friends and they are welcome—had stayed in their house the night before. Marion and Fulke were away in the city the night before, kept too late by a meeting to get home. There were two candles in front of Marion's photograph on the piano. The picture, in a Russian headdress from girlish days, resembles an ikon. I said fancifully, 'I did it myself,' but that was for Michael: he loves her."

Baruch smiled to himself. "I have never been there," he said.

"That, perhaps, set me off into a strange and long dream that lasted till morning, except for one wakeful hour."

Baruch looking at her found it strange to see that she was suddenly in high spirits. She began taking the pins out of her hair, and let it down. It was long and curling, and gave her a soft, bright, feminine look.

"A wind came up," she said. "I woke and I immediately said: 'Winds of the night arise and wander over wide earth all restlessly.' I felt as if I were outside with the wind and as if leagues and leagues were in my bones."

"There has been no wind here for a week."

"No? They rise there in the night and go down by morning: it is very high."

"You are often at Marion's house?"

"I am with them at the meetings. It's very uncomfortable for me at home at present. The Communists are prominent with the seamen, and my family is very respectable, you know; they don't want to have the neighbours look at them coldly. Mother and Father are very kind to me, they say nothing, but I see they suffer. I simply stay away from home when I am organising. When I get too sick, I go home till I am well enough to go on again. Then—the Folliots are such good friends. Marion—is very good; a good woman to women."

She laughed :

"This morning I told Fulke that I dreamed that walking in my sleep I put the candles back in front of the photograph. He was disagreeably impressed. Why?"

"That was a curious thing to dream," said Baruch idly.

"Marion said so. In fact, it affected her badly and Baruch did not like it—I mean, Fulke did not. An instant of curious understanding and hostility can spring up between you and your dearest friends."

"Are they dear to you?" asked Baruch.

"Both, but differently. I am sometimes jealous of Marion."

Catherine flushed faintly. Baruch thought, "I have imagined before that she was sweet on Fulke." Catherine said, "You are sometimes very quick, Baruch, and sometimes very blind."

"I am not very good at character-reading. But women are much better than men in that, it is their business; they don't learn any profession, but they learn to sniff," said Baruch. "I underestimate the profound capacity for evil, jealousy and hate in men. Nevertheless, I remain an idealist. I still believe firmly that another state of society is possible where such passions would be bred out, where, rather, they would not be evoked."

"The sombre passions exist in all men and women," said Catherine distinctly; "only, they could be turned to nobler work."

"I see no need for them," remarked Baruch mildly : "I cannot understand them, almost. I am too simple, I regret it sometimes."

Catherine got up off her chair impatiently and walked round the room, approaching the table where the drawing lay. Above lay the "Gloss—to Marion!" She saw instantly the phrase, "in your company . . . brought together by my love. . . ." She turned

146

her back, took a book from the shelf and read a page, but her hand trembled so violently that there was a rustling sound. What is Time? what is Time? said the book vainly. What does that matter? said Catherine to herself; a life is short, there is more than enough to fill it. She put down the book and went and sat down quietly on a chair with her eyes gleaming, liquid, speaking a thousand times more than her mouth could have, and, lost in passion, began, without thought, to do up her hair again. Baruch, in misery, stared at her, his hands on his knees, his lower lip trembling with rejected consolations. He could not understand how she could have come to dispute him with Marion, as it seemed. He began to glow, and said in a low voice:

"Catherine . . ."

Catherine smiled and said quietly:

"You should have been with us last night, comr'de. Fulke spoke well and Whiteaway spoke more to the point. You should speak yourself. I heard from Marion this morning that there was a 'manifestation' after outside the Folliots' house. The inhabitants gathered outside Fulke's roses, and sang 'God save the King' in scared, after-dinner voices. They gave three cheers for the King, and withdrew in dubious dignity. It sounded so odd on the bush road. The neighbours complain, and the Folliots expect the police at any time to visit the house for contraband literature. Twice the offices of the *International Worker* have been raided, a publicity stunt by the Labour Party."

Baruch said nothing. Catherine continued anxiously, as if telling a private worry:

"Fulke is getting run down. He told me last night—we walked a long way through the rain together; he says he guesses that this struggle will go on through the centuries as now. Poor Fulke, with his small shoulders, worried about the struggle of centuries. But it shows he needs a rest: he is always so courageous."

Baruch made no answer. Catherine raised her head and remarked:

"You don't appreciate Fulke sufficiently, comr'de. He works hard. He has his mannerisms, rather charming in so downright and bluff a set, but they are not a sign of dilettantism. He is

147

honest."

"The evening comes down quickly in these parts," said Baruch, peaceably looking out at the yellow and orange west.

"What do you say to the Folliots?"

"If I must say what I think," said Baruch, "they are romantics. They would be delighted to have a police-raid. Ever since their marriage they have had nothing but splendid adventures with the police and frontier-guards, and have always got off scot-free, of course. Fulke's father is a rich amateur collector of paintings. Marion's people are high up in the Government service in England. There are no romantic scuffles with a policeman in the life of the working-people. It riles me when I see Fulke get up before a body of bleak-faced, whiskered, half-starved men and get off his cheese-cake eloquence and well-bred witticisms. I don't care if he has passed a merry quarter-hour with a traffic policeman in Moscow and discussed breakfast with Lenin. He is too darned well-bred. What the deuce does it matter to them whether he went to school with the Conservative Prime Minister, or not? They want to know if he went to school, like them, with poverty and labour, and for what close-weft dissertation on low life he was received to the doctorate. True," continued Baruch mildly, "he has some good impulses, and even from his inept work the party may get some good, while he stays its friend. We are all imperfect lenses for the sun of human liberty to shine through : in the clearest it shines like a flame, in others artistically, as through a prism, in others murkily, and with specks of dark. In some those specks of dark are as a host of midgets darkening the face of the sun, as they can when they put themselves directly on the eyeline. But, Catherine, Fulke is weak. He will give up sooner or later to comfort or vanity, if no worse. For, on my honour, if I had to pick out one man amongst them all who had the style, graces and talents of a prospective *provocateur*, it is Fulke!" He had flushed and stopped now, biting his lip, in anger.

The air became drawn as if congeniality was drained out of it. It was so in fact. Catherine's dark, clear-cut face and glassy eyes showed the emotion, not visibly, in ordinary terms, as by becoming bloodshot, or watery, but they rather revealed the unillumined interior of her mind swept clear with gusty passions, purged of hesitation, personal regard and love. She receded from social contact, and grew pallid with angry and scornful thoughts. Presently into that chamber of her mind rushed a torrent of sounds, the noise of her heart and her temples beating louder and hotter. A black shadow disengaged itself from her heart and flew up into her head, shouting hate, hate, disgust: thus she looked on him.

Baruch went ashy pale, and sat sorrowfully mute, like a child.

It became clear that she was ruled by her impulsive passions which ever strove with her intellect for mastery. Strange cross-currents and maelstroms in a mind; storms not easily predicted but fated when seen. "I am totally alien to you, and you will never concede me to have your insight. Masterful, resolute and courageous mind, frail, tempestuous and scarified brain, lean, dark form, what will you come to at last? There is no place for you here, there is little understanding for you; but there is for you, as with me, some admiration and sympathy. You win it at the point of the sword: you woo for no favours, you courtesy for none. You are a sword, a reaping-hook and an alpenstock, a goblet. Your will is keen and brandished hither and thither every new moment; it cuts in a thousand directions. The full and golden grain of our most charming traditions fall before you; by your own strength you have climbed out of more than one dark, icy abyss, and by your frailty you will yourself be crushed in the dark hand of fortune, and your martyr's blood will stain the ground. Perhaps it will blossom the next spring."

Their duel was over in a few minutes. Catherine stirred as if out of a pose.

Baruch said: "Catherine, I am sorry. We spend all our lives watching each other, like cats: we understand inwardly, but speak old stuff. You are unhappy."

Catherine sighed with tears in her eyes but would not apologise.

"My character is to undergo. Everyone and everything I meet is the further instrument. You, too. If I find myself in a calm I have a brainstorm, a fit of tears, based on nothing, to break it;

thus, I am born to strive. Under many hoods and hats, we are all the same creature all the time trying to make its way out of a thicket. There are cuirassed guards waiting to hack us down at every thinning of the bush, so we try to escape, as a bird, a bat, a floating vampire head, a shadow, a skeleton, a deer, a rat, and what you will. Stability, that is the only character we have never—but we are always in that state of delirium, folly, passion or drunkenness, which is our life. Such a life is without time, it is out of the presumptions of clocks. We are willing to cast away our life because we are always at the end of it, every moment is an experience. We are willing to begin anew because our strength is always fresh. We are insensible to great disasters, because we have met them often and often on our path in company with death; they are old acquaintances. We feel small things so sharp because they mock our heroics."

Baruch went to the window and looked into the dusk. He said, in a sorry tone:

"Go abroad, if you can. See if you can join Saunderson's party to the Balkans. Get a real cause to fight about. What do I see on your red dress pinned there? The badge of the Kuo-min-tang? Do you know their function in young China? To impede the path of revolution, for example. But to you it is only another flamboyant cause by means of whose symbol you can irritate your folks at home and your vis-à-vis in the tramcar. Isn't it true that you sang with the Salvation Army several times to irritate some atheist friends, who pressed you too far? Catherine, what are you doing with yourself? The most glorious, and the bloodiest and most serious work is open to you, you who never had a home or work. You can be a martyr and for the sake of liberty; you can with your fire light some cold, shivering hearths. Drop the Folliots, whatever it cost you. They are both opportunists—they will use you for their sentimental ends, and will despise you while they deplore your fate. Marion is a beautiful woman, but an unconscious prima donna. She will see that she is there to get the bouquet in the end, and will knock anyone down who tries to get it away from her. You are madly in love, all the time, and you imagine you are in love with any number of sad little pedants and posers in a backbiting circle where your passion is a subject for conversation over buttered toast."

Catherine was white. Baruch turned to her and took one hand, saying in an over-dramatic voice:

"You are a pure artist—don't you know yourself? What is all this knocking your head against suburban brick walls? You take the last possible drop of pain out of everything. You are a born soldier also. Can you hear the young guard of the proletariat marching through the turpentines in the Folliots' valley, among the singers of 'God Save the King'? Up there, it is too nice. I know—you see— I have been in their valley, but uninvited: I spend some Sundays there. I admit my weakness—Marion's charms took me there once and I got to like the place."

Tears shone in Catherine's eyes and her expression was bitter.

Baruch continued, without looking at her:

"You wake up at night in a comfortable home with red roses in the vases and the head of Eros on the wall. They are K. of K. roses. I looked, I saw the label—you know what a poor botanist I am—you wake up with your dark hair curling on the pillow, dreaming you are a happy woman like the others, your sisters. You hear the wind roaring up the hill through the eucalypts, in the darkness is the trampling of armies like locusts, trampling to your ear through your long hair. Why, why these retreats, these gentle dreams? We will win, soon those who can carry a battle-flag will have a host behind them; the host is there now, waiting in the twilight of morning by the wayside, after a long bivouac troubled by dreams and sickness. What are you waiting for? Do you want to be a dilettante heroine like Marion? Less successful."

Catherine's face was covered by her two brown hands. She said slowly and distinctly:

"I am too weak; I haven't the strength. I would die of exhaustion and get nothing for all my troubles, and have no friends and nobody to say what I had done."

Baruch burst out:

"You have an impatient irritable mind: you bite everyone's head off—that is the sign of strength frittered away. You must move on; otherwise you will live to old age, true, die miserably and as respectably as anyone at the long dry end of a rut. Leave the country, leave this country, at any rate for a while. Or go up country—but that is too easy: you would soon be back with your gang. Gold has to be looked for with fanaticism and thirst. You can only speculate in it sitting pretty in the city. I remember the night I said our professional rationalists, relics of the R.P.A. era, before-the-war heroes left dreaming behind the battlefield, now help to keep up the belief in God, because they give some life to a dead idea by fighting it. You kept screaming at me, 'What is God? What do you mean by God?' All the way home you kept hacking at the notion: what is God, define God. It was senseless, but a wonder how you were enraged: no one could say anything the way you kept it up. That's an example of your way of behaving. You need refreshment."

She stared at him as if he had shown her that she was only a bag of bones imagining itself to be a human. He ended:

"After all, Catherine, do you expect ever to be happy? Do you want to be happy as women are, bound to one spot of earth by the delightful chains of ceramics, carpets, cobwebby laces, a marriage ring?"

Catherine laughed shortly:

"If the truth were told, yes; although I would fret against them."

Baruch shook his head.

"You can't get that, you're not the sort. Then get something out of your lovers. I knew a girl who learned eight European languages perfectly from her eight lovers. But you won't; no. Otherwise you would have done it. Yet you should give your magnificent passion exercise, since it is your sole and jealous interest. It is your way of living: exacerbate existence!"

"You don't know what you say: Baruch, all is a theme for exposition to you."

"No; I study you passionately. I cannot see lives wasted. Joseph is another marked one. Joseph does not exist, but he can come to life. That strange, delicate, translucent mind, is a larva of a mind; I never saw a person so confined with so little prejudice."

Catherine said rudely, laughing:

"Simply a tranquil stupidity. He receives every impression with the same indifferent interest, like a mirror. Yet, it is true; it is true, by Jove, what you say. His dimensions are ambiguous, he has no depth, but he is very profound, nothing can sound him: you can see an infinite distance, if there is one to be reflected, but if you attempt to travel there, you strike an inviolable surface."

"That is true," said Baruch, "a good image you have there."

"Joseph has no understanding whatever of the muscles and nerves of the world. So he rarely smiles, for he sees no humour, that is to say, no shifting of the natural order, no obscurity, gleam and veiling of the plain world in fancy; but if he is in company and somebody cracks a joke and everyone laughs, then he will laugh, to oblige; or he will sit there for a few minutes after smiling, oblivious of the rest of us, until he finds out in what way it was wit. No, sometimes he smiles quietly to himself: that points to something personal and silent in him, but he smiles rarely. However, sometimes doubtless some strange fleeting fancies stir in his brain, and he sees us in a new light: but it is slow, it is like the secular action of the hills and littoral, rising and falling. He can weep of his own accord, and so perhaps he has a sad understanding of his position, that he is a cipher. Once we were going up the North Shore to see Mother: as we left the tunnel at Wollstonecraft, the fading light from the west fell full upon Joseph's face—it looked aged and grief-stricken, and he is only twenty-one: it was more than that—a drained face, full of want, penury and hopelessness, but not despairing, a submerged face. You can see the same on middle-aged working-men in repose at the end of the day. I saw his life is out of my ken and reach: he is beyond salvation: I never attempt to trouble his repose."

"I doubt it," said Baruch warmly; "you see in him the refinement and senescence of all parts through the decay of the family blood? I sense in him a sombreness and passion which I have never yet seen exhibited, but expect to. The quietest and simplest man can develop endlessly: even the lifelong sleeper can be awakened: it is this dull life he leads, the Church and the univocal opinion you all hold of him which retards him."

"You love him?"

" I believe I do. I love a humble man; when you walk the streets all the well-dressed people have such inflated faces."

"I don't love him: patience, stupidity, irritates me. He is part of the human scenery to me, as I said, of the same stuff as the hills and as slow. Not like my brother Michael, a remarkable character, he. He does absolutely nothing, he is positively an abstract personality; he shows an inner struggle to union with himself and his counterparts; Michael eats his own flesh."

"That is not unique," said Baruch restlessly. "They all develop this prodigious flowering of the sensibility and aimless intellection. Don't admire it; wish, rather, that he were like Joseph."

"It's a type you don't understand or feel any sympathy for. Yet I'm surprised; you're a paper-eater, yourself!"

"We'll discuss that, later," said Baruch, smiling. "Michael is aged, too. (I only saw him once; I may go astray.) But it is the chronology of his own lifetime. A small intelligence wasted even in early youth by a disequilibrium of passion. There are such people, wretched, weak, who have no destiny, but are marked out for an eccentric life."

"H'm, h'm," concluded Catherine, with an ostentatiously considerate eye on Baruch, "when you strike right, you strike home. Michael *was* very strange: and only I know how strange. He was my *alter ego*."

"You'll tell me all that some day," said Baruch politely, examining her wild, romantic, exaggerated pose.

She looked him over, and picked up her hat. "Good-bye!"

"Good-bye!"

Joseph often went home with Baruch for tea. He looked noncommittally for a long time, the next evening, at the drawing which Baruch was working at, called, "La Femme s'échappe de la Forêt," showing a naked woman with agonised contortion of body and face bursting through a thicket, tearing her thigh on a splintered tree, while a boa constrictor and a tropical vine loaded with large lilies hung before her and impeded her.

"Queer," said Joseph; "what does that mean?"

"Woman escapes from the forest. It means, the middle-class woman trying to free herself, and still impeded by romantic notions and ferocious, because ambushed, sensuality."

"I don't understand."

"Your cousin Catherine, for example."

"Is that Catherine?"

"She is an interesting character. She was here yesterday. She had something on her mind, but I don't know what."

"Was she? She is a bit—eccentric; yes. But she's always very kind to me. I don't know why she can't settle down, but I suppose there's a reason; something in the blood."

As Joseph went out he fell into the arms of Withers, who was entering quietly, or who had been standing there in the dark of the landing. Withers embraced him violently, turned him about, and pushed him into the room before him.

"It's early," said he; "you're in no hurry, you've got no rendez-vous with a sweetie, have you? Perpend while the Professor decorates the themes of injustice and sings the threnody of capitalism."

Joseph loosened himself petulantly. Baruch's glasses gleamed and his opulent personality, gracious, smiling, flattered, considerate, revolved through a dozen facets before he spoke.

"Come in, thing of evil, and sit above my chamber door: Poe would have been twice the man if he'd had you to croak for him. Well, what's the latest news from the front?"

Withers grinned. His rat-teeth showed through his moustache. He bestrode a chair with his back towards Joseph, picked his teeth with a match, and said through the corner of his mouth:

"I stick to Chamberlain, because I like to scrap; Chamberlain doesn't like to scrap, but he does it for me."

"That's matrimony, son. Wasn't I saying the same, the other day, Joe?"

"We're both so feeble. We hold each other up like two drunks, who can't put one foot backwards or forwards for fear of dropping the other and dropping himself."

"At the same time, if Chamberlain gave you your £60, you'd duck, wouldn't you, despite the pshawcological problems?"

Withers looked cunning.

"If Montagu gets him low enough, I hope to get him to make me a partner before the final collapse. Then the buyer will have to treat with me as a partner, and I've got enough evidence on Montagu to make him treat me properly. I'm no slouch like Chamberlain. I pretend to do everything Monty wants—but I keep my eyes open. Then, I've got Chamberlain. You can put a man into bankruptcy for a debt exceeding £50; that's my lever for the partnership. I'll end up owning the business, you'll see, and then, presto, you'll see a reformation. I'll become respectable, never go on the bend, marry my landlady and settle down."

"Excuse me," said Baruch, "while I go to the W.C. for a breath of fresh air, as my old boss said on a famous occasion. You don't get much sleep o' nights, do you, thinking up these Machiavellian schemes?"

"I don't sleep well," complained Withers, "but it's chiefly due to toothache and neuralgia in general."

"Go on," said Baruch, "I recognise the origin of this fiendish ingenuity. The malady is fiscal and your plans vain. If you had £100 clear would you feel like this? Or £20 even, and a good suit of clothes? I am Professor Teufelsdröckh from Weissnichtwo; clothes will do the trick. Invest in a suit of clothes and you'll get your money and be able to beat it, without giving yourself headaches. Go on, Tom, do it and leave the chap. He's corrupting your morals. This stupidity is obsessing us. God knows, I am leaving as soon as I get my boatfare, but I advise you and Joseph, and especially you, to get another job at once. Best from all points of view."

Joseph said, "You are leaving!"

"If I left him," averred Withers, suddenly serious, "the poor beggar would go bankrupt; and he begged me not to."

"What happened?"

"I told him to-day I was quitting. He caught me by the arm, told me what an innocent he'd been till twenty-five, never touched a girl or a drop of drink, but that hard luck had made

156

him shifty, trying to overhaul the banks and Monty and me. But that I was his true bosom friend, his mainstay. His apparent confusion of mind, he said, was methodical, no, diabolical, for it deceives Montagu: but all the time he's looking for the flaw in Montagu's armour. Oh, ho, ho, I laughed at that; Chamberlain, the demon for strategy. Well, a lot more like that. He would pay us all to-morrow although his wife and child should have no food in the house for a week (it's probably more or less true); called me his good Tom, and said he knew he was a trial to me, 'but you are caustic, Tom'; said that without me he would be beat; the banks had him, and Montagu was rotten to the core and only wanted his blood, but Montagu gave him play while I was around, for some reason he couldn't make out—psychological, no doubt.

"I pushed his hand away, keeping a stiff upper lip, because he began to snivel. I said, 'No, I must go, I should have gone long ago, and I want my money. I am rotting here and I am not getting any younger.' I told him some plain truths about Montagu, what a fool he was himself, and how his own business was down at heel, and how he sponged on Chamberlain and would certainly ruin him and go down with him, for all his bombast.

" 'Look at the other day,' I said; 'didn't he steal money from Graham? Well, it's been the same history with hundreds of people already, to my knowledge.' I had all the fatuities of the garrulous person who's held his tongue till it burnt a hole in his cheek. Finally in comes his lordship.

" 'What's the trouble?'

" 'Tom wants to leave me.'

" 'Go then and God bless you,' he says lightly; 'let him go, Gregory, he yowls so much he makes me tired in the end. Mendelssohn will keep you afloat for a while: I don't know if he's not the best chap you've ever had.'

"Chamberlain can't resist any suggestion from the old man. He wavered, then said, 'All right, Tom; if you feel like that. I don't want to stand in your way, but I don't want you to have any ill feeling. It's true Mendelssohn's dependable.'

"Then I got mad. 'All right, you let me go?'

" 'Yes,' he said uncertainly.

" 'Good, you'll regret it,' I said. I shouted, 'When is it con-
venient to pay me, eh?'

" 'At the end of next week, if I can scrape the money together.'

" 'Well, you'd better scrape it pretty fast. Otherwise . . .' and
I went, leaving it in the air like that to worry him.

"After all these years he has kicked me out : he would never
have done it, if Montagu hadn't come in and given him his cue.
As for Monty, I never expected it; he's cooking something up
against me. I'll get him, though, too."

"Good heavens, you asked for it," said Baruch. "But it's done:
don't yield to the temptation to go back."

Withers laughed, twisted the match in his mouth again, and
said :

"I came down the street feeling cheapened and poor like a
woman unexpectedly deserted by her man."

Joseph laughed loudly and Withers bit his fingers in a kind of
cattish anger. Baruch hastened to soothe Withers. Joseph took
his hat again, got up darkly behind Withers' chair and almost
limped to the door to show his disapproval and dislike. Baruch
cried, "Don't go, Jo," and Jo hesitated. At last Withers mumbled :

"Is it true? Did he speak to you about taking my place?"

"Of course not," said Baruch. "Don't be foolish, Tom. Ough,
what a fellow you are. In a moment you'll be inventing
Machiavellian schemes against me too : and I'm such a little chap;
it's easy to polish me off."

Withers looked up gaily, then cast a dark look at Joseph,
betraying too plainly his desire to be left alone with Baruch.

Joseph said good-night over his shoulder and went out, closing
the door briskly. Outside, he stood still for a moment. The voices
had struck up again in Baruch's room. His departure caused no
comment, and Withers' feeble-spirited distress seemed to receive
an attention which Joseph had thought his own person alone
excited. He buttoned his coat and dawdled downstairs, leaning
against the wall. At the bottom he found his *casus belli*; "I am
leaving as soon as I get the boat fare." Baruch had said it
casually—thus Withers knew Baruch's plans better than he knew

them. He thought of the midday colloquies in Lachlan Place, the long evenings in Baruch's room, violent discussions in which Baruch had taken part, flooring them all at the end with his argument and apt memory, wiping the floor with them all by a final conclusion of force and brilliance, and then coming quietly and working beside him. Joseph then quaked with a sudden dissolving pang, and when he reached the bottom stair, in darkness, he felt he must rush back to the door, so close to him then, but which would be so inaccessible at midnight when he was sleepless, and ask some question of Baruch which would bring a reassuring answer and break the bond now existing between Withers and Baruch. He stood with one hand on the banisters, rubbing the back of his head, looking at the outlines of furniture gradually becoming visible in the gloom, listening to the radios downstairs, and from time to time trying to make a decision. He actually climbed the stairs once more and stood for some minutes outside the door straining his ears, although taking no notice of what he heard, fascinated by the splinters of light shining through. When he collected his wits, he heard Baruch say:

"Why, it's a perfectly healthy emotion to wish to kill anyone who is in your way, simple, effective, very: and don't tell me you wouldn't sleep like a child the night after, if you were sure the police weren't on your trail. Then, what harm would you do? There's no other thing will neutralise that sprawling creature with his mate who softly engulf everything. If it were not so natural the murder taboo would not be so fearfully strong. I am not like that, I admit. I can never hurt a person without suffering agonies myself. I am not like 'Bel-Ami'—well, it's done, and it's done, so much the better. I cannot even tell a person bad news: but I can appreciate anyone who has the nerve, killing an enemy or a nuisance. Why not? life is after so much the gayer and freer. And look at you with your cold blue eyes—you don't care for a soul."

Withers laughed.

Joseph listened miserably to Baruch expanding his joyously macabre notions and funambulesque morals to an infinite number of listeners through numberless years of life in other places and other societies. Joseph felt fall away from him the last undervestments of pride. He wished to be angry, but he breathed heavily as he went away from the dearest creature in his life. Outside on the dirty pavements, greasy with a hot spring shower, looking sidelong into the sordid living-rooms open in the heat, he knew that he was one with the vilest of the poor and corrupted. He hated Baruch whose good digestion and security of future let him ride all storms. There were tears in his eyes. When he got home he found that Catherine and Michael were there, and had been there for supper. Michael proposed to stay with his aunt and uncle a few days. He knew the fishing spots, he knew the fishermen, who had not changed for many years. When he was thoroughly disgruntled, he came to stay with the Baguenaults, kept Joseph company, and went out by himself spending long days on the reefs and fishing rocks.

Joseph recounted to Catherine his evening at Mendelssohn's. He said clumsily at the end:

"He has just proofed a new plate. The chief figure is a woman— he calls it 'The Free Woman'. I don't like it much; but he explained it to me: the free woman is like you, although you are not entirely free."

Catherine caught her breath.

"What is the woman like?"

"What is she like? I have almost forgotten. She is—she has no clothes, she is coming through thick bush. She has long hair and is rather thin."

"Long hair?"

"Long black hair."

"And what is it called?"

"A woman escapes from a forest, or something like that. I told you, a free woman, but not quite free, a woman who is having trouble in getting free. You know Baruch: he is rather sentimental about women. He told me, 'You should not ask too much about the woman you love, you should believe in her. It is more important than in religion, to believe in love.' He's very sentimental. I don't see any difference between a woman and myself."

"You're right," said Catherine, but left the table and went and walked about in the garden in the cool evening breeze.

"What's Tom Withers like now?" asked Michael. "I haven't seen him since before I went to the war. He was a card then : I'll bet he hasn't improved."

"A silly sort of chap, always scrapping, never satisfied, and always got a complaint. And a regular, er, er, what's the name?— Munchausen. The tales he tells!"

"He hasn't changed," said Michael, smiling.

6 🔊

Backchat. Acerbity of Winter, effrontery of Fulke;
the recognition of Marx postponed. Catherine wanders.

JOSEPH and Baruch went after work to the club-room of the
Workers' Education Association, in Rawson Chambers, and sat
there idly by the window looking out at the city workers streaming towards the Central Railway Station, at the trams grinding up
the ramp, and away to the left to the Darling Harbour goodsyards.
Night settled down slowly over the streets and the lamps flicked
on. The people were all wilted at the end of the long hot day, but
they hurried because they were hungry and they were anxious
to get their shoes off. Sometimes they went in pairs and the man
carried the girl's shabby paper case; sometimes they did not go
straight home but had something first. The ill-lighted greasy chain
restaurant opposite was full of people eating ninepenn'orth of tea,
pies and toast. Joseph also yearned for tea and pie. He had come
up to the Club to have a bite with Winter before they went to
Ross's. Joseph did not want to go to Ross's. It is very cool on
summer evenings in Fisherman's Bay. Joseph only wanted at the
moment to sit by this cool window fanned by a harbour breeze,
looking out at the twinkling city and the last hasty movements
of the packers in the boot establishment opposite. He listened to
students and workers making tea in the little kitchen behind the
stage. He was glad to hear Baruch's voice at some distance, ex-
postulating with someone in the passage; he was glad to hear his
cousin Catherine's voice at some distance, disputing with someone in the kitchen behind the stage.

The windows were ornamented with coloured papers which
Catherine had bought and affixed. Catherine had also stencilled
the bold bright designs on the huckaback curtains to the windows,
had painted cubist designs in the "Russian genre" on the stage

curtains, and arranged the stage decorations and costumes. With scissors, brown paper and paint Catherine had done her best to imitate on an eight-foot square dais the decorations of the new Moscow art theatre. Joseph could still hear her now, back of the stage, describing some political meeting, or some speech, in her excited high voice, going off into peals of laughter, in which she was joined by the gruff, mollified voices of tea-drinking men. He heard Rawson, from the Trades Hall, ready, assured, blatant, a political opportunist, whom Joseph called a "real smart-alec", Milt Dean and Heinrich Winterbaum, both softies and intellectuals. None of them ever spoke to him at all.

Three women school-teachers did basketry beside Joseph, getting ready for a Labour Party fête, and discussed mentally defective children. One said, "When I look at them, I can't believe they'll go to heaven." Two or three solitary persons looked through the bookshelves and asked advice of Mrs. Carey, the old Communist Party militant. The soft air blew over Joseph's face, he felt unspeakably glad and at peace. How depressing to have to go to Ross's on this sultry night. If Ross, that great Labour Leader, who had been in gaol, and had fought a case against the Commonwealth Government, should address a word to him he would sink through the floor. He would appear a perfect noodle. On the chair beside him, someone had left a book—Strindberg, "The Spook Sonata." That sounded funny and Joseph started to read it, but it was very dismal, and reminded him of his mother and father: too dull. Joseph swam off into fancy and watched the trains shunting in the Darling Harbour yards; all he could see now were the tail-lights and red smokes. At the next window two young girls were talking. One had bright golden hair, which curled round her temples and neck. She said:

"Pumblecherri is the one genius the University has: always liquored up, of course. He spoke last night on Beauty in Art. He struggled out of the flies, half-seas over, of course: 'Ladies and Gen'lemen,' he says, 'I represent beauty without art, that is wild art, art in the state of chaos, art unborn, for if I came to you sober,' he said—he admitted it, quite unashamed—'I would be mere imitation of the concept man, that is, scholastic art, rigid art, than which is better the mirror reflecting the sun with prismatic faults, the photograph translating a blue water as grey smudge: but if I came as I dare not come, that is, completely tipsy, I would represent beauty and art, that is an approximation to the concept civilised man, his living portrait, but interpreted, and interpreted in a formal medium and traditional style, by means of a revolt against both.' It was something like that, but beautiful. I just felt beautiful. He makes you understand. 'Well,' he said, 'let's get down to analysis and flout Keats.' What did that mean?''

Joseph could no more understand that than Chinese. Everybody here spoke some kind of a learned dialect. Still it was interesting to listen. Such things he heard as he could never imagine; his tongue had never learned to crawl, let alone gallop like that. He ran his tongue along the edge of his teeth. His imagination began to move. A funny head he had that would sometimes move without warning. He saw in front of him a copy-book double-ruled, and in copper-plate, *'Qui vult decipi, decipiatur'*; likewise *'Magna est veritas, et praevalebit.'* That sounded very stupid; it did not help him at all with these people. He was sorry he had spent his lesson-hours learning such things. He could just as easily have learned, "Beauty without art, wild art . . ." what was it? Such moonshine; and now he wasn't in a position to say a word to a soul on earth except his mother: and mother, talking about soup and the people who didn't go to church. "By God, I'm a man, what did I learn this tommy-rot for?" he cried to himself. "I had better go to a class," he whispered to himself, looking out in the dark. He still thought of the University grandly mounted, as on horseback, in Camperdown, as a kind of holy place, holy and exciting. Things happened there that amounted to the legendary. There was the famous young surgeon who died, who lectured before European congresses, almost at Joseph's age. There was Pumblecherri, the wild art lecturer, who was allowed to lecture though drunk; there was Garnet Gotham, who had been a father to the students in his little round-tower room and had been kicked out for having a mistress, so they said, but really, it was whispered, for being a Communist. Was it possible, a professor?

Their heads, too, are like little round-tower rooms and no one knows what goes on inside. There was Martinelli who had come from Java and the East Indies, looking for traces of the "bridge" in the flora and fauna. Now, by the mere recalling of their names, Joseph felt that he knew something; he was learned. Baruch had been pumping him full of anecdotes the last few days—no, that was what he was talking about all Friday evening, while Joseph was looking in the shops. It came back. Perhaps these classes were not boring, but were brilliant. He could wake up and get out of his sad rut. Baruch came back at this moment, dragging a small man who looked like a new-laid egg. "Here is So-and-so," cried Baruch; "I've told you what a collection of gramophone records he has." The little creature began to chatter in a strained, feminine voice. — in the back of the Roman Café were great doings: Martinelli was always there smoking, Pumblecherri always there drinking and spouting, there were Lindsays galore, Young, all the artists and intellectuals, Handley, the Rhodes Scholar, who had shoulders like an ox and who was writing an elucidation of Marx for working-class students.

"Come along you two, come along," urged the little fellow.

Joseph looked at his coat involuntarily.

"Don't worry about how you're dressed," protested the little fellow; "who cares? it's the feast of reason and the flow of soul." He made a beck to some one back of the stage. "Oh, it's too bad," he continued, stamping his foot; "there's Catherine backstage, looking like La Tosca, with roses in her arms; I absolutely promised to bring you back those paintings, absolutely Raphaelesque. Watkins said, 'You should carry through whatever you start: you'll do something magnificent.' God, these women with their primeval force, their unregimented talents. God, when I think how giddy I am and I take a person like you, a female Caesar would positively cross the Rubicon twenty times a day; and I see how you hold yourself demurely nun-like in the background, or else go round with a purple tragic air, Cassandras predicting the fall of the human race because they have no children. God, I positively weep. We men are nothing to you girls and you let us impose on you. God, it's terrific; a real Euripidean situation."

165

"Don't be a fool, Dacre," cried Catherine, for the little creature had had a romantic mother and was named Dacre Esme Eugene —the last name is immaterial in such a man, for every one calls him by one of the first.

The young woman said:

"It is an indictment of her mind that she loves him so madly. What will he be? A W.E.A. professor?"

"Yes, I said in May, he has a responsibility towards her. She probably came to him untouched; to her he is Dionysus, the divine, inspired youth of men. Men want something different from women. To women they are the fertilising item, spring, corn, trees, Ra ascendant: to men women are a means to become initiated."

Joseph stared. What sort of women peopled the world; what sort of an ignoramus was he? No wonder he made no progress with them.

The people at the window said:

"Did you hear the latest? Ferry is touchy about his name since the last 'Hermes.' In Fiz. yesterday Shaw pronounced the e long. 'Mr. Shaw, my name is spelled . . .' ' I know, F for fornication, E for exotic, R for reverse, R for rural, Y for youth,' said Shaw. Naturally he was kicked out. There's trouble now: the Dean had him on the mat. But it's frightfully obvious. 'Don't be surprised at his manners,' old McWilliams said to James when he got his scholarship and had to work with Ferry; 'old Ferry is one of the old school and then an old bachelor; he has a rather sentimental interest in young men, having no sons of his own.' I call that the *esprit de corps*, being very neat, don't you?"

Joseph looked sadly at the people at the window. A dunce is a dunce. They rattled on.

"When Young begins to expound his theories of expression," insisted little Dacre, "God, you see the world in different colours. You see lakes, nymphs, moonlight, portal, colours, as you never saw before. You see Art shadowed by ritual, by spring fertility, by poetry."

Joseph imagined himself in some such centre now, as he looked out at the vasty, brilliant night sky. He saw the De Rezske tobacco smoke floating around them and cloaking them in a sort of Young dream, the glitter of lightning as derision-wreathed mouths opened and gave issue, like the smoking clefts of rocks of volcanic countries. He imagined himself making a timid remark, for his brain was opening, in this exotic lingo, exotic the word, and everybody receiving it seriously. After all, with borrowing some of Baruch's expressions, and Baruch that good friend would certainly not object, he could perhaps make a remark even to these———

" . . . voyagers to Cytherea . . ." proclaimed Dacre in his fluty voice. This happy dream dissolved into the present, and in the present stood Winter, just come in, with his built-up boot, his threadbare suit, little ratty face and his bulging pockets.

"Come and have tea?" said Winter, looking over Dacre and Baruch with scorn.

Martinelli and Bedlam dissolved into the tea-steam. Joseph said hungrily:

"What did you bring us?"

Winter had just been paid, and had bought three pies, three rolls and three bananas. Catherine, who had a soft spot for Winter, brought out the cups of tea.

"Hullo, Jo, where are you off to to-night? I see you in better company than you've ever been!" She smiled at Baruch, "Thanks to you?" and departed again into the loud region beyond, where Rawson, that skite, was shouting:

"Wait until we corner them in Caucus on Tuesday. A pound to a penny, Donnelly will never get the local committees resolution past Me!"

Much disorder. The Catherine wheel spun and sputtered again. Milt Dean said spongily (he was thirty-six and a bachelor):

"Have you read Mrs. Dora Russell's book on Free Love?"

Joseph and Winter, two humble, hungry and modest creatures, sat dumbly before all the people waiting for their class, before the book-lovers and stray people who eyed them furiously, as if glad of something to fill in a dull half-hour, and they ate their pies, bananas and rolls.

"Yer coming to Ross's after the meetin'?" said Winter.

"You bet," said Joseph, more willingly, since he had eaten. He would never have had the nerve to refuse Winter, in any case, short of a toothache. On the way out, Winter said:

"Folliot's there, and I expect him to speak. I don't like him, I'll tell yew frankly."

"My cousin knows him — Michael Baguenault."

"Oh, him — oh yes. We've got a good number of chaps belongin' to the Seamen's Union sheltered down at the Hall. They sleep there, and they're fed as best we can manage. It's important we should all help them to stick out. Some of them'll be at the meetin' to-night. If yew look about yew'll also pick out, I think, some plain-clothes Federal Police. Any working man can tell them in a minute. But don't expect to hear anything inflammatory: Fulke don't want to taste gaol."

"I didn't know we were going to a meeting first."

"O' course. They're makin' an election issue out o' us, the bluebottles; d'ye know the Cockney word? It's all ridiculous, as there're only about two thousand real true-blue Communists in the Commonwealth. That's why every true workin' man like yew, especially yew in the printin' trade, that has so much influence, should stick to the movement. Don't yew realise the fate of the working class depends on men like yew, quiet, honest, severe-thinkin', who don't join for no personal pride, or Bohemian quirk?"

"I don't think it's right to make trouble," answered Joseph, troubled; "there is always trouble with workmen anyhow, nothing but strikes and award disputes. I read in the *Sun* that there were more strikes last year in Australia than anywhere else in the world. Why do you chaps do it? For advertisement, I think. It's to advertise your ideas to the workers. But it isn't the right way. You should do it quietly; you can vote, can't you? I think every one should vote and say what he thinks; then if they're in the majority, they win."

"How much per cent. is necessary to win?" asked Winter irritably.

"Well, I don't know; more than half, I suppose?"

"So, if fifty-one per cent. of the people vote Communist, we'll have Communism?"

"No, there'd be fighting, I suppose," said Joseph, "'cause there's fighting always."

"And if seventy-five per cent. won, there'd be Communism?" insisted Winter.

"I suppose so."

"Do yew know what Communism is?"

"Well, it's equal chances for all," said Joseph wearily.

"Not at all. It's the dictatorship of the proletariat. The proletarian, that's yew. Can yew imagine yerself havin' somethin' to say in life? instead of obeyin' yer father and mother, the church, yer cousin, admirin' the intellectuals like Baruch, goin' to College to try to get a little better pay, knucklin' under to Chamberlain, keepin' yer mouth shut, bein' too poor to have wife or child, to buy a decent coat or eat good meat every day—imagine, instead o' all that, yew've got a right to say how the business should be run, how the machines should be improved, the workin' hours altered to prevent yew gettin' tired. Imagine yew bein' able to go up to the head o' the State, Sir Spinach Spinach, then Comrade Garlic, and sayin', Comrade Garlic, yew don't know a goddamned thing about printers, and he listenin' to yew."

"That wouldn't happen, ever," said Joseph decidedly; "I don't know enough."

"And suppose yew was taught enough, from the time yew was a baby, instead of goin' to school and learnin' goddamn nonsense that helps yew nowhere. How did these other chaps learn? 'Cause they had well-taught fathers, or went to expensive high schools. Not yew, yew poor oppressed workin' man. It ain't hard to learn."

"If I'd been taught a lot; but I'm not smart," said Joseph sadly. "I couldn't learn much and you can't count with me. I'm badly off because I'm not too good, but the majority of working men do pretty well. They have homes, they go to the races, they drink beer. We aren't so badly off; it's not right to stir up a land."

Winter responded irritably:

"Let me tell yew here and now that Terra Felix Australis, this waste and sleepin' land, this lazy dago land, whose volcanoes died and whose rivers dried up millenniums ago, is on the edge of a social volcano. Because why? we're primary producers, and we feel every oscillation of the markets as a cloud the wind. Because why? because the shadder of the N.S.W. Corps still blights the wheat-fields, because we've all got to work here to keep four thousand elect and fifty thousand mean little rentiers in the boardin'-houses of London. Because 'their Whitehall' is breakin' the sheep's back."

"The Australians," said Joseph, harking back to the sententious-ness of his old mother, "are lazy. They don't like to work; there's always been labour trouble in this land. Like the South Africans, too."

"There always has, thank God," said Winter, "because we're the seed of rebellious men, all the martyrs of the nineteenth cen-tury Trades Union England, all the men who stole bread rather than see their wives and children starve. That's the sort o' men we are; that's why we don't knuckle down to the man who wants us to go in rags while he gives his wife a fur coat and pays for his daughter's whoring parties."

"But we're better off, with the basic wage, with the arbitration awards, and everything, than almost anyone," said Joseph, shocked.

"We're better off than the darkies growin' opium and rice and rubber in the F.M.S. who can't even pay for one meal a day. But do yew consider yerself so well off that yew don't need any more? Yer satisfied as yew are?"

"No, but that's an accident. Chamberlain . . . Then look at the Labour Party here. They can do practically anything, and look at the scandals."

Winter threw up his hands.

"La Rochefoucauld said, 'Yew need a little madness to get out of some situations.' Here is one. That madness is revolution, and for yew it's a tap on the napper to wake yew up."

Winter pulled out of his pocket a paper on which he had listed the names of fifty capitalists in Sydney who had made a profit, 'or surplus value', to the tune of more than £5000 net, some going up to £20,000 net, that year; there were more to come.

"And a lot of it's concealed," said Winter. "Where does it come from, the £5000 cool?"

"They earn it."

"Fool," said Winter: "wrung out of our necks. The sweat yew drop in yer stinkin' shop is minted; yew don't know it. Why, because yew were put under ether in school, in church and at home. Yew don't know currency when yew see it. If Chamberlain ran round in his borrowed car for a hundred years he couldn't sell his labour for a loaf of bread unless yew were all there to work the machines to produce the print. He could use his brains for a hundred years and turn nothin' out of it without yer hands, brains, bodies, wills."

Joseph felt surprised. This acerbity — Winter was poverty-stricken, and had had a horrible accident once, the spoke of a delivery van had run into his leg, and perhaps his leg always hurt him. He had no use for the dignity of work, endurance, saving. Joseph felt his heart thud. Winter sounded right. He had had no idea that these ideas were actually a passion with anyone; with Baruch, of course, but Baruch was a phenomenon, but a plain poor working man like Winter.—He felt a great thirst and desire.

"Where does that car come from?" exclaimed Winter in excitement, with bony fingers gripping his arm. A Hispano-Suiza with the initial letters "IA" flew past.

"Italy?" hazarded Joseph.

"Out of yer belly, or the belly of some Italian brother of yours. Think that there's a man exactly like yew, doing yer job, thinking yer thoughts, poor, a Catholic, ignorant, beggarly, in Italy. Out of his purse, that is his belly, it came. Yew dropped it as yew skedaddled to work or back home one day, like an improvident cat havin' her babies in the fairway. Do you suppose *his* profits suddenly bloom like the rose at the end of each half-year?"

Joseph thought perhaps they did.

"Don't yew realise they are collected coin by coin and drop by drop every minute of every day of every week in the year? I mean drop of blood by drop of blood, bead of sweat by bead of sweat. Yew look pretty pale at the end. But the Hispano-Suiza has come into the world, neat, natty, lacquered, steel-fitted, with foot-warmers and a radio set installed, and along with it a whole host of strange creatures, the gargoyles, griffins, bloodsuckers, ghouls and flitterbats of the latter days, gramophones, bath-heaters, radiators, wireless sets, electric stoves, other things that neither yew nor yer mother will ever see, that feed on our thin frames invisibly, as it were."

Joseph looked terrified at Winter, sidelong.

"Do you work more than Chamberlain, or he than you?"

"We work harder!"

"How is the money divided, and the comfort?"

"Unfairly," said Joseph in a deep voice. They argued it out. Joseph was often lost in thought, trying to reconstruct his shattered "job" as the atom of the economic world.

They turned once more and came to Communist Hall. The name was scarcely legible. Young working men lounged in the doorway. They went up a small wooden stairway, at the top of which was a pamphlet stall, and into a room with a high stage, furnished with schoolroom forms. Round the wall some of the seamen were already sleeping, with their coats under their heads, and bits of blankets and variegated rags over them.

In came Marion Folliot the magnificent. Baruch, standing by, said, "She takes up so much psychic room!" and with her, little ironic Fulke, very pleased with himself, saluting everyone with "Good evening, comrade!" The meeting immediately assembled, the sleepy seamen getting up from their benches. Fulke came forward. Catherine Baguenault sat in the side-benches beside Marion, and both women gazed intently at the stage. Fulke said:

"Mr Wellborn" (the Nationalist Prime Minister) "is fighting you for a principle — and interest, as you are fighting him for a bed and breakfast according to principle. The opponents are well matched. But Mr Wellborn has a disadvantage, he is a gentleman. You must not blame Mr Wellborn. I went to school with him, and the dear fellow was along with me in Trinity College, that was near seventeen years ago. At that time he was thinking of taking orders, and if he had he would at this moment be sitting in some Paris restaurant swopping *mots d'esprit* with fashionable actresses and dragging in Jesus Christ very adroitly to honour the

172

cloth. Think of it, he has to drink the tea served in Parliament
House, and be bored with the speeches of vulgar Labour politic-
ians with a twang and faulty grammar. Mr Wellborn was always
what he is now, a prize boy. I remember when he was in the
sixth form of the private school where we were educated — in
Sydney, if I may be precise. It was a school for the wealthy, and
I was not then aware of the lowness of my birth—he was Captain of the School and Speaker of the School Moot. He always
made the speeches he makes now, and was always requested
to reply for the school when the Rt. Hon. William Bluebeak
came to visit us on Speech Day, and say, 'Dear lads, looking
at your shining faces, I think of the time forty years ago when I
sat on those same forms . . .' and so on. And I, by misadventure,
was always, as now, in opposition to Mr Wellborn, and they did
not trust me to mention the crimson thread of Empire in the
Speech Day oration.

"Now all this preamble is to show you how very little Mr
Wellborn must know about economics. Like the celebrated Aus-
trian economist, he begins by discarding his silk-lined overcoat.
'In summer, I can do without that,' he says; 'poor men, to begin
with, are men who do not have silk-lined overcoats to discard in
summer.' Then he moves on and shivers as the terrible, although
quite hypothetical, case occurs to him — that of a man forced
to go without an overcoat in winter. 'The rebels in the world,' he
says to himself, flipping his hands and drawing his chair into the
sun, 'come from men, alas that there be such, who do not have
overcoats even in winter.' But you, comrades, have never had an
overcoat probably, and you begin in the other direction. You
begin by saying, 'Will I so much as get a crust of bread to carry
me through to-day?' and overcoats are a hundred miles above
your heads.

"Mr Wellborn means well and was trained in a very expensive
school. But as he is, all the members of his class are, and as he
thinks when he discards his overcoat, think all the well-inten-
tioned members of his class. There is not a man among them who
has suffered hunger, want, cold, mental distortion, scholastic
want, thwarting of the simplest and most powerful desires. All

comes to them freely, and they believe it comes by the force of their will. They live in a mystic world based on a free allowance of bread and jam. By some mysterious process their larders are always full. To them, the world should be like that; and if your larders are not full, it is because you have managed badly. 'My great-uncle was a humble labourer,' says one of them, and assumes that every humble labourer could have been a shipping magnate by integrity and hard work. But that is contrary to reason . . .''

Thus little Fulke, rapidly, sibilantly, smiling, with effrontery. His paper the *International Worker* had twice been seized by the police. Winter said, sensing Joseph's confusion :

"I don't think it's quite the style for the seamen."

Joseph was restless.

"It's hard to understand. Why doesn't he stand on both feet?"

At the end the seamen applauded respectfully, the women warmly. They knew they were listening to the editor of the Communist paper whose presses had twice been seized by the police, and who might any day be put in the jug. They were the very tail of the workers, ignorant, wretchedly paid, put-upon and misled, and now, owing to the strike, almost starving.

Whiteaway sprang up, a man just come over from Canada by way of the Pacific coast of the United States. He jumped up on to the platform and said, "Let's talk about practical things." His tone was not very complimentary. His voice was dry and his stuff matter-of-fact, but in ten minutes the audience was mad with enthusiasm. Some of the seamen put gruff, dry-throated and clumsily phrased questions to him; some applauded him every two or three words, like pepper-shot. He answered the interjectors rapidly, like a man who has to catch a long-distance train. Catherine argued with him about immediate Labour policy — no good in continuing the strike, let them mediate now and strike again later on when there were more funds in hand. Winter found out he had lived with Lenin in exile, and although the joy of speaking to a man who had lived with Lenin illuminated his face, he asked serious questions — "What did Comrade Lenin think would be the immediate Labour history of Australia? How would the traditional Trades Union movement develop here? Would we continue to be betrayed by the P.L.P.?"

Fulke sat smiling on one side and Marion brooded over him, with her hand on his knee.

After the meeting the forms were pushed to the side of the room and the seamen immediately rolled themselves up to sleep. Joseph wished there had been a canteen there; he was very dry. Perhaps Ross would give them tea. Outside they met Tingle, secretary of the Seamen's Union, and one of the two rival heads of the Trades Union movement. He went with them to Ross's house, along with the Folliots, Catherine, Baruch and Winter.

Joseph, who perhaps expected to see a monk's cell decorated with pictures of the labour-class heroes and martyrs, and a Trades Union vatican of books, was disappointed to see an ordinary middle-class home, with photographs of the family, muslin curtains, bric-à-brac, and a modest yellow-braided Mrs Ross who was fussing because her baby had been crying all the evening. Nothing, thought Joseph, is as I expect it. I must get my bearings in all this world.

"Crying for a good reason," said Ross, grinning. "He probably knows what he is in for when he grows up. His name," he said, turning to Joseph, who was distrait, "is Jacob Karl Marx Ross. I gave it to him to allow him the opportunity of being well reviled when he grows up, and that through no fault of his own. When that little feller is a big 'un his name will mean something to the whole world."

"Naturally you postpone the recognition of Marx for a generation; always one ahead," said Winter bitterly. Ross believed in conciliation tactics; Tingle wanted to threaten a general strike and disable the country entirely for a week.

"You can't bring all the unions out on every frivolous excuse," argued Ross.

"You've got to win this strike, or be beaten so badly that you'll make a retrograde step of ten years," insisted Tingle.

"If I'm allowed to be personal, I think it would be interpreted to your discredit, as a political move," cried Ross.

"I don't care what you think: I'm facing the situation at the moment. Every day the harbour's tied up, it's a loss of seventy thousand pounds at least. Everything's picketed; there are about three blacklegs on the waterfront. You've got the thing in the hollow of your hand; and you want to go up there without real authority and attempt conciliation. Browbeat 'em, get your votes, go up with the threat of a general strike and you'll bring it through this week."

"No, the unions won't come out on that. You're risking the Labour organisation for a bit of fanfaronade."

Joseph found it hard to follow their quarrel; the undercurrents of jealousy carried it along. It all made Joseph very tired, but he had the feeling that he was expanding in bone and muscle.

He went home by the last tram. At the top of the hill at South Head he looked out at the water, dark on either side, and the multitude of lights in City and suburbs. He tried to think of the homes they represented, the discussions which went on all day and night on all sorts of problems foreign to him, of the division of these people into "classes", "interests"—all that he had heard filtered through the network of lights. He was very sleepy.

"It is awfully complex," he said to himself, sitting alone in the back compartment of the tram of which he was the only passenger. "I wish I had been born a clever chap."

His cousins Michael and Catherine bubbled merrily in that soup. Through the stew of these energetic and disputatious people, he saw a white figure emerging in the distance, that of Winter's commonwealth of workmen, in which he would be somebody as well, and the warm blood coursing roused him for a few moments. He smiled.

"Catherine is right," he thought, "and Michael is wrong." Yet Catherine was extremely simple and rather crazy in ideas, but easy to talk to, even simpler than Winter, whereas Michael was subtle and involved; and though both were Socialists, Catherine was poor at definitions, whereas Michael could discuss the meaning of things for hours together. Again Baruch cut across them both, being more sanguine than Catherine and more subtle than Michael and more learned than Winter, loving at once revolution, refinements, the farthest reaches of deduction.

176

"Baruch," said Joseph to himself, "is the sign x in man; x equals—anything; the unknown quantity." The warmth still increased in him at these first steps, and he wondered if he could ever lose himself in the worlds of Catherine, Michael or Winter; he thought it likely if Baruch remained long enough in the shop to turn his head. But Baruch was leaving. "He is so brilliant, we will hear of him," said Joseph, with the light of pride in his eyes. Baruch had his reward. He could not be so persuaded by the dry, prickly discourse of Winter.

"I don't like him," said Joseph; "he is not suave."

In the morning the world appeared no different. The yellow morning passed gradually, events passed like the shuttering of early moving pictures, all was normal. He did his work, and no commonwealth of workers appeared in the offing.

"I must be a man with no passions for my private trouble," he said to himself.

Baruch was doing his work with a Gioconda expression; was he without passion? No, he was all passion and he showed it; but Joseph realised that that transparent creature lived behind thousands of glass shutters which oddly transmitted his contours; he resented it. What were those shutters? Refinements of sense and intellect which he got in a different society.

"Bah, money, there you are," said Joseph; "it is the same all over the world." In his conversation appeared pleasant sophistries and an independence of his meagre present which were only treason to Joseph bound for ever to the same turn-table.

Baruch looked at Joseph and saw his thin dark lips pout. He said:

"Giuseppe mio, what tune did Fulke the Fiddler play you last night?"

Joseph replied grumpily:

"He's no good, I think. He's too well brought up. A man called Whiteaway was there; he's practical."

Baruch continued:

"If you go often you will have plenty of problems of personality to solve. These glib, rhetorical speakers sometimes fire the men but more often betray them. Follow the interest of your class.

Become your own tactician, your own Caesar. Don't be afraid to criticise the speaker. Don't become refined, Joseph, your clerical training was a bad start, you always incapacitated yourself by believing in refinement. You could be a fine antique that way, but the workers would stick you in a museum. You can't follow Fulke or me. You must think for yourself. For preference, listen to those of your class who speak simply, without the flowers of rhetoric, without jokes, without cleverness; none of these glancing, glinting, slithering fellers. I ought to be a leader myself," continued Baruch in a depressed tone, "but I can't stand too much discomfort, and I want to be a scholar. You see, it's harder for me than you. The reigning bourgeoisie offers me prizes."

Withers began to laugh :

"Mendelssohn is right. Truth in the dumps. I've always said he'll be a rank failure, he'll fall between two stools."

"He won't," cried Joseph, outraged.

"You say that because you want to see him on top, you like him, but you'll see," said Withers, biting his moustache in a catty rage.

Joseph said no more, but he was solaced. He was a slender creature, no apostle, no originator.

"He's like me, a foredoomed failure," said Withers, acidly.

No reply.

"A wanderer, a rolling stone gathers no moss, and doesn't want to gather any, but no house is built on top of it," emphasised Withers.

Joseph mournfully held a sheet of paper up to the light to examine its texture.

"Baruch is brilliant," he said at last.

"Of course, he's brilliant. He's brilliant—I'm not saying he's not brilliant, I know he's brilliant : but brilliance doesn't get you anywhere. It's character, it's will. And then you have to be a bit of a fanatic; not to see too many sides of a question. Like a friend of mine. I don't like So-and-so, he said, because he sees too many sides of a question; you can't look at a man's belly and behind at the same time. You've got to take sides."

"He takes sides," Joseph said.

178

"Of course. Because he can talk like a Burke, and grin like a Chinese idol so that, whatever happened, he could make himself a place; he's brilliant. But it's not conviction, it's just involuntary. It's not heroism, it's not foresight. He knows the coming world of demagogues is made for tikes like him."

"You're jealous."

"I'm not jealous : listen, you've just met the smartest man you ever met. You're bowled over. I've had experience : he won't go far; he's a weakling."

Baruch had been straining his ears but had heard nothing. He sauntered closer.

"Well, I had a letter from my uncle this morning, telling me it's all right, he has fixed the place as secretary to Farmer, the industrialist."

"Where does he live?"

"In the States; in Baltimore."

"Will you go?"

"Will I go? Joseph, I've already booked my passage : I'm dying to go."

Withers went away tee-heeing.

"What's Withers laughing up his sleeve for?"

"He's jealous," said Joseph flatly.

Baruch's happiness was easy to see. He would be political secretary to an aspiring industrialist who foresaw a more highly-mechanised industrial system. For Baruch, it might be the beginning of a political career. He said to Joseph :

"Horace Greeley was a printer, Benjamin Franklin and Henry George : the last wrote after having been a political secretary. There were lots of others."

"William Caxton," said Joseph, and reproaches himself for the contraction of his heart. He tells Baruch, in a minute, how glad, how joyful he is that his problems are solved. But his heart sinks to think he is losing his prospective Greeley, Franklin or George. Why does his newly-cemented world have to be broken up?

"You deserve it," said Joseph slowly.

"You deserve it," said old Williams, standing by and grinning like a Cheshire cat, his cheeks flushing at the idea of what can be accomplished by youth. "Joseph and me," said old Williams, "will stay here, year in, year out, and watch you in your meteoric career. One of these days we will say, when you're member of Parliament ('Congress', said Baruch), we knew him once; he worked side by side with us."

"He'll only remember you with a round flourish as picturesque examples of downtrodden men," said Withers. "He'll be a liberal reactionary, then."

"You love to rub salt in a wound, Withers, don't you?" said Baruch, with glistening eyes. "Why is that?"

"I'm a dog," said Withers, returning to his work.

Baruch immediately bubbled over and talked long and periphrastically. Chamberlain coming in invited him to lunch. Montagu came in, and with dignified bonhomie invited himself.

"I'll be taking advantage of your political relations one of these days."

At the end Baruch was brought to a stop by the trouble and pain he had noted for some time in Joseph. The others went back to their machines. Baruch took Joseph's hand:

"I'll be very sorry to leave you here. I've never met a more candid or serious man."

Joseph trembled, turned away, and started to go on with his work. Baruch circled so that he stood in front of him again, plunged his regard into Joseph's sombre and chagrined eyes, and dismayed, went back to his own machine. Clickety-click, clack-clack, clack-clack, said the machines. Baruch began to smile to himself and a tune burst from his lips. Joseph bit his lips. All the morning their two minds cantered between the two themes, the joy of the one, the sorrow of the other.

Would he like to go to America? wondered Baruch, and then concluded: "How could anyone expatriate this one-rooted plant?"

In the afternoon the close sky clouded. They could have worked with their shirts off. In the evening the rain poured down.

The same evening Baruch and Joseph went to the University to their lecture on light. The Central Railway was blinding wet, the bars crowded and steaming, the tram-tracks congested with trams, motor-cars, home-goers. Electric signs made the vapoury circus brilliant like a house of smoky glass. They rattled in the tram down George Street West full of bright cheap shops, dentists' parlours with red tasselled curtains and cheap-jack stores of every variety. They alighted at the University steps, near the Men's Union, and tramped along cuttings and new roads past the Teachers' College.

"I made a mistake," said Baruch, "I was thinking of something else. We should have got off at the Vet. School instead of the Union."

He pronounced the names with a familiar fraternal tone as if he had spent long years there. He dearly missed the years of post-graduate and professorial work he had promised himself already when a schoolboy. Joseph tramped along in silence. They squelched through the fat clay ruts and grass. There were lights in the Medical School and a faint glow in the Fisher Library still. Out here the wind raged, the rain ran down into their socks and their necks, and streaked their uncut hair. The trees lashed about and the few lamps tossed on their stalks. Frogs croaked in the basement of the Teacher's College and in the University Oval. Faint lights gleamed, as in castles over the bog, in the Methodist and Presbyterian Colleges. They fought their way over the cinder-paths and marsh leaning against the wind, towards the new Physics Building. Joseph was sick and feeble, the Bovril did not keep him going more than half an hour or so, but Baruch, with pale forehead and dripping body, with hat turned down all round and burning hand, hurried him along. They came to the door at last.

They walked a little way along the corridor, their shoes making a squashing sound, past 'the hat-racks and feebly-lighted walls. The installation was recent. They came round a corner into a mountainous demonstration room, painted white, immensely high; at the back a panelled wall rose far over their heads. Joseph, who had expected an ordinary class-room, felt transported into the temple of some rigorous superhuman cult. It was like sitting on an artificial hill. A sarcastic man with horn-rimmed glasses, black hair and wrinkled forehead watched them roundly all the way from the door, so that Joseph tripped up the first step and sat down abruptly in the first row. The man was one of those whose sole distinction is a crushing stare; he was in his element, no one could resist him. But Joseph thought Science was looking down on him. This man, when he felt well, when he came out from a not too arduous day, clerking it in a Government Department, would walk stiffly along the street, in his shiny black suit, slaying passers-by with glances of penetration and scorn. This was his sole joy in life, and he exercised it all his life.

An aquarium was let in, in the centre of the long yellow demonstration desk. The desk was crowded with small aquaria, mechanical models, retorts, tubes, glass rods, lantern slides, models of the most beautiful and fantastic imaginable glass-blowing, a dry cell, two microscopes, a magic lantern, a magnet, a knife switch, a bottle with three spouts in the side, a spectroscope, two sheets of optical illusions.

The lights were placed high, too high, and were too bright. They had had the lights on in the workshop since three o'clock on account of the storm, and their eyes were bloodshot; they blinked continually. There was an assistant, an old fellow, bowed, curiously menial in black, with a mean loose smile, who kept shifting the lantern and bringing in things from a laboratory on the left with a cunning servile air. The blackboard, stuck naked in front of them, was empty there for centuries of time, it seemed. Joseph sat dazed, bitterly regretted the evening lost and the long journey home through the wet, his ankles soaked round his boots, and his flushed forehead. Feet scraped, people hung up mackintoshes and closed umbrellas with a flop; the room was cold. There were fifteen people there and others walking in with shabby, nervous assurance, dressed in the drab, bad clothing of struggling workers. They stared at the blank blackboard and struck up subdued conversations. Joseph started and stared at a thin, oldish woman with straggling hair, who came in in a waterproof hat. It was his cousin Catherine. She looked round disdainfully, immediately saw Joseph and came across to them, with her masterful voice raised. There were now twenty persons. Someone walked about creaking, laughing, distributing papers. Joseph put out his hand and got a paper. "Join the Evolution Society!" The distributor was the Secretary, a middle-aged workman, with greying hair and a clerical turn to his dress. "Evolution is an established principle in Nature, but it has enemies in human thought. Do you believe in Evolution? If so, join us and help spread enlightenment, destroy superstition which is retarding man. If not, come and hear what we have to say. Are you sure you are right? Lectures every Wednesday. 'Evolution in Society.' 'Evolution in Nature.' 'Geological Ages.' " Joseph turned and stared at this assembly of poor learners. Did they all, actually workmen poorer than him, stone-choppers, linesmen, spend their nights worrying about Evolution? His life must have been spent in a morass. He was the last of the last.

Baruch laughed; that laugh! It would soon cease in his ears for ever. "It is Christian anti-Christian!" said Baruch, crumpling up the notice. Joseph stared in front of him and went over minutely the details of the day. The stooping, black-swirling, frontally-whirling blackboard absorbed him, with its black minion discreetly circulating. The pains in his belly had stopped, everything was yellow, spewy, faint, watery, sick, before the high electric lights, the blackboard, the dry, hungry air. He looked upwards, drew nourishment from the wavering reflections of the aquarium on the ceiling, remained transfixed, staring upwards.

The conversation all around, rising slowly, more confident since Catherine arrived and the Secretary of the Evolution Society had passed, came to him in waves: "The Kitchen Committee is badly managed—Mrs Jones tells everyone how she met her husband and tries to conceal her wig by always wearing hats—Wyn Bates believed in free love till she got a boy—My next book is coming out in a limited edition, de luxe, two guineas the copy, few but fit, as they say—Yes, Nietzsche is still a draw with the submerged intelligentsia—. . . in the Esperanto Club debate, really obvious—Major Barbara, Dora Russell, mental tests, Dr Warner said . . ."

Joseph touched Baruch, who was laughing helplessly at something he had just said himself, and exclaimed softly:

"Do they all know each other? You feel like an outsider!"

Ah, the only thing in life was to get home, have some bread
and milk, see the windows were stuffed against the storm, get to
bed and sleep. There was a stir:

"Here's Mewler, Möhler, here's Mooller, Mueller . . ."

Silence. The black menial stood bowing by.

"Ladies and gentlemen, it is going to be harder for me to speak
than for you to listen to me. I understand that you are students
who have not had any tuition at all in physics, chemistry or
mathematics, that you probably know very little about those
things, except what you have had to learn for your own trades.
You must interrupt whenever you do not understand. And try to
understand what you do not understand. A boy at high school
learns certain basic acceptations: if you are not cognisant of
these principles—they are not truths, but acceptations—you will
not understand me. They are so much accepted by me, that I may
assume what you absolutely ignore. You must stop me when I
do that."

He wiped his forehead. Silence again. A soft voice, a man of
medium height, with an ivory forehead, ivory silk handkerchief,
ivory silk evening shirt. Silence again, reflections on the ceiling,
little vanes turning in the tubes, the water in the aquarium, and
silence, silence.

Joseph in a moment felt that his soul was built on a firm stone,
as he had not felt since he could remember. He felt isolated and
light; his head was flushed a bit. The rushing trees have died away,
the agony, the griping, the fire in heart and limbs is soothed down
and asleep, the wet ankles are a pleasant sensation, the brain is
washed in aquarium water. He was joyous, alert. He half turned,
and Baruch's sloping, fleshy dark profile invaded the white world
and stayed there still, immobile, with the soft underlip drooping,
still shadowy, dreaming in the reflections, in the golden lights,
water and silence. "If he goes, I will not be able to understand a
thing again!"

Mueller switched out the auditorium lights, and nothing
remained but the light underneath the aquarium set in the desk.
Mueller took a glass rod and touched the water: the reflections
began in the darkness with a sudden flurry, freckling and flowing

out and out, larger, paler, shadowier, and dying down the walls. A spasm of love clove everyone, plunged into their hearts, light shot up their midriff in a glass tube between two dark lungs, they expelled light into the air. "Ah!" cried the class.

The submerged cave was swimming with light and air and filled to the ceiling with pellucid waves. The reading-lamp alone glowed on the desk. The professor stood there, a magician, in medium height, with gold cuff-links and glass rods, gleaming glasses and ivory silk handkerchief.

"Look up again!"

He stirred the water again, and this time his exposition came settling down through the waves, pouring through the room, turning, glinting, falling on the counter, growing up into the physical being of Mueller, to whom they presently all turned, a raven flock with pale heads. He stood in the half-light, a man of words, a heavy-grained man of flesh and words, no magician, but a man in evening-dress with elegant, clipped speech.

"Study their brilliancy and size when they begin and when they reach the limits of the screen: continue to watch them while I speak.

They glared at the lights above.

"What you see is the action of light waves: light is emitted in waves from a radiant object, as from this globe, and in waves passes through space and matter . . ."

He turned on the light and worked a little serpentine mechanical model which showed the action of waves: he showed them a manometric flame. He described the chemical constituents of light, showed them the prismatic distribution of light into elements, made the blacks in the prism significant, described the composition of the atom, the electronic universe, the weighing of the stars, the blasting of an atom, chemical affinities: enough in an evening to send them home in a stupor, drunk with learning. But he expounded with a clear dry passion which shook them and etched his lecture on their memories.

Joseph half-turned to Baruch, his eyes shining.

"It is wonderful; I never knew . . ."

Joseph perceived through a great door in his mind's eye, a sort of internal cathedral, in which the five senses were as five ogival windows; it was the slow and stable architecture of the universe, in which all was perceptible, computable. His heart throbbed: "All can be seen, discovered: it is not chaos." He saw a vivid unfolding in thousands of series, spathes unfolding into innumerable buds, cubes developing infinitesimally, groined arches ricocheting infinitely, leaping higher and higher, and the incommensurable perspective of mountainous universes building without builders. He saw thousands of concentric cubes, kingdoms of crystals ascending from needle-tufts to Dolomites, hierarchies and hosts of peaks like the hosts of the empyrean, orderly dissolutions and reformations, like armies in battle, polarisations, crystals in deposition like forests of leaves, chemical affinities resembling human love, the universe in the electron resembling the solar system. The universe seemed more perfect and orderly than it did to the lecturer. He breathed quietly and joyfully, the world fell into order and the furniture of his mind moved mysteriously into the proper places—like the marshalled benches of a class-room, like the austere reading-desk of the lecturer. At the demonstration of the inflexibility of the physical order, he felt more a man, freer. He turned again—Baruch's dark hair and white thick-skinned profile leaning on his hand, looking melancholy downwards, the symbol of free thought without regulation, of dispute, confusion, sophistry, of man's untold aberration, anarchy, waste, disappointment, whose relation to him was as a chemical affinity, but dimmer than the relation of the atoms, and troublous, round whose radiant attraction his little dark world had for a time swung out, this strange profile impinged on his demonstration-world, spoiled his gaiety. Darkly, with a pang, the bottom fell out of his jerry-built heart.

He turned to the lecturer again.

"Not to mislead you, I am rubbing out these diagrams, which are symbols and do not represent any existing thing. They are a convention for something not understood . . . these things have never been seen, they have only been divined by rods, screens, jets of metal and vanes in vacuums. The newest is not necessarily the best. . . . I am not dogmatic, do not you be . . . theories do not grow out of date. . . . Our course will not be dramatic as to-night's lecture has been. It is for sober students."

The class applauded faintly, not sure if it was correct in a lecture on physics.

They paddled round getting their cloaks and umbrellas, and left in a sort of scrimmage, a shameful collection of dillydaddles. Compared with the universe, they were in a disheartening disorder. The black-coated servant continued to sneer as he put away the apparatus.

The rain had stopped; they walked to the quay. When they came through the little park of Lachlan Place, Joseph said:

"I had better go and get my coat: I left it in the place."

"Funny," answered Baruch; "the lights are on."

"Chamberlain's working late over his accounts."

He came out in a minute:

"Funniest thing I ever struck. Montagu and Withers are there by themselves going over the accounts. Perhaps Chamberlain's gone out for a walk. They didn't look pleased to see me."

"They're cooking up something. Perhaps the bank manager's coming down to look over the place."

"I'm goddamned tired."

"I hope it's fine for our picnic Saturday."

"What picnic's that?"

"I didn't ask you, Jo? What a shame. You'll come along. It's the crowd. Your cousins will be there."

"Where to?"

"The Lane Cove River, I think. Go on the spree for once; you never have any fun."

"All right, I'll see. Good-night!"

"Good-night; see you to-morrow."

7 ✒

Under the eschscholtzias. Montagu a skunk, Withers not a
social type. Castaways in a busy harbour. Brother and sister.
Examples of the long thoughts of youth; a mediaeval tyrant.
The sons of Clovis. Catherine wanders again.

ON SATURDAY a fresh breeze blew under a sun-drenched sky.
At twelve the city was full of feet and wheels; at two, pigeons
picked at dung in the centre of the principal streets, the untrodden
macadam shone blue and the air was clean and still. In the week-
ends, during the six months' fair season, the whole city empties
its workers like a shovel emptying nutshells, on to the beaches,
river banks, bay, green suburbs, to the tennis-courts, boat-races,
horse-races, baths and public reserves.

Baruch and Joseph hustled out of the office, putting their coats
on, and smelling of soap. They sat down in the little park under
the tiger-yellow cannas and the eschscholtzias. The dark humus
exuded a honey-scented moisture in the heat. The heat soaked
through them and the wind flitted over the blades of grass.

"We have time," said Baruch when they had eaten their sandwiches; "let's walk round the sea-wall."

"We'll go and see the animals in the Gardens," said Joseph.

"If you like, but I hate animals, with their thick furry foreheads, and moochy caged ways."

"There are monks too," suggested Joseph with sympathy.

"All right, we'll peek at the little monks. Funny," he continued,
partly to himself, "how the monkeys obviously recognise that we
are another sort of ape. But with us, there's a shape, here's a
shape, everywhere a shape; and nothing but a strange coincidence,
a bizarre collusion of Nature and Irony. Then, their pure stupidity
might have taught us we're animals; look at us, smells, diet, love,

188

fighting, defecation, the same. We could invent God in our image, but not animals. Very dull indeed, our respected ancestors. You might say the mind of man has only just begun to blink up out of the primeval ooze; he has no more mind than that clod, or that century plant there, slow blighter. The same as a century plant. For years and years, four generations, he laps up sun, rain, air, juices; grows a big stalk, looks important, and then puts out a flower once in a hundred years. What happens? A marvel: everyone runs to look at it. Whereas the rose that flowers four times a year gets no applause. When we get a bright idea once in a century, how we applaud ourselves. With much ach-and-krach and hitting each other on the head we fall, after thousands of years, below the ant, who works in pure Communism. And for that we consider ourselves the dandy of creation; something with a soul. Of course, what else could explain such remarkable achievements, but the Intangible and the Unknowable?"

"You would say," said Joseph cautiously, "that a monkey is a sort of imitation of men in nature; a freak, like the mandragore root."

"I'll get you a book on Darwin's theory," said Baruch.

"He rejoined the Church at the end and said that all he had done had been a mistake," remarked Joseph doggedly.

Baruch looked at him intently.

"Funny; you have such a clear mind. You wouldn't say that if you knew anything about it. I trust in your clear mind."

Joseph kicked the pebbles on the path. Blarney.

They saw a man, a familiar figure, throwing bits of bread to the black swans. It was Withers.

"Hurro, Tom!" cried Baruch joyously.

"Lo!"

"Not grouchy at present?"

"No fear. You must think I've got a rotten temper. I have, but I've been sitting half an hour in the sun, there, out of the wind. The sailing-boats look like bonnets bowling along the water, from there. It makes even the old girls sitting, palsied, acid, disappointed, unresigned to old age, it makes even them sweet-tempered. One's been entertaining me with the history of her life, to amuse me because I looked lonely, she said. After all, compared with her, my troubles sound like an attack of the jim-jams, that's all. They have to pay rent, too, after all, and they have to eat, and dress means more to them than to us, and if they don't get a boy every one calls them an old maid: and if they go astray, wow! what ructions! That old girl looks strong and fat, but she thinks of nothing all day long but that she is an old maid, with no one to care for her, no one to leave her money to buy her quarters of tea, no grandchildren to come and look at her tombstone. She can't sleep at night for thinking of it. The old don't sleep, anyhow. She's ashamed, she told me, she never had one man. She's sorry she didn't take a man off the streets, a truck-driver, anybody; can you imagine it? Well, it put me in a better humour; it's terribly funny. And you feel, what a breed! Who stops them from breaking loose? There's no actual law; and if they all got up on their hindlegs and broke loose together — he-he, Lysistrata reversed. It's their own fault, after all: enterprise bred out of them since the wigwam, I suppose. Well, I don't give a damn, it's not my business; but it gives me the pip. Men and women, the world's yellow and a pack of beggars. I reckon we need discipline. It must have been better in the martial ages. There weren't too many people either, they got killed off. And the women had several husbands. Ought to be like that now. They wouldn't cackle so much."

"Gay and gallant as usual," cried Baruch.

"A marriage in the family," said Withers, turning and walking with them; "Effie's marrying her Dave, from what I hear. Good thing too. Wonder the boss hasn't gone bust a hundred times already. I'm feeling rather more bouncing myself. Dave'll probably make a go of it. He's going to run the business, you know. He's put up some money. The bank has taken his guarantees and Montagu's. I've learned a thing or two. Montagu and I went over it last night (when you came in, Baguenault). I'm keeping my eye on that bounder just for the good of the family."

"Thanks," said Baruch drily.

"Montagu, a skunk, dyed in the wool, tipped the bank off — he knows the manager personally — that Chamberlain was not good for his overdraft. Chamberlain was crying this morning, after you left. 'But what's a bank for but to give you credit when you're stuck? A man don't want it when he's in the funds.' 'They've kept on extending it, Greg says loftily: 'but I'll try to persuade the manager, if you'll hand over all the books and let me see what can be done.' 'Gladly, old man,' and he gives him his books, a shameful display. 'Go now, Montie, I'm too hard pressed: luck's against me.' We had him on his knees. He's so ridiculously proud of his little tinpot press; that was our cue."

"What's the game?" put in Joseph.

"We'll be part owners, and the overdraft is extended. Chamberlain's out altogether. I don't know all the details. It's the only way I see of getting my money back. Effie's willing; we spoke to her secretly. Her head's screwed on right. Her mother has a bit of land with a cottage at Blackheath; they go there at Christmastime. Effie'll get her mother to sell it. The money'll go into the business when Dave Jonas and Effie are married, to pay the overdraft, as a wedding present to Dave; besides, they owe it to him, for the car, or at least some of it. Only one consideration, that Chamberlain, that big slob, is eased out. He can look around: he's no good for this business. He can work as foreman if he wants it."

Withers laughed long and softly. "I'm a good manager; they play into my hands."

"The business is his pride," said Baruch mournfully. "What will he do when he finds he's eased out, and by his daughter, son-in-law, wife and two closest friends?"

"Didn't he give me the boot?"

"He's just the sort of man to jump over the Gap."

"He might," said Joseph slowly. His mind travelled to Fisherman's Bay. There two nights ago, when he came home, a rowing-boat was tied to one of the piles of the wharf; in the rowing-boat a tarpaulin covering the body of the Gap's latest victim, a bankrupt shop-keeper.

"He looks back at his life," Withers went on canting, "and says, 'I've always been a good fellow, really good, never done harm to a fly. People have always liked me, I was Grand Master

191

of the Lodge; I had the best credit in town. I can't understand how all this has come on me, how I came to have an overdraft, to sign notes for Montie, to sign notes at the garage, to have this big debt. I don't know how I came to deceive my wife or let my daughter run wild with a young man. It all came on me; but I don't know how.' Touching! 'That's funny,' he continues to me this morning (he was slightly shicker, weeping), 'I was such a good young man. Until twenty-five I never told a lie, touched a drop, or even went with a girl. I was really pure. I went to church twice on Sundays and used to take the Sunday School out into the fields, fields we call them, and tell them stories in "God's own tabernacle", I used to tell them. Funny, I always loved Nature and my fellow-man. I'm weak, not bad,' said he. God, I had to keep blowing my nose into my handkerchief to keep from laughing at him : but I was irritated too. I could have brought my fist down on his red tear-bleary face."

"You must be sorry for him," said Baruch. "He's not a bad friend to you, apart from the fact that he absorbs cash like dry-dust water. But you knew that."

"But don't you see? If I'd had my own money in my pocket, I could have gone shares with Jonas on a proper basis. Now I'm practically a slave. They have me in a vice. I can't move. If it weren't for me, seven years ago he would have been ruined, the customers would have thrown back every bit of work. The business is mine; my blood's been poured into it. I've run all round the town, I've managed everything. It was me got the new press out here on credit, and got it through the Customs. I tell you, it's my business, practically speaking, and now to see it whistled into Montie's pocket, my own business! I always expected to own it. I would have married Effie, if she hadn't got tied up with Jonas, but I'm a stinker myself, and can't foist on a young girl a chap that's likely to see the blue devils any night. Rotten luck. Always defeated, always defeated, with my brains! I'm the smartest man around there. No wonder I'm fuddled half the time. I wish I'd been some imbecile old woman who didn't know an overdraft from a hole in the ground. Their idiocies. Men have a tough life. All fighting, and at the end nothing." He looked sourly at a young woman trailing languidly in front of them. "Lot of fowls. I would have married Effie: she's a nice kid, but loose like them all. I know she's been the mistress of three men at least. And all that fancy business. She'll stick at nothing. Lively."

"We should have struck long ago," said Baruch regretfully.

"No, I don't strike. I want to run things my own way. I'm not a whining underdog, I want to be manager, I want my money. I'll make my own way or not at all."

"Well, our relations are stereotyped," concluded Baruch drily. "This identical situation occurs in hundreds of small shops, because we're not organised. You're too good to strike, you want to run other workers. Joseph's priest won't let him strike. You're intriguing with a man you know to be a pig, Montagu; I'm counting on getting away to America. That's the great secret: how does a small minority oppress a large majority? — we count on making a getaway. We don't realise our whole life is bound up with a million others: we're all individuals. We believe in God, luck, astrology."

"Aw, don't begin that," said Withers bitterly. "I'm not a social type, true. I don't give a damn about my fellow-workers. To begin with, I don't want to be like them, or live in a commonwealth with them, or vote with them, or argue with them about some idiotic politics or Socialist theory. It gives me a pain in the neck. And I don't want them to worry about me. I like to be alone and I want to die alone; no comrades for me, thanks. And I'm not going to sign on with a lot of hot-headed fanatics who want to upset everything, out of jealousy, because their brains aren't good enough to get them on. Nothing but 'the State'; the State should do everything, feed them, their women, their kids. I'm a man. I want to fight my own battles. But there's another reason: I'd better tell the truth, or you'll be after me: I'm not so heroic; it's not that. I just don't want to fight, I just don't want to. I've had too much trouble. I don't want any more, with going to arbitration, or with rioting, or with strikes. I want rest; I want to make a bit of dough and sock it away so that I'll have a plug to chew when I'm old and sour. I'm no pioneer or working-class martyr. All that makes me sick besides. They're all on the make, or so badly

O

off they couldn't be worse off in gaol: so they get into gaol. And I keep a level head, too. I don't run after the first demagogue who gets up on a soap-box and shouts, 'Liberty, Equality!' It's a lie He knows as well as you and me that there isn't any. Look at Joseph; with all the equality and liberty in the world, he wouldn't get on as well as you, Baruch. Nah, you can't change human nature, or differences in brain, or cunning. Then I like to think for myself. Your Socialist Parties have credos like the Churches; as for the Communist Party, I'm dashed if I'm going to spend my life at a party's beck and call, doused by a secret conclave of Doges, taken down by some little duffer of a secretary who only wants to get, by making himself big in the eyes of a few mahogany-heads, a position he couldn't get by hard work, and who's only anxious to get a soft Government job under his particular type of Government. Certainly, turn the old ones out and put the new ones in. Smart, that is. Nah, nah; leave me alone. Besides, I could join your things, but I'm not a hero; if they clubbed me on the napper, I'd yell for mercy straight away so that I could go back to my natural element crooking my elbow at the corner pub. If they started to torture me I'd split on the whole gang and anyone else who came into my mind. It's a fine show, your revolution. After all, own up: you only stick up for it because you know you'd be somebody in a revolution, you have the capacity for demagogy. As if the workers haven't enough trouble paying the rent, without getting themselves into trouble with the police and bosses, getting locked out. There's plenty of unemployment; they can always find scabs. Look at the wharves now; swarming with scabs. They'll all scab in time, and your fine Folliots don't live too hard, do they? And I bet you'll be different when you get a nice pozzy with Farmer. You can't change human nature: you'll always have jealousy, squabbling, and greed."

"There are other traits in human nature," said Baruch. "As you know yourself, your arguments do not shine by their originality, but I'm not going to fight with you now. It's too ridiculous."

"Yes, leave me alone," agreed Withers. "If you don't want me to get narked and nurse my grudge all the afternoon. You know me, Baruch, I'm not meat for your fry. You don't take me in."

"All right, all right. Let's be getting along, it's nearly two-thirty."

"When you get older, you'll know the world better. The capitalist system is here for a jolly long time yet : you'll see. Wait till you get your job as political secretary, too : you won't be so keen for starting study circles and strikes."

"I understand," said Baruch.

"I'm as good a Socialist as anyone, but I'm practical," said Withers.

There was no reply.

"I'm a good Communist too, if it comes to that, but I use my eyes," Withers finished irritably.

He was silent as they walked back, round the bay, towards the wharf, where a launch, already half-full, awaited them. Baruch looked down at their dusty feet, at Jo's boot curiously fixed with wire — or a hairpin, he decided, after examining it sideways for a moment. Wither's face had hollows, the eyes were sunken, from drinking the night before, the temples were fatigued. The expressions were rather the same, although the physiognomies were so different. The faces were almost lifeless in repose as if after they had been created in their idiosyncrasies, they had been lightly stamped in the same press. There was no sparkle; only an expression of endurance of hard luck. In a moment Jo cried joyfully, "Yes, that's our launch, there's Catherine and Michael!" and Withers, looking up, took on a livelier expression. They all had packages, contributions to the table.

They set out from the shore, the first slow chugs in the shore-water setting their hearts throbbing. The week was over, the week-end began auspiciously. Aft, they sang "Ramona". Baruch laughed with Nell Waters, the friend of Kol Blount, a tall, plump, energetic blonde of twenty-four, an ardent Socialist, a school-teacher, with a clear, sallow complexion, tinged with her night fatigues over exercises, and large brown eyes, ringed with black, due to her weeping, as some said, over the improbability that Kol Blount would ever be more than a stone. Catherine was there, ill and dull, her nose reddened by the wind, her yellow skin shining. She had not washed because she had slept the night before on a shakedown in the Salvation Army shelter. She looked down unmoved at holes in the back of her stockings, at her dusty shoes, her faded flannel dress, too hot for such a day, the stains on her skirt. Only her nails, which were almond-shaped, were polished, but had a little line of dirt since yesterday. She had brought some great thick sandwiches, cut for her by a laundress she knew and had lived with sometimes. This extreme untidiness and roughness came over Catherine once every two or three months. Although she had only to go home to have all the comforts possible, to eat, sleep in a soft bed, bathe, and dress well, to be petted and rest in the garden, she preferred her vagrant life and raffish experience. Some acrid ambition stung her. She was in a fever at these times. It was not safe to speak to her much, she withdrew from argument: she paled perpetually with suffering, her eyes swam in a brilliant liquid, she cried aloud in a tempestuous voice, instead of speaking, or else turned her back on the company, her lips purple.

The tune died in the hiss of spray: sailing-vessels scudded past. From a ferry-boat came the sounds of a band. Conversations were going on all around.

Heinrich Winterbaum raised his voice:

"The great are only great because they glorify vulgar themes."

"Shunt that," responded Withers from the other end of the boat. "You chaps with your low highbrow talk will drive me frantic. I'm going to tell a dirty story to get you into the right frame of mind."

Milt Dean, the paid secretary of philanthropic works, looked severely at Withers and kept on speaking to his girl:

". . . a kind of sentimental involution. He prefers classicism to revolution, due to a crystallised system of inhibitions beginning with timidity as to self-expression in early adolescence . . ."

Winter rested his high-boot along the seat and proclaimed in his harsh, small voice:

"Who told you the English are slaves? Chartism isn't dead. But the movement's too full of prospective Fergus O'Connors. Lenin said the revolutionary movement was unpredictable in England; the English dock-workers were the first to strike to prevent arms being carried to the White Russians. The English are free, they are a free people. We are the sons of free men, a very great race: and their economic understanding is not matched by any other people. Adam Smith himself said, 'The real price of all wealth is labour.' "

Baruch began shouting joyously, "He also said in the same chapter, The real price of wealth is corn, gold and a healthy day's work. That that poor bastard ever became famous shows that few people could read or write in his day . . ."

Milt Dean kept on severely droning, ". . . in juvenescence man only perceives one vital principle in himself . . ."

They laughed, clattered and shouted each other down like a lot of cormorants quacking as they plane over the water for fish, talking on a rock while they dry their wings.

They disembarked in some pleasure-grounds up the Lane Cove River. Heinrich took their photographs as they hung round an uprooted tree. The sun set later on in a pomegranate sky; the smooth narrow river was like cloth of gold. They made tea and ate fish just caught in the river by some peaceful members of the party. When dark came rapidly, as it does in those latitudes, the owner of the boat lighted lanterns along the roof and they sat in the dark, feeling the breezes, listening to the creaking of wood and the lapping of the shore-water. The breeze went down, the heat increased and the insects of the night flew. Country Night, with her uttering owls and pale surf of meteors, eased their troubles.

Going back in the launch they sang sentimental songs. They chugged between the dark fleets of ships tied up in the strike. A few lights hung among the decks and fell dully on the still dock waters. On one ship, bound for the islands, some savage sailors danced round a brazier placed over the hold, clapping their hands. At the sight of the girls and youths on the launch they cried out, laughing like parrakeets, making obscene signs with their dark thin hands, their vertebrae and ribs standing out in their starved bodies as they rolled and gesticulated. Lascars in dirty rags hung over the high pontoon decks, silent, dark in the dark, only their yellow eyeballs rolling. A thicket of short masts stood up on the starry universe, the hawsers wheezed, the incoming tide clucked on the weed-grown rusting bottoms. A tug puffed beside a small vessel, chains clanked and ironmongery rattled, a man shouted and was seen standing high, in the red light of a lantern, against the deep sky. The vessel was an island trader putting out with scab labour picked up round the wharves. They all looked at it with aversion as if at an unclean thing. Even Withers said slowly:

"By Jingo, when you see that little sneak crawling out, you wonder what they've got inside their hides, the scabs."

Baruch and Catherine laughed in the dark, but Catherine's laugh was impertinent, exasperated.

"A queer lot of men, castaways in a swarming harbour; a ship of the damned."

"I'd like to join them," said a dull voice, "to see what it is like to join a lost ship, to be with the lowest of the low. It would be strange company. Can you imagine them eating together, sleeping together? The berths below teeming with lice, the food stinking ih this weather, rations of rum served out to keep 'em happy till they clear the Heads, and in the back of their heads the idea that when they get paid they're going to clear out at the next port; no responsibilities and absolutely not wanted here: exiles. I wouldn't mind it at that. You know, I'm not too sensitive to moral issues, when I've seen what I've seen. And then it must be a relief to be with a lot of perverse dummies, whose backs aren't always bristling with righteousness."

Michael was speaking. They turned cold faces to Michael, but he was sitting in the shadow aft and they could only make out his form. Catherine cried sharply:

"Suicide would be better. I can understand a person wanting to live alone, but not as a class, or social traitor."

"I have no class," answered Michael. "I am a man alone. I don't know what you are all raving about: it doesn't touch me. You can't shame me."

"Leave him alone," said Withers. "When a man postures there's naught to be done. Listen, blokes and girls: do we take something along with us to Blount's house? We can't expect Mrs Blount to provide for this caravan."

They went out to Annandale, the poor suburb in which the Blounts lived, carrying more packets. Kol Blount sat in the lemon circle of a lamp. His mother had finished clearing away and was washing the dishes in the kitchen. Glasses were set out on the tables with several dozen lemons for lemon-drinks. Mrs Blount came gaily in, complimented each one, called them "Boys!" "Girls!" and tripped happily back to the kitchen, where she had put her darning-bag. By housekeeping and cleaning she had supported Kol since his babyhood, when he had fallen off a table and injured his spine. She had had hopes once or twice that the bachelors she worked for would like her style. She was musical, sang about her work, dressed brightly, with high heels, and cared for them like a mother as she often told them; but the veins in her hands and legs were now badly swollen, and her heart was bad with running up and down stairs. She hoped to open a cheap boarding-house for students and poor teachers, presently.

"I'll let you young folks talk your hearts out," she cried gaily, and they heard her humming tunes from *Floradora* and *The Geisha* to herself in the kitchen. She was not unhappy. She had preserved her son for herself alone, and she always said, with the airs of a young girl, "My son has his mother for a sweetheart." Never wife or mistress would come to disturb her maternal possession. She had been unhappy with her husband, who had left her two years after their marriage; she wished he had been like his son in temperament. "Kol was never interested in women," she told them all happily, and sometimes added, "Nell Waters is like a sister to him: I often wish they had been brother and sister."

Catherine misanthropically went into the kitchen to help Mrs Blount. They heard, in the living-room, the talk rising in spirals, culminating in a clap of argument or laughter; falling. They heard whispering in the stone passage—lovers in the dark, or plotters ready to spring a surprise on the band. Someone appeared at the door. It was Michael, who stood looking reflectively at them, as if he had come there to be alone and not to talk.

"Are you staying to-night?" asked Mrs Blount.

"No, thank you."

"He was here all yesterday and stayed last night," said Mrs Blount to Catherine. "Your brother is wonderful company for Kol. That's a sort of joke. They're not really very gay; just lugubrious company for each other."

"I know," said Catherine.

"What long faces! Go and join the other children," cried Mrs Blount. "You don't want to stay here and hear an old woman's gossip, and I know you don't like darning stockings, Cath."

Catherine went pale; her eyes flashed, she put down the basket she was holding and rose. Mrs Blount did not see her expression, and Michael manoeuvred himself between Mrs Blount and his sister. He followed her out, and said in a low voice:

"What are you flaring up about? You're touchy, I don't know why: it's true, isn't it? You've got holes in both your stockings. If you must be a rebel, you'd do better to go bare-legged."

They were in the stone passage. Catherine wheeled on Michael and struck him furiously on the temple with her fist. She seized his throat with both hands and said in a strangled voice:

"I'll kill you, I'll kill you, you, you . . ." She was demoniacally strong and forced him into the dark corner under the stairs. He collapsed and stayed there cramped, on his haunches, while she ground his head against the wall: her eyes started out of their orbits.

"Don't be a fool, don't be a fool," he kept whispering through his compressed throat.

She let go suddenly and stood back, grinding her teeth, with her hands clenched.

"If you ever dare say such a thing again, I'll kill you."

"You're afraid, or you would have done it then," said Michael coolly. "I don't worry; I've always known you were a bit cracked."

"You dare say that, Michael. Oh, Michael!" She began to cry: she rested her forehead against the staircase and sobbed.

"I always knew it; that's why I loved you," affirmed Michael. "You are not like the rest of the world, you're mad. With you one can be free, one can say anything, nothing is absurd or horrid. I didn't have to expect a trite reproof or cheap witticism as with the others."

She looked at him, trembling.

"Michael, I am terribly unhappy: my heart is bursting, that is why I have to go mad. Anything I do is to avoid the abyss in me; I want to fill it by leaping to death, like the Roman centurion."

"But now, that's changed," answered Michael. "I'm too old, Cath. My youth has gone and I've nothing to keep myself going in maturity. I can't be bothered getting married, having a home, a social circle. I would retire to a monastery or a cave in the desert, which is what I always wanted to do, if it weren't so bloody out of date. If I could I'd join a desperate expedition, one to the North Pole, if I didn't hate the cold (but I don't want to die of congestion), or one to Central Africa, if I weren't afraid of being eaten by a lion. Would you come and get eaten with me?"

"I wasn't joking."

"I'm not."

"You sound pretty silly to me."

"Of course. We've got older and madder, Kate, but along different lines. A long time ago you were really my sister."

"If I could dash my head against the wall, I'd do it; I can't stand all this."

"Why don't you marry some chap, Kate? You like plenty of men. You don't have to stay married; after five years you can hop it."

"No one wants me for a wife, and it's serious with me: I want to be loved and leave of my own accord."

"Well, you see, with me it's different. I wouldn't mind if I never saw another soul in my life, starting from this hour."

"You'd better go in and see Kol Blount. You're easier in your mind when you're with him. I'm going for a walk. I'll see you in a day or two."

Michael started for the kitchen.

"My throat's hurting, I'll get Mrs Blount to give me some liniment and put a rag round it so that they won't see. A nice scandal!" He laughed.

"And I'm going for a walk. You don't expect me to be sorry," she said furiously. The door banged. Someone put his head out of the door.

"Who went?"

"Catherine," called Michael. "She's got the jim-jams: leave her alone."

"I knew she had them all day," said one of the girls.

"Poor Kate! If she would only settle down! She's very artistic, if she'd only settle down, as you say! . . . She's had a lot of experience! . . . Politics is a hard life for a woman! . . . Well, if she liked it, but it's a *pis aller* for *creation*!"

The chorus arose from her friends now sitting on cushions around Kol Blount in his long chair. A very young girl, a kitten, innocent and foolish, related that she liked philanthropic work and had been collecting for some hospital fund.

"There was an old man there with a beard, nice enough. He said, Wait till I go upstairs and get some money. It was beginning to rain and he said, Aren't you getting wet? Eventually, he seduced me inside the door . . ."

A shout of laughter. Some of the young men rolled on the floor clasping their cushions and thumping the floor with them from time to time. The girl looked surprised, thought it a tribute to the humour of the story, and went on:

"Coming back, at the top of the stairs he got 'a bone in his knee'. He fell to the ground, like this, on one knee, and, with his eyes rolling, held his hand out to me, with the money in it. I started to rush upstairs; he struggled up, but slipped near the bottom and upset me on the mat. He had to help me up, but he was furious. He stuck the money in my hand and pushed me out of the door quickly."

The gentle virgin told this without a blush on her Sèvres china face. The boys could not contain their guffaws, some got quite red in the face, others gave a deep guttural note of enjoyment and then fell silent.

"Win, you are a fool," said Kol Blount. "Seduced is something quite different; you mean induced you inside the door."

"Psychological mistake of the first order," cried Milt Dean

delightedly.

"Everyone's absolutely full of mistakes like that, but it's a blessing: you have to let yourself go, otherwise you'd go crazy," opined Fayre Brant, the young university student with whom Milt Dean was in love.

"I think it should be admitted freely in society. I know chaps and girls who play all sorts of love-games quite freely, and they're all artistic; it's good for the free expression of emotion. Some friends of mine belong to a repertory theatre, and in between Ibsen, Barrie, Galsworthy, they amuse themselves in the dressing-room: they have what they call *libido games*. They get frightfully pepped up for their dramatic scenes."

"It's fascinating," said the young girl, "simply fascinating. Do you mean to say it really develops the artistic instinct?"

"Aw, haw haw," began one of the young men, "some of the chaps were turned out of their lodgings in the middle of the night, in the Glebe, you know, old Ma Brown's place. She's a bit off her nut, because her husband died when she was thirty, a year after they were married. She likes to take in young bachelors, but she goes mad if they have any girls in, and she writes letters every week to the Dean. Last week, in the middle of the night she thought she heard cries, thumpings, dancings backwards and forwards over the floor in all the rooms. She got up furious, and found the chaps all asleep as it happened. Only a window was open, as one of the chaps was out on the spree and hadn't come back. She turned them all out into the street in the middle of the night. The chaps all went to the Dean and told him she has hallucinations, so they're having her sent to an asylum."

"Next door to my place," began one of the older girls, in a low, thrilling voice, "is a satyr . . ."

"The devil take you all," cried Kol Blount. "Somebody make the lemon-drinks. Bring the lemons here, and if anybody starts out on the subject again he'll get lemon in his eye."

"Don't be a nark," said a young boy, a law student, with rosy cheeks and chestnut hair, the same Joseph had seen in Phillip Street, and whose name he did not know. "Don't be a grandmother! Listen, I had an adventure. A girl. She has a lover; he's a shipping magnate and he keeps her, but now he's in Melbourne for a month. I found her crying in the park because her father's gone bankrupt. She wants to marry the shipping magnate but she's too poor. She told me I'm the only one she's ever lived with except the shipping magnate. And her mother, father, two sisters and brother know all about it: would you believe that? I tell you the world's not the same any more, parents are getting more liberal."

"I hope she leaves you your shirt," said Kol Blount drily.

"What, you don't believe it?"

"What do you take me for?"

The law student looked crestfallen. "It's not possible; she's so honest."

"In one of the Scandinavian countries," submitted a young law student interested in sociology, "they suggested having State fathers. I think women need it."

"It would be a good idea," said Withers, interested. "Like that old woman I met in the park."

"You're very kind to women," remarked the girl who had been snubbed on the satyr story, primly.

"Let's have a debate on it, impromptu," put in the chestnut-haired youth excitedly. "I'd love to hear the girls debate a thing like that. You know, they never really discuss their own affairs; you never know what they're thinking."

"You must admit that women are really becoming free," said Milt Dean in his dry voice. "Our mothers would never have even listened to such things."

"What rot, Milt," cried a girl. "The Victorian girl in eighteen yards of flounces represented a tiny section of middle-class society in a tiny couple of decades. The great mass of women never knew these post-Stephenson and pre-Ford notions."

"What I detest about your mixed parties, Kol," said Michael, "is this man-woman discussion which goes on for ever. Turn 'em out."

"It's eternal," said the satyr girl drearily, turning her too-thin face to Michael, "the eternal man-woman question, the eternal struggle."

"There are no women," interposed Baruch flatly. "There are only dependent and exploited classes, of which women make one. The peculiarities are imposed on them to keep them in order. They are told from the cradle to the grave, You are a female and not altogether there, socially and politically : your brain is good but not too good, none of your race was ever a star, except in the theatre. And they believe it. We all believe these great social dogmas."

"Where would be feminine charm?" said Milt Dean, his dark cheek mantling with passion. "I don't want to marry some big husky who shouts orders to wharfingers six hours a day. I want a woman who waits for me at home, who knows how to arrange knick-knacks, who gives me children and wants to bring them up for me, to teach them at her knee, to look after me in sickness, to close my eyes in death."

His sweetheart looked a little embarrassed and retired into the shade, while there were shouts of "Mediaeval! Tyrant! Patriarch! Marry a children's nurse then!" The satyr girl said softly :

"You are right, Milt, that's what most women want to do." She had been in love with Milt secretly for years.

"I don't care for equal rights, for political powers, for legislation," said Kol Blount sternly from his chair. "A person should be free, entirely, absolutely free. If they must fight to settle their rights, let them fight, but let no man have power over another. If they work together, let them work together in mutual understanding with common profit; but let there be no power. I hate power; it is the destroyer of the soul and mind. It produces all those crooked, sick and wretched people I see around me."

"Do you mean us too?"

"You, too. Then you don't have to live in these forced confrères, of family, school, society, union, government, nation. You have your own mate, or mates; you assort yourselves, not according to class, that detestable and degrading economic prison, but according to the temperament, will and talents. What beauty in life? Life would have a curious taste, even at its lowest, perhaps a little dull, but satisfying, like drinking your own tears."

"A vegetable or mineral philosophy," remarked one; "not for creatures with legs and fists."

"It is the natural one, suitable for inanimate things as well as for us. Inanimate! I am that, and I should be outside all human laws and restrictions. Imagine my misery. To see your fatal errors and degraded manners and have to live among you, have to carry you in my breast like a diseased heart. Perhaps that is why, by the bitter irony of bitter fate, I am as I am. I could do too much harm, I could lead you all back to anarchy; look at me : shackled, tied, garroted. I can't see free people (there must be some), I can't see where to start, in which country, climate, nation. I only live with a lot of slaves and pigs of Circe. You live like niggers, glad of your bonds, and licking the hand that whips you and singing to the Lord to make you meek. God, I can't stand it any more—year after year. From being a baby to being a schoolboy, from schoolboy to manhood, and always sitting here fermenting thoughts, and never able to stir. I say aloud in the middle of the night, Free me, free me, force that sometimes comes to paralysed limbs, to the numb, weak, dying. I pray for the house to be burned down in the night so that I can get frightened and get up out of my chair and run. I would go away a long way, as far as possible from this room, and this street and its sounds, of carts and postman and trees and school-children."

"I would carry you on my back," said Michael in a low voice, with tears in his eyes.

"Michael would go," said one of the girls with a disagreeable grimace of satire : "He just said he'd be a scab. It was all we could do to stop him jumping overboard the launch and swimming away with the Fiji islanders!"

"I can understand it," said Kol Blount bitterly. He shut his eyes and pressed his hands to his face. Michael sat as if he had not heard these words. Presently he got up and went into the passage, where he sat on the steps biting his nails. One of the girls busied herself with the supper, and presently they were all chewing and drinking. Michael listened for Blount's voice but did not hear it. He returned to the door, and saw Blount starting at him, waiting for him to come back.

206

"I thought you had gone out," said Blount.

They had turned the light out and lighted a candle on the roll-top desk, relic of Kol's father. It fell on the black headless venus which dominated the room. Some were crooning sea-chanties, some revolutionary songs. The young men and women had drawn closer together in twos and threes. Some people left. Michael, who had eaten some pickle and nut sandwiches, an invention of Mrs Blount, began to have gripes; he was in every sense soured and upset. They heard him vomiting outside in the passage. When he came back Kol's face was hidden under his hand. The guests teased him:

". . . ill-digested theories of the evening . . ."

"At least I don't ingurgitate it again like some young puppies. . . . ."

Kol's face came back to him and rested on him, blank, melancholy, curious. Baruch left now, taking sleepy Jo with him, to bunk with him for the night. Among the scattered guests, looking at books, talking fitfully in the corners of the room, Michael made his way to Kol Blount and said:

"I won't come and see you again on these evenings. It doesn't suit me: I can't stand the discussions, so many voices. I have a feeling like lead behind my ears and in my temples."

"Go upstairs and sleep!"

"I never sleep here," answered Michael, pacing restlessly up and down behind Kol's chair and round and round, fiddling with the tassels on the window-curtain, kicking against the footrest of Kol's chair. "I never sleep any more. I have such bad dreams."

"What dreams?"

"Nothing special to relate; my father lying in a pool of blood, long black spectres coming in through the crack of the door, forests of serpents, dismal rivers flowing without end, as in the 'Sons of Clovis', at the Art Gallery."

He stood looking down at Kol. Kol raised his eyes to Michael, smiling faintly, anxiously. An old-fashioned picture of the sons of Clovis, hamstrung, deathly pale, floating bound on a barge down a ghastly grey river, had been taken by them for a picture of themselves. Michael scratched at the plush of the arm-rest.

"I didn't want to stay; I only stayed to please you. I had a rotten evening. You must like it, for all your cynical air. They swarm round you."

"Out of pity and aimlessness."

"They pity you and despise me; a nice situation."

Jessica, the satyr girl, seeing Milt Dean with his arm round his sweetheart's waist, came up and said with brave coquetry:

"Michael, take me home, will you? It will be good for you: you are in the dumps, and you're never gallant. I'll initiate you into good manners; you needn't be afraid of me. Come along."

"No, I won't," said Michael, frowning. "I don't know if I'm going home, and anyhow I'm not going with anyone. I need a long walk; I'm going out of my mind with this buzz round me."

Suddenly Catherine appeared in the passage, coming from the kitchen. She made a startling figure at the door, pale, breathless, her hair in wisps, her eyes blazing.

"Michael, you've got to come home with me. A man followed me in the street. I got out my hatpin and held it ready and stood under a lamp and he was afraid; but I'm nervy, I don't want to go out alone again. And I want you to come home with me."

"A pity you women don't wear breeches, then you wouldn't be followed: you've earned them," said Michael. "I'm not going home and I don't care if you don't. You seem to be able to pass your nights pretty well nearly anywhere: you've got lots of friends. Why didn't you go with the Folliots half an hour ago? I'm a Timon to-night, I am not obliging anybody. I've obliged too many people too long. I'm going on the spree, if I haven't lost the art. I'll see if I can pick up some whores and some booze, anything to wash out the flavour of this."

"Good-bye," said Kol Blount. "You'd better go, if you feel like that. Send me a note when you have slept it off."

"I may not sleep it off."

"Don't be so tragic," said Catherine sharply. "It doesn't suit you to be a ham actor. You've got stomach-ache or something of the sort; I know you." She smiled cheerfully at him to get a smile out of him. "You have a poetic temperament, Michael!"

"Thanks for the general good opinion," answered Michael,

"but none of you will see me for a long time from to-night. I'm going to look for something I lost."

"Where did you lose it?"

"On the seashore. When I was a little boy."

"What was it?"

"The notion that life was worth living."

"Aw, cheer up; don't be so tragic," said the few guests left, laughing and raising their heads to look Michael over.

Michael said, "I was a serious rum little cove——"

"Chekhov . . ." supplemented one of the hearers, smirking at his neighbours.

Michael continued, biting his lip:

". . . I had plenty of fun running round the beach, going fishing with the fishermen, but I didn't like school, because I couldn't take a joke and schoolboys are cruel little blighters. I used to row over in a dinghy to talk with the night-watchman on the dredger called the *Cormorant* that always tied up in Fisherman's Bay. The old chap's name was Watson, and he used to give me nips of brandy and ask me if I had any sisters. I told him I had a nice sister, Catherine. He asked me, What sort of eyes has she, what sort of hair? I thought about it then for the first time: I told him, Black eyes, long black hair and her eyebrows meet right across the front. He said, I'd like you to bring your sister to see me, and every night after he asked about my sister. He was very lonely, sitting on deck smoking, his safety lantern swinging on the railings, the tide lapping round the flat-bottomed dredger, waiting for me and my sister to come. But I never wanted to take Catherine. I was hurt he wanted to see her so much and bothered me about her. Then I realised I wasn't the only person in the world. Catherine was rather a Tartar at home and wasn't much in favour with our parents; she was a tomboy and much more athletic than me. Things became dull for me after I began to grow up. The only times I remember that I really enjoyed were the days we were taken in to see the Eight Hours' Day procession. They always have fine weather for Eight Hours' Day. And I used to love the bakers' floats especially, with their giant loaves; they seemed to come straight out of a land of food, sun and flowers in their aprons and caps. I always wanted to be a baker. Upon my soul, I should have been a baker. A baker feeds the hungry, he deals likewise in the symbols of life and contentment. What I imagined was a yearning for spiritual things, later on, was a yearning to knead dough and smell new-baked bread and hot ovens, to smell yeast and paraffin, to be respected and respect myself because the housewives respected me. But I had to be something clerical, a teacher, clerk, scholar, student, something soft-handed, at any rate."

"In teaching you get corns whacking the lads," said a young male teacher. "It's not lily handed, and you get corns elsewhere getting more kicks than ha'pence."

"To be continued in our next . . ." said Withers. "You weren't cut out to be a humorist, or Scheherazade, at any rate; you escaped those two lily-handed fates. Say, Michael, cut out the wailing. Come and we'll guzzle lemonade in some Greek joint. There's no beer to be had at this hour of night, and naturally Kol doesn't think of laying it in."

"Right-o," agreed Michael. "And I'm not coming back. Good-bye, all; we'll meet in a better world."

He was laughing now continually. Catherine looked at Kol Blount, raised her eyebrows, and said under her breath to Kol:

"There's nothing the matter, it's just nerves; nothing will happen to him. Don't worry."

"Ah, you know me, don't you, Kate?" said Michael, overhearing and looking at them sidelong. "Very well, and you've a woman's instinct, and I'm a transparent beggar anyhow, without any guiding principle, easy to read. Kol can manage me, you can read me. Why not? It's no harm; it's no impediment in my slipshod slide to a sloppy end. It makes no difference to some kinds of men."

He was silent a moment, knitting his fingers and getting paler. They began to look away from him indifferently and talk amongst themselves. Michael continued violently, to their astonishment:

"But there are some things which are too much, said at the wrong time of day. At the fatal moment a cast match can let off the train and blow up the magazine. I'm a river of tears inside,

210

from the top of my head to the soles of my feet. I can hardly say why—it's misery, misery. The world is rotten; if you amuse yourselves, it's because you are too dull to know what's going on under your noses. You giggle and flirt; it's not for me. I want to die. I'm too tired to make believe life's worth living any more. If I were a baker or shoemaker, it would be different, but now I couldn't be, I'd get bored; I'd want to be walking round with a lay preacher's air, talking pseudo-Socialism and questionable humanities."

"C'm on," said Withers, taking his arm.

Michael went and stood beside Kol Blount's chair, taking his limp hand in his:

"Good-bye, dear Kol," said Michael earnestly.

Everyone stared; some began to smile.

Kol looked at him with compassion, with inquietude. Catherine stood by, all still in the poor light, a sketch of a woman, but dramatically poised, her mouth half-open, checked by surprise. Michael nodded to her and moved away, ignoring the people he had to step over to get to the door.

"Michael," said Blount in the silence, "come here!"

"What?"

"Michael, think of me! What would I be without you?" He spoke in a bantering tone, but he looked strained.

"I think of you," said Michael. "If it had not been for you, I would have gone before this."

"Where are you going?" said Catherine sharply.

"Good-bye, Blount!"

Kol Blount put his hand on his heart, looked fixedly at Michael and uttered no sound. Withers jammed on his hat and made for the door. At the gate Catherine caught up with them.

"Michael, what's the matter? Are you ill? Where are you going at this time of night? Tom, you see he's in no state to go with you. I wish you'd take him home and put him to bed."

"He doesn't want you with him," said Withers; "he has too many goddamned mentors. Let him go on the razzle-dazzle for a day or two. Struth, a man needs it."

"Stop butting in, Kate, you're a nuisance," said Michael.

She grabbed his arm.

"Listen to me! Don't act the goat. Wake up, you're acting as if you're asleep. What's the matter? You haven't taken drugs, have you? You seem to be out of your wits. I've been thinking about you all the evening. No man followed me, that was the other evening. I came back here solely because I was worried to death, seeing the way you've been behaving."

"If I'm out of my wits, they're poor wits and I'm brighter without them. If anyone picks them up on the pavement he'll take them for Chinese puzzles, not wits: so I'm out of wits, and in some sense. Tatterdemalion looks better naked. Good-bye; never mind where I'm going. Withers doesn't know either. You don't have to follow me. I don't want it, and if you do follow me, I'll lead you a nice chase and drop you. You're a girl after all, there are some places where you can't go, thank God."

"I'd go anywhere to look after you at present."

"I'd like you better if you weren't always the hero-woman," said Michael with cruel intent. Michael smiled at Mrs Blount, who had come to the gate. "Good-bye, sweetheart; if I don't see you soon, it's not because I don't appreciate your nut and pickle sandwiches and your welcome." She gurgled with pleasure.

"What the deuce is all this leave-taking?" shouted Kol Blount from the window, where he had been pushed by a guest. "Is he going on a liner in the morning? You women see a man off even when he's only going to the pub. You like it, it's your traditional right. Come in here, Mother, and Kate, you come in."

"That's it," called Michael, "I'm going where there ain't no traditional rights, or sociology. Good-bye, and my respects to the Seven Deadly Instincts and the Thirty-nine Acquired Characteristics."

He ran down the whitened stone steps and out through the wicket, laughing sillily, with Withers after him. They went down the street rapidly, slapping each other on the back and guffawing. Catherine was as white as the steps. She didn't return to the room, but looked down the street after Michael.

"Don't follow him," said Mrs Blount. "When a young man goes nutty, you've got to let him go. But take my tip, he'd be better if he were married and settled down. All that stuff he talks only means one thing, he needs the responsibility of a wife and kiddies. He'd make a lovely father."

"I suppose so," answered Catherine, "but it's hard and he's rather queer."

"You're both very queer," responded Mrs Blount, laughing fondly.

Catherine, cut to the heart, said:

"He's never been unkind to me before these last few months."

"He didn't like your friendship with—er—er—your friend, you know, dear! Brothers are so foolish; they look after their sisters like little girls."

"You're a nice woman but an idiot," said Catherine. "At any rate, good-bye. I won't go home. He won't, certainly, and I can't go and lie in a comfortable bed, with mother bringing hot soup to make sure I sleep, while Michael's gadding in all sorts of corners."

"Sleep here!"

"No, rather in the park!" She laughed in her high voice and banged the gate. Her footsteps resounded in the silent street.

But Catherine was wrong. Michael left Withers at the railway station and went straight home and went to bed. His mother came in several times during the night with shaded lamp to be sure he was still there. Balm was laid on her heart at each sight of his face. She thought:

"It's so unusual; perhaps at last he's come home, my wandering boy." She went back to bed murmuring to herself, with tears clotting the ragged lashes of her old eyes. "So much trouble," she whispered to herself, as she lay awake through the night, "a good boy, all the same."

But Catherine walked by street, lane, lamp-post, policeman, picket fence, suburban church, dark shut factory and green grave-yard, passing through several sleeping suburbs until she had lost herself. Her heavy-soled flat shoes clapped on the asphalt under dead windows and closed doors. She had come out without money, having quitted her job in the laundry the day before without being paid. She had spent her last penny on the fare at

213

the launch-picnic and had counted on having Michael take her home or lend her something. She got her bearings at last, and after walking another half-hour came to a shelter in a very poor section, where benches were provided, on which one can sit, stand, lie, or do anything one wishes. There was a dirty lavatory on a landing, a wash-basin, and a bench with a gas-ring on which the vagrant women there could cook anything they liked, if they had anything to cook. In the morning they could work for the charitable institution and thus earn their breakfast; there was no reason for them to starve. Lying on the bench, at rest, because with the lowest and lost, with the degraded, unambitious and debauched, Catherine reviewed her life. But there is no need to go over all that, with her. It had always been the same, though the scenery had been different. She remembered a strange scene she had seen from Baruch's window the evening she had been there. A Chinaman was rolling in the dirt of the backyard with a filthily-dressed middle-aged woman. Was it this afternoon she had seen the same woman walking in the street down by the quays, accompanied by a sailor, and carrying a black bag, a bottle of milk, a bottle of beer, and with a large, round maternal belly? Thinking of this, tears began to course down Catherine's face and she murmured to herself:

"In the lowest places I find my answers: I've fought all my life for male objectives in men's terms. I am neither man nor woman, rich nor poor, elegant nor worker, philistine nor artist. That's why I fight so hard and suffer so much and get nowhere. And how vain ambition seems when you look at it, unambitious." She looked round the room, lighted by moonlight filtering through a faint mist, and saw strange attitudes, a large hip bulging through black clothing, a bag, a bonneted head, a cadaverous young face with disordered hair. A baby's faint wail began and one of the women rose. She sat directly between Catherine and the window. Catherine saw her bent head, straggling hair and full blouse. She gave her breast, grey in the gloom, to the crying infant. The women stirred and protested at the noise, which ceased again. Catherine sat up on her bench and looked at the young woman, until she had finished.

214

8 🐟

Michael recalls his adventures, lets out a secret or two,
goes to church, is advised to marry, visits his relatives, sees
the early-morning fishing in Fisherman's Bay, and
brings the chapter solemnly to an end.

IT WAS SUNDAY, his mother's favourite day; she had been up since five o'clock pottering in the garden. Convinced that Michael had come back to the fold, she smiled at him all through breakfast and began to congratulate him on being home again. The Mayor had given her a hint that week about the dangers of subversive company, and the iniquity of the striking seamen. Michael was known to frequent the Folliots', prominent in the strike. Mrs Baguenault took her son into the garden, and when they reached the well, said:

"Are you better now, Michael, more settled?"

"It seems so, sensibly improved, there is no comparison. When I first came home from France, I was at odds with everyone: even last night, I was with a crowd of young frauds, frothing at the mouth with heavy sententiousness and sensuality. I realised that I could get nowhere with them. So I came home. Perhaps you can get me out of a mess, Mother?"

"Michael dear, Mother will help you: you're a big man, aren't you? but only my little poppet to me. Poppet, mother could die of joy to see you here again, and not with that worried face you usually have."

"Well, don't die. What am I going to do?"

"My baby! Well, perhaps if you would do something at home a little while each day in the daytime. If the Returned Soldiers' League can't do much, you can always have preference over other men by saying you've been to the front and been wounded.

There's the Education Department—they're glad to get returned soldiers."

"H'm! with my record; the brutes crawl all over me."

"I don't worry about your future: you'll get on. Don't you remember, Poppet, how you were always studying and drawing too? You used to do beautiful designs, too. You remember the time you went to the Technical College for a competive entrance examination: you all had to draw a fret pattern, and yours was the best? There are lots of things you can do. Oh dear, I always used to say to Father, when he wanted you to go out and play football, Don't worry Michael, he is immersed in his books." She looked brightly and amorously up into his eyes and rubbed her cheek against his sleeve. "Such a rough sleeve: my little Poppet used to wear velvet suits, think of that!"

Michael frowned pettishly at the baby-name. "For the love of Mike, that's myself, don't call me Poppet: I'll brain you, Mother, if you do. But I remember the rest. Well, what suggestions have you, Mother?"

"The girls are both going to America to study. And Catherine . . ." she sighed. "But if you are with us Father and I could be at rest in our old age, even if everything doesn't go well and we aren't able to leave you much money. You know, Father lost a great deal in this amusement pier company. You could live with us and look after the financial end, the mortgages, the rents, and so on. Later, when you feel like it, you could find a nice quiet girl, a home girl, and get married. Father and I have been looking over the girls we know. There's Pauline, Mrs Astrid's girl; she's young yet, but you wouldn't get married for a couple of years. There's no hurry about that. But your father is not a young man. We were talking about you last night. You can imagine that it seemed like a message from God when you came home unexpectedly. I said to Father, God has answered us. Then, we don't insist, of course. If you have some girl in mind, a good woman who would make you a good wife, bring her home, dear, and you can settle down right away. You could stay with us. Father and I would give you the top floor, or half of it, and have a wall put in. It would warm my old heart. A new daughter. I am an old woman. I may die any day; I would like to hold my grandchild on my knee."

"Well, I don't want a kid. Why should I bring a kid into the world to live through sixty years of troubles, when he can avoid it all and never know what he's missed?"

"That's childish, Michael. You were always so insensitive to others' feelings when a boy, although sensitive in other respects. At any rate, a man like you wants a good wife to settle him, to soften him."

"Bad women do it quick enough."

"What's that I hear?"

"Mother, be a realist. Don't try to satisfy your grandmotherly cravings through me, I don't want it. I am making my way slowly out of a mess. I was never too strong in the upper storey; they muddled me completely on the other side. You know one lung is baddish, and I am restless and feverish because of it. Leave me alone, there's a good girl; you always want to settle people. It's so stupid. And you have always been so unquiet about me, fluttering about me like an anxious hen. Even when you say nothing I know you are sitting there, fearing, hoping, brooding on things I know nothing of, talking to yourself in your bedroom and kitchen. It's too queer, it's upsetting. Women when they get old are frightening—no wonder men believed in witches. Even a young woman like Cath—if a young woman curses a man or hates him, she does it like a witch and her face is drawn like a harpy's: there is something in their sharp, transparent faces and bright eyes: queer breed—bad company for a man. . . . Listen . . . did you love my father?"

"Michael, what makes you ask such a thing?"

"When I was a child you used to brood over me and suddenly clasp me to your breasts. It embarrassed me to feel the soft round flesh inside your blouse, it quite turned my stomach. I wanted to run away from you. But you did it so, crying sometimes, that I once or twice knew something was wrong. And I knew Jimmie Halland was adopted and his adoptive mother mushed over him because she was barren. I thought it must be that, but couldn't make it out."

She got out her handkerchief and wiped her eyes.

"Don't cry, Mother, please, please."

He left her and began walking up and down in the back garden. She went slowly, with her slight stoop, to the veranda, and looked at him bitterly: "A hard boy."

He knew her comment, having often heard it, and bit his lip. It was his habit to get momently dark or gay. He came to the steps of the veranda where she sat, and stood half in the red and blue light shot through a coloured-glass window, with his eyes cast down, fretting the boards with his boot-toe. He laughed; and became sombre again.

"Your family were a lousy lot, never knew their own minds; that's what's the matter with me. Look at Grandfather trotting round the world with a change of socks in a rucksack, leaving his wife every third spring to go prospecting, or just globe-trotting—feather-brained, unreliable: what did he get out of it all? Nothing; but he thought himself no end of a character. And look at the others, running about to prayer-meeting with their noses in the air, showing the whites of their eyes and dressed in black, getting their wives with child with their hats on their heads and a prayer book in one hand. And the last generation, your brother a holy jo, preaching and praying, and the distant relative who is a philosopher never heard of outside his university town— an idealist, peuh! In general, idealists—you don't know what that means: it means having enough money to pay the baker without having to earn it, and—no sense of touch, like me."

"If you could only get a good, steady job, Michael dear, and stick to it, you would be happy. You soon get into the way of working regular hours; there is happiness in routine. All these ideas don't mean anything, they only mean you're nervous and worried because you have nothing to think of and think all day of your troubles. I am a woman and know what I'm talking about. And don't sneer at my relatives, please. If they gave their wives many children, it was honest. They believed in God, they supported the State, they paid their bills, they were respected. They wouldn't have understood a man like you who makes his friends in public-houses."

218

Michael guffawed. "Gosh, all you say is so unreal, Mother; where have you lived all your life? In cotton-wool? You don't exist."

"It's all right, don't worry; I exist all right. I've had plenty of troubles . . ."

"Don't tell me about Father's early struggles, and about Catherine's running away from school, etc. I know all that: that doesn't help."

"An honest man earning his daily bread is happy and doesn't worry about things that don't enter his work. Running with journalists and strike-leaders, and immoral riff-raff . . ."

The old lady bridled, looked to see Michael watching the sky dreamily over the fruit trees, nodded her head to herself and once more wiped her eyes. Michael smiled benevolently over her head, passed her his own large handkerchief, and said:

"You want to know about my girls?"

"If it's something you can tell me, Michael."

"No side, Mumma: if you don't listen now, you'll never hear."

An intense curiosity brightened her face. "A son can talk to his mother."

He made an offhand gesture.

"Do you know the fate of an idealist? He has no sense of touch. He is in a solitary cell; he watches the country through the grille. The birds fly past, the people work, sow, harvest, bring their wives and sons to labour the fields, the harness jingles, the storms fly, they sleep at night. His hair gets yellow with never sleeping, and the gaoler—even his step never comes near. The spiders pattern his clothing with their webs, his footprints are only marked on the dust of the cell."

His mother's eye began to wander; she smoothed her dress.

"Into my cell three women came"—the old lady became as still as stone and lifted her bright eyes direct to his, which were cast aside—"the first undid the lock: I could have eaten the dirt she walked on; a girl like—I would have killed a man for her, and thought of doing it. The second—took me into the fields, but at night I slept in my cell; she was the nearest and the farthest away too. The third I met when I was far afield: it was a loveless

adultery. I didn't like it, I came back to the cell. I spoil everything I touch because I was born without hands—like poor
Blount, for all practical purposes. To act is for me to do something awry, to stop the machinery, stick my heel through the
scenery, gaff in the acting, forget my lines. What is the effect of
all these desolatingly stupid dull acts on the mind of a man like
me, do you think? You have no idea, a simple old woman : it is to
alienate the spirit. You prefer to seek a world where these
accidents don't happen. Perhaps in an intrepid man even a crime
is beautiful, deft, neat, and the most ghastly serves his purpose,
but in an irresolute man like me the least thing goes astray and
I am immediately surrounded by yelling faces of mockery. A little
crime, like an adultery, grows apace once planted in the rich
earthy world and mocks my barren soil with its majesty. It is
fecund, worldly, better than me, it is something I feel too sick at
heart to care about. I don't want to do anything, I don't want to
produce anything. My deeds and crimes—I have done some—are
no more a part of me than things in the moon, but they do themselves through me and then destroy me, or having left me, leave
a thin shell—you know, like the cast skin of the cicada crept
from the earth. They cut me off from man and will not even leave
me in my funambulism. I am too delicate, quiescent to benefit by
my own fantasy. I have immense visions, and I can't even be
bothered looking at what is passing in my mind's eye; I prefer
to sleep. But one cannot sleep, so I swing like an empty bladder
flapping in the air between this world and the netherlands."
    The old woman scrutinised him closely, as if he were a stranger
sent by a friend.
    "Why did I say that?" continued Michael, leaning his head on
his hand. "When I was a boy I dreamed I was hung by the hair
in space and swung over the earth in a sixty degrees arc. The
earth swarmed with people who fought in a claypit and all fled
from it when it became, a second later, a battlefield running with
blood; a road or river ran by writhing with bodies and blood.
But when I swung near, they were only penny china dolls
with red cheeks like you put in the pudding. Nothing was real
when I came near. And when I swung away, at the end of a

pendulum, they came alive again in their blood and dirt. The wind blew on my body like a knife; they fought faster and faster and yet my body flew ever farther and farther away into un-imaged space. It came from my heart; my life has been revealed to me in dreams. I remember hundreds of dreams, some of them dreamed in childhood. I would like to go on telling them all to you, it is such an ardent pleasure for me to talk about them; it is as if I were eating honey, and instead of clothes I wrapped myself in a vestment of sunlight. The veil is thin between me and the spinning chamber of the fates; when I die I will go there and dip my hands in the unwoven raw material of life, for once."

He threw back his head and laughed; he took her by her hands and said:

"Really, Mother, I would love to do it. There is no joy I ever had like the joy I had this moment imagining it."

"How foolishly you talk! There's not a practical idea in your head."

He bent over her and looked down at her, her grey hair, the wrinkles round the eyes and lips, the sunken temples. At the serious, tender look, she drew in her breath sharply but said nothing.

"Poor old Mother, poor old woman, with your cuckoo son, baffled that although he has no wits, he escapes your under-standing, sorry you couldn't have kept him always in your skirts. You understand nothing much, in an atheist age you still pray, you sit with a priest, you like to think of the time you will be underground with the termites, worms and unborn larvae, the roots of the exploring trees, the rivulets of rain seeking a bottom. You wander about cemeteries with a bunch of flowers, lovingly clearing gravestones, throwing flowers out of flower-pots, read-ing inscriptions, weeping over the memorials to wives and mothers, making your acquaintance with the dead so that you will have gossips there from the first day. You are happy; you have made yourself a hearth and home even amongst the dead. I must die soon and I hate it. You will be easily buried with a few shovelfuls of earth, because the cinders of all your years gone are on your head, but I—with my cold flame always replenished,

I am sure I will walk at night."

"Oh, don't say such a thing!"

"I will walk looking for what I can't have while alive. You never wanted happiness and you cannot understand the thirst for it, for extreme happiness, even if it costs the lives and fortunes of two or three people. I loved you once when I was a tiny little boy and you gave me milk, my heart still beats with your warmth. You are the only creature that was ever tangible to me; perhaps I loved you."

She whinnied in a delicate little joyful way, and drawing him to her, put her head against his waist. She thought, as women do, that it was all over, that the masculine stress was past. He kissed her tenderly on brow, neck and hands, and taking up his hat in the hall, went out towards the gate.

"Take care of yourself, my little son! What time will you be home?"

"I can't say."

"Not late."

"Perhaps late."

"Where are you going?"

"I don't know. Perhaps to Joseph's at Fisherman's Bay, for tea, but I don't know."

"Don't be late."

She sighed and shook her head. But he did not return; he stayed at his cousin's all night and got up very early on Monday morning.

The house was still asleep, so he went up into the "barracks", that is, into the military reserve. The frank aromatic smells of scrub, garden and sea reminded him of early days, forgotten in the middle years of life; he had a memory of soft dark hair falling half across a pale face, not easily recollected now, for he was so old, not the face of any one, he thought, but the blurred visions of years. When he was a child, at this hour, he would come out into the garden with a trowel to dig where the worm and slug tracks lay silver all over the ground from their night business, while sparrows hopped and jabbered in the oleanders. Or else he would go up into the barracks, pursue weed-grown passages, and look at the seagulls scouring the ribbed sea. Even now the early summer day was idle, simple and companionable, and made him feel a little boy for a few instants; but there was an older thought in its red shadows, and the restlessness of the coming heat stirred already in the small dry plants; the season was on the verge of husky maturity.

The blood-red sun rose through a thick veil which stretched some hundreds of feet above the horizon. The water, shining like oil and burnished metal and bearing oil traces from the ships at Garden Island, ran irregularly round the margin of the beach; the tide was midwaydown—in an hour it would be fit for fishing. No ships were in the harbour, the houses were shadowy, the water was a clouded mirror. Michael began to sweat, even on the hill where a faint breeze still moved. The city lay far off, folded in morning lavender. Presently the first tram ascended the hill by the Gap, there was a clatter in the cook's galley in the pilot-ship, the workmen came aboard the dredger; outside the heads sirens, bellowing like the royal bulls at the Easter Show, called the pilot. A fisherman with two dogs went wading along the beach, and Pegleg climbed down the steps and unlocked the boathouse. The chimneys began to smoke in hotel and kitchen leanto; the reveille, so fine and clear in the hill, woke the camp. All began their morning work. Michael looked at the still smokeless chimney of the Baguenaults and walked through the military reserve where the barbed wire fences are tangled and broken. He circumvented the hill full of ditches, grassy trenches and doors into the hill and came to Lady's Haull, where a fisherman stood on the bluff shouting below. In the bay three fishing-boats were driving in the salmon. Beyond the salmon was a ring of dolphins, the outside the shark which had rounded the salmon up, cleaving the water with dark fin, restlessly patrolled the bay. A warship entering the harbour straits saluted the port; the hills reverberated and the dolphins plunged. Michael went through a gate and by a broken grassy descent to the shale platform under the inner light. In fine weather, with medium tides, this is a fine place to spend the whole day, with the ocean singing in the ears, the rare clouds flying overhead, ships dipping into the swell as they pass in and out, with a fishing-line swinging in the bottle-neck pool where fish move fluidly or nose out from the kelp weeds, dark wirrah, spotted kelpfish, rainbow parrot fish, eels and octopus. In storms the whole platform is a sheet of foam, broken by the slaty ebb and all the cries of the deep in the plunge of the decuman.

The *Turgot*, a new motor-ship, carrying wool, which should have cleared at midnight and had been delayed by a sea-cooks' strike, went out, sailing into the morning before his eyes, taking the long Pacific swell across her bows, with the pilot-ship dancing before her like a cork on the water. The *Turgot* carried a Scandinavian crew which had not been affected by the general water-side strike. Now she danced out, with her tall, blond sailors on deck. Everything was pure and sweet that morning. There soon sprang up a strong sea-breeze which still freshened from the south-east, blowing up the welt of cloud. Michael walked among the brilliant rockpools where the boys kept alive the fish that they caught on the reef. He managed to climb on to the farther platform. The swell was increasing despite the low tide and fair weather, and he got fairly wet and stung with spray. North Head with its graveyard above the quarantine station stood out clear in every detail in the lucid summer morning.

Line fishermen were fishing on the sheer, slippery rocks, over whose polished shoulders the deep swell rose and withdrew without foam. He sat down on the stinking rocks, dry-salted since the last storm, perversely sniffing, for people who live in fishing villages get to like strong smells. He remembered the last time he had sat on the edge of that triangular fishing-basin. That had been ten years before. Mae brought him down here, took off her shoes and stockings, lifted up her tennis skirt, and paddled in the standing tide. She had been so merry that her laughter bubbled over the edge of the rock and fell in globules into the water and was carried out to sea. The afternoon sun, coppery, lay in flakes on the sea. Then she walked back with him in the gloaming, and the officers of the permanent staff coming home to their weather-board cottages in the barracks, greeted them in the dark. They dawdled home, smelling the sea, the marshy lawns, the Norfolk

Island pines, the trickling rocks, and hearing the scattered chorus of frogs. Michael wondered now what would have been his history if he had married her. He dipped his fingers in a fissure full of starfish, setting the starfish in a row to see them creep gingerly back to the fissure. The fishermen caught a few rockfish, and a great blue groper stood up two or three times inside the wave about to break foamlessly on their rock, but he managed to get out of the undertow and disappeared. They sensed him nosing round the rocks there, just outside, protecting his fine blue skin and fins; they rebaited their hooks, looked for firmer footholds on the boulder, but he got away.

The fishing was good. Michael got up to go to his cousin's for his lines. He would not be able to fish for several days thereafter because a storm was clearly coming their way from far out on the Pacific. The tide hummed ominously round the coast; the wind blew regularly. He started to split cunjeboy and put the red and yellow meat in an old tin. His fingers were stained red; he washed them in the pool and saw the hungry anemones close on the juice and fragments. Dawdling over the pools feeding the anemones, he became too sleepy to go back for his lines. He retired under a big rock, boiled three or four crabs, and fried a fish given him by one of the men, and fell asleep in the warm blowy noontide. When he awoke an hour or two later the tide was surging through the mile-wide straits. It was getting too rough to fish; he had missed the tide. A coalie putting in from the south sank behind the waves in a frightening way and reappeared regularly, running in on the rollers.

"The storm will come to-night," called one of the fishermen, passing him on the way home.

"A coupla days, I should say, it will last," said another.

"So long," called Michael.

"So long," replied the men and waved their hands.

"I'll go up to town," said Michael to himself.

He found Heinrich Winterbaum at the offices of the *International Worker*, borrowed some money from him, and as evening came on he visited several public-houses, stood drinks to several unknown pals, and was thrown out in Market Street.

drunk, at six o'clock. He wandered down to the "Tank Stream" Press and picked up Withers, whom he found looking gloomily through the window at the evening crowds.

"Let's go and get shicker," suggested Michael. "But I warn you, I haven't got a cent. I drank it all already."

"I have," said Withers, "and I'd shoot my grandmother to break the ennui. Let's paint the town red."

"Orright, good idea, let's paint the flaming town red."

Withers took Michael home to his single room in a lodging-house in Woolloomooloo.

"Let's ask in Mendelssohn," said Michael.

"No, he doesn't drink, no use. He's a mollycoddle of purest ray serene."

"Yes, a mollycoddle; can't hold his drink."

Withers took a pleasure in seeing his friends stewed. They both got undressed and sat round in their shirts drinking and singing. Towards ten o'clock Withers dragged Michael to his feet and shook him.

"Heh, you're drunk. Get dressed; we'll go out wenching."

"No, too drunk."

But nothing could deter Withers from a debauch. They staggered along Castlereagh Street, Michael leaning on Withers' arm. After they had walked a few minutes they crossed a young sailor flushed and embarrassed, with two street-walkers on his arms, one old and one young, both haggard and both drunk. "Come on," cried the old woman, dragging him towards an aperture in the wall between two large buildings, "just a little way down here." A lamp glowed over a door at the end of a whitewashed passage. Michael began to giggle. Farther along a toothless young woman with painted cheeks hung with heartrending tenderness on to the arm and coat of a vain pimp who looked over his cigarette at her, and preened himself at her worshipping smile. Despite the sea-wind and the great cumulus clouds massing, the summer heat started out from every doorway. But the curtains were beginning to float out of the topmost windows.

"Come along," urged Withers, going down an alley.

"You bet," agreed Michael.

Michael awakened the next day about four o'clock in the afternoon, in Withers' room, feeling ill. He dragged downstairs, received a black look from the lodging-house keeper, and went into the street. A bitter wind was blowing, the sky was black, the street-lamps were on. The ships docked in the port creaked, and the virginia creeper on the terrace fronts lashed about. Michael found a shilling in his pocket, put there by Withers certainly, and went into a pub for a drink. When he came out he was sick in the gutter.

"I must rest somewhere," he kept saying to himself. He had a season ticket to the north-shore suburbs where his family lived. The Folliots lived on the same line, a few miles beyond. He walked through the evening bush, glistening as the sun set through a rift in the heavy clouds. He followed a large gully, half-cleared of its turpentines and eucalypts, along the bed of a small stream now bearing away in its waters the rubbish of dry months, and went up through flowering scrub to the lower fence of a descending orchard and private wilderness he knew well. There the Folliots lived. There was no sign of life, no clothes on the line and no light. He sat down for a while in a summer-house at the top of some steps and waited for the sound of voices, or a car drawing up. A lost chicken came piping madly down the wire-netting fence looking for an exit. Michael caught the soft little thing and said, "Silly little beggar, silly little beggar," a dozen times tenderly, while its heart pumped hard and it squeaked. He went up with it to the chicken-coop. The house was closed. Then he remembered the Folliots had gone to Melbourne for the week. He went to the rain-water tank, removed a brick from the base and took out the key of the back-door, left there for any homeless or unhappy friends who should need asylum.

Michael made some strong tea, with condensed milk, and ate some cold veal. A dust storm had arisen on the road outside the house. This road ran on the ridge between two deep valleys. After the dust came the trampling of heavy rain up the gully, and the storm was upon them. There was a storm also creeping upon him from another quarter, and he could feel it rising. His

227

pulse beat hard, his small heart began to suffocate him: he was fevered. He ate some dry bread and presently located the good port wine that Folliot kept for his late night-work. He drank a lot of this port, lying on the divan. There was a drawing-room grand piano in the sitting-room, a polished walnut table, and on the piano a photograph of Marion in Russian headdress with her black hair falling thickly on each side. On the wall next to the cushioned bow-window was an obscene etching called "The Débutante", show a voluptuous leering maiden, dressed in a transparent skirt, being led forward by a hairy gnome. Michael looked at this and began to laugh a little to himself. Just off the sitting-room was Fulke's study. Michael rummaged in there to find something to read while he drank, and came out with *The Golden Bough*, a large book by Havelock Ellis, two or three by Adler, Freud and Kraft-Ebing. These looked particularly interesting, as they discussed erotic practices and perversions. He laughed again and said: "I'll knock 'em dead yet at Blount's." The reading-lamp gleamed on the hexagonal sides of two brass candlesticks placed on the marble mantelpiece on the other side of the room, and two long-stemmed champagne glasses, greenish, with black dancing figures.

The rain continued and it got darker. Michael got up restlessly, flinging the heavy books helter-skelter on the divan and floor. He began to play some music lying on the piano—Gounod's "Funeral March of a Marionette", "The International"; Marion had not gone very far with her music, being too impatient and having little ear. Then Michael began to pick out old tunes he had sung in the army and songs current in England when he was on furlough long ago, idiotic tunes with two sets of words, one for the women, one for the soldiers. Things quite forgotten began to crowd back upon him. He had made a hit with Marion when he met her in London because he had known nothing about Communism and was romantic and had taught her the real words of the songs. Which songs? He remembered. In his fumy brain memories began to assort themselves into a dream of a night such as this that he had passed in a deserted house near Bapaume during the war, and an inn, too, but he could not distinguish the inn from the house nor either from the house Fulke and Marion were staying in at Golder's Green when he met them in London. He supported his bursting head on his palm and rested against the piano.

The storm thundered on the side of the house and the rain seeped in under the sashes. The street-lamp was lit. He went to the window and looked out at the country road, the tall bush with lathy branches lashing from side to side. Under the lamp stood a man. He whistled, and an older man, only protected from the storm by a scarf and a waistcoat over his ordinary clothes, came out of the scrub, while a third, looking like a tramp, slouched across from the Folliots' front fence, easily, with the air of a man who takes his own time. They stood under the lamp scarey, blowing to tatters, the lamp-light tossed from cheek to cheek on three rugged and whiskered faces. They did not appear to speak, but in a moment began to spread out again and moved along the road. Michael recognised them for an old family of wood-poachers who had stolen wood out of the government forests, and had done bushranging in the old times. Their family was almost destroyed by gang feuds with competing logrollers and bushrangers. The feuds exist to this day.

In the wall of the house opposite a red-lighted blind appeared and disappeared. The men came back along the road, crossed over and walked along by the house—beleaguered, beleaguered. The lamp-light from the street fell across curtain, floor and mantelpiece, and on to Marion in the Russian costume.

Michael fetched some candles and pulled the curtains. He slept for a moment on the piano-stool, full of dreams. It seemed a strain came from the piano, "O tannenbaum, O tannenbaum, wie treu sind deine Blätter . . ."; the Socialists sang it in London, with different words, but that was how Marion sang it. The aspect of the room changed a little. The ceiling was eighteen feet high, the curtains were of yellow tapestry, the lustres hung from a painted and gilded oval where cherubs floated between balustrades on a blue sky. Voices, and people like milky glass moved about the room, faint sounds of joy came from them. At a distance soldiers were singing; Michael shifted his ear out of his cupped hand to hear better what was going on. The only light was from the two candles in front of Marion's picture, but the room was full of windy sound and the storm beat in. He looked at Marion—how young she had been, mild and soft—looking at the picture he could perfectly recall his sentiments of those old days.

Two women came to him and beckoned him to his feet; it seemed Withers was laughing behind him on the divan. Michael plucked their arms, they all ran about the room. They clustered round him again, and he invited them to drink. Although he poured out three glasses, the women did not drink, so he had to drink the wine for them. He poured out wine again, and this time they drank, but they only drank with him; they would not sip it till he raised it to his own lips. There was a murmur of laughter from the piano under his hands. Someone played the tune of an obscene song, somewhere out of sight he knew a girl was sitting on a soldier's knee, pulling his ear affectionately. He knew that on the wall was a mirror festooned with gilt and decorated with paper roses, and on the ceiling was now Leda and the swan. He didn't care for obscenity. He was engaged in watching the eyes of the two women, who would certainly go away if he did not insist on them staying, by staring at them through the palm of his hand. They were very voluptuous women and only lightly dressed. It was disconcerting, but he couldn't get his eyes off a certain movement. They had black eyes and thick hair. He wanted to ask them if they were sisters, but felt too sleepy. He began laughing loudly to amuse them, and then they got up and left him. There was no one else in the room, which was the Folliots', and only a small grand piano stood before him.

"And to think—" said Michael, but before he finished he saw a strange person standing in the room. He came closer to the mirror and recognised himself. He began to laugh. Before he had finished, the younger woman of the two came back to the door, her bodice undone, and struck an inviting attitude, bared her teeth in a sort of smile, and left him, banging the door after her. He stayed in a maudlin state for a while, murmuring phrases over and over. His voice rose higher, he became agitated, and getting his feet together began to move about the room, posturing and acting over the scenes that were passing through his mind. The door opened—someone poked a vicious, thin inquiring face round the corner, smirked, said, "Oh, sorry," and went out again. Withers sat on the divan in his shirt, baring his yellow ratty teeth to drink, but Michael was sick of him and didn't want to hear his silly discourse. A silence. Later he heard whispering outside the door. He listened attentively, staggered to the door and threw it open.

"Come in," he shouted, "come in; you bloody well can take me, take me; but I won't go back, I'll shoot myself first. Court-martial me, but I won't go back." The piano gave out a crash of discords as he slumped on to the keyboard. He straightened himself up.

"Mustn't drink any more : I'm a bit shicker," he said to himself, and tried to keep his eye from twitching nervously. "I'm a bit upset," he emended. He went to the hall door and looked out. He came back into the room and shut the door carefully. He stood uncertainly in the centre of the space beside the fireplace, his humped shoulders, baggy unpressed trousers, and legs thrust wide apart, giving him the appearance of being blown out with spleen. His wild dark eyes darted back and forth and up and down over the walls cobwebbed with dark and light; his chin jutted out and his lower lip hung down trembling. He was really alone.

The heavy rain driving from the south shattered its lances against the glass door at the back. It came in noisy gusts battering and chattering at the panes, in the chimney cowls, whistling behind the closed grate, and ceased suddenly, leaving the guttering to drip into the night. Now again he heard the heavy roar of guns, far off and sullen, and he was not sure that it was not the thrumming of blood in his temples and breast. In the fire of his brain the hurry and confusion of the retreat he had been in, near Bapaume, ran itself over and over with black footsteps, and in that stormy night where the light flared unceasingly, his eyes still strained to see the men he was with; they all expected to be killed, they were all afraid like himself.

"Like fowls waiting to be killed—what are we waiting for? I can't stand it—let's go up and get shot down now," he said to the man standing next to him. The man did not answer; he looked like a pillar of mud, and might have been asleep on his feet, dead of fright or cold, or merely occupied with his own thoughts. An officer passed along hurriedly; it was a desperate retreat—no one would get out of it alive. Michael did a simple thing : he ran away and miraculously escaped, the only one to escape. He ploughed his way through mud and water, holes and debris, and after hours of running, crawling, hiding, he took refuge in a grange. When in the night rain came into the grange, making rivulets all over the floor, Michael climbed through a widow into the large kitchen of a farm. The farmer, with half his things packed ready for an alert when the soldiers swept past in retreat, rushed down in his white night-shirt with a revolver, shot at him in the half-dark of early morning and got him.

"Let me out," yelled Michael; "I'm not stealing; I'm a soldier looking for shelter," but the enraged farmer kicked him out into the cold. His savings were in that kitchen under the hearthstone, and he was convinced to the end of his life that Michael was a ruffian stealing his way back from the lines to safety. Michael thought over all this, as he had many times before. No one knew, not even Withers, who liked to worm out your secrets when you were drunk and who remembered them even if he was drunk when he heard them. Michael was picked up after, wounded (by the farmer) after wandering about in all directions. He found himself on furlough in England, and there met the Folliots. They respected him as an honest militant; they immediately started to try to convert him to Socialism. He pretended to be converted for the sake of Marion.

"Why not?" he had often said : "it's all a game, mine or theirs. And as to the rest, they told me I was a pawn in the financiers' game—not so much as they think, not the pocket hero." He sighed. "I'm a coward, but that's because I'm neurasthenic—there are lots of situations I'd face that many a man wouldn't. Rules don't mean anything to me. I want what I want and don't recognise rules. I'm a man; man made rules, man made cowardice and courage, their ideals. I'm another sort, only not in the majority—that's all."

His head ached: he formulated his thoughts very slowly and with great pain, but he was forced to keep thinking it all out.

"I understand my own situation perfectly," he said.

He walked up and down the room holding his head back and front with both hands as if to keep the brains in.

"I shall burst a blood-vessel," he said to himself. "It will burst; this can't go on."

He sank to his knees beside the piano-stool and tried to rest his head on it, but got up again; thousands of hot needles stuck into his brain.

"Am I going cuckoo?" Is this how it starts? No wonder they shriek out, madmen, if it feels like this." He had to think.

The pain rushed over his head in great waves, his head was on fire, the roots of his hair burned. It poured into his head stronger and stronger.

"Let me break a blood-vessel; I can't stand this any longer. Let me pass out, I'd rather die. Now I know what it is to want to die."

He began to laugh, holding his head and pacing the room. He felt remarkably sane. He stopped in front of Marion and stared at her with tear-wet cheeks, but he was crying for pain.

"Anyone," he said violently to the photograph, talking aloud to keep his mind off the pain; "you would take anyone you wanted when you wanted them. I came at the right moment, that was all; Fulke was in Manchester, and I was ersatz-Fulke. And here my head's been splitting all round the town for a couple of years on account of you; and Fulke pitying me for an unfortunate lover. But you're lovely, Marion, sweet, a woman, little Dooky—ugh, I'll go mad with this yet. I've got to get out of it, it must pass away. How long will this night take, how long can the body keep up without sleeping? If my head would only burst, at the back where the skull is grinding."

He muttered continually to himself. His reason struggled over a vast battlefield, it seemed, advancing and falling back in front of the floods of pain. He visualised this battle as the one he had escaped from long ago. When his passion and pain swept forward, he saw running men advancing over the field and silhouetted on the skyline once more. Then as each gust died— for these microcosmic conflicts raged during the noise of the driving rain—he remembered the real battlefield once more, and sometimes remote and sometimes growing nearer and clearer every minute, and right at hand, he saw the miserable and condemned band, eleven men. What if he could meet them all one day and find they had all done what he did and been saved? They would look at each other joyfully, a camaraderie of saved men. They were the only brothers he could ever hope to have. But they were not living. He would like to meet them. Barker, a man he had lived with for months, the easiest kind of man to live with—what a pity he was not alive. He could have told him everything and gone off with him somewhere, out of the world. He would shake off the torpor of years if Barker were still alive; he would go anywhere in the world to meet Barker. He would never get these headaches again. But Barker had died the night he ran away, overcome with nausea and nerves, as now. Barker was the pillar of mud. Dust now. Their faces were white and childish as the dark smoke-black warriors of Satan rising from the mud surrounding them, shouting inaudibly, waving their arms tall as forest trees, horribly blown out and lacerated, some with their eyes gouged out, each with a gun cocked. He could not run back to them now over all the space of ground and all these years. He had run too far; better to stay where he was. They were all done for, he too, no doubt. It was enough to have come here through the rain in the crack-up of the earth. Chaps got medals for the same thing done in the other direction. There was the levitation of the lights all around; he had been unconscious part of the way, didn't know what he was doing, a nervous type with signs of tuberculosis that should never have been sent into the front line anyway. It was not treachery; they were dead for sure by now, and he would have been; for nothing. Let him sleep, only let him sleep, only to lay his head on no matter what, log, mud, chair, stone, stump, rut, and sleep for a night and day. Their faces were white in dream; the lights burst and flamed. Michael

234

pressed his hands into his head.

Silence fell again. The candle-flame wavered and grease dropped to the piano-top, where it ran to the edge and formed two small white stalactites. Outside the water rushed from the guttering and spurted upon the sodden earth. Two running past the door splashing. The wind sighed and the door creaked. Did the handle turn? Surely the door moved? No. His eyes moved from the door to the window; he suspiciously watched the wine-stains which had somehow come on the wallpaper near the table—the shape altered just as his eyes reached them. No, it moved no more. Something in the room continually whisked out of sight. His eyes darted from wall to chair; he paused where the palms dangled over the divan, in the alcove. His fearful regard rushed over cornices and mouldings, over carpet, polished floor, waxed piano tail, to the corners where the feeble shadows moved up and down; then back to the handle of the outer door. His eyes narrowed and he watched the handle for at least a minute, but certainly it did not move while he watched it.

He rushed to the door and flung it open; only the black night confronted him and the damp air blew in. The moon must have been shining, for lighter patches appeared in the sky, showing up the summits of gigantic rain-clouds swiftly advancing from the south, bringing another blast of rain. He shut the door again and the windows rattled. He must pull himself together. He was going crazy, definitely batty. Why shouldn't he go batty indeed at last? No one had ever thought him too sound. Besides, he had had too much trouble, born unfortunate, lived queer.

"An ordinary life," he said aloud, "is like that crack in the floor, mine is like this," and he wavered up the crack, sometimes treading on it, sometimes wide of it.

"I am a yelled, that is yelled, yellow—what? Why?" It had been the forlornest chance and what the devil; but why couldn't he tell even Kol Blount that he had run away? It was so reasonable. Why did he have to have a blind spot? It was Kol's fault, he knew no more than an old woman, he understood nothing, ranting there in his chair about moonshine. He sat down on the piano-stool. The handle moved. No, the wind blew—then again,

Marion lying naked, laughing in a wide, white bed, with a flowered quilt, in the house in Golder's Green; Marion even weeping because he had not taken her out to dinner. He smiled a little—Marion, the heroine of so many adventures, whom every man looked after, had wept for him. And for that he had run away, no doubt. No one knows where life is leading us.

But then how he had agonised after her these three last years, playing the fool for everyone to see, latterly insulting Catherine who was so visibly hurt. Oh, heaven help me, he said, my head is bursting this time, and in fourteen layers already like a Russian doll. Listen to the footsteps outside and the shouting. Why shouting? There was none; there was no battle here, nothing, that was a dream. Lord, the pain he had suffered; it seemed to be going down now a bit. And for nothing. Nobody makes bread out of blood, red bread—red bread, what is that? The poor in Europe eat black bread, Barker and the ten others would make flour lying in the fields, wheat with the rust, undoubtedly, and tassels high in the wind above the head of the dead; and the dead sleep well. The skulls of the dead are cracked by the roots of wheat; they are emptied out—pollen-dust, golden. Now, was Fulke in the next room, entered softly? You could never tell with that secretive, blond creature, what he knew. His eye was on him—good reason, good reason.

Michael still stood in the centre of the open space swaying. How did he get there again? Presently he sat down in the arm-chair and ran his fingers through the thick plush. The rain came again; it stopped, and presently two or three voices began outside, lowered. Michael took no note of this, his glance fixed on the reflection of a candle in the polished wood. He was really asleep.

He awakened and found the candles burnt out, the room dark. He took the photograph of Marion to the divan, covered himself with the cushions, and fell asleep with the photograph in his arms.

On Tuesday morning he borrowed some money from Winterbaum at the *International Worker* and went dawdling about with Lancyman, a leading reporter on the *Guardian*, friend of Fulke's.

236

He fought the British in Ireland during the civil war, and went to gaol for it; he fought New York cops in Socialist demonstrations, but was now a retired war-horse who liked to jingle the bit from time to time. A droll lot of stories Lancyman had to tell. He travelled all over the world, and wherever he was, in Rio de Janeiro, in New York, Paris, Shanghai, London, he found a mare's-nest of dissolute Australians who lived by journalism, stock promotion, defrauding of dowagers, confidence tricks, marrying of landladies, cadging of drinks and general cheap exploitation on the basis of their easy-going and taking manners. Lancyman got to know these fellows for amusement, sometimes lent them money. "I prefer a confidence man to a bobby," was his last word. Withers clung to Lancyman with delight, hanging on every word that came from his lips, and would have been only too happy to meet this down-at-heel Australian international, which perhaps only existed in Lancyman's imagination.

Michael laughed all the morning. As Lancyman paid for his drinks, Michael still had some money. He went out to the Rosebery ponies, put his money on every alternate race. He won in the first race on a horse called Trickster, and successively put his money on The Card, Lucky Streak, Artful Dodger, Jerrybuilt and Tinsel, winning on four, and coming out with £15; a chap who had all the racing sheets and several tipsters' envelopes hung on him enviously to cadge the fare home and a drink at least. "What's your system?" he kept on asking, and after he had had a drink got quarrelsome and pugilistic. Michael slipped out by a side door and left him in the pub, which was considered a dirty trick by all there assembled. The bus he took landed him near Elizabeth Street. He went past the Mint and the back of Sydney Hospital, and looked with affection at the morgue with its gloomy motto, and trailed past with melancholy delight the houses in Raymond Terrace. He came down through the Domain to the harbour, mud-coloured at present with the constant wind and tide running in. A coastal collier was putting out. Some young boys leaned over the side pointing out bits of familiar landscape—perhaps harbour lads running away for a bit of sea experience as they often did. He went down through the 'Loo

(Woolloomooloo) among the homing crowds with their galoshes, umbrellas, and spoiled hats, and up into Paddington, past the small provision shops and public-houses now getting rid of their customers at closing time. Old women without underclothes sat on the gutters, thin children played with cats and dogs, all skinny and covered with sores, and boys with their scooters and home-made wagons tore along the grey slimy pavements, while some of their mates, little lads with bright eyes and matted yellow hair, hopped on crowded trams selling the evening papers. Opposite him were three terrace houses with twelve-foot front-ages. They were built about 1850 by a builder whose affection for the old country had induced him to reproduce on a new free soil the worst slums of Camden Town. They were numbered 10a, 10b, 10c, 10d. Each front had one dark door and one curtained window. Mingily, dingily, the little houses looked on the squalling street. The dull face of 10b became agitated, the black door flung open, a middle-aged woman dressed in bits of skirts shot through the door and the little iron gate, and finding herself on her own property, the public street, stood shouting insults in a rum-ruined voice to her unseen enemy. After a few minutes she began to totter up the street in the direction of the public-house. The children gathered round, jeering. A black-dressed woman appeared in the door of 10b, and answered the insults with prac-tised replies. She banged the door. The insulted rushed back with a dodging stride to cry, "Thief, . . . I'll get the policeman." After a minute the dingy curtain fluttered, the window opened, and a couple of small bundles shot out, hit the pavement with a clatter and crash. Bits of china lay over the pavement and some silver and cutlery spilled into the gutter. The children stood round, delighted. The outcast picked up her property, crying drunkenly over the broken cups and teapot, "I'll get you, you . . ." and so forth. The window shot up again and the black-dressed woman shouted to the assembled street, "She made up to my husband; she slept with my husband, the dirty street-walker; she ain't got no man and she tried to steal mine. I'll throw her into the street too and beat her into pieces." The window went down, and the dull face of 10b became quiet as a stone again. The inhabitants

238

of an old two-storey house and the workers pouring out of a factory near by, assembled. A woman put out of the public-house, tired of insulting the publican, zigzagged over the street, her skirts hitched up at one side to her waist, her drawers, grey with age, dropping below her knees, her stockings about her ankles. The children were hilarious; no pantomime approached this spectacle. "Come along," shouted the second and took the arm of the dispossessed one. They quarrelled about the degree of their intimacy and relative position on the social scale. The watchers in the two-storey house applauded. A man with a cap, silk scarf and brightly-striped suit, baggy at the knees, came past, laughing at his success with the girl hanging on his arm. Her front teeth were out and the roots seemed blackened; there were lines radiating from her mouth in all directions. She was dressed with a certain amount of coquetry, had no rouge, a neat waist and new shoes. The watchers in the house shouted prompt, explicit and offensive advice to the two. The man planted his girl at the corner of the street and retired to a distance to watch her game; he spent his time chalking designs and legends on the cement wall of the factory. The woman with the dropping drawers left her dispute and sidled up to him.

"Want a good time, dearie?"

The crowd went into shrieks of laughter. She came over to Michael.

"Are you flush, dearie? I've got a nice room."

Michael, who had been staring enchanted at the scene, smiled at her hideous face and forked out a pound-note.

"That's to keep away from your room; buy yourself some new drawers."

The crowd applauded him and started to follow him down the street, when the arrival of 10b's husband retained them. 10b's husband, a tall, rubicund workman, looked scared to see the people round his house, said, "What's the matter? Anything up? An accident?" Many voices informed him. Michael hurried away. What to do all this blamed long wet summer night? He was sick of the gang, the Folliots out of town, the boys in the press all boring, he was too tired to go out on the spree with Withers. On

239

the walls someone with a firm hand had written, "Down with the Masons", "Damn the Jesuits", "Expel the Jews". The public-houses were breeding drunken humanity as fast as lice. The sun went down behind torn clouds, the sullen short evening preceded night for a few minutes over the city. The names of the winners of the day's races were scratched on the walls by happy gamblers, remnants of tipsters' envelopes lay on the pavement, men greeted each other with the time honoured " 'Oo won?" He was lonely. The city was at tea; smells of sausages, stews and cabbage were everywhere. He went down to the "Tank Stream Press", but Withers was gone. Only Baruch and Joseph remained, heating bovril, and eating sandwiches on the lavatory bench.

"Hallo, Michael; you look down in the mouth, what's the trouble? Come along o' us to-night? Professor Müller, the gentle-man Democrat, is lecturing again. He looks up at the demon-stration room with a slightly fearful look as the most courageous David might look at Goliath. At any rate, this is his first stone against the Goliath of proletarian ignorance. Since the soap and steel companies and technical colleges turned out first-class engineers and chemists, the University must climb off its green horse and blow its trumpet where the masses can hear; the old golden Laputan mysteries don't work. The subject, you know, 'Light, or My heart leaps up when I behold a rainbow in the sky'. Mr Words-Allworthy would have been destroyed by a few lectures on light—he would have deserted the over-chlorophylled lakes for the dry light of reason, perhaps. Come along, Michael, there's nothing so soothing to a brain-storm as a contemplation of order in the universe. What if the old firms of N. & T. (Nineveh and Tyre), S. & G., Troy & Babylon, and so on, have bit the dust, the ninety-two elements have always been there. A pity we didn't spend more time on them before. Hannibal could have crossed the Alps by express train. More dry-eyed speculations and fewer thunders of tears in the style of Messrs Root and High-Cockalorum (of course you know them, Racine and Corneille), would have advanced us a few millenniums. We would have missed a few fine examples of delirium tremens, paranoia, and schizophrenia, and Freud would have been on the bread-line from the start, but we would have had more ox-eyed Alices, sleep-bearing Hebes, prolific Joves, literature would have gained. I remember my old Professor Muffanduff, formerly of Ekaterina-slav, now of Oregon, Oregon, used to say that Helmholtz was the night-light of infant mankind. Here, a sandwich—the bovril is ready."

"No thanks; I'm not hungry."

"Been boozing?" inquired Baruch sympathetically but perfunc-torily, because he knew it. "Yes, you're hungry, yes, you are, you've got a soulful look and you're almost on the point of com-mitting suicide, aren't you?"

"I can eat if I want it," said Michael. "I won fifteen pounds at the races."

"Beware of spring," admonished Baruch. "More suicides are committed then than at any other time, and also at the various festival days and commemoration days. On those days the appeal of light is small; it seems to show too plainly certain motes in our brothers' eyes, or holes in our own ramshackle spiritual tene-ments; girls look like perambulating Astartes; boys look like fish-eyed egotists. Why is it? We can stand the first blow of winter, the coalman throwing coke down the chute, for it means so many months of chilblains, so many colds, so many dozen handker-chiefs covered with snot, so many blue-fingered mornings getting up at six, cursing at the family and running for the boat with a red nose. But, you think, all will soon change, it will be spring, something good will come in spring, a rise in pay, a nice girl, someone to love you, someone to notice your remarkable, in-grown talents. But in spring, no chance more for a twelvemonth; then it is too plain that things are going on as before. Yet around you are chaps with new girls lovely and fluffy, or jolly and loving, or little and easy to deceive; there are chaps with scholarships going to new schools or abroad, boats going out to foreign countries just awaking in the outlandish way they have, with their trees all bare sticks and all that; there are houses with new coats of paint and spring handicaps. I know what's in your mind, Michael, cheer up. We can't lose you yet; we can't do without our spiritual comforter."

R

"Comforter?" asked Michael, smiling.

"Surely, comforter. You're the cement of all of us, the only chap whose complete life-history is not told. Without you Kol Blount's barnyard would have no charm, no shadow, no mystery; you're the poet of life to us."

"Oh," said Michael coldly, with a far-away look, as if calculating something like the price of soling his boots. "What's concealed probably isn't worth telling."

"Don't say that," urged Baruch, "an insignificant thing may fill a man with passion. Lives wind their way out by curious bypaths. You may have noticed, official drama is so fearfully unsatisfactory because of its big gross themes. Everyone knows it doesn't represent their own feelings at all. There would be a row if real situations were reproduced; it would undermine the State. The State is built on grotesque comic-opera conventions which no one dares mock at."

"Yes, too right, it is," agreed Michael, energetically. "I know something about that."

"Well, are you coming this evening?" asked Baruch. Joseph blinked and looked at Michael with a dull face to discourage him. He was pleased to go with Baruch alone.

"Come on," said Baruch.

"No, thanks," said Michael, frowning; "I see I'm not wanted. I'm going to blow in my smackers."

"You're wanted, but don't come if you don't want to. At the same time, you'd like it. Jo did."

"No, I—I have to go to a friend's house. I remembered just now—it's a birthday party, or engagement party or something. Is there still time for me to buy something? It might not be bad— they generally have claret cup, champagne, lobster, the hostess is free and easy and a good sport. Yes, I'd better go there."

"Good, good," exclaimed Baruch. "Yes, you'd better go there, go and amuse yourself; one makes aphorisms on death at a feast, truisms at a funeral; it's the aphorism that helps the cat to swim, the truism is the stone that knocks it under. Oftener we change the more constant we become; the more we reflect other people, the clearer our personality emerges. Do you want any more in the same line of goods? I am the old wives' dictionary unabridged and revised. Go and act the fool."

"It's known to be my habit, isn't it?"

"Of course, you really are a fool, Michael. I always say, I'm glad to know you. I know I've touched rock-bottom. I can measure humanity upwards starting from you. You know that."

"You found me pretty low, eh?" said Michael, smiling ingenuously.

"Absolutely; with you, Michael, the world would be a pit of shifting shadows to me, but on you I plant my ladder and mount to the light. At the top I find——"

"What?"

"Other creatures just like you; it's very strange. But then we're in the antipodes."

"Then I'm top and bottom and tropics too. It sounds so familiar. I'll tell you a funny thing about myself, Baruch."

"Yes."

"I never thought of a joke in my life that went off. Yes, I think of wonderful jokes and laugh at them myself, but when I tell them, everyone stares at me anxiously or lugubriously. I go home and repeat what I have said to myself; it sounds perfectly good, and then I repeat the things other chaps palm off, and they don't sound half as good. That makes me simply despair. It means there is something else, a sort of animal success which I haven't and can't get. Another thing, when anyone twits me or insults me, I can't stand it; I want to cry or kill them, or commit suicide. Even if I answer back it does no good. I go on thinking over the insult for weeks and crying inwardly. It kills me, this wounding and this hatred, it stirs up in me. But other people are not like that. They give back as good as they get, and everyone is happy. People like to quarrel—they only insult to stir up a little fun. But to me, it's like murder. And all the time I feel foggy."

Baruch was silent : Joseph stirred uneasily. Baruch said finally :

"You must have suffered to feel like that, that is the reason for your fogginess. You ought to get a steady situation of some sort, get married and get a job. Get a loving wife, to begin with."

"Wonderfully original idea," said Michael discontentedly.

243

"Well, I think I'll take myself off after making myself undesirable. Perhaps I'll meet my fate at the party."

"Hey, come on, it's late," cried Baruch, getting off his stool. They grabbed their hats and rushed off. Michael followed them deliberately downstairs.

He walked out towards Double Bay. His friends lived there, on the heights. A white-lined cloud, flushed with the afterglow, now appeared large and rapidly driven in the south under the covered sky. A damp wind arose, puffing strongly. The clouds turned black and drove towards the zenith, the harbour seen from the heights of Paddington banded red, purple and grey, grew dark. The night sky still shone with a few stars in the north. The ships creaked and swung at their anchorages. Winches squeaked and chains rattled as they were anchored fore and aft to withstand the coming storm. With quiet long strides up and down the hills of Darlinghurst, Elizabeth Bay and Double Bay, Michael went, smelling fresh gardens, looking at the little households behind lace curtains under silk lamps. Trams rattled past and soft-running cars; lovers were in both going out towards the Gap, Rose Bay. Sometimes he passed the red spark of a motor-car halted in a side road, with its blinds drawn. "Yes, spring is dangerous," he said. Presently a wide dark stretch lay on his left hand, and brilliant tennis-courts lighted by swaying arc-lamps arose on the right. The dark patch was the Rose Bay golf-links: his friends lived just above them. A car passed him, with boys and girls singing "There's none so classy as that young lassie", and stopped several doors away at his friends' house. They rushed up the steps, shouting "Coo-ee", and the hostess appeared.

"It was so lovely of you to come. Ellen's waiting to see you." He saw through the open window Nancy, the minister's daughter; Victorine, who was marrying the son of the house; Pam, a little flirt who had just announced her engagement to the minister's son. Someone tipped him on the shoulder, and he looked round to see two boys and a girl with shallow laughing eyes and long lashes.

"Michael, if it isn't you! Can't you scrape up the courage to come in? Or are you going to throw a bomb?" She explained to

244

her two cavaliers:

"Michael's *awful*, he really does throw bombs. He's a Communist."

The boys looked at him suspiciously, and all three left him standing there. In the side-passage the garage door was softly opened and closed. From the piano inside came the song, blown out brilliant on the gusty wind, "I said goo'bye, but I didn't mean goo'bye."

Michael laughed and moved away. "Ellen! Engaged now: used to be ten years old with mousy hair."

A smothered laugh came from the garage.

"I'll shove off," said Michael.

On a vacant lot near, two figures hastened into the deep blackness under the paling fence to avoid him. He went on, remembering that a poltergeist was bothering a family round about and had placed bloody hand-marks on new-plastered walls in vacant dwellings. A few streets away a policeman stopped him and asked him questions, under a lamp. Before he went away, he asked the bobby:

"Who're you looking for?"

"That feller who raped a coupla girls here the last few weeks."

He went on. On one side were the dunes, on the other the links, on both sides the waste of water. He stood between two heights. The sand blew into his eyes. The black sea and black harbour seemed to threaten the neck of land; he could hear the long surge over the sandhills.

A young fellow standing near a street lamp came into its light, while approaching Michael modestly. His small hands were manicured, his fine wrists and delicate neck were blackish as with coaldust, but his hairless face, with oval cheeks, was pink and powdered. His eyes, large and timid, looked appealingly at Michael. Michael brushed rudely past him. The boy retreated to the fence once more to wait. Michael heard steps, the boy coming after him, he thought, and he looked back—only a tram conductor going home from the depot.

Going up Rose Bay hill by the side of a well-planted estate that looks over the harbour, he passed an old man, carrying vainly a beard, long, silver-grey and well combed. His aspect was mild but troubled. His hands were clasped over a silver-headed stick. He walked rapidly like a man who has been busy all his life. His long, sensuous, finely-modelled mouth worked, as if he muttered or were nervous. His round back bobbed fast down the hill. The old man hesitated as he passed Michael, lifted his dark glance, his two hands carrying the silver knob, and seemed about to speak. But it was such a slight gesture, that Michael could not be sure. A hundred yards farther on he passed a tough, in poor clothes, who also stooped as he walked, but as if to hide his bad face, repulsive concentrated eyes and thick jaw between his broad shoulders. He walked rapidly, steadily, with a broad soft foot, as if that were his habit also. Michael walked again a hundred yards, stopped, and looked uneasily back, but the young man and the old man had gone down the hill and round the corner.

He thought no more about it, but in the salt fierce wind he shivered. There were so few lights along the road at this point. He said, staring constantly ahead at the dark, "To the alien eye, odd sights." A tram rattled past, bringing comfort with its commonplace passengers. Its light disappeared up the hill.

"I will go on and sleep in the Bay," said Michael. He was tired, and sat down to rest on one of the seats provided along the tram-route. He thought:

"To-morrow I can get a regular job, perhaps, if Fulke is back, or Lancyman remembers his promise. But I'd rather take a boat to Samoa, Hong-Kong, Shanghai, Singapore, Cochin-China. It's lovely there in spring, the cosmopolitan crowds, the gutters like canals, the street-sellers, the little girls in tea-houses, the blue sky, the dogs, leprosy, tigers, temples. A man should be able to loaf at my age; it's too late for him to make a career, he's settled for life, if he's a bad 'un, he is, so there's nothing to do about it; should be pensioned to loaf."

He looked down at Fisherman's Bay in the distance. A liner, in evening dress, with all her rows of lights, made towards the Heads; the pilot-ship ran before her and waited for the pilot just outside the Heads. The harbour, freed from the strike, lived again; the liners prepared to leave. A ferry visited the near wharves and rolled in the swell; her long rows of lights rolling, scurried towards the Bay.

"It's the eleven-thirty," said Michael. "I suppose Joseph is aboard, coming back from his lecture."

Two girls, walking home from the pictures, came towards him, discussing with ecstasy the attractions of a cinema star. They looked at Michael in a doubtful way when they came close to him and hurried their steps a little.

He took out about ten pounds in notes and small change. "Silly not to have given it away and so many people need it." Near the lighthouse stood an old whitewashed stone house of two storeys, large and old-fashioned, like the one little Annie Pennergast lived in when he was a little boy. A light burned in a back window; he heard a baby crying. He looked through the cracks of the paling fence. A dog barked. A woman, dark, thin, flushed, dressed only in a calico chemise, nursed a young baby. The room was painted in yellow kalsomine; on another bed lay a man and a child of about eight.

"Hey!" cried Michael. The dog barked furiously. The woman started and listened. "Missus," cried Michael, "just a minute." The woman strained towards the window and grew sallow.

"What is it, Annie?" said the man in a childish, sleepy voice.

"Shut the winder," said the woman. "I thought I heard a voice."

"You're all nerves; it's the wind."

The woman put the baby down, rushed to the window, closed it and pulled the blind. The dog continued to bark. Michael went softly away. As he came out on the road, a man came up, started, and hurried his step.

"Pardon me," said Michael.

"What do you want?" asked the man, at a distance.

"I want to give you some money," said Michael. "I don't want it."

"You get out of this," said the man; then relenting, "Go home and sleep it off, mate." He turned round and quickly got out of sight. Michael sat down to wait. After a very long time during which the lighthouse ray swung over his head, turning and turning, a boy came along on a bicycle. He had no cap, but wore a noble pair of motor-goggles. His bike was shining with rain, his yellow oilskin shone under the lighthouse beam.

"Hey, feller!" called Michael.

"What do you want?" asked the boy fearfully, stopping.

"I want to make you a present," said Michael, advancing. The boy watched him steadily.

"Here," said Michael, "ten pounds, not forgeries. I don't want 'em. It's a weakness of mine to give away cash. I'm a millionaire, or almost."

The boy looked anxiously at the money.

"You won't be, long, if you give it away," said he.

Michael smiled.

"Take it, son, I'm not kidding you; I'm giving it to you."

The boy took it, took out his little purse and stuffed the money in.

"Thanks an awful lot; I don't know whether it's a mania, or not, but it's a windfall for me," he told Michael cheerily and earnestly. "You're shicker, though, aren't you?" he asked woefully.

"Not on your tintype," said Michael, "just eccentric. I'm going to commit suicide."

"Oh, don't do that," said the boy. "No, you're not. Fellers with dough don't commit suicide. Well, I'll be going. Good-night, and thanks very much."

He tootled off down the hill whistling.

Michael sat down on the seat outside the barbed-wire fence. The whole sea was in motion rolling into the land. He did not know how long he sat there, but he thought of very little all that time; his mind was as dark as the weather. He looked up from his seat. The harbour lights still blinked in the channel: the tramway lights still swung on their suspension wires, and very low in the west a faint glimmer in the sky announced the setting of the moon. It must have been about four o'clock in the morning. He began to walk towards Fisherman's Bay. In a few minutes he reached the top of the road near the signal station and lighthouse, and turned off the road across the sandy cliff-tops strewn with tough little yellow-flowering bushes, to look at the weather, which had surely come up again. For the last two days the horizons had been red and misty morning and evening, and the sea had been gathering force in mile-long rollers which plunged with a slow booming into the caves under the roots of the village. Now the wind had much increased, and when the squalls of rain came from the black clouds overhead, it blew exceedingly hard and the short squalls followed each other like blasts of shot. The sea was running high, and although all was black, at the foot of the cliffs, which are bold and bluff, he could see the dusky white breach of the surf.

At this part of the cliff there is no fence, but the sand and sandy mould, bearing short coarse grass and dry ti-tree, ran to the crumbling edge. One looks down along several headlands, all bleak, low, with surf at foot, into the stormy south. Although the weather was dark, an imperceptible illumination had begun, the morning breaking far down and far behind the cloud. The outlines of the Southern Heads with their surf were clearly distinguishable.

He passed the lighthouse, going down now towards the bay. Above him rolled the pale limb of the wheeling light, hooded in flying spray as it turned out to sea. Next was the flagmast through whose loose strings the wind roared.

The military reservation fence goes to the brink of the cliff. Michael climbed through and looked down at the sea, at the earthy ledges, and at the cowled and formless cliffs below him. He wrapped his coat round him as he wished to wrap the deep sea round him and its sleep fathoms down. He wished to sleep, to have the water sing as now for ever in his ears, and the inextinguishable anguish in his mind to be hushed. So he stood fixed, with fixed and troubled look cleaving the sea, in whose heart he had always found more repose than in any human heart, which understood his miseries through its own rages and revolts, his inconstancies through its tides, his longings through the bottoms grown with various plants and barnacles from foreign ports, and the turbines ploughing its waves.

The wind sways him like the rooted plants and grasses, whistles through his hair as through the pine trees opposite : he is already no longer a man but part of the night. The pine trees crowded him to the ledge, the light wheels, down underneath is the howling parliament of waters deciding on his fate. The gusts on rock and ledge as spirits hold his heart in their shadowy hands and squeeze the blood out of it; darkness only runs through his veins now. He takes a step nearer the edge, and at the same moment this idea splits him from head to foot: "What if I should fall upon a rock?" He falls into the sea, the wave a moment later cracks his skull against the submerged pediment of the cliff, and his brains flow out among the hungry sea-anemones and mussels. It is done; all through the early morning the strings of the giant mast cry out a melody, in triumph over the spirit lost.

9

In memoriam: a mass, a dream, a strange narrative.
A new love.

THE SECOND STORM passed over in a night. The day broke
clear, blowily under a sky full of torn drift. In the evening Joseph
was too tired to go to the College, and the deck-hand had to
wake him up when they came to the Bay. Frowsy with sleep, and
with patches of ink on his face Joseph jostled a comical, blonde
factory-girl getting off the gang-plank, and was surprised to see
the young girl smile at him.

"You didn't hurt me," said she. "You were asleep, weren't
you?"

"Yes, I was," replied Joseph.

"You must get awful tired to fall asleep like that," said the
young girl. "I know; I just pray for five o'clock to come, so that
it's only an hour to six o'clock."

Joseph laughed and look at her. She had a little nose, Wedg-
wood blue eyes, and straight if whitish hair which hung round
her like a mop. When she laughed she showed all her upper
teeth and the gum with them, but she looked kind and frank.
She was of middle height and wore high heels.

"Without those heels," thought Joseph, "she would be my
height."

"Gee, it's awful windy still," said the girl, as they came near
the Gap and the gust brought down a few drops of spray.

"Yes; well, I've got to turn here," said Joseph.

"Good-bye; I catch the same boat."

"Good-bye."

Joseph walked round the beach-path in profound astonishment: she was a nice girl and she liked him. He hardly noticed

the beach children jumping in front of the shop saying, "Oo-hoo, Joey's got a girl!"

He went towards the steep hillock down which boys sped on their scooters. The kitchen lights were shining over the green; warm odours of meals floated in the air, full of spray, and darkness was escaping from its hill prisons, from the troughed water and from the sky of spent storm-clouds. The telegraph lines sang loud.

As he climbed the street once more towards the cove, he saw his father waiting for him at the gate, with his patch-face still against the vines.

When Joseph came up, his father said, articulating slowly, as if disturbing himself with a long contemplation:

"Did you read the evening paper?"

"No."

"Well, Joseph, an accident happened to your cousin Michael: go into your mother, she is upset. Everyone in the Bay knows."

Joseph licked his lips.

"What is it?"

His father replied in the same tone:

"Your cousin was found dead outside the Gap this morning. On the rocks, washed up."

Joseph leaned against the gate-post. At last he said, "I'll go in," and walked softly and uncertainly into the passage. His mother heard his step, called "Joseph, Joseph"; he went to her and fell upon her breast. When he had comforted his mother a little, at last, he left her dozing and went out to get himself supper in the kitchen. He was very hungry. He cut some bread, with cheese, pickles and cold meat, with tears rushing out of his eyes and down his throat till he was nearly suffocated. He wiped his eyes with his inky handkerchief. Then he set about washing the dishes which had been left over all day. The news had been brought early in the morning.

He was surprised that he was not shaken. He moved like a machine, quite transported by the strangeness and unbelievableness of Michael's death. He imagined the conversations now going on in every house in the Bay, and tried to understand how disgrace, which he had long accepted as his own, had fallen on his whole family. The idea upset him: the misery of life spread too far. He seemed to be in a dream from which he would soon wake, to find the moon shining and the sleeping noises of the house coming through doors half-opened. But the gas continued to flare up and bubble, the broken sky was filled with rushing flocculent clouds. He put the plates in their places, shining discs sliding one behind the other, little counterfeit moons in mundane array; he swept up the floor, the bits of fluff scooting about in the various airs coming through chinks in the old cottage. He listened to his father and mother speaking low. The gate opened and shut loudly; there was a step in the hall, and Catherine stood before him, pale and tattered; she must have sat outside on the boat during the journey down. Her eyes were ringed with deep black. He heard Catherine go into the room and speak to his mother, and her voice break. He heard his father's step, shortly after, as he passed for the sixth time along the half-mile of the barracks road. His father opened the gate at the bottom of the garden and came up to the kitchen, where Joseph was hanging out the towels to dry.

"Son!"

"Yes, Father?"

"Do you know why he did it?"

"I don't know, Father."

"You saw him pretty often; you saw him on Saturday."

"He was acting queerly on Saturday, But he often did. If you want to know what I think . . ."

"What?"

"I think he was bound to commit suicide."

"Ah, pshaw! No one is bound to; there's always a reason. It was the low-down rotten company he kept."

"Who knows?"

His father went out again to the road. Presently Joseph heard him turn down the steps to the beach. The weather was clearing up wonderfully: at present the moon was shining. Joseph went and sat on the back-step. It was a tragedy, but he could not fix his mind on it.

The night was now clear and resonant, the wind died down.

A high tide clapped round the rocks and against the boats drawn high up to the stone wall. At the change of moon the weather and women change. It was full moon; Catherine herself had changed. She was full of vigour, her voice rich and powerful like a man's. Joseph turned down the light in the kitchen and looked up the dark barracks hill where the frogs were chirping. A young man and woman passed down the military road between the white guide-stones flickering in the moonlight. The young woman was small, but wore high heels which tapped clearly in the hill. If she had worn low heels she would have been smaller than the man : why did not women like to be little and neat? A tremend-ous surge of joy rose in Joseph. He began to think, Michael, Michael, I should be thinking about poor Michael. Michael had lots of trouble with women. There were things he had heard alluded to but had never known rightly. Michael had run after women. Joseph went into the room Michael occupied when he came down to the Bay, the spare room under the attic roof, where the window blew in. He sat down in the dark and felt the unblanketed mattress. He put out his hand and began touching the familiar things standing on the bedside table, running his fingers softly round the edges. He felt the embossed frame sur-rounding a picture, some girl Michael had known before he went to the war, he believed. Who? A patch of moonlight began to move over the groined attic wall. Joseph's arm shot out without his intention, there was a fearful loud crash, and as he started to his feet he crunched the small pieces of broken glass. His cousin Catherine spoke down below, and his mother cried out in a voice like a kitten's :

"Who's that? Who's that? Is that you, dear?"

He heard his cousin's voice, strongly, like a man's, soothing his mother. He went out into the garden and walked among the sweet-smelling flowers. Wearied out, he sat down on some sacking at the end of the garden, then laid his head on the grass and heard the fishermen's voices from over the Bay quite close to his head. The footsteps of a soldier going past the fence seemed to pass over his ear, the clear air and the earth making a micro-phone.

254

When he got up in the early morning, the grass was full of the crepitation of snails: he was soaked with dew and cold as ice. He went in and began to make early morning tea for the household. Catherine said:

"Joseph, are you up? Put on your coat and come up on the cliffs with me: I want to look at the sea."

That night always seemed to him a night spent in another planet, so strange and unearthly it was.

The following Sunday the Baguenaults, dressed in sombre dress, attended a mass of special significance being held in St. Mary's Cathedral. They sat down under stone trees among cartwheels and spindles of coloured lights, and waxen creatures, men and children, in black and purple, moved lights, censers, tablets and vases back and forth. The congregation entered quietly, like thoughts of a past life entering meditations. Michael's relatives thought ceaselessly of his death and wept, and Michael's spirit embraced them and the towers and foundations of the cathedral in its gigantic folds. But Joseph, crouching apart, with eyes open and hands at his sides, knowing the Mass, heard different words and different plaints. He had been Server of the Mass when a child with decency and piety, and now attended for the last time. He held his hands joined, and saw the little boy come from the sacristy preceding the Priest. The child at the altar placed himself to the right of the priest, made the genuflexion, took the wand, lifted a little the alb of the priest as he mounted the steps.

"I will go unto the altar of God."

"To God who gives joy to my youth."

"Judge me, O Lord, and choose my cause from that of unsanctified men; from the wicked and erring man sift me."

"Because thou art, O God, my strength, wherefore wouldst thou repulse me? and wherefore should I walk sadly, when mine enemy afflicts me?"

"Give thy light and thy verity: they led me forth and to thy sacred hill and in thy tabernacle."

"I will go unto the altar of God, to God who gives joy to my youth."

". . . wherefore art thou sad, my soul, why tormentest thou

255

me? . . ."

A man can die from such tormenting. Joseph sank his head in
his hands; his mother sobbed. His father's head rested on the back
of the *prie-Dieu*. I have never seen anyone die. I saw Michael's
body lying under a tarpaulin in a dinghy on the beach on Wednesday evening, and the children gathered round like flies. As
round a dog's body. Dogsbody, that is no one: Mr. Dogsbody
he was . . . he used to go fishing and now he is dead.

". . . till the end of time."

"Amen."

"The Lord be with you."

"And with your soul."

"Lift up your hearts."

Joseph looked at his mother; the black satin ribbon on her hat
rose towards the priest. Black satin ribbon, you do what you're
told; you're a good Catholic, but you don't know men's hearts.
But Michael would have difficulty in lifting up his heart: it is
dissolving, running away in brine and blood. Joseph's mother
turned a briny blue glance upon him, and her black cotton-gloved
hand fumbled for his sleeve. . . .

"Lead us not into temptation,"

"But deliver us from evil. . . ."

The sun shone in the transept, and a visitor, with lifted head,
perambulated slowly round the chapels, his soft footstep making
a vagrant comment on the Mass. Outside the grass flicked silver.
That has nothing to do with it: I've never had temptation in my
life and never done evil, said Joseph, but I'm poor and unhappy,
and might just as well as Michael jump off the rock. I'd sink in
the sea, the end of me; who would care? I would just be dead
like a dead seagull.

". . . Till the end of time."

"Amen."

"The Lord be with you."

"And with your soul."

"May they rest in peace."

"So be it."

At the end of the Mass, his mother took his arm. They filed

slowly out, with the drab mothers and gay girls, between the yellow sandstone pillars. "That's better," said his mother: "now I feel better. I prayed for Michael all the time, and I am sure he will be pardoned. But I will have a mass said for him in the cathedral here. Just one. I have the money. The priest will do it." Joseph was silent. "What do you say, Joseph? You will be server, won't you? For old sake's sake?"

"No."

"Why? You feel badly?"

"No; he wasn't religious. He would have thought it was foolery."

"He didn't know; we shouldn't speak of his errors."

"I don't know either. I can't do it."

"Take the holy water."

He made the sign of the cross.

"This is Sunday: it doesn't seem like it to me any more. I never wanted to commit suicide; perhaps there are lots of things I don't know: who can say Michael was wrong?"

"You know quite well that Michael was—drunk when he fell off the cliff."

"So they say."

"Come home. Catherine'll have a nice dinner ready. You'll feel better after dinner. You're upset."

"All right."

After lunch he said to Catherine:

"Let's get out of here. I've been up to the cliff every day since Tuesday. I've changed. I can't be in the face of that blue, always changing sea, so wide and pagan; looking at it and thinking Michael was washed about there on the rocks, I feel that the end of the earth is the end of time for us."

"When I've washed up we'll go. But don't try to explain to your mother."

"I've told them, but they don't believe it."

"So much the better."

"I've been to my last mass."

"Good."

At about the same hour Marion and Fulke visited Kol Blount, astonished to find himself so long alone, to apprise him of the death of Michael, a secret five days old. When they came in to the quiet room, swimming in light-barred gloom and fresh with the fat summer breeze, Mrs Blount arose quickly with her darning and gave them chairs.

"He doesn't know," she whispered with dramatic emphasis, and wiped her eyes. "Poor Michael! a dear boy—like my own son."

"What are you whispering about, Mother?" called Blount, "is it a surprise party? I'm bored to tears. Come in. I'll bet you have Michael with you, the dog, keeping me in suspense like this for a week."

"No, Michael is not here," said Fulke.

"Don't think you can fool me," said Blount. "Now you three be seated. Come on in out of the passage," and leaning out of his chair, he pushed forward the chair beside him where his reader usually sat.

"He is not here," said Marion.

"He will soon be here. All the afternoon I have thought about him and am sure he is coming. It is always the way: I know by telepathy."

"How that dog howls," said Marion.

"It has been howling for a week," said Mrs Blount; "it makes my blood curdle. Since Tuesday, imagine that!" She cast a significant eye on the Folliots.

"Since Sunday, it's a spoilt little tyke," said Kol Blount. "The owners have gone to Cronulla for a couple of weeks. The butcher's boy feeds it every morning and evening. When it hears a step its moans are simply desperate. I'd go in and bring it here if I had a leg, but Mother won't touch any one else's property, will you, Mother?"

He laughed.

"I'll risk it," said Fulke. "I'll bring it in to you. It doesn't bite, does it?"

"No."

"Come and show me the way, Mrs Blount."

"If you'll take the responsibility, I'll be glad. I'm a neighbour, I have to be careful."

When they had gone, Blount moved his head nervously from side to side and squirmed as if trying to throw off a serpentine oppressor. He began to speak quickly and hotly, like a person talking in his sleep:

"Marion, I'm glad you came; what a dream I had last night! Was I too rough on the people last Sunday? Milt came to see me on Monday night with Fayre Brant and told me they were engaged. Tuesday, the night of the storm, no one came. I knew you were in Melbourne, so didn't worry: besides, the weather was so bad. But about four o'clock in the morning I had terrible nightmares, waking dreams rather, had to call Mother to sit by me, and I heard Michael's voice distinctly, calling 'Kol!' through the storm. But only once or twice. It is very hard for me to shake off dreams with my way of living. Last night I dreamed two great gondolas paddled by rival boatmen ran side by side down a wide turbulent river, with a few stars and low clouds above. Above rose giant pillars of cloud into the evening air. On one of the boats was I. On the prow of the other lay a gallant with white hair, bleeding and gasping his last. Round a body trailing in the water, several people bent and mourned: not yet a body, however, it still breathed. I embraced the dying man, half lifting him from the flowing water over the side of the vessel; the gondoliers leaned on their poles and had forgotten to strive. As I embraced the man in the water, a stately phantom rose over the body of the gallant and cast its hands upwards. With the same movement one of the women, Catherine she was like, rose on her knees and lamented bitterly; then the phantom, it was Grief, flung its arm out, and the second black-haired woman, who was like you, Marion, rose up and flung out her arms, lamenting. But both were unconscious of the phantom that mounted into the air and mingled with the pillars of vapour from the clouds. At the same moment the gondolier pushed the other ship angrily forward, the wounded gallant sat up laughing, the drowned man at our prow fell into the depths of the canal. We rushed on into the dark but he had long outdistanced us.

Underneath in the canal, now become clear, I saw Michael smiling at me. I told Mother that, I was so impressed, and she burst out crying."

Kol Blount looked at Marion, waiting for a word. Marion was much disquieted by this dream and looked out of the window for Fulke. Yet she was a little relieved that he had been prepared for it by dreams.

"And why not?" she said to herself. "Their life was nothing but a dream, the whole world, their fever, their failures, their love was nothing but a dream and incoherent when told. He was a man who could attach no one solidly to him."

Kol's long arm tugged her skirt, from his chair.

"What are you thinking of? You have such a profound look!"

"Nothing much."

"Have you seen Michael?"

"No. Kol, tell me, what do you expect to be the end of Michael?"

He looked intently at her.

"I don't know."

He would not help her. She had rehearsed the opening of the confession for days. The clock struck four. She heard Mrs Blount making tea in the kitchen.

"No one has seen Michael for days."

He said nothing. She had expected alarm, questions, and they would have helped her along. He malignantly disappointed her, and brooded, caressing his cheek and chin with their two days' growth of stubble. He thought Michael was dead drunk, and they had come to clatter about it. A bitter hard expression was levelled at her, saying, "You like to see a man downed, don't you?" Marion listened impatiently for Fulke's step.

"What has happened, Marion?"

"Michael will not come here any more."

"He has gone abroad. Don't say it!"

"No, he is . . ."

"He is what?"

"He is — listen, Kol, give me your hand — he is dead."

Before she had finished speaking he put up his hand quickly

260

to ward off the stroke.

"Michael!"

He let his hands fall on to the arm of the chair, his face fearfully convulsed; then he sat still. She put her hand on his knee, for he did not wish to hear a word. He patted it gently, but in a few minutes he began to shiver, long convulsions from the depths of the Cimmerian cave; beasts howled on the remote rim of the world; the planets went whirling over the edge; horrible forests, black, mountain-perched, mossy, cloud-soaked at the end of existence, began to toss. All the time he sat shivering, shivering in a Chinese contortion of black and white, white face and limbs and black eyes. She heard Fulke, thank Heaven! coming up the path.

"Fulke, Fulke!"

Fulke looked, and rushed across the room.

"It's all right," said Kol Blount, "but I didn't expect it. At least, not so soon. Wait a little while in the kitchen with Mother, will you?"

"Let's go now," said Catherine, when the washing-up was finished, to Joseph. The two old people were sleeping. The Bay was full of rowing-boats, people in light clothes walked all over the roads, green Vaucluse, with its white palace and rich bungalows, sparkled beside the blue water.

"It's a lovely day," said Catherine. "We'll take the boat in. I want you to come and visit Baruch with me: we'll have tea somewhere in town. I want to go on the spree a bit; I'm going into an asylum to-morrow. You'll think I'm crazy, perhaps, but it's the best thing for me, the way I feel."

"An asylum? What for?"

"I want to rest, and I can only rest where people are allowed to be queer. You wouldn't understand how upset I am over Michael: I'm supposed to be without much family affection. But I want you to understand. You're not a bad fellow, Jo, and you take people at their own estimation, that's why you have faithful friends: there's no spite in you. But those others, half of them are stuffed with spleen, spite or gall. Every one in the asylum pities the insanity of the others. And they teach handicrafts there. They are kind people, the insane, easy to live amongst, easy to humour, and if cranky, no worse than plain men."

"Oh, I couldn't. But can any one get in?"

"No, I have a friend; a doctor who will certify me unbalanced. And I am."

"Do it if you want to. I don't think it crazy; you know best what you want. I'll come and see you."

When they reached Baruch's bachelor room in Woolloomooloo, they found him absorbed in books. He seemed annoyed to see them; then he sprang up.

"Catherine, I'm delighted to see you. How do you feel?"

"Rotten, thanks."

"You must; did any one know Michael so well as you?"

"No, I don't think so; I am sure not."

"Do you know why he died?"

"For want of breath."

He gave her a shocked glance.

"That's a funny thing to say; you know I'm your friend. Did it concern the Folliots?"

"You will never know that."

"I know it already. But I don't press you. Only, I had a real affection for Michael. It was entirely unexpected to most of us. Perhaps not to — some woman."

He gave her an inquisitive glance, half theatrical, to force her secret. He thought, She dislikes Marion; what is the real basis of the jealousy? Catherine laughed aloud.

"Baruch, you're cunning, you're devious; but you wouldn't know my tale if I hadn't come to tell it. I'm going into Forestville to-morrow, to rest and for psycho-analytic treatment, and I want to begin to unburden my soul now."

"I'm sorry to hear it; I don't believe in that treatment."

"I do."

"Good."

There was a silence. Baruch fingered the pages of his book, reading a line or two. Catherine turned towards him impetuously.

262

"Would you be interested to hear the private history of Michael?"

"Very much."

"I warn you it is strange and long."

"All the better; most lives are stale and short."

"He was Mother's illegitimate son, and knew it quite early. Our money came partly from his father, an eccentric surveyor, mathematician and astrologer."

"Whose mind was so much in the stars that he didn't know what he was doing when he walked amongst men."

"Yes, Michael arrived in one of those off moments. He was intended to go to the University because Mother had a romantic feeling about him, the bastard son of an eccentric man, quite evidently a genius . . ."

"One of the great race of mahmzers."

"What? Well, Michael was emotional and sensual; he was first attracted to the Church, you probably can't imagine why in this country which doesn't exactly favour cloistral gloom and where every one thinks of the price of wool. His mind was lost in antique Celtic fogs: he drew designs in his odd hours, and had a very sweet imagination, *mittel-Europäischer*, *mittel-alter*. He used to dream about colonies of angels and vast buildings whose columns had scaly winged feet. He told me every morning when he waked what he dreamed. I used to lie back, shut my eyes and see it too. He collected prints of Dürer and mediaeval artists, but he didn't like anything modern. He bought a wooden replica of a peasant Christ found in the Tyrol, a most grotesque thing, to have in his bedroom, which he had painted white. But it wasn't to pray, it was the grotesquerie, the bizarre monastic flavour, a shock in a suburban bungalow. He met a girl in the Bay called Mae Graham, a teaser, and he could not tear himself away from her even when she married. I imagine he committed adultery with her. He met Withers before that, and Withers liked to tote him around; he was the same then as now.

"He would always go out walking with me to tell me his dreams. He insisted on having a photograph of me, and said he walked with me in dreams. He left it at some friends."

263

She looked at Joseph.

"I broke the frame the other night by accident and put it in a drawer. I did not think it was of any use."

"You were very close to each other?" said Baruch.

Catherine was silent for a while. Her powerful tragic sense changed the small room, even in their eyes, to a theatre. Baruch remembered her scenes as if he had seen them stereoscopically. And this, hardly believing, he called Catherine's narrative.

CATHERINE'S NARRATIVE

We were hearts united—before the war.

Before the war. But I thought it was finished when he returned from the war, until a holiday we spent in the country. Once we went to Tuggerah Lakes during a vacation. We used to walk along the beach about seven miles to Norah Head where the lighthouse is, and back, over the soggy sand. The mouth of the lakes is always filling up. There is a sand-bank in the centre of the entrance lake, the tide runs out fast through thick mud channels on either side. It is very treacherous at the ebb. The sand-banks, too, at the mouth of the lakes often drop off sheer into the water. The water is like an aquarium underneath, and you can see the fish ten to twenty feet down.

Behind the bungalow is low dense scrub, eucalypts, bottle-brushes, she oaks, and in the back-yard a tree with large white trumpet flowers of the nightshade family, I don't know the name. In the bush we sat every day before lunch and tea and Michael read me his poems. The place is damp, mournful, magnificently lac-coloured morning and evening.

One day we rowed to the island, which is covered with trees and dripping with damp. We got out, tied the boat to a stump, and went in amongst the trees one behind the other. Michael walked in front, because I can't bear to have anyone behind me— so I could not see his face. We continued to walk along over the leafy mud. It was quiet except for the ring-necked doves roucou-couing right up in the tree-tops and some curlews on the opposite shore—they have a dismal human cry.

264

I said nothing. I was thinking about the meeting I was organising out at Double Bay. Laverty, the local secretary, was rather rocky and indifferent because I was a girl. Michael kept on walking in front of me. The island became silent except for the squelching mud. Michael's dark raincoat, gawky saunter and black hair seemed to stretch out into the undergrowth. He pointed out things with a bit of stick, without speaking, but he kept on, starting to speak on some subject which he was revolving in his head, without ever making anything but a coughing sound, as if he had changed his mind and started off on a new track. A sea-fog had drifted in; the rolling vapour fell on the island. We plodded along aimlessly in the wet, cloaked in our ideas—it got darkish, blobs of water dropped from the foliage to the earth. I began to think about Michael, that if he walked long enough he would miss the path and walk off the island into the water, struggle in the mud four feet thick, be drowned and so end his unhappy, useless life. I wished he would. He was so dark and cold, like the moon; I felt the fire in me by contrast. If I had had a true brother, I thought, I would have had a companion; he always failed me. I thought, I will never get anywhere while he is a drag on me. He spoke to me,

"Do you think it is auspicious that my dearest friend is the paralytic, Kol Blount? What do you think of that?"

"I think it's a mistake," said I.

"If Blount could walk, he would despise me to-morrow. No one, you all think, could have a true affection for me."

"Everyone is loved," said I.

"Even Blount and even me. But they flatter themselves. If he were free he would leave them all. He is a better man than all."

"He is a brilliant man, but whether he's better than any one of us—it's difficult to prove. He gains by his immobility. You over-rate him. I prefer an active man as a companion."

"Even you despise me. It's strange, isn't it? For a long time I endeavoured to be human. What is the solitude of a man? Not that he is a unit, but that he is a fraction. In my solitude, as a boy, I migrated people to the sky, peopled the dark spaces with bodies. I talked to the stones and the sea, the stones in the house

265

answered me. I spoke familiarly to the furniture in my room and everywhere in nature and in the building materials of the city, in cast nails and puddles of lime, and underfoot, I saw a movement, a breathing, upwrenching, freeings and unhappy motion : I felt the trees had the souls of men prisoned, nature was full of gagged voices. Isn't Kol exactly like that?"

"Yes, I understand now."

"No. I lay on my back watching a shining, futile ant fussing through green thickets of grass and climbing gigantic stalks to surmount them, instead of going round the roots—immense energy for nothing; next day he died and was tugged back to the ant-hill to be eaten. But the grass thicket and the ant-hill themselves were alive, creaking tremendously in my ears; I never heard, except in a storm, such a roaring in the air. There is a blasting like that in the uneasy silence of Kol's sick-room."

"Is that it?"

"No; there is more. I went at night in the Inner Domain where it overlooks Garden Island. The tramps were there rolled in their caves, their fires were extinguished, and they were like dead leaves, or bad fruit fallen out of the trees. No, they were shadowy emanations from the ground, abortions. They were not alive, but the trees were alive. Awfully they began to move and bend over me; they crowded together in their congregations and unholy intercourse began. I was as invisible to their senses as their speech inaudible to my outward ear.

"When the wind comes off the bay, as it often does at nightfall, when a scurrying and rushing of feet, a series of flurries and cat's-paws comes off the hills, then they burst their cataleptic dream, with what horrible memories and unspeakable ideas drunk up out of the earth with the dead encysted in its flesh, I do not know, but I was always afraid at that hour. Yet the trees were more alive than the men. Woe to the man who has the soul of a tree : such I am!

"At last I could no more persuade myself I was human. I ran out into the country at night, on to the fire-scorched and blackened hills, where splintered boles and spaded burrows of little animals trip one up at every step. There are snakes in the long grass. I passed by sleeping farms and orchards where the roosting hens clucked and the dog shook his chains and barked. I looked for a stray sundowner or homegoer late at night on the road, a man going early to work to hoe the turnips, put in the potatoes or pluck the hairy caterpillars off the grape-vines, or a country boy coming home late from a country dance, overcoat on shoulder, drunk and whistling; but none I ever found, or if I found them they passed by with only a word.

"I thought I might fall in with a beggar or a thief, either is a human relationship, but I met no one. In the street, in the evening, the women only looked at me over their shoulders and trotted on. What is the mark that puts everyone on their guard? A child sees me and looks at me solemnly and reflectively: 'Look, Mamma, look at the funny man!' But there's really nothing funny about me, is there?"

"Nothing at all," I said, without looking at him. As you know, though, he had an absorbed, fanatic look, with his thin cheeks and eyes too close together. In Naples they would have said he had the evil eye.

"There is something," continued Michael. "What? I am a man: I can't see that deformity, it is not physical. Yes, my forehead is dark and my cheeks sunk in with the many nights when even sleep forsakes my bed, but there are thousands like me, in the crowds of workmen and students going to work in the early boats every morning, with every cast of forlornity.

"Do you remember the summer I was seventeen, I went into the country for the holidays and came back the next day, without saying why? I came to a town and drove down by pony-trap from the station. Oh, the radiant bush with eucalypt leaves and the stench of undergrowth exuding aromatic oils, the red tracks winding down the hills towards cabbage-tree palms, through cycads, the blue sarsaparilla vines and boronia plants, their juices bubbling in the hot air. We came towards the water. Newly-varnished rowing-boats were drawn up in rows against the stone pier; no one was there but me. I was whistling with pleasure. There was a hut verandahed, and roofed with blinding unpainted corrugated iron, hot, red and silver under the hill. That was the

place I had come to stay in. A woman with moon-white hair
and yellow face approached with a rake along a row of worm-
eaten cabbages, bare-footed; she had no teeth. After her, in rags,
came two children, yellow as wax. She grins, 'Do you want
cabbages? I'll have to arst my bruvvernlaw.' She sends her husband to her brother-in-law's hut: for they have only one pair
of trousers between them. They find out what I have come for;
they stare. It is a mistake. 'But you can stay,' she says obligingly,
'ten shilluns a week.' The floor is only made in one room and
stacked with fowls' excrement: as I come out by the back door,
I see the brother-in-law having his bath, quite naked in a tub
under a water-spout. 'We wash 'ere,' says the woman. 'No thanks,'
I say. They all stare after me with lugubrious, disappointed faces.
'I jest killed a chicken,' says the husband; 'you better pay for it,
all the same.' I paid for it. When I came home, I looked at the
day's paper: there was the same advertisement. I never knew
what went wrong, but I know that where I was mixed up a thing
something would be wrong."

"That's funny, not tragic," I said, and laughed, remarked
Catherine.

"I suppose there are people who can't stand any sort of rebuff
or shock, but it's outside my world," said Baruch. "However,
what happened then?"

Michael began to get more excited. He said:

"I went another time with my friend Chaunter on a motor trip.
We were to cross the Divide and go into the great plains. We
were in the foothills of the mountains at night. The low shrubs
moved soundlessly in the breeze and the broad road stretched
away among the undulating uplands for many miles, now lost
in shade, now shining in the moon on some far hilltop, or curving
between brush-lands with rough edges, like a bird's feather
dropped in flight. The car moved swiftly and silently mile after
mile. Presently the ridge declined and great areas of sand
swamped the vegetation. It was midnight. We stopped the car
and walked a bit in the fresh air before turning in. We presently
lost sight of the car and came to flats like dried lagoons, caked
and split with salt.

268

"We had now left all vegetation behind and nothing was to be seen but sand: a strange desert, a desert as wide as the earth, strange, strange," said he in a high-toned voice. The very notes produced a disturbing sensation, mysterious and ominous. The curious diffusion of light elongated his legs and spindled his waist.

"We trod over the sandhills for twenty minutes, bewildered by the illimitable moonlit wastes, sunk in thought, silent, scarce hearing the screech and whirr of the trodden sand, our thoughts rushing round and round as if we inhabited a nightmare. What are those sounds that the mind alone hears at dead of night and when the wind is still? The full moon was now in its zenith: presently a chill wind rushed out of the eastern horizon, out of the darkness, and gathered darkness above it; it wandered about the desert and ever grew in sound. At first it was like the calm full tide in a deep anchorage, murmuring against the chains and bottoms, but shortly it moved towards us upon the hills with a profound murmur stirred up from the bowels of the sand, and hidden caverns I know not where; and at last it roared upon us as the storm in the high wooded mountains, and a thousand imagined terrors found form in sound and gloom; we stood in light but we were consumed in gloom: and then again, it had passed and gone off on its wild errand and we were alone upon the waste.

"A flake of air fell past my ear sighing 'Gone!' At my side was nothing but a violin planted in the sand. 'Look yonder!' said the air, and the air became full of sounds, thicker and thicker, and the air began to roar and the sand to whirl and we were again in the full blast of the sirocco. In the following storm, which was a minute's entire length, he bowed beside me, above, around, like half a dozen goblins; looked like a violin, scraped cries out of his own stomach, turned into a mandrake, withered and swelled. The cloud of dust was full of people, rushing past with songs and kickings, old mutterers singular and angularly breaking into yells, bad children, fairies, old professors, confessors, aiders and abbesses, two legged palsied palimpsests, clerks, sharks, narks, shades, suspicions, university janitor, spiral-horned rams, stock exchange rampers, rabbits, whorlie-whorlies, willy-willies,

269

whories, houris, ghosts, gouttes, knouts, ghouls, walking-gourds, grimalkins, widdershins and withering wights, but in such a horrid, enlaced, perplexed, twisted and lolloping rhythm as I shuddered to look upon.

"As for him, fantasy filled him; he shouted, waved his legs, sang; he swayed the people into five lines and a key signature: he took it into his head to do a once-about, and in the shut of an eye, the place was deserted. Then the moon shone, all was still.

" 'What is the time?' said he. There he was at my shoulder. We walked on and neither of us said anything. He limped a little. 'I trod in an old rabbit warren,' he said, and pretended, I suppose, to know nothing of what had passed. But he left me the next day, and I never heard of him again. You doubt me? It was so; the ranges of human experience go beyond human belief. All my friends were like that. There's Kol Blount, ironbound in his chair, like Holger the Dane.

"The third occasion was this. It was fine weather, the night before was a night of brilliance, with the stars swimming in the sky at great altitudes and the black bush like the rough hair of a beast; many legions of stars swarmed at a heavenly height, especially when seen over the neighbour's wall. It was in 1919, when I first returned from the war and felt reborn.

"The sun rose in the morning, as I saw it, for I was awake all night, with a crest of twenty fine rays. The air was chill with the first breath of autumn, the small sunflowers turned to the sun above the transparent water at the bottom of our gully slope, and on the pond in our house the waterlilies, the nymphae, were not yet awake. The face of the creek was silvery where it had lain quiet all night, until the light slowly dawned upon it and turned it pale: thick autumnal dew on the grass. I got up early.

"I thought of the sea-mist, like this, that crawls over the gunners' tents with sudden drops and on the leaves of our valley and on my pillow, swaddling all of us in its grey coverlet, as if to march off with us under its cloak. I decided to go up on the northern rivers. I took the night train towards Newcastle and got out at a place not far from Brisbane Water, where if you stand on a knoll called Berry's Head, you can see on one hand in the distance the white waters of Brisbane Water like a handkerchief in the grass, and opposite the grid of orchards on the slopes, the high pale range beyond, and to the north the fruit-bearing valley, with pine-nurseries and vineyards on the way up to Wyong. I know it well.

"Well, it had blown up dirty weather when I got there and I could hardly pick my way along the road, which was only rolled clay. The trees were clashing and the road strewn with branches. It was dangerous walking; although I had intended to come on to Tuggerah, I knocked at the door of a cottage, and the owner, who had a sailor's ruggedness (and a sailor he had been, sailing from London Pool at twelve), let me in. He had a poor orchard, which cost him money. Williams was his name. A kerosene lamp lighted his kitchen beside the dying fire in the built-in stove. He was waiting for the doctor, his wife being very ill with pneumonia and his daughter lying in the other room with a childbed fever. He was a gentle man, but it was freezing in the house and he had no extra covering, nor would I have put him to the trouble of housing me. So I went out again on to the back road towards a house he named. The road ran down a hill between orchards to an old house with all the rooms built in a chain of rough-hewn blocks, long ago quarried by the convicts. In front of the house was an old Araucaria Bidwilli pine, where a convict was hanged, or beaten to death, or caught by blood-hounds, I forget the story. But there was no light; and as I went down the hill, I felt cramped and faint, so I sat down on the clay bank and listened to the lashing trees and crying plantations. Overhead the clouds were black and scurrying; a flying fox flopped off the tree beside me.

"After a while the wind stopped, the storm became more resigned. I looked towards the stone house and thought I saw a light. 'Is that house awake after all, then?' I said aloud. In answer, there sprang up a loud wild yell which seemed to come from the tree or house and from close at hand. It continued for a short time and died down into a whistling and a sigh over the paddocks. My blood stopped running : I thought to look upon the material-ised face of horror, but nothing more came. That cry of inhospitality and solitude is still in my ears. I turned away from the house which had gone black again, and walked all night through the rain.

"Thus I became afraid; in the nights I lay awake unable to sleep for the beating of my heart, which thought every sound a foot-step coming to my side, and which beat faster at the following silence. I resolved to become less human, then I should not miss people so much. I called up the brutish spirit of solitude, saying, Put all sound out of my ears, drive me out with pricks and salt to walk the streets at night, let me wound bitterly my only and dearest friend, start with affectation at his simple words, suffer slight from his unintended innuendoes, give me a dry sharp voice, so that I will be entirely alone. Aggravate and embitter my sorrow with every expedient at your service, and you will not do enough. Your torments are weak compared with those I can invent for myself. Yesterday my cousin Joseph looked at me and laughed in my face. I walked three hours in a fever wishing I had screwed his neck. I saw nothing for three hours but the blood running out of his nostrils. You would never lose my soul as I can lose it, old bit of rubbish that you are. Get out of this, take yourself off, hoppygo devil, with your stage effects, trumpets and storms, you dumb jackanapes with two ideas and a black coat perched on your back, quite devoid of subtlety.

"But so perverse in everything; out of the vice into which I wished to sink, a new life came up into my nostrils. The world imagines that virtue and courage are honourable, because it benefits thereby, but for the possessor and doer they are vile error and sin; they destroy his humanity. The giver-up, the sacrificial agent, the atoner, the ascetic of the body will hereafter have no more restraint in his imagination. His desires flourish as their denial is pressed down; what they lack in satisfaction, they put forth in the fruit of understanding and sensibility. Then when they have fitted him to understand it, they destroy his virtue and make him the subtlest connoisseur of his own destruction.

"I thought my heart would burst my body, it so strained at the chain and wished to augment itself: I burned inwardly and my life flowed three times as fast, so that I could not see any motion in the world, except things blowing in high winds.

"This was what I thought, but this was the perversity—I saw Catherine through a new lens, and thus I am mocked : my destiny is stronger towards unreality than life."

"Michael was silent for a while," said Catherine, "and I thought : Who is this Catherine?"

"Who was Catherine?" said Baruch.

"You are serious and sympathetic," said Catherine; "I will tell you what followed."

He said : "Why is there so much darkness in the world that even the sun can only illuminate a small part of our day, at noon? There is dewy darkness in the forenoon and dry radiant shadows at midday and dusk pregnant with imaginatory forms in the evening, but all through the day, thus, the kingdom of dark remains and lies in a guet-apens for the time it shall reign. Also in the mind there are very few things which are bright and clear, but the greater part of our day is spent in internal dark—and what of the inenarrable night sessions of dreams? If you dig in the earth, it is dark within, despite the gold and fire contained there. If you penetrate beyond the diffusing envelope of air, the heavens are black; if you even look into the heart of a tree, darkness seems to rush forth as you cleave the bark; thus man goes upon his way peering. The greatest occasions of life are made mysteries, such as birth, love and the adoration of God— the womb, dark and without air, the earth, the same; light is but a temporary star in our existence. Birth strikes the eyeball and says "Let there be light!" I often wonder what makes a child come forth for something which he knows nothing of : does he see a sudden flash of light in pre-natal night, and hunger and desire it thereafter? Surely darkness is the condition of man, and light is all he thirsts after, for the Kingdom of Heaven is said to be all light, and it takes a very austere and not a fortified mind even to conceive of Hell without *light*.

"So a candle is a lovely thing, so I am ravished when I look at the starry way, and limpid Jupiter in the early evening; and also your eyes, Catherine, in their exceptional lucency, and your form, which is all darkness and white, the eternal contrast and composition of the world."

I was terrified. I said: "Michael, hush! What are you saying?"

He said: "It is not permitted, in this part of the world, to a brother to love his sister. He may grow up with her and become familiar with her ways, and her thoughts, the way she speaks, but he may not love her except coldly and indifferently: he may not love her as any stranger whom she accidentally meets outside may love her. The reasons for this prohibition, unnatural and cruel, which brings it about that brothers often hate their sisters, are among those nameless mysteries and darknesses I was speaking about.

"Whereas, as I was born unnatural, I have come to love my sister as myself, for you are myself, but everything appears in you with a greater perfection, and all that is dark and light in you is the very reflection of my own thoughts, my mind and my desires. A man cannot *love* himself, but all men do, and so there is no satisfaction in the world, for we must clasp another body, informed by another spirit to ourselves.

"But I love you not for myself, but for you. I cannot explain why in this or that way of speaking, and why in your expressions and glances there is such exquisite pain, such sudden revelations, as if I discovered every hour a new beauty in your face which is so familiar. But so it is, and so I am in love with you; not you, but that which is like you in me. I am lost because part of me is sundered from me for ever.

"You look at me in horror, fear and speculation, but your unquenchable beauty reflected in me, your sun, my moon, move in accord; you cannot hate me. Your silver eyeballs gleam, your silver brow and the lightnings of your aspect. Put your face in your hands. Because you are not beauty, you are terror, you are destiny, what is destiny but death, and what else are you? If I ever kissed you, what would I have under my lips but the very substance and moment of death and dissolution?

"I have no meaning in ordinary life, and this is what releases me from being silent about my love. and it is what makes me love, perhaps, the image of myself: it is a hunger and lust for death at root."

274

He said this to me while walking slowly in endless circles round the island. He stopped once or twice and looked at me, and then turned round again and walked on, almost indifferently, as if he spoke about something impersonal. I did not know what to answer. He did not want any answer.

We rowed to the house. We only spoke on that subject once again in our lives, that was the other night at Kol Blount's house, and then, by allusion. I endured it for a few months and almost believed what he said: I lived in a sort of amazement, so that the sun did not have the same colour. Then I changed. I met a lot of people: my own world emerged. Michael went away from home, and when he came back and joined our circle I saw he was running after Marion. He knew her abroad.

Catherine was silent.

Baruch unwillingly stirred himself and remarked, "Then it was Marion!"

"No, it was I."

"How did you feel? You must have felt strange."

"Didn't you understand? I loved Michael: I have always loved him. I tried to make plans to go to some other country where they would not know we were related, but all these fantasies went up in smoke; besides, Michael would never have done it. It would have made the thing too real to him, he only wanted to play with the idea."

"Faithless to each other, you all are," said Baruch abruptly. "You can't believe in a sincere passion. All crazy and all seeking outlandish vagaries to distinguish you, a true oddity seems a disgrace to you. You bark like tykes when a true nonesuch arrives among your eccentricities. I must say, I'm moved by your tale, and I don't think his feelings misplaced either; he could have found no one but you and Blount amongst all his friends."

"How lovely you are, Baruch!"

He looked in the glass, pulling a whimsical face.

"Nobody can think so. What a face!"

"You know I mean in nature."

"An insult, then."

But he fell silent, moved his chair and looked out of the window. Presently his eyes fell back to his book, and he kept stealing glances at it.

"Excuse me," said Baruch presently, seeing his two guests sitting still side by side, not willing to move, "I can't get that tale out of my head. It's really so peculiar."

"I'm going," said Joseph, seeing Baruch absorbed.

Catherine did not move.

"I'm not; this is my last night amongst rational people."

Baruch turned his chair round and looked at her.

"I thought you were going into the asylum voluntarily?"

Catherine began to cry.

"I'm ridiculous," she said, "don't take any notice of me, but I'm wretched. I don't know what I want, and I don't really want to go into the asylum, but it's the only place where I have a home when I'm cranky and cracked. If I were always in touch with a person like you, with a golden sanity like yours, I wouldn't think of such things."

"The Folliots are quite sane," said Baruch gently, smiling.

"I'm mixed up in too many emotional relations with them. I was in love with Fulke at one time, and I disliked Marion at others for her trailing Michael round. You can understand."

They talked for a long time about odds and ends, while they felt the blood rushing through their hearts to a new measure. They talked automatically and disjointedly and unnecessarily, so that the conversation would soon drop and a silence would come when they could look at each other with full glances, questioning and responsive, understanding, hesitating. They grew more corpulent spiritually, they felt stronger, they grew to their full height. Innocent fancies filled them, they had a temptation to speak with a familiar simplicity which made them smile to themselves. They lived thus for several hours.

"I feel better," said Catherine soon. "I wish I had not arranged to go to Forestville, but now I must. I am going to help with the instruction in the workshops."

"Don't go," said Baruch.

"You won't be here long, Baruch. I can't antagonise them. I must have a haven to go to, when you are not here any more and I am upset."

"Do I really make so much difference?"

"Of course."

He touched her hand. She got up and put on her hat.

"Well, I am going home. I am tired out, and I have to pack a little bag, not much. I must see Mother, for I have told her quite a different story, that I am instructor at the asylum. Thanks very much. Good night!"

He came downstairs with her, and at the door made a stiff European bow.

10 ⋘

A chapter of accidents: two poor men in gaol, Montagu skips,
three poor men without a job.
Jo's mother sums up.

IT WAS a steamy white Friday towards the end of September.
The weather promised to be exceptionally hot, the afternoons
shone copper, the meteorologists announced a drought, and the
people in the west had already had a succession of days at one
hundred and ten degrees in the shade. In the city they were glad
of the wind off the water. Joseph went up in the morning to buy a
cheap bathing-suit in royal blue at the fire-sale shop, "The Hive,
Where Biz Hums". There were always plenty of bankruptcies to
supply the "Hive" with cheap stuff. "With the 'Hive', you can't
go naked," said Joseph's mother comfortably, when daily inspecting its advertisements.

Joseph spread out the royal blue bathing-suit on the window-
sill and contemplated it. Baruch came in, jubilated.

"Am I dreaming? Have you bought something, something
absolutely unnecessary? Boy, aren't we rich? aren't we smart?"

"I can't go swimming without, especially with a girl," said
Joseph, rolling it up and busying himself about, with his back to
Baruch.

"A girl! You close wretch; you've been keeping a girl from me
all this time. I might have known it when you appeared with a
new tie last week."

Joseph grinned, then said in an offhand manner:

"Don't tell the boys, there's a good chap. You know what
they are!"

"Why should I tell them? You know I don't talk about people's
affairs. A man's business is his own: I never interfere."

Joseph, happily engrossed in his work, whistled under his breath. Presently he heard Baruch's voice at the door.

"Mr Montagu's not here, this is not his office, we haven't seen him since last week. Will you come back in half an hour when Mr Chamberlain is here?"

A thick-set man of middle height, with a well-tailored grey suit, hat on his head and hard inquisitive glance, looked down insolently at Baruch, and put him aside with his hand.

"Let me come in. I've got a warrant."

"Show it to me," said Baruch.

The man thrust a paper at him as he shouldered past him into the office. Baruch followed him in and asked:

"What's up?"

"A lot," answered the man. "What do you know about him?"

"Nothing," said Baruch. "He comes here from time to time, sometimes as a client, but he doesn't give us much work, and he hasn't been here for a week."

"Pretty thick with your boss, eh?" asked the detective, looking at the account-books and putting his fingers casually on papers lying round the office.

"As far as I know, it's a business acquaintanceship," said Baruch carelessly. "Why, what's up? Someone after him?"

"Too right!" answered the man.

"What charge?"

"Wouldn't you like to know?" The man grinned, "Eh, sticky-beak?"

"It's a human weakness," laughed Baruch. "What makes you go in for the career of detective, eh? A genial impulse to know what's going on in whited sepulchres, coupled with the timid bloodhound's abstract scientific passion to know where a smell leads to."

The detective put his hat on the desk, and lighting a cigarette, tilted back in the chair.

"You're wrong," said he. "Everybody has a down on a detective: but we're the servants of public morality. Look how we dig up crime. The place would be overrun with smugglers, burglars, rapers, murderers"—he waved his hand—"cheap swindlers, counterfeiters, Communists, drug-runners." He smoked hard on his cigarette. "People like a bobby because he's in the street, you can hit him on the head, or run him down when he's not looking, but no one likes a detective because he's a wise bird and gets up in the morning earlier than you do."

"Funny," said Baruch, "it's every boy's ambition to be a detective at one time or another, isn't it? Not mine, though."

"Yuh," replied the detective, not abandoning his pose of careless self-mastery. "When they're young, they're smart; when they get older, their minds gets routine. Now to be a detective, you've got to be fresh, you've got to think of the unlikely, the bizarre, and you've got to get an oblique way of looking at human nature. And you've got to know human nature. Now I know all types of men. Some are obvious—there's a signboard on their mugs which says, 'Don't trust me!' Others are quiet little fellows that you'd give the management of your estate—if you have one," he added, winking at Baruch, Joseph and Williams. "Others are big hail-fellow-well-met, frank-looking blokes, they're the confidence-trick sort!" He paused. "In fact, I've got a private little theory: I've had plenty of experience and I know human nature."

"The theory of a man about his own business is always illuminating," remarked Baruch earnestly.

The man lighted another cigarette, and looking Baruch straight in the eye, said gravely:

"My theory is that every man is a potential criminal: there's no difference between criminals and honest men; it's just a question of how tight a corner you're in. There's plenty of crimes, light offences and ghastly crimes, that are never known by anyone. That's why we couldn't manage if we had twice as many secret police in the service."

"You ought to write detective stories," said Baruch. "How do detective stories appeal to you, a detective?"

"Rotten," said he energetically. "To begin with, things never happen the way those writers describe them, and then you get better stories out of the papers every day. I don't know why they don't take stories out of the papers or police records. And then you have to know police methods to describe it right. They make so many bloomers, I can't read them: I put them down in disgust."

"What about the murder of Marie Roget, and the murders in the Rue Morgue, and the Purloined Letter?"

"Yuh, Poe, you mean? Well, it's not possible they would have missed a letter if they'd ripped the place to pieces. Still, he would have made a good sleuth. No, it's too easy; an author makes up a plot, he knows the answer, and then he finds it out. It isn't like that in real life. A chap has four aliases, three passports, he's not stupid, but smart as hell, he's up to all the dodges in creation: and there are a lot of criminal businesses that have a perfected technique, like—printing, banking, anything you like; drug-running, for instance. They have organisations bigger than international banks, Governments get mixed up in it themselves sometimes. Like in—well, you don't know about that."

The detective stopped talking. "Well," he concluded, "it's a career, it's a career, but a hard one. You usually run up against a blank wall. In detective romances they're always solved one hundred times out of a hundred."

"You ought to write some detective stories, on the basis of the crimes that aren't found out and aren't solved."

The man looked wise. "When I get through," he said, "I may. Or when I get more time; I've often thought of it. I thought of a good scheme like that; start a paper giving half a dozen unsolved mysteries a month—real ones, mind you! Then offer prizes for the best solutions. Don't you see? The hidden criminals would often write in for the prizes; they know the solutions, don't they? They usually need the money. It's a peach of an idea. But you need money to start the paper."

"You'd run it for private profit?"

"You bet. I'd become the Sherlock of Australia; no one would know how I got the info. I'd run the paper under an assumed name—take some smart feller, who knew how to write—you, for example—you could run it from the printing-office; it doesn't need any editing, I give you the stories. A peach of an idea; but don't worry, they'd soon find out and stop my scheme."

"It could be done," said Baruch. "It's a first-rate idea. To begin with, criminals are proud of their little feats when they don't get pinched."

"Of course, that's my idea."

"Listen," said Baruch. "It's hot here, isn't it? A pity there's no window in the office. Do you want a whisky and soda?"

"I don't mind."

Baruch began to get out the bottles and glass, saying quietly:

"I don't care twopence about this Montagu or whatever his name is, I've only seen him a few times, but he strikes me as a bounder, and as you say, he's got 'Don't trust me' written on his mug. But I'd like to know what he's been up to; is it misrepresentation selling his antiques?"

"No," said the man, taking his glass, "I can't tell you; but it's not that, it's worse."

"What, smuggling?"

"Don't ask," said the man. "I can't tell you. You'll know soon enough."

"It's all right, it's only 'insatiable curiosity'," said Baruch, grinning. He hesitated a moment. "Some more whisky?"

"All right. I don't turn a hair at a bottle even. I've got the levellest head in the city."

"Do you think it's going to snow?" asked Baruch.

"What?"

"Snow?" said Baruch.

The detective winked at him. "You're smart, feller, aren't you? I certainly would have you to run my paper, if I could get it started. You've got a taking way that is just the thing. You'd make a good crook. Professional adviser, eh?"

"No," said Baruch, walking out of the office. "It's my honesty that makes me charming; without it, I'd have no appeal." He called the boy and started his machine.

Withers stalked in gloomily, and presently the printing-room was working at top pressure.

"Where's the boss?" said Baruch. "There's a visitor waiting for him."

Withers looked at the visitor, gloomily noted the glass beside him.

"Looks like a dick to me!" said he. "They've got 'private detective' written all over their faces. With suspecting everybody and regarding the least accident as a stepping-stone in their career, with each brutal murder and desolating embezzlement of the funds of widows and children meaning a new star or stripe for them, they get mean, ferrety faces: I hate 'em."

The detective got up and circulated sedately, with a casual expression, round the machines.

Fulke Folliot appeared at the door, looked for Baruch and came in saying:

"I've got a job for you, Mendelssohn!"

He saw the stranger and stopped, looking him over. He turned casually on his heel and beckoned Baruch into the office.

"Come in; I want to explain to you what I want."

When they got in, Fulke said, leaning over a bit of paper on which he sketched with a pencil:

"That fellow belongs to the Federal Police. I've seen him before, and it's my business to know their faces."

"I know," said Baruch. "He's in the drug squad, I think."

"I'm always running into them, it's rotten luck. I'm fated to run into the crew," said Fulke. "Look here, it's a pamphlet I promised Winter to bring out. You know his pet study, the profits raked off by local capitalists, each year? By the way, you know he's in quod?"

"No!"

"Yes, on a charge of sedition, inciting to riot, etc., for a speech he made to seamen at the Union's offices, on Monday. They wanted to get someone, and didn't dare take anybody important; I nearly expected it to be me."

"Oh, you don't have to worry," said Baruch peacefully. "You'll get let out if any over-zealous blue takes you up."

"What makes you think so?" asked Fulke, flushing. "I've been in gaol before this."

"And will be again, perhaps," answered Baruch easily, looking up at the motion of the big press. "But we must both realise that we are makeshifts so far as the workers are concerned. We are not workers and don't fight with the bloody ardour necessary,

283

and it's touch and go whether we'd sell out for a nice home and quiet life, if we thought the Capitalist system was going to last our lifetime. You have an income; it's a philanthropic hobby with you, just as Christian works are with Milt Dean, that's all. And you get a travelling allowance by it."

"The uneducated working classes have to be led by devoted men from a wealthier stratum," said Fulke stormily.

"But our career is miserably short," said Baruch heavily. "It's not our class. We are fighting a battle with our own class who hate us and our poorer brothers who suspect us. We don't trust each other. Our own people regard us as rats that leave thinking the ship sinking: we are homeless men, the dispossessed of the world. Dispossessed! Because we straddle two ages; keen-sighted for the same reason. What is there to do but to throw yourself heart and soul into the elucidation of the present tangle? But do you or do I want to do it? The world is still full of promise for young men of the middle class; perhaps it will not be in ten years—we don't want to lose our last chances. But the shadow is already on us. You have no children—because you don't believe in your future. I don't even want to marry—I don't know if the system will even last fifteen years. Our Catherine is in a lunatic asylum. Which one of us has plans for the future? We are lost men, for a hundred years the world belonged to our fathers, intelligent scheming, smart combinations in the business world paid a hundred times over. A clever man had only to turn his attention to the exploitation of raw materials or a single invention to make his fortune. There were swindles, but they were small in turnover and return, and rare compared with great merchandising businesses. Now, the merchant world is totally disorganised—only protection, confidence tricks, swindling, can make giant fortunes or keep Governments afloat. Great robbers can only flourish in dark ages. We are their poor relations. Dishonest is our business, dubious our future."

"Well, throw in your lot with the working classes; you are a working man and with no personal fortune and no relations to speak of," said Fulke.

Baruch laughed uneasily. "I was born to the idea of success.

284

I shall perhaps, even here, or even in America, never see the triumph of the working classes. I can stand that idea, but not yet; when I am older, when I have been disappointed and worn by the career I have chosen, I will be able to. At present I am full of hope. I expect to get a lot of experience in politics and finance, I may be enabled to repeat the history of Henry George."

Fulke smiled.

"Henry George? Yes, why not? But these wild fruits have not much savour; it is better to submit yourself to a strict intellectual discipline, follow a principle; we need men of your calibre."

Baruch looked cold.

"But not in my state of mind; I can't do it yet. I must know what is going on on the other side of the fence. Working men don't know it. They should. They should know that their enemy is resolute, wide-awake, informed, armed—and in what manner."

"I sowed my wild oats years ago, and they weren't worth sowing," said Fulke, debonair, friendly, smiling in a peculiar manner at Baruch's bent head.

"I am sowing drought wheat to come up in lean times," said Baruch sombrely, over his cogs and spindles. "The lean times are coming. Give me the material for the pamphlet; is it all here?"

"Yes; get it up in as cheap a form as you can. Ask Chamberlain to donate it; see if you can persuade him."

"There's no hurry?"

"As soon as you can; I want to take Winter a copy in gaol."

"I'll give it to Baguenault."

Folliot waved his hand round the workshop.

"So long, boys. I've got to skip."

"Goo'bye," said Withers as Fulke went out. "That's a nice fellow, Baruch: I know you don't like him, but you underrate him. Let me tell you, a couple of sophisticated chaps like that are what they need in the Labour Party and the Communist Party: they have no illusions about how you get things done—practical men."

"There's a lot of difference between the means of the Labour and the Communist Parties," said Baruch, smiling.

"I'm as good a social theoretician as you," cried Withers, who was slightly tipsy and smoked a new cigarette every two minutes, his remedy for tipsiness.

"What time does your boss show up?" inquired the detective, coming out from the composing section.

"Ought to be here now; he's late," said Withers agreeably, offering the detective a cigarette. The detective looked Withers over and smiled.

"Thanks; I'm used to waiting, but you waste plenty of time."

"Here he is," said Joseph from near the door.

Chamberlain, haggard, hurried in through the doorway, his habitual stoop exaggerated. He nodded quickly to Joseph and began scraping through his papers in the office. He rang up Jonas, and asked him to come over immediately; then noticed the detective, came towards him severely, and in passing, said to Baruch:

"Why don't you show visitors into the office? I don't want people in the work-rooms. Yes?"

The detective followed Chamberlain heavily into the office, and said something to him in a low voice. Chamberlain looked scared, motioned him to a chair, and mechanically beckoned to old Williams to wash the glasses.

"He's a close friend of mine, of course," he said. "But what's the matter?"

"Where is he?" asked the man.

They talked for some time, and Chamberlain gave the man some more whisky. When he had gone, Chamberlain came out into the press-room wiping his forehead and looking worriedly at the work going on, without seeing it. When he had made the rounds and consulted with Withers, he went back to his office and called Withers and Mendelssohn to him.

"Boys," said he, "I'm in Queer Street. I might as well tell you frankly; it's the best way out. Now put your heads together and see if you can think up something. It's this way. Dave Jonas will be here in a moment, and I want you to know what he's done for me before he comes so that you can think up a way to save us both. I've had an overdraft at the Bank of Seven States extended for two years, and they wouldn't extend it any more unless I got guarantors. Montagu wouldn't get them for me, but

Dave Jonas, a lovely boy, I wish I'd had one like that, a corker, a true friend, a friend in need, you know, endorsed me for his own part for £100. Now he will have to pay the £100, and it is all he had in the Bank; he expected to marry Effie on it. Of the rest of the money, Withers endorsed me for £60, the value of the house. His house, though, has a second mortgage; he already advanced me in cash the £60 it was worth. It is empty and he will have to give it up. Montagu gave his name for £40, but Montagu's paper was purely *pro forma*; it was really a credit in his name at the Bank, because he had an understanding with the Bank."

"Well," said Withers, "your wife's got property for £200 and more up at Blackheath. Get her to sell it; after all, we advanced you the money on that understanding, that she'd sell it."

"Of course," said Chamberlain, smiling weakly. "Well, here's the rub. She wouldn't sell it for me. She said it was to set her daughter up in life, when she got married. You know we've been separated, bed and board, for years and haven't spoken for twenty-four months. Well, Montagu went to her, as on my behalf, and explained to her a dirty scheme, in which Effie was supposed to have a part. She was to sell the property for Effie, deposit the £200 in the Bank in her own name. The Bank was to threaten to sell me up, force me to reorganise with Jonas, Withers and Montagu as partners, and renew the overdraft to the new owners." He looked with reproachful eyes at Withers. "Montagu managed to persuade Effie, my own daughter, and a good girl, that it was best for me that I was a ne'er-do-well, and the only way to save me from myself was to do it. Effie persuades the mother and gets me to sign the papers, telling me the money from the sale of property is for me. When I ask about the sale, they say there are technical difficulties, and I keep waiting for the sale to be completed and wonder that the money isn't coming along, when I'm nearly mad for it, and wonder that Min, my wife, isn't more cordial to me after making the sacrifice for me. This morning, Effie breaks down and begs me not to bear her a grudge and so forth, that it is you that's buying the business. and that it's just the same, only Jonas, Withers and Montagu are running it. I trembled when I heard that and burst into tears like a cry-baby. They tell me the £200 from the sale of the property was deposited on Saturday. Effie agrees to get her mother to give it to me. At last I got down to the Bank to try to stop the affair, knowing how crooked Montagu is in all his dealings and not hoping he will be better with Effie than me, and I find that although Montagu received the money on Saturday at the Bank and made believe to go into the manager's office with it, they know nothing about it, unless my guarantors pay up, or else there'll be writs out for them; the Bank manager's being sent on long leave. It seems Montagu's account shows many irregularities: they're going to put me into bankruptcy. Now this dick who was here tells me that, from all appearances, Montagu's skipped: and I imagine with the £200 odd that Min got from her land: poor stupid woman. She can't speak to her husband, she has to trust a crook like Montagu, and throw away her own, Effie's and my chances of commercial success. Now, boys, think quick. Otherwise, you'll have to come and feed me with biscuits every Saturday through prison bars."

Withers looked white.

"And I'm in for £60 I never had. That was fraudulent, of course, but I did it for you, Gregory. And Jonas, where's he going to get his £100 again, once he's put it up for you? He's indebted for the car you run, to the garage. You've sunk the crew."

Dave Jonas appeared, his plump waxy face sunken, and dark circles round his eyes:

"What's up, Greg?"

Gregory explained the situation to him. Jonas studied the flooring for a few minutes, and said:

"Montagu came to me Saturday, said he had to fly the Commonwealth because they were on his tracks. He admitted he was mixed up accidentally in some drug-running business and said he needed the money urgently to get out. I lent him £50. He gave me two cheques he'd received that afternoon, which I put immediately into the Bank, value £37, and two post-dated cheques from his partner, Willis, the auctioneer, for the rest. This morning the Bank telephones me to say the cheques are worthless. I rang up Willis, and Willis says they aren't his cheques. I only know that

I've been cooked and that we're in a nice pickle."

"The filthy swine," began Chamberlain, but Jonas put his hand irritably on his shoulder.

"Don't start that, Gregory. At bottom, it's you that's got us all into a hole, and our own impracticality second. Now what's to be done? Montagu's not to be considered. He's in Western Australia, New Zealand, or even Honolulu, by this time; or he may have taken a coastal boat and got off somewhere in some little port. He's a smart chap and can pass himself off as anything, not to mention that he's been in almost every business in the world and knows the tricks of the trades. We'll have to fight the Bank if they don't listen to our tale of woe."

Chamberlain added: "Another thing, in my mail this morning I get a notice from the Customs telling me that a consignment of Chinese vases and banners is waiting for me in bond. Will I try to sell it? Or refuse it?"

"Don't take it," said Baruch. "It's a trap; if the feller was mixed up with drugs keep away from his merchandise."

"Aw, don't be melodramatic, Baruch: Monty was too smart to do that sort of business. I don't believe this drug story. If he told it to you, Jonas, it was a lie. He never told the truth straight out in his life. He told you that perhaps to keep me off the goods until he can get them."

"And invoiced to you?"

"Well, perhaps he'd done that before his mess. I don't know; I can't follow his tricks. A snake is a poker compared with him. I s'pose you're right: all right, don't touch the stuff, Dave."

There was silence.

"Give me the invoice, Dave," said Chamberlain, "I'll nose round down there and find out what it's about: I'm *persona grata* with a couple of the chaps. I've often been down with Montagu in the car to get things, every week practically, and they all know me."

He reflected again.

"Not so good, eh, if Montagu's in a mess. They'll nab me as his pal."

"You're putting your foot in it if you go round to the auction rooms," said Baruch.

"I'd like to find out," said Chamberlain. "Listen, boys. Mind you, if I could get those goods, and there were drugs in them—I could get it through easy; they all trust me, they know I'm honest—drugs sell for fantastic prices. I could perhaps save the business with the money I'd get. We could easily find an agent. Bribe the police-johnny who was just here. He'd take it: I know that sort of mug—'Grease my palm' written on it."

They vetoed this phantasy with scorn.

He fiddled round disconsolately with his papers and went through his files to find some old bills of Montagu to compare them with the present ones. He put together all his statements, letters and notes from the Bank and went through them with Withers to discover discrepancies, oversights, differences of dates or amounts on which he might found a countersuit against the Bank.

"I believe I've got them," he cried once, but after arguing with Withers, put the slip aside and went on. The sweat beaded their foreheads; Withers got angry and began chewing his moustache.

"It's a fool business: you're stuck," he said. "Why don't you go and tell them what a hole Montagu's landed you in? they're men, they'll give you a bit of time."

"Time!" cried Chamberlain, suddenly desperate, "what would I do with time? I've had time, haven't I? No one can do with time what I can, make hay of such quality and in such stacks! You irritate me, Withers, I wish you'd try to think of something."

"Go and see the directors, point out the culpability of their manager, threaten a scandalous countersuit for conspiracy, based on your wife's sale of property. Anything. Have I got to think of everything? and suffer too!" said Withers, in a huff. He threw down the papers. "I'm not going to wear out my neck trying to find some little technicality to catch them on. It's their business not to have technical errors, and it isn't you who's going to find the first one. Go on; throw yourself on their mercy. Tell 'em you'll give up the business and have me or someone else manage it. Let 'em put in who they like. They won't get anything out of selling you up. The clients are yours, the clientele like you. Go and tell 'em."

Chamberlain looked up. "I will," he said desperately; "I'm sick of this."

He jammed on his hat, and they saw him hoofing it wretchedly past the window towards the Bank, which was a few blocks away. They did not see him again till the afternoon. They came in from lunch and found him sitting at his desk, his hat beside him, very red, while a collected, dark, elegant gentleman promenaded round the work-rooms. When the men came in, Withers inquisitively went to the office and started whispering to Chamberlain.

The heads of the workers, pink ovals marked with black, appeared round the machines and over the composing tables and out of the binding department. Old Williams, who had been pottering about in the storeroom overhead, came downstairs following the visit of the dark stranger and tiptoed up to Joseph, saying behind his hand, "What's up?" Withers bent closer to Chamberlain, very red, and threw up his hands.

"I expected it! What am I to do?"

He came out lugubrious, almost decrepit with spleen, and walked about the workshop saying to each one discreetly, with a certain bitter pleasure:

"Boys, you're sacked. He has to close the shop until the Bank decides what to do."

Baruch went on working; Joseph stopped his machine and ran about trying to confirm the remark, and ended up at Chamberlain's office door, saying:

"Mr. Chamberlain, is it true, we have to go?"

"Yes, I'm through, I'm ruined. They've done for me."

Withers put a couple of questions to the man from the Bank, but did not get very far. He came back and sat down on the window-sill, gloomily smoking a cigarette. Presently he walked up to Baruch.

"Come and have a drink. Why should we work, when it's all over with us and with the boss?" He threw a contemptuous glance at Chamberlain. "I could have run it beautifully for him. I'm more mercenary; that is, I have more business sense. I would have made money. But his goddam vanity spoiled it all, he had to put his finger into everything. Everyone knows him for a fool in the hands of an adventurer. That's the way we end up! You're leaving, aren't you? Easy for you."

"I've bought my boat-ticket, the funds came from Uncle Herman, thank goodness," said Baruch easily. "I sail in three weeks."

"And we've got a week to go," said Withers. "I've a good mind to join Jo's cousin, over the Gap—if I hadn't come through tighter places. Thank goodness, it doesn't mean much to me where or how I live."

On the same day the week after, Joseph was looking for a job. The printing works had been closed temporarily while the Bank's accountants went over the accounts and recommended a policy. Joseph went home to tell his mother and father how he had got on that hot day, walking the city. Summer was in the air and the new leaves of the gardens were burned at the edges. The house was full of bits of leaves where his mother had been burning off dahlias in the garden, the sky was purple and green after sunset, and a rich, roasted fishy smell was in the air. His mother had a saucepan of hot water on for tea and was sitting in her old cane rocking-chair eating bread dipped in Worcestershire sauce, when he came home.

"Well, my son?"

"Hallo, Mum."

"Tired, boysie?"

"A bit, Mum, and a bit down in the mouth. Don't bother. By the way, I saw Withers. I know his favourite pub. He says the Bank will put him in charge to run the place for them. He's a sort of softie, but he always manages to make out because he'll work for anybody that has the juice. He's going to try to get the £60. Jonas has paid £50. Is there any tea in the pot? I'll make some fresh. Wait a minute."

"How did you get on, Jo?"

"I went to the three places in the paper, and I went to the Labour Exchange in Castlereagh Street. There was a whole queue there. There's a printer near there, by the way. They used to do the same work we did; I knew them, so I dropped in and left my name. They wrote it in their address-book, but the typist told me they do that with every applicant."

"Cheer up, sonny, you'll get something to-morrow perhaps. In a country like this you can't starve. After all, it's not like the old country."

"You think so? There are thousands out of work. You should have seen the people waiting—for anything."

"I know : but there are a lot of misfits who don't like to work permanently, not like you."

"You think so? You've been in the kitchen all your life, Mum, you don't know working men."

"Well, I know you're a good worker and honest, and you speak nicely, so gentlemanly, and then you're a good Catholic, that's a recommendation."

Joseph smiled, and looked at his mother tenderly.

"Well, old Mum, it's better to be in a job than to be out; you don't mind what I take temporarily, do you?"

"No, but you've got a good trade. You should work at it."

"Yes, but for the time being, I'll try anything that offers."

"What is there?"

He hesitated, and then said quietly :

"I tried to-day for a janitor's job, in Ranse Brothers, the big general emporium."

"I'm glad you didn't get it!" Her lips shut hard.

"Something to keep me going till I get decent clothes. I'm no picture as I am."

"Seven years you've worked at it, and now to take the first lazy man's job that offers."

"I didn't take it—and you and Father depend on me having something, don't you?"

"Yes—but a janitor! My son couldn't be a janitor; I won't have it. I'll go out and do dressmaking like I did when I was a girl."

He picked up one of her rheumaticky hands, with its black swollen veins, and laughed.

"You couldn't make a bob at your old Irish dressmaking! And

I'm going to work for these old hands, no matter how."

"That's true: well, if it's god's will. But you could try harder."

"You don't trust me much: you don't think much of me, do you, Mum? But you see all other poor boys in the district without a job doing the same; in fact, the majority of them are hanging round the wharf and round the beach."

"You're a good boy, but I suppose it's because you're my son and I know you. And then all you young men get finicky. It's these labour unions: they make the working people discontented; they all think they deserve something better. Look at your cousin Michael."

Joseph looked at his mother sadly.

"I know, Mother."

"Michael had plenty of brains. He could have been anything, he could have got into the Government service and got regular pay with advances every two years. But after the war, when he came back, he got in with that set. I always told his mother he'd be better when he settled down. He never settled down, and I even heard from Catherine, your cousin, that he was fond of a woman in that set, a married woman. They're such a terribly immoral set, they condemn themselves. Imagine in our family: it never happened. But your aunt, although I've never said it, is rather light-headed. A boy is what his mother is."

Joseph sighed: "All right, Mother."

"His mother told me he had become an atheist."

"It's true."

"You see! He was a bright workman, he went to classes, but Catherine had a terrible influence over him: she's so headstrong. It makes me sick to think what a mess your aunt made of her children: she's a silly woman, rather flirtatious, I knew she was, in the old day. But she cried once, and told me she had an affair with a man. What a country; and her so well married! Her husband used to worship her."

"Uh-huh!"

"But Michael! No, I can't always understand it, I can't understand it. I asked Father Bingham about his case. I had him say a mass for the repose of Michael's soul, although . . . but he was

294

such a fine lad. I often wished he was my son. He liked me better than his own mother. It's funny, you know, he told me more than he told her, when he was young. I often thought she was jealous of me for that. So clever; and look at the way he ended."

"Yes, horrible."

"They say it was on account of this married woman."

"Who knows? They talk scandal. I don't think so myself, and I knew him. He was a queer man, and he was ill."

"I can't understand it at all. There are many things in the world that are a mystery to an old woman like me. I do my work in the house and garden, but all the time I am thinking about Michael—I frightens me—with your Mr Chamberlain going bankrupt, and Mr Withers in such trouble, and Mr Montagu with the police after him—who would guess? I can't understand it. Never mind, the world is all the same, and you'll never get on except by luck; all dishonest. But I think of you, Jo, how you are so good and trouble has come on you too. I don't understand it at all. What justice is there in that? How do we come to be mixed up with such people? It's a bad business. Life's hard.

"I will tell you, Jo, you're my son. When I was a young girl, there was a young man, a student, who loved me, but I had no money, so his parents wouldn't let him call on me. I ran away to another village, and then he married someone else. I married your father after because he was coming out here, and I wanted to get away. Your father's been kind to me, but my life has been spoilt by thinking of that sorrow. I had you, Jo, you were a consolation to me, but I lay awake so many nights thinking of my sorrow that I feel as if there were too many tears in my life. All because of a bit of money. His parents were landowners, they had five horses and two farmers working for them. He loved me all the time, but he married a young girl whose father had a shop in town. She looked pretty at her wedding with the silk dress they bought her. But he sent me a note telling me he would always suffer because of me; and in ten months they had a son. I thought I would drown myself; but I ran away, and met your father. And your father—well, he took me because I was a hard-working woman, he saw that, and he has always been a just man. No, I have never been happy in my life. I concluded the Lord sent us here to work hard, to till his soil, to save, to be honest and pious, and in the end he will gather us into his bosom and we will have rest. That is what I thought, but seeing so much trouble, there are moments when you doubt. That is the worst of all; so many years gone and perhaps you have been wrong all along, perhaps there is no one looking after you. Then, I have seen some happy people, but people like you and me, my poor son, are never really happy. It's not right, it's not according to deserts; it's often according to hide. It is not easy to understand. Blessed are the poor in spirit; but the proud inherit the earth."

She looked at him rather timidly. He smiled at her and took her hand :

"Mother, I know."

He and his mother sat drinking tea till night came on and his father came home. Then they lighted up and had tea—bread, butter and jam, cold veal pie, hot potatoes and many cups of tea. Afterwards, Joseph washed up the dishes and folded the table-cloth while his father smoked on the back veranda, and his mother went across and spoke a few words to Mrs Whortleberry, and came back quite radiant, saying :

"Well, there, Mrs Sanders' baby turned out to be a boy; another boy. She said it would be."

The children raced down the hills on scooters, the boys were still playing football in the dark down on the "Lawn Tennis", and the clatter of tea-plates came out of the open windows in the houses around. Presently the radio sets were turned on, people sang, other people went past to the pictures, the ferries went in and out of the wharf with a ting-ting, ting-ting, bringing home crowds of young people from work, and later, lovers who walked up to the Gap, and evening set in.

Joseph hung about a bit, picking out some tunes on the piano: Massenet's Elegy, "As pants the Hart for Cooling Streams", "The Indies" Waltz, Rachmaninoff's "Prelude". His father came in and sang some old French tunes with him in his tuneless voice. They then turned out the light and sat at the window looking at the high afterglow : it still lighted dimly the brass bowl on the table, with a dragon spitting fire and playing with a sunball after the Chinese fashion, and Michael's photograph, the one taken in a sailor suit when he was twelve. Presently Joseph excused himself, saying:

"I'm going out for some cigarettes."

He walked slowly along the back road and went along by the Gap; the cool breezes blew in from the ocean. Presently he reached a new stucco semi-detached cottage on the Heights, near the signal station. The little blonde girl lived there. She was sitting on the veranda knitting, but when she saw Joseph sauntering carelessly past, she waved her hand, put down her knitting, and jumped off the veranda.

They walked up and down the paths and Joseph realised for the first time how attractive the small front gardens were with their cement paths and standard roses.

I I 🖎

The seventh poor man leaves our shores. A kermesse, but
nothing to startle the modest. A madman contributes a tale
of beauty and horror. Kol Blount makes a complaint.
End of a love affair. And Baruch's last night in the antipodes.
End and beginning.

CATHERINE taught design in the workshops of the insane asylum
at Forestville. One Saturday Marion Folliot arranged a party of
friends to go out and visit her. The afternoon was fine, the beautiful gardens of the asylum were rich with flourishing arbours
and parterres; the inmates sat about in groups, mildly, talking
peacefully, like all other people. Catherine came out in her old
grey dress, woefully wan and dark-eyed, and smiled with anger
at seeing them all there.

"I am not sick," she said. "I don't want visitors as if I were an
invalid. You all know what is the matter with me."

"I brought you some papers and some chocolates, Cath," said
Fayre Brant mildly, giving them to her.

She went pale, and put the gifts in the branch of a tree they
were passing :

"Thanks, I'll collect them."

She turned her dark eyes to Baruch and Fulke Folliot, smiled
painfully, put her hand to her heart and led them all down to
the grassy wilderness at the bottom of the park, beside a rivulet
spanned by a rustic bridge.

"It's pretty here; let's sit down and talk."

They brought out some sandwiches and lemonade and passed
it round. Catherine designed the sort of conversation she wished
to hold by asking Fulke long questions about Winter, still in gaol
but to be released in three days. They began to criticise Winter's

raw theories, but Catherine presently held up her hand and said:

"Baruch, I'm sorry, I can't stand it! Let's talk about something else."

Marion, watching her with pity, whispered to Fulke, and Fulke piped up with:

"We'll all tell you tales. 'Soldier, rest, thy warfare o'er.' A soldier has good cheer, a good time, company, a long pipe and beer in between trenches."

Catherine smiled at him:

"If you feel up to it, it's a good idea."

"Listen," said Fulke, putting up his hand. "Here is a very odd story. A captain of a tramp steamer held up here met me the other day and told me that his ship got swept away off to an island off Stewart Island to the south of New Zealand. He had a cargo of pine on board and was loaded, as they always are, to the gunwales. He had broken a flange of his screw and was hobbling along looking for the nearest port, perhaps Invercargill; they rigged up a sail aft. One day at daybreak they sighted land, and came up in an hour or two, with the soundings showing a rapidly-rising shelf, to a low, rocky shore where the dispirited cliffs seemed to have given up hope of vegetation and to have lain down with worn flanks to die. They cast anchor, greatly astonished, thinking something had put out their compass. The weather after sunrise was fine, and a high mountain arose some distance inland, purple with light vapours, and topped by granite palisades of a strange character. They landed and followed a watercourse inland. In the distance they soon saw a city walled with a sort of Saracen wall, but unattainable on account of deep and continuous marshes, broken only by small reefs of sand on which cottages were built. Only at a great distance ran a cause-way about three miles long, straddled by an arch. The sun burned so hot at midday that pigeons, cockatoos, and likewise a family of black swans, and pelicans migrating over the marsh, fell roasted alive in hundreds on the roadway or sank in the marsh. Many were spitted on lightning rods, weathercocks, finials, flag-poles and other points, and the roofs were crowded with chimney-sweeps, roof-menders and lay-climbers like bartenders and hungry midday clerks eating roast pigeon and swan. One particularly savoury dish was a baked pelican containing a mouthful of broiled fish and a bellyful of fish in ragout. Those that fell into the bubbling and steaming marshes were boiled, and had a very fine taste coming from the excellent mud. The trees of the region were fearsomely marked with large footholes scratched by a giant feline animal, and once they saw at a distance a striped creature like a hyena with the markings of a tiger. The crew took fright at this; running at full speed, they passed over the causeway, and soon reached the walls of the city, but in measure as they approached their eyes began to water, their stomachs to turn, and the more delicate began to belch along the highway for the strong smell that guarded the town from enemies. They then perceived that the turrets which rose from the battlements at frequent intervals, to the number of three hundred and more, counting only those in sight, were so many stools used by the soldiers and townspeople . . ."

"Impossible, your manner of tale-telling," said Marion peremptorily. "Look at Catherine's face, she is green with boredom. Change, I say; Catherine, you!"

Catherine's lips curled in a dark smile; she took up:

"Over the causeway galloped an apprentice on a black charger. The itinerant sailors stopped him, saying, Where are you going so quickly? The apprentice, wild-eyed and foaming at the mouth, could hardly wait to reply, but as they held his bridle and would not let him depart, he told them, I am on the track of a secret which will turn this marsh into abundant vineyards and this water into wine.

"I come from a far country where on a plain covered with blue linen grass, prisoned by thousand-foot ranges, is a black imperishable stone with five words written on it. No one can read them—what is the meaning of the words? Those who read them will be as rich as Midas, all their lives, but without his troubles; those who half-perceive their meaning, fumble at the secret and drop it half done, will have their hearts pierced with a golden sword and drop dead, and their souls will fly free in the air. The words are in an unearthly tongue. Travellers cross the mountains on foot, on camels and horses, bringing with them dogs gone mad with thirst, and blacks chained together by their necks, to carry home the treasure. The travellers have planted their staves in the soil of the plain which is now like a vineyard with the staves. The soil of the plain is barren and glitters with mica and with bones, polished to ivory by the rough tongues of hungry dogs—but none can read the words. When they stand at the top of the hills, the valley is alive with activity. There they see the buildings and towers of a mine, with flags flying and trolleys scurrying along a mesh of rails; they see glass roofs, heaps of slag shining with flecks of gold, yellow clearings, new houses with bush above them, heaps of sulphur and silver; and by night, the blinding sparks of furnaces and foundries with smoking funicular railways. Farther afield is the flash of the axe descending in the forest. But when they come into the valley all is silent, naked, untrodden, windless. There is perhaps for the young a field of heath and daisies, a pile of rock and patch of rosy pigface, a patch of daffodils, a light copse. They lead their animals on foot down sun-latticed pathways into a receding distance, they pass hundreds of ruins with nettles beside. Along the paths run dark shapes, foxes, panting dogs and a black fellow or two with poisoned spear, but these are only the shapes of those dead. And the yellow dervish spirit of the desert patches beckons them on the other side. If they pass through everything, ford the mirages, come through the suffocating middays, they reach the black stone, and there they pore over the letters of gold, the five words which mean nothing, however much they know of languages, witchcraft or archaeology. Forms pass them—a golden-fleshed woman floating on a cloud of lilies, a boat sailing in the air with blue cloths, a riderless horse wrapped in gold and roses, a flood of silver, a well of transparent oil, a mountain of diamond, a nugget in a rock, a strange fungus growing on a tree. They lift their tired, red-rimmed eyes from the inscription, and that moment it vanishes. When they look around there is nothing there but a shivered boulder, and in the valley is nothing but sand, fire-blackened splinters, the funnels of ant-lions, the traces of scorpions, naked bushes covered with red flesh-devouring ants.

They retrace their way and die at the foot of the hills, for the most part.

"I had a mirror, said the boy; I found it in a cave where once a witch lived. She had only one eye and perhaps that mirror was her eye. It was blue and oval and viscous to the touch and lay among her old rags and bones. I held up that large blue mirror over the stone. They looked in, all, those cracked and grimy scholars. There were people from the British Museum there, men who had dug up Tutankhamen, or perhaps it was not he, but another, people from the Smithsonian Institution, from the Linnean Society, all sorts. In my mirror they looked, a thicket of stubbles and whiskers, and in it they saw the blue country, the black stone, the new visitors approaching on asses and the sun flashing on the inscription. And in the magic mirror I read a translation of the five words. There was a catch in it—it was only the clue to another mystery but the five words were . . ."

Catherine started and stopped, looking at a tall sombre man who was eyeing them from a row of pines.

Baruch went on, heedless:

"Io an qanat, reed pariah!"

"What does that mean?" questioned Marion.

"Nothing at all, that's the beauty of it, it fits your case perfectly."

Catherine beckoned to the stranger, who had been wandering previously round and round the pine-walk, treading deeply and thoughtfully into the thick layers of pine-needles and casting envious, curious, friendly glances at the group. Catherine whispered hastily:

"A friend of mine, an inmate."

The man approached, smiling, with dignity and saluted them, bowing to the women.

"You are telling tales?" he said.

"Yes."

"I will contribute mine, a tale of beauty and horror."

"Do so."

"It is the solution of the magic phrase you spoke of," he said to Baruch; "I also saw that stone."

302

The man sat down cross-legged just within their circle, and lifting up one thin arm, began :

"When the dove cleaves the sky it sheds a clear equal light on heaven and earth which fades into crepuscular gloom in which some flower, some far-off tower, some cleft in a mountain-head, some milestone, some beetle hovering between cloud and field, some sound of a bell rung in a distant village, some whitecap in the bay, appears instantly, glinting, and as soon is lost. After it comes the complete night, full of beating of breasts, falling of cinders and pacing of floors, when the sea draws back and the hideous submarine floor is revealed. Only a brief memory of the paraclete flies across a welter of beings pouring towards the deep in a cataract of grimaces, brandished arms, legs in a windmill, grinding teeth and a rain of carcasses, bile, convulsions, and of wounds, eruptions of viscera, and of monsters, falling for ever through the black humours into the gulf.

"It is very dark all around me. The pages in which I read this tale turn velvety and crisp at the edges like burnt paper, they are dusky yellow, but the letters burn black on borders of red and white in the fire.

"The aloe and the paraclete, it says, are the summer lightning of sanity, white in the sky, but immediately wrapped in smoke in the lower regions and stifled on earth. Reason flowers as slowly from as dark a root and dies as suddenly. All else on earth is lost in the cries of the demented, the prayers of the religious, the murmurs of old women muttering their vengeances as they go along the streets after a lifetime of disappointment." The inmate's face was covered with sweat. He ended :

"I see the world browbeaten and struggling in the dust under a sulphur sky; they scramble in the marshlights and sink in quicksands. Hermit-crabs and octopuses issue out of bony wrecks, ribands of flame out of the shrunken mouths of sunburn castaways rolling on beaches in a spasm of thirst, barnacles close the seams of coffers holding fortunes.

"Stealthily in the background a giant hand draws back a magnificent Chinese curtain, embroidered with towers, waves, coral caves, dragons and cities, the fair outward false semblance of things; and as the iron-browed prognathous monster with sloping temples turns his face over the hurly-burly, 'Disorder, Lord of the earth,' shout the last survivors and quail under his fearful eyes."

The inmate stopped with pale face and wiped his forehead with a silk handkerchief.

"That is my story. I know a lot of tales like that, but I cannot tell you any more at present; there is such a heavy weight pressing on my head."

He got up, left them with graceful gestures and took himself off by the pine avenue. Catherine was pale, with bright eyes. She flung herself on the grass and began weeping loudly.

"What is it, Catherine?"

"That is my life; only a madman knows it," she said, and became silent.

Baruch stared uneasily, took out his handkerchief and wiped his forehead. He turned to Kol Blount and remarked under his breath:

"If I don't forget all this at once, I won't sleep to-night. I have to think of sane, material things all the time, or I see blue devils."

Joseph stared at them all with uncomprehending eyes, and said aloud:

"But the man is absolutely mad."

"And we are half mad," said Catherine, with a sort of lamentable smile.

"No, I'm not," protested Joseph. "I don't even know what he's talking about. It doesn't give me the shivers. It simply doesn't touch me."

They smiled at him. Joseph thought to himself:

"Here all these months have gone past and they are *still* talking a lingo that has no meaning to me. But why should I learn it? They are all throwing fits and I am calm, a dummy, but calm." He smiled quietly to himself.

At that moment, for the first time, he wished for the presence of Winter, that reasonable, raw, sane friend. His mind flew back to the little economic essay of Winter's which he had printed himself. Winter in gaol thought of the state of the workers—

something easy to think about and understand; these people found it quite reasonable to talk with lunatics. Very odd, somewhat unpleasant. He noticed that his coat was touching Marion's dress, and shifted a little, disliking her robust form.

But Baruch said at present:

"Insanity has no more excuse for existence than tuberculosis."

Kol Blount fingered his pocket nervously for a few moments, and seeing that they had all fallen silent, took out a paper, saying in a stilted fashion:

"This is the last time we will all be together, perhaps; friends are dropping off: Baruch is leaving, Fulke and Marion are going to England to live quietly as good middle-class people, since they came into their money; I will be quite alone, it seems. I have a sort of 'In Memoriam' written for us all, but begun after the death of one of our close friends. Shall I read it?"

"By all means."

He began to intone, his pure baritone finding sufficient room in the tree-lined wilderness:

"Thus sang Michael when with opened eyes he streaked upwards towards the Pleiades.

"When in the dim ante-glacial world, monsters rampaged in mountains and seas, a white body rolled in the leaden flow, a nameless land rose from the steamy abyss, awash, awhist and away; and there they made their stamping ground, mammoth, roc and dinosaur, by Java, Malay, Celebes and swimming the Timor Sea.

"Mountains split, graciers crept, floods froze, forest fell, ice flowed, earth whirled white in moonshine, the northland was in twilight, hairy men and beasts fled south to the meridian. The vomiting volcanoes extinguished their breed, rivers congealed, lands fell into silence and sleeping creatures died. Seas sank and the water continent solitarily uprising preserved them alone and an antique race of men.

"South without land to the pole, in the rough swilling sullen sudden surly southern ocean, last post of the land world, thence south to the whaleland, to the penguins and seals, to ships shrouded in ice, from Land of the Eendragt, to Aurora Australis,

v

to undiscoverable shores, and mist, fog and snow. Hang out your lantern, old Wrecker, and pick the bones of the clippers; guard your magi's treasure, sound the fog-horns, breathe, blow and bellow, rip, roar and hollo in your salt torrents; your treasure is sand, that is the lot of misers. False and silvery Venus, who rose likewise from the sea, will guide the adventurers here.

"The youth who then uprose flying with glistening foot over barren hill, sandy stoop, salt inland sea, snowy crop, northern jungle, southern scrub, blue mountains steep, long sea-arms and creeping affluents, over ironstone lodes, coal mouths, quartz jetties and free river gold, barren hills teeming with silver, limestone ridges, opal hills, saw much that affrighted his eye, rolling white under black lid.

"He cast his boomerang at the wild cat and striped dog in the southern thicket, the night-waking opossum, the platypus, echidna and dasyure. He looked forth over the thousand-isled Pacific which ten years could not explore, strewn with reefs and beaches as the sky with stars, and the foam of the coral reef like the Milky Way; and saw the tides and seasons changing with the moon, not wild, but with a mild and musical flow, filling the bays and lagoons with green weed, nacreous shells, fish and cuttle-fish, over which the sun rose bright and dripping with dew from the seas and sand-dunes.

"He heard the surf thundering under sandstone bluffs, the frail mists meeting with sighs, intermingling and floating over the face of the sky streaked with morning, fragmented, dissolving, disappearing—or was it ghosts of fleets and wraiths of sailing men?

"Sometimes bold Malays cast on the broken shores and among the perpendicular cliffs found their way into the enamel waters of the Great Barrier Reef, or discouraged fled back to the islands again, or were lost in sudden gusts of the Gulf, or sank slowly down in the green Timor Sea among the pearls, crabs and calamary, or swirled by hot currents, passed by Trengganu and Samarak and had their bones picked by auks and penguins in the China Sea.

"Now the land was more desert and had risen yet more barren from the spume, sea-smoke, salt and shine, ringed on the rising water-line with shells, salt-crystals, wrecks, bones, pearls, weed: hardy, valiant, rib-apparent, hide-burnt, wind-bitten.

"The native youth bound his brows with eucalypt, damara, cedar, araucaria, cypress pine, his limber loins with the ferns of lower valley and sandy crown : he broke open the red seeds of the cycads and ate their flour. His swart foot shone in the pools and water-holes, dried by droughts, and there disturbed the trout and lazy ceratod. There, among flocks of cranes and waterfowl, he saw the gaudy jabiru and the moon-swimming black swan, the crane, spoonbill and the whistling duck, the ponderous pelican, and the sunken grey plain swarming with hawks, eagles and crowds, while over the sea, gannet and albatross breasted the grey amongst the gulls, and the sea eagle with gleaming belly fled upwards from aerial Lilliput.

"He chased the kangaroo, and the wild turkey from its incubating hill, heard the curlew and the boobook owl in solitude and the deep throbbing of the frogmouth's throat; started from sleep beside a native camp to see the flames; heard drums and stamping feet and brandished spears, the deep bell-notes of males in unison and the cries of women, heard the dogs, and far-off and groaning in the ear of the initiate fresh from trials and vigils in the bush, the bull-roarer; saw the medicine men and feathered dancers challenge the unseen, saw slow fancies creep into the brains of night-watchers, swollen with fear and magic, and the dark man's torpid blood produce broods moulded on air, and like his form with mean powers of gods and demons. Down in the dismal swamp the bunyip shrieked with the bittern, and the serpent writhed amongst uprooted trees in floods.

"He sometime stood upon the hills in winter and saw the grey rains drift across the flats, climbing the hills, and blind and grey with agelong wandering, thrust their bristles into his skin; saw the sun rise on the Murray and the mountains go up in smoke and the creeks rush down in rainbows, roaring over debris and naked rock, and the leaves burn red, and the pastures under water and dispersed tree-clumps, last haunts of the drooping rains, resound with frogs and crickets. The cicada shouted through the forests, shouting after rain, outsinging frogs, birds and torrents, shouting to the sun after three years underground; their tympani beat as they smelled the conquered land, each one crowned with jewels.

"Centuries passed and the black tribes followed the rains from north to south, east to west, eating the wichitty grub in famine, tree-bark and eucalypt: sometimes the dusty desert pregnant with rain flung out green children, sometimes the land was burned to a rind and the black tribes wandered many arid leagues.

"Catholic Spain, proud Portugal, sent their sailors steering for Solomon's Isles, the Moluccas with fruits and china bells, and the jewels of the unconquered uncatholic uncommerced new world. Captains from Holland and the North Sea unwound their wakes upon the waters of the world. Fires were lighted, murder done, ships cast away, cargoes plundered, robbers clothed in silk, rafts seaswept, women lost, sacrosancts profaned, mutinies smothered, hostages taken, chartings made, short-lines plumbed, reefs struck, wreckers enriched, the Chinese rolled from port to port, the Kanakas perished in the cane, mountain bluffs were climbed, the blackfellow destroyed, the plains bore flocks, the desert of spinifex spouted gold, the new world began. And after all this notable pioneer tale of starvation, sorrow, escapades, mutiny, death, labour in common, broad wheatlands, fat sheep, broad cattle-barons, raw male youth and his wedding to the land, in the over-populated metropolis the sad-eyed youth sits glumly in a hare-brained band, and speculates upon the suicide of youth, the despair of the heirs of yellow heavy-headed acres. What a history is that; what an enigma is that?"

The madman at this moment approached solemnly, with quiet dignity, and cried: "My blood is running back to the sea. Out of the sea I rose, you have clipped my wings, I cannot rise again. I must drink the salt of the sea!"

The company sat silent. They heard as a harp twanging in the air for some time after Blount finished. He had begun quietly, and when the first measures took the audience by surprise, a wild strong high note broke into his voice, as in a young man's where the boy's voice and man's are blended. He leaned towards the circle and fixed his glance upon some member of the company

308

for long moments. Catherine had risen from the grass, and sat composed and silent, her eyes roving about the sky and trees. Sometimes the person he fixed shivered, or withdrew his fascinated gaze in an embarrassed way. At other times the person felt a wild, rich, angelic joy as if the universe were a globe of light and his face being approached to the tenuous globe, the light poured through him: it was neither the subject, nor the words of the bard, but the tone of his voice, his passion, his rapture. Everyone thought again of Michael and wondered how such an ordinary person could have aroused so strong a passion of love in Blount. At the end, after a few minutes of perfect silence, during which one heard some faint evening sounds, of beetles winging and a bell ringing for vespers, movement began among them like the rain come quickly from far off over roofs in the summer night. Blount stirred himself, and said:

"Why are we here? Nothing floats down here, this far in the south, but is worn out with wind, tempest and weather; all is flotsam and jetsam. They leave their rags and tatters here; why do we have to be dressed? The sun is hot enough; why can't we run naked in our own country, on our own land, and work out our own destiny? Eating these regurgitated ideas from the old country makes us sick and die of sickness. Are we vultures to eat the corpses come down here to bleach their bones in the antipodes? This land was last discovered; why? A ghost land, a continent of mystery: the very pole disconcerted the magnetic needle so that ships went astray, ice, fog and storm bound the seas, a horrid destiny in the Abrolhos, in the Philippines, in the Tasman Seas, in the Southern Ocean, all protected the malign and bitter genius of this waste land. Its heart is made of salt: it suddenly oozes from its burning pores, gold which will destroy men in greed, but not water to give them drink. Jealous land! Ravishers overbold! Bitter dilemma! And lost legion! Our land should never have been won."

The evening shadow was falling across the party. Fulke and Marion wheeled Kol Blount into the upper part of the garden and stayed a little while yet, talking quietly among the flower-beds. But Catherine and Baruch walked in the far alleys, went out

309

across the adjoining paddocks, and inspected the workshops. In the workshop where Catherine taught design and woodcarving, Baruch sat down on a little table and said:

"I am tired with so much walking. I am all impatience to be gone. That's the truth. Well, Kol let himself go this afternoon. I understand they are going to make an experimental case out of him in one of the hospitals. A Macquarie Street doctor thinks he can be cured. He should never have been in a chair all these years, it seems; a pure case of neglect and poverty. He's a forceful character. Are you sure of this afternoon's event? Or are they the last sentence of the legend? Now there is no more of your brother left to be revealed. What an underground life was that! These deaths and youthful suicides show the fearful tension in which we live. That is what my aim will be, to prepare my understanding for the next step. My old self dreaming of academic scholarship I leave here with you, brothers of my past, in the antipodes. What will you do? Think of it! Wednesday I am going! Ah, how sweet life is after so much trouble! I am no more in uncertainty as to what I want to do—Ranke, Fustel de Coulanges, Marx, all that is going on, I will have at my finger-tips; in ten years I will be a citizen of a future state."

Catherine, fingering the tools of the workshop, said sombrely:

"I hear what you say. Take this knife; can you strike it into my heart without the blade glancing on a rib? The pain would be less than I feel now, my veins would not thicken faster, my eyes not be quicker filled with blood. Yes, while you spoke, I saw as a door open in your speech, leaves drifted in and outside were barren leaves, and nothing but the white bones of death everywhere. I have nothing to look forward to. You are leaving me; in that, I strike the irrevocable, the irretrievable, an absolute of life beside which death is a shiftless, temporary state. Are my lips black? They feel black, as if the venescence coiling the ambushed snake, Terror, which is eternal and circles the world, in the ocean as the ancients thought, for the ocean is also bitter, black and encircling, had already shot into my blood through its black fang. Nothing can satisfy my spleen but to fall into the terror beyond death, but let me only escape the terror of living through so many unhappy loves."

"What is it? Oh, what is it?"

"You are afraid."

She laid the knife on her wrist, the skin resisted, then yielded, and the blade sank into the flesh. Her face was stone-white but her eyes welled like luminous jelly. Blood rushed out. She withdrew the knife and the flesh lay apart like the walls of the Red Sea divided.

"Your hand will wither, perhaps."

"I am withered."

"What have you done?"

"Your renaissance is too hard for me, there are too many pangs, and your new world is too sane for me. Why? Because I have no seed; I am a freak of nature. To me your science, labour-and-bread humanity is too stable."

"Why, I imagine spring fever will always send the clerks and farm-boys roving, and good citizens will go on the bust; there will always be poets; what has that to do with it? Look at you, dripping blood on the floor! Here, bandage your arm with my handkerchief—it is not very clean. Why did you do that?"

"I meant to show you the bone, but there is too much blood! I feel the skeleton under the flesh. In all this time I have not felt any pain in my arm, although it is coming now. 'They are alien,' said Nietzsche, 'so alien that they cannot even speak their difference to each other.' When you speak of the new renaissance, I am thinking that you are going away and that I will never see you again. When you are considering the governance of future states, I am despairing because your relation to the world is dearer to you than anything else—yet it is that in you I love. You are the best man I ever met."

"But you said nothing of this until to-day!"

"No, it has been growing on me. You are like sunlight, a natural thing when you are there, strangely and universally missed when away."

Baruch dropped his eyes but could not help ejaculating:

" 'The light of the world!' Oh, women are great lovers. But you will love someone else. Do you realise the relentless ambition at the root of all your loves?"

"Yes, of course."

"I am sorry. I am leaving you, you love me. You must stay here and I must go. What is to be done?"

"Nothing. I will fall in love with someone else, who is brilliant, ambitious and roving."

"You will forget me."

"No; I love passionately still every one I have ever loved. If I only fish their image out of my memory and look at it, feel all the old passions stir."

"Strange girl that you are. You will always be in trouble; you had better get married."

She looked at him derisively, said:

"Don't worry about me, I'll pull through. Let's go back. The bell will ring in a minute and you will have to go."

As they came up the cement path between bushes of roses and coxcombs, the bell rang, and the visitors streamed towards the gate. They all said good-bye to Catherine, who accompanied them to the gate. Baruch said in a troubled voice:

"I will write to you."

"Do," said Catherine, smiling graciously.

He wrote her a letter the next day. She put it away with a few other letters in a small black lacquered box.

It was Tuesday evening and the eve of Baruch's departure. Joseph, Baruch and Winter walked down to the Union Steamship wharves to look at Baruch's boat, and afterwards had a beer at the "Three Bells" public-house, where there were also at the moment a negro pugilist, an English sailor from the Argentine, two Italians and two little blonde girls.

"Come with me," said one of them to Winter. "It'll only cost you half a dollar."

"No thanks," said Winter, "but I'll have a beer with you."

"Married?" said the girl.

"No," said Winter.

"You're a nice feller, I'll do it for nothing," said the girl.

312

"No, thanks," answered Winter. "My friend here, he's going to America to-morrow, so we're just going to walk round the harbour a bit."

"Gosh, I wish I had his luck," said the girl. "They say Bunos Airs is a good place. Well, tootaloo, bon voyage."

The young men walked round the semi-circular wharves into Woolloomooloo Flat, and climbed the tall stone steps into the Inner Domain. A cargo boat was coaling and loading: her derricks swung from wharf to hold, and a coaler shot coal into the bunkers. A full moon had risen over the southern shore, the blue slowly-breaking light illuminating the water far and wide, but still too low to light the grassy mounds of the park. The workshops on Garden Island were working full blast with hammering and tapping, and in between the three companions and the Island a full tide ran in, audible to them even on the top of the hill, with metallic musical blows against the piles and stone quays. Above the sky paled.

"When I was coming in this morning," said Joseph, "the gardener was burning off in Admiralty House. You don't see it, you two, but at this time of year the rocks are draped with flowering creepers which trail in the water. The gardener had thrown the trash into the corner, and the smoke from the fire drifted up into the shining air, like a sacrifice to a sun god. I could not help thinking our radiant city should make sacrifices on holidays, as in the old days."

"The sight of a large city always stirs me almost to prayer," said Baruch.

"I always feel most a man when in the city; in the country, I am almost afraid, there are no voices out there," remarked Joseph.

"That reminds me," said Winter, "of the last camp. Did you hear about the dryad? One of them, out in the bush, heard music and, looking for a long time, discovered a lightning-struck tree, from which the music came. There was a soft wind blowing backwards and forwards, as it does on a slope or in a hollow, so it was supposed that a natural aeolian harp had been constructed. The camp had got into a poetical mood down there by the sea, with the bush around it, and without sitting round the fire for

313

long starry nights—you know our climate and living out of doors, and the simplicity of our people, make for animistic belief—so there was an expedition to the haunted tree that night, but although they found it after a lot of hunting in the dark, it was silent. Yet the wind was up. We visited it after, but apparently we never went in the right wind, for it was quiet, except if you put your ear close, when you heard noises like you might hear in any tree. There was a lot of discussion afterwards. Mrs Hanngartner, you know, believes there are souls in nature."

"We are not far from India here," said Baruch. "If you were simpler people, and had not the drawbacks of public education, you would probably become star-gazers, tower-builders, and use the astrolabe. It is not for nothing you build an open circus on the hill at Cremorne to await the second coming of Christ. Your deserts, if you had no ships, would be full of eremites, sun-worshippers and sandstone temples, with your mystic northern breed transported to the Tropics."

The moon was now in the central heavens and following them as they trod. They walked through the shaded Domain past the side of the Art Gallery where appeared the names Cimabue, Giotto, Botticelli and Michelangelo, to St. Mary's Cathedral, where they saw a light through the windows of the apse.

"Let's go in and sit down a bit," said Baruch.

Only Winter demurred. He hated the smell of incense and the bad paintings.

"Ecrasez l'infame," he said bitterly.

"Hush," said Baruch, out of respect for Joseph, but Joseph was indifferent to Winter's feelings.

Joseph took the holy water as they went in and genuflected when they crossed before the high altar, out of pure habit. He would do it to the end of his life. There was no one at all in the cathedral. They presently came behind the high altar and stood in the shadow beside the painted bleeding Christ. A servant of the cathedral, without seeing them, passed rapidly in felt slippers from one of the doors and began to take money out of the offertory boxes: "Chink, chink, chink, clink-a-clink, chink, chink"—into his hand. A silent hostility emanated from Winter, but Baruch smiled and waved his hand at him. Joseph shifted from one foot to the other and seemed asleep; the wasting candles dropped into the sockets and those that remained the attendant snuffed. He then passed round the other side, and after him came a priest. The priest passed by, and the three companions, tired and chill underfoot, sat on a dark bench below the altar: in front of them the Mater Dolorosa sorrowed over her crucified son, and Saint Anne and Saint Joseph stood one on each side.

"It makes me sick," said Winter; "let's get out of here."

"I understand how all this came about," said Joseph, out of the dark, to Winter's great surprise. "People sense some sort of inevitability, and try to run with destiny. They think destiny can be supplicated."

They sat there for a while, speaking occasionally, softly. It was very cold in the cathedral, and the flagstones struck ice into their bones. Out of weariness Winter fell asleep. Joseph looked at Baruch's ghostly face and said:

"I must look for work to-morrow."

"Go to Withers—he's not a bad sort, he'll try to help you out. That's his hobby. He likes old friends, too."

"You are lucky to be getting out of it."

"I've got to work hard at the other end, Jo, to keep my job."

"You can do it easy enough. It's been interesting listening to you, Mendelssohn."

"Yes, I'm a kind of endless gramophone record, a wax matrix that records the ideas of the times; not inspired."

"No, you're an awfully good chap; you've done a lot for me. I'll always remember."

"I've done nothing, you've done it all yourself—you've got brains, Joseph. What have I done?"

"Through listening to you and Winter I know where I stand."

"You have found that out. Is it worth while knowing?"

"Yes; I'm not a missionary like Winter, nor an intellectual like you, understanding every step I make. That must be queer, though, to know what you are doing. I'm not selfish and scheming like Withers, and not a straw in the wind like Michael. I don't get into dramas and excitement like everybody else."

"What are you, Joseph?"

"This is how I think of it. I'm a letter of ordinary script. Events are printed with me face downwards. I will be thrown away when I am used up and there will be an 'I' the less. No one will know. The presses will go on printing; plenty more have been made to replace me. History is at a standstill with me. That is what I am. I see my life, after all; I know what I am doing, too, in my way. Even you and Winter don't see yours as I see mine. But I realise everything is against me, as my smallness and oddness show. There are—as they say in the Bible—hierarchies and hierarchies over me economically and intellectually, and I shall never rise against them. I know now as much as I can ever know, and that's due to you and Winter. Perhaps Winter can still teach me a little; but it's slow. Every single power there is has over me a—sovereignty, jurisdiction and dominion—that was something you said the other day. 'Do machines have children?' that sentimental fellow Milt Dean said one day when I was at Blount's. I am a machine. I am the end of my race."

Baruch glimmered in the faint light under the great west window. He thought of Catherine sleeping with the insane, and saying she too was a sport without seed.

"It's curious I should not have known Michael well," he said. "I never got to know him."

Joseph looked suddenly at Winter, who coughed in his sleep.

"You know, Winter's in bad shape. He shouldn't be sleeping here in the cold. He nearly died last winter, and the last spell in gaol knocked him up."

They got up, and knocked a long time on the door leading to offices of the cathedral. At length, an angry priest came and let them out into the warm, brilliant air of midnight—everything was drenched with moonlight from horizon to horizon. They took Winter home and Joseph stayed with him. Then Baruch trudged home himself. He sailed at midday the next day, but nobody was there to see him off, for Withers was at work, Winter was ill, and Joseph had got a temporary job cutting sandwiches in a lunch-room.

316

Endpiece

Joseph goes home late.

LAST NIGHT the storms gathered round the moon and the wind blew whirling cones of sand and dust about. Over Middle Head was the pale rosy light of the bushfires. The trees raged in the park, which is always turning back to wilderness; they lifted their arms and tossed in the darkness of the under-cliff. The souls of trees are freed in storms, they struggle, arise and commingle in the lower air. Wild flutings, reedy laments and cries of inhuman passions fill the ear. The gale trumpets in the distance, and they tremble as if before the trampling of sabaoth. Let the wind-buffeted man run past with his overcoat squatting on his back and his hat running along of itself before him; he is out of his elements. The children of the storm strain and howl, taking no notice of him and oblivious of his world in their recital of lugubrious mysteries, earthy deeps, lost rivers and subterranean caverns.

The leaves clashed together with their opening cry, "Kastelaison, Kastelaison," and the storm came. What was the history of Kastelaison? But the wind has changed; that is for another day.

The wind blows straight out of the black sky, the moon is one day old, the stars and white-caps leap together. The distant roar of the caged lion in Taronga Park charges the air in a quiet with a single shock of sublunar pain, a prelude to the gale's second onset.

Now between Joseph, this traveller hurrying on with head thrust forward, and the nearest star something moves which may be a silk mesh such as conjurors used. Underneath is a giant gulf in which rushes the sea: the stars appear therein with intermittent flashes. The threads of the mesh appear and are woven of the bodies of flying men and women with the gestures interlocked in thousands of attitudes of passion. Thought flies along their

317

veins, they move and gesticulate with old motions lost in memory.

"That was long ago," sighs the traveller, his head still bent. Now the web trembles, now the threads are free and they swing out into space, feeling their way in universal shade and bearing their own light like the rayed bottom-fishes. They sit on saturnic moons, they sway far out in the interstellar spaces. Suns brighten and flash!

"Long ago! Now it is only like a dream from which you awaken and feel tremulously near to tears without knowing the reason," murmurs Joseph, as he hurries along the cliff-road towards his cottage. "Why were we so shaken then? Was it because we were young?" He shakes his hair out of his eyes and rubs his furrowed face. He is a small, rugged man, and the ill-willed moon peering through thickening vapours throws his odd shape fantastically on broken rocks.

The wind blows up again from the south; the curtain of cloud rushes across the immense sky. As it blows, the delicate beings aloft shiver, they wither and fall apart like thin dry leaves, they fall to earth and perhaps fall into the sea. The sea is fretted with a thickening web of shade, the dark pours into the sea. What were those creatures? Men, or dreams, or magellanic clouds?

The roof of the sky opens for twenty seconds before the titanic wind; he stands erect on the scaffolding with stars in his hair and sends the birds' nests rolling. Then all is dark.

Roar on, O Pacific sea, and blow the golden weather in with morning; in the dark bad deeds are done, pillows are wet, hearts despair; in the morning everything is resolved. Underneath sleep and snore in their beds the hutted people of the Bay, like dry leaves fallen from the heavenly tree. Far out at sea ships move on towards the port that they must enter at dawn, and all night long goes wheeling through the wet the long ray of the South Head lantern to keep them off the blind openings in the southern cliff. Seven miles away signs swing and windows rattle in the city, the boats strain at their anchorages, the poor people who sleep under the wharves in Ultimo move their rags closer to the bank, and rats leave their holes.

The traveller hurries on, thinking of the warm stove and his

318

wife. He reaches the wooden doorstep at last, the door comes ajar, he slips in; but the wind and the night enter with him. He shakes out his rough woollen coat, and some leaves which fell in the park fall on to the hearth. He sits down and takes a cup in his hand, but it trembles, and a brown stain spreads over the tablecloth.

"I had a hard day," he says apologetically. He is tired, but the wind is in his ears. "I saw Withers," he says, and thinks again. And so he sits long into the night with his hand in his wife's hand, and tells her the history of him, Joseph, of Michael and Catherine, his cousins, and of many others who surely live no more: for they cannot have a sequel, the creatures of our youth.

And thus he begins:

"We were seven friends, at that time, yes, seven poor men . . ."